Savage Planet Embrace
Savage Planet Series
Book 1

Kassie Keegan

Copyright © 2022 by Love Planet Publishing

All rights reserved.

No part of this book may be reproduced in any form or by any electronic or mechanical means, including information storage and retrieval systems, without written permission from the author.

Book Cover & Character/Place Illustrations by Gleiver Prieto, Artist-Illustrator

www.gleiverprieto.artstation.com

Savage Planet Series Logo by Maria Sarmiento MASS, Graphics Designer

Instagram: mariasarmiento_mass

Titles and Branding designed by Deranged Doctor Design

www.derangeddoctordesign.com

Editing

Amy Briggs, Editor

www.editsbyamy.com

Re-Editing

Waddle Editing Services

www.waddleediting.com

Dedication

Thank you, Mr. K, for your unfailing love and encouragement.

You are the model of affection, devotion, and desire for all my heroes because you *are* my hero. And my very own sexy beast. Rawr!

S, K & T, your love and support mean the world to me.

Alana, phenomenal friend, what a delightful ride this journey has been! Thank you for everything.

GP, you bring my vision of this world to life in beautiful style. Thank you.

Sharon, Kristin & Annalee, thanks for reading as I dreamed and crafted. Your advice is golden!

Morgan, not all heroes wear capes. Some have red pens and really cute laughs. Thanks for making a tough job *fun*!

This book is dedicated to all those who have stepped out into a free fall with your hair on fire, screaming to the sky 'I'm HERE!" Not knowing where you'll land, but knowing you'll have a great adventure along the way! Time To Be EMBRACED!

Also by Kassie Keegan

Kassie Keegan's books are available on Amazon and in KU

Savage Planet Series:

Savage Planet Embrace

Savage Planet Secret

Savage Planet Discovery

Savage Planet Destiny, Finale

Savage Rescue Trilogy:

Savage Planet Rescue

Savage Planet Recovery

Savage Planet Redemption

Savage Quest Series:

Savage Quest: Lord Rawdon

Savage Mist Series:

Savage Mist: Arden

Savage Mist: Astor

A Confession

Dear Esteemed Reader,

I need to make a Confession.

I am addicted to Capitalizations and hyphens.

I love them! I've tried to walk away from them, but every time I did, it only made me want them more. So, now I simply accept my needs and their presence in my life. I revel in the dash and Cap, using them with pleasure-filled, reckless abandon.

You'll see Capitalizations and hyphens everywhere, and I even Capitalize and SMASH words that have no business being smooshed together. And italics. *Oh*, italics are *yummy*. It's a free-for-all, y'all!

Perhaps you'll think to yourself, "Did she really mean to do that?" The answer will always be, "Yes. Yes, she *did*."

And let's not get started on apostrophes…

…

…

No, LET'S!

A Confession

The Lio have a whole naming system that uses apostrophes.

Like, when a gorgeous Lio male from a 'Fiel Pride is being introduced, there's either Bon, Pon, or Lon in front of the 'Fiel.

"Bon'Fiel" means this muscle-bound, silky-furred, beasty-male was born on Lio HomeWorld. "Pon'Fiel" means he was born in a 'Fiel Pride on a Lio Fleet traveling the Known Galaxies. "Lon'Fiel" means he was born on a Lio Colony World. A Lio knows all that just by the letter that begins his PrideName.

And when a *Prime Ambassador* male gets mated, the entire Pride is so excited everyone changes their PrideName to start with Argen, Pargen, or Largen. It's a big deal!

And I use lots of wide, open space for the words to breathe.

Yeah, maybe I have a vicious hate of dialogue tags, but that's beside the point. I have dear ones who have difficulties reading, and a wall of unbroken text is intimidating. I hope experiencing these Lio Adventures is super-smooth and effortless.

Check out the Glossary of Terms and Character Summaries at the end of the book, too!

Enjoy the Journey! Stay Savage!

~Kassie

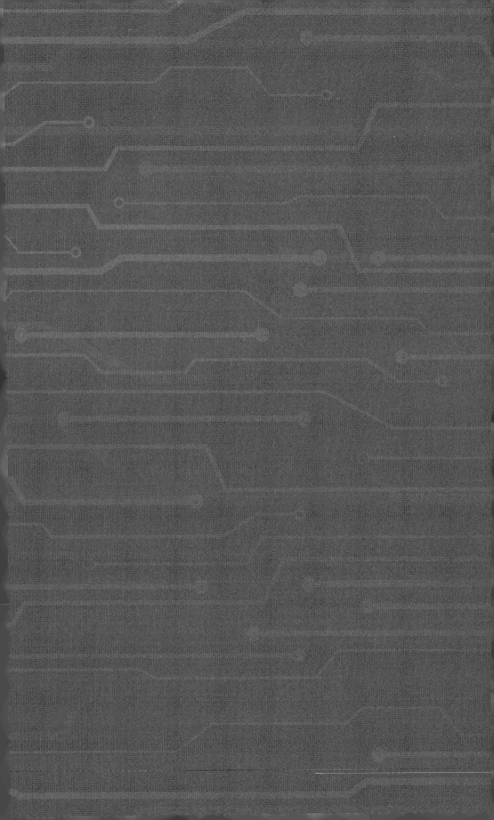

The Lio

When humans advanced into the Space Age, they encountered the Lio. The lion-like humanoid beings who seeded the Known Galaxies with the beginnings of life, allowing Worlds to develop according to their evolutionary presets.

Earthers worked faithfully alongside female Lio Nessas and male Lio Nels, eventually leading the Lio to sponsor Earth into the Galactic Alliance, becoming a Protectorate of Lio HomeWorld and their Fleets.

When the Cataclysm occurred, and Lio could no longer produce female young, the Galactic Alliance rallied to find the cause and cure it. But their efforts were thwarted at every turn.

Earth sent scientists boosted with Lio genetics to live, study, and work on Lio HomeWorld. Creating a new race the Lio called Honored. So named because they honored their commitment to the Lio race.

Men became Honored Nels. Women, Honored Nessas.

Through miraculous Happenstance, some called Fate, the Lio found a solution. An Honored couple fell in love and MateBonded with a Coalition of Lio Nels, producing the first female young since the Cataclysm.

Honored are treasured by the Lio. Without them, the Lio would no longer exist.

Kassie Keegan

Thanks to the efforts of the Lio Inquiry Office, human men and women eagerly apply to the L.I.O., hoping to be chosen for genetic boosting to become Honored.

Doing so gives them extended lifespans, added strength and abilities, and untold opportunities to create lives for themselves that would have otherwise been impossible.

Chapter 1
Daniel

Gaze riveted, mouth dry, Daniel Shaw's heart pounded as the Space Transport's gaping maw of a bay door gratingly opened, announcing their arrival on Lio HomeWorld with pops, screeches, and hisses.

The familiar smell of filtered air ripe with the scents of mechanical fluid, ozone, and the surrounding travelers was now washed with delicious fresh aromas a SpacePort 'Rat' like him, with newly enhanced Lio-boosted senses, had not experienced.

Daniel anticipated this moment for most of his life. Growing up and surviving on SpacePort Arata with his mom had been a struggle. Holographic Story Videos, StoryVids, broadcast from all over the Known Galaxies, kept him sane. His favorites had always been the Lio StoryVids.

As a kid, tales of adventure and valor depicted by the Lio and their Honored Mates captured his imagination. Those stories gave him hope for a family. One with strong Lio Mates, all loving a woman who adored them back. For a place in a Pride, where he would never be alone again.

His mom, Lauren, knew his hopes, saw his avid interest, and encouraged him. Before her sick, worn-out body took her away from him, she insisted Daniel apply to the Lio Inquiry Office, which amusingly shortened to L.I.O. They'd laughed about it. She taught him to find joy and keep it despite hardship.

Many applied for selection, but did not meet the Lio's mysterious requirements, making Daniel feel like being chosen was a long shot. It shocked him when tall, statuesque, golden-furred, and golden-eyed Abassa Itakah from Lio HomeWorld arrived, seeking him out.

Abassa Itakah kindly instructed him on the basics of Lio culture and stayed with him through his genetic alteration on SpacePort Haddou.

They'd sedated Daniel for his gene-altering injections, which boosted his genetics, and during the insertion of his Mimetic Mineral Shield Disc. He awakened literally a changed man, his skin a light-gold, thicker and tougher than it had been. He didn't need glasses, and his human body hair, although still not furred like native Lio, was velvety soft.

Despite appearing mostly the same, Daniel's abilities became wildly enhanced, especially his sensitivity to energy sources around him, which grew exponentially. The Lio helped him harness his new skills, acclimate to being boosted, and taught him how to use his Shield.

When Daniel was ready, Abassa Itakah sent him by Space Transport to Lio HomeWorld to begin his life as an Honored Nel.

He'd worked so hard and endured so much to be there, the failed hopes of his parents to live in a fresh, new land making it more poignant.

Exhilarated, Daniel felt the weight of the moment, this turning point of stepping foot on an actual planet for the first time. A World he chose.

Taking a deep cleansing breath, he shivered as he emerged from the cool, dark internal Dock of the Space-to-Land Transport onto the blazingly bright Arrivals platform on Lio HomeWorld.

A promise to myself fulfilled.

Daniel experienced the weird pull of gravity on his body, feeling heavier. He walked carefully, feeling the precision and weight transfer of each footstep.

Looking out at the intensely blue sky, golden light blazed across his awareness, warming him, his eyes drinking in everything he saw as fast as he could process it.

So, that's what an actual cloud looks like.

He stopped walking, amazed by the view.

Two moons!

Squinting briefly into the sun, Daniel then peered down at his own exposed arm and hand, alternating making a fist and extending his fingers while rotating. His new Honored skin shimmered in the sunlight, soaking in the warmth.

He'd wondered if sunlight would hurt, but it felt pleasant. It felt necessary.

I will not give this up.

Suddenly a delicious, unfamiliar scent registered on his senses, then a different heat hit him like a blast. It blazed deeper than the sunshine. It came from inside him, the burn starting in his chest, concentrating around his heart.

The raging power deepened, pulsing outward through his limbs, clouding his thoughts as sensation overwhelmed him, before zinging upward. Sizzling through him from the crown of his head all the way to his toes.

Daniel crowded close to the platform rail, needing to anchor himself, facing a sea of fast and trendy Land Transports parked on the field.

He breathed deep as the flames burned hotter.

Am I dying? Did something go wrong when I got boosted? Is the planet killing me?

Daniel gave himself to the fiery torrent.

If this is it, at least I made it here.

Kassie Keegan

He clenched, then released his fists, his head dropping back as he surrendered to the hot, glittering rush. As he relaxed, allowing it to take him, the burning gradually eased into a manageable, pleasurable warmth.

He raised his head.

Could this be what coming home feels like?

He stopped trying to make sense of the overwhelming, unfamiliar feelings, simply letting them churn through him. However, one part of him stirred to thick, throbbing life.

What the actual fuck? I'm getting a hard-on!

Chuckling, Daniel moved his short, cape-like Chalel further forward to cover the evidence of his arousal. The rest of his lightweight clothing hid nothing.

Guess I'm happy to be here!

Taking long, deliberate breaths, getting himself back under control, his mouth watered at the lingering delicious scent. Its fleeting notes were complex and enticing, overpowering all the other scents invading his senses.

I want more.

He turned toward where he perceived the source was, eyes searching, to no avail. The smoldering heat in his heart flared in intensity, burrowing into the core of him, morphing into a noticeable but tolerable ache. He rubbed his chest over the throbbing discomfort.

Daniel ignored the bustling crush of other travelers around him, wanting to take action.

What am I going to do? Leap off the platform and make an utter fool of myself for a smell?

He wanted to do the right thing here, to respect his new home and their traditions. So off to Arrivals he would go. Still, Daniel lingered a bit, rubbing the gnawing pang, hoping to catch one more hint of the intriguing scent.

Perhaps it was a flower.

I have to find this flower!

He knew one thing for sure, Lio HomeWorld wouldn't be boring. All these experiences in his first few moments, despite being uncomfortable and different, only confirmed to him he made the right decision.

I am home.

Chapter 2
Aubrey

Tucked up under the wing of the latest high-end Land Transport, Aubrey Newton Bon'Fiel was in her happy place.

She and her fellow Transport-enthusiast buddy, Stealth, took every opportunity they had to see the sleek new vessels. A flashy one much farther down the line captured his attention.

She inspected a sharp little beauty's newest features, drooling at the idea of getting her eyes on its yummy power core, when she sent a casual, incurious glance to the people meandering down to Arrivals several hundred feet away.

A furious blast of animal magnetism hit her, making her freeze, completely unprepared for its impact.

Despite the distance between them, Aubrey absorbed every painstaking detail about the alluring Honored Nel who transfixed her. His presence spoke to her, resonating as clear as a bell.

The teeming travelers surrounding him disappeared from her awareness like smoke.

Emerging from the shadowed exit of the sleek Space-to-Land Transport, the Honored Nel glowed. His pale light-gold skin gleamed in the sunlight, complementing his soft-looking short, wavy brown hair, a few shades lighter than her own. He had a close-cropped mustache and beard.

Tall but not lean, having 'meat on his bones,' as her friend Talia would say. Sturdy. He moved with the ease and confidence of a man right where he wanted to be.

Oh, I like him.

The pearlescent shimmer around him made her blink as a hum of sexual interest swelled within her. She licked her lips.

Hmm, I want to taste his shimmery skin.

Aubrey savored the enticing moment of attraction, then mentally shook herself.

What is this?

These were not feelings she was comfortable having. She'd never taken one glance at a male and started panting with blazing need, not even for her three Lio Nel shadows, Léandre, Jovian, and Commander Ferrand.

My body is on fire!

Unable to stand, an audible buzz overtaking her hearing, Aubrey dropped heavily to her knees, concentrating briefly so her Shield protected her flesh from the rough ground.

Breathe. Just breathe.

Aubrey intently focused on the compelling stranger as he paused at the lip of the Transport before striding onto the Arrivals platform. The moment echoed her own experience stepping onto Lio HomeWorld.

Is this his first step ever on a planet like mine had been?

Exquisitely attuned to him, she saw him shiver as he moved forward. She understood the slow, careful movement of his limbs as he acclimated to planetary gravity, his face wondering, eyes darting from one thing to the next.

Kassie Keegan

He appeared happy, which pleased her. She couldn't help but chuckle, watching his open enjoyment.

The man wore common Honored attire of airy, light-colored, loose-flowing vest, leaving his beefy, muscular arms visible, and trousers with comfortable sandals. He had a half-length, green Chalel cape with gold shapes and designs draped loosely over one shoulder.

Squinting into the sun, a small smile lit his face, shifting into a full grin as he stared down at his own arm, turning it this way and that, clenching and unclenching his fist.

He sees the sheen of his skin.

Aubrey remembered her own first moments in the sunlight.

I wonder if he sees the surrounding glow, too.

His grin became rueful.

What are you thinking, fascinating man?

He was so authentic, open, and expressive.

Show me more, handsome.

Abruptly, a different deep heat burned through Aubrey. Starting around her heart, shooting outward like a starburst throughout her body, centering in her core. She ached with overwhelming, burning arousal, which scared her.

Her gaze remained locked on him, and even at a distance, she noticed her Honored Nel's throat swallow, realizing she swallowed at the same moment.

Are we connected?

If they were, it strangely comforted her.

He stopped short, mid-stride, near the railing facing her direction, taking a long, deep breath.

Does he feel this, too?

The movement of his chest said their breathing was syncing, hers slowing down and deepening to match his. His fists clenched-and-released, his eyes closed, then his head tilted back with a shudder.

Is he alright?

His head came back up, and he adjusted his cape.

What happened?

Her gorgeous glowing Honored Nel opened his eyes, his gaze scouring across the myriad Land Transports surrounding her. She knew he would not see her in the privacy of the dim shadows she knelt in. However, he seemed to sense her as deeply as she sensed him.

She perceived him seeking her in the hum of her gift.

Intriguing.

The crowd of travelers surged around him, urging him forward. He resisted the flow and lingered, searching. Finally, reluctantly, he walked to Arrivals.

Aubrey stayed frozen on her knees, burning brightly with need.

Chapter 3
Aubrey

"Aubrey."

Crap!

Stealth's smooth, deep voice came from behind her.

"What's wrong?"

She couldn't move or acknowledge him. All Aubrey could do was blink her eyes and burn with arousal.

She felt Stealth crouch beside her, hearing the subtle grind of soil shifting beneath his weight, knowing he watched her closely. He didn't touch her, but she felt the hum of his attention and heard his concern. In her peripheral vision, she saw him track her locked gaze to the Arrivals entrance.

"Are you hurt?"

Stealth audibly inhaled.

"I don't scent blood."

He then growled thoughtfully.

"Hmm…No, blood, but oh. Abah-Sah, you scent of…"

Savage Planet Embrace

He stopped mid-sentence.

Aubrey lost sight of her Honored Nel, no longer able to catch her breath, hands clutching the front of her coveralls. She felt helpless, making tiny keening sounds in her distress, caught in deep arousal.

Her eyes closed, overwhelmed. Aching. The unrelenting hum of sexual need threatened to take her under.

I'm going to die.

Stealth spoke slowly and calmly.

"Listen to me. Can you hear me? Nod if you can."

She nodded the tiniest bit her head would allow.

"I will help you. You are locked into your Call to Mate. This is natural, as it should be."

Aubrey mewled, rejecting this was in any way 'as it should be.' Refusing even the notion she was Called.

She'd worried this day of reckoning would eventually come. Dreaded it too, thinking perhaps she could ignore the Call. She'd been so wrong.

It's impossible to ignore.

"I am pleased to be with you, sharing the blessing of your finding your Honored Mate. Do you accept me as your Shumal, your Protector and Guide?"

Shumal.

"May I touch you? I will help."

Touch... me?

Stealth moved to block her view and look her in the eyes, compassion in his gaze.

"I know it's intimidating. Even Lio Nessas are intimidated by a Mate-Bond, and they have fangs and claws. But I swear I'll make sure you stay safe and healthy. You'll be in control of the Mating, no matter how out-of-control your Mates' beast-natures make them.

Stealth's tone firmed.

"I'll protect you. Take care of you."

This can't be happening.

"You must consent, Aubrey. I can release you, but only with your permission."

Consent? What is he talking about? I'm dying here.

She finally pushed breathy words through her tight throat.

"Don't let me die."

Stealth spoke reassuringly.

"You will not die from this. Do you consent? I only need a nod."

Aubrey nodded.

This is *happening. No escaping it now.*

He moved, wrapping his strong, golden-blond body around her from behind. The velvety pelt of his muscular arms felt silky against hers. His palms covered her hands where they gripped her coveralls.

Nestling her into the curve of his frame, Stealth brought her back and rear into complete contact with the front of him.

Aubrey cried out, all of her nerve endings firing at the same time, threatening to take her under into unconsciousness. Stealth's reassuring words kept her with him.

"Shh. I will help you. You are not alone."

He buried his face in the crook of her neck, huffing a deep breath. Stealth shivered.

"Breathe, sweet one."

Slowly, Aubrey realized his undemanding embrace helped her cope with her body's chaos. She began breathing easier, uncurling, and sitting up some so she could expand her lungs more. He followed her movements, supporting her with his strong, lean frame.

"This will be quick and intimate. It's natural. The way it should be."

Stealth's familiar, calming scent comforted Aubrey as her body went haywire.

"Being your Shumal is an extraordinary gift I take seriously and treasure."

Stealth guided one of her hands to her breast and the other down to her core. She groaned at the exquisite pressure at the source of her painful arousal.

He pressed her hand perfectly over herself, his grip pressing her palm hard against her heated center, beginning a fast, firm but gentle back-and-forth rub. His other hand directed hers to pinch her sensitive nipple.

"Stealth. What? Oh!"

He crooned.

"Yes. That's it. Let the pleasure rise. Ride the crest."

Aubrey let go, coming gently with a deep groan of relief, sparkling sensation pulsing through her in roiling swells. She rolled with the waves, grinding into her hand, supported and driven by Stealth. His body followed the current of hers until they slowed and finally stopped.

Aubrey relaxed back into him with a sigh, able to move freely again.

With a contented, calming, rumbling purr, Stealth rubbed his cheeks and jaw along hers and over her shoulders, scent-marking her. He chuffed a breath against the crook of her neck, then placed her hands on her thighs and held her in a warm hug, continuing to rumble contentedly, patiently waited as she came back to herself.

Kassie Keegan

Aubrey suddenly stiffened.

What did I do?

She was dying again, only this time her heart shriveled in painful embarrassment.

I'm not like this! I don't want Stealth. He's my friend.

Stealth hugged her tighter.

"No. Don't. You're okay."

A tear dripped down Aubrey's cheek, her eyes still closed, scared to face him.

Stealth leaned to the side, angling to see her face.

"Look at me."

She shook her head with a tiny jerk.

"It's okay, Aubrey."

She opened her eyes, staring blankly ahead as more tears sluggishly welled up and trailed down her cheeks.

"Please, sweet one. Look at me."

She sniffed at his cajoling.

"I'm not letting go until you look at me and we talk."

Taking a bracing breath, she rasped a response.

"I guess they will find us here in a week span because I am not dealing with this, Stealth."

But I have to. Ignoring it won't make it go away.

She cleared her throat, taking another fortifying breath.

"What is happening?"

Stealth rubbed his furred jaw against her in a cherishing gesture of comfort, wiping away her tears with his velvety fur, giving her a soft squeeze.

"You have been Called to Mate."

Urging her to face him, he grasped her slim hands in his large ones.

Stealth had startling bright turquoise-blue eyes with a contrasting deep blue, almost black, rim around the irises. They narrowed thoughtfully, his lion-like face serious, head tilting to the side as he assessed her.

Not wanting to focus on her problem, Aubrey focused on her friend and his unusual coloring common to the 'Salel Prides. His fur shone a light creamy gold color everywhere, even on his chin, chest, and abdomen where Lio were usually a snowy white.

His long mane was gathered into a thick, straight, pale-blond trail of silk, braided back from his face, reaching past his butt. He'd told her once that a golden 'Salel's mane grew fast and was ritually cut.

Stealth had an aristocratic face with a smaller, more defined nose than most Lio Nels, influenced heavily by his Honored Nessa grandmother's human genetics. His eyes were a match to his grandmother's, too, with the addition of the dark-blue rim.

He had pale-gold, silky chin fur, slightly longer than his other facial fur. She saw glimpses of his fangs as he spoke to her. He wore a sleeveless vest and loose trousers, more commonly worn by Honored Nels, altered for his golden-tipped tail.

Pulling a strand of her straight, long, dark-brown hair off her sweaty neck with a gentle finger, Stealth roused her from her wandering thoughts.

"You discovered the Honored Nel you've been waiting for. You knew this would happen eventually, didn't you?"

Aubrey's eyes bounced between his as she processed his words.

"My Honored Nel… Mate."

She felt this truth in her bones.

He nodded.

"Yup."

Stealth loved the Earther slang her cadre taught him. He gave her a smile, his eyes twinkling with humor and affection as she fell back from her knees onto her rear.

Taking a deep breath, Aubrey lifted her knees, bracing her elbows across them. She dragged her gaze away from Stealth, back toward Arrivals where the Honored Nel had gone. She still thrummed with a low-level hum of arousal for him.

Stealth brought her face back to him with a curved finger under her chin.

"This is a natural part of your Call to Mate. I am thrilled to be your Shumal. It is a sacred honor from Abah-Sah that I take seriously. Prime Cassian will also be pleased your MateDance will begin so soon after his rise to Bon'Fiel Ambassador."

Aubrey's eyes widened, thinking about the towering, buff beast Prime Cassian. The guy was 'extra' in every way. Bigger, stronger, faster, and frankly hairier than any other native Lio Nel male she'd seen.

Aubrey shook her head.

"I didn't know *this* would happen."

She put her hands up to her still burning cheeks, so glad they were in a private area away from the bustling crowds, hidden deep in the shadows.

"Your Call is strong. A beauty to behold. I look forward to Witnessing your MateDance."

She rubbed her face, then gaped at him.

"Witnessing… Um. Am I finally going to be told what happens at a MateDance after the 'Dance' part?"

Stealth's grin broadened.

"Depends on the Abassa or Abassan overseeing the Ceremony. I suppose the 'kitten is out of the sack.'"

She snorted.

"It's 'cat out of the bag.' Do you even know what you are saying?"

Stealth laughed, shaking his head.

"No. I do not understand why small felines go into fabric pockets they must escape, or why such a term is used for secrets being revealed. I like the word 'kitten', though. It's cute."

She sighed.

"You are trying to distract me."

"Yup. And it's working."

Aubrey gave him a rueful grin.

"You are a good friend."

"The best!"

He sobered.

"However, I am now your Shumal, as well."

"I don't know what it all means. Please, tell me."

Stealth touched his chest as he spoke.

"By their wisdom, Abah-Sah has seen fit to bless me as comfort and Guide through your Call to Mate. I will stand with you in your need and protect you from harm should your Mates' beast-natures overwhelm them. I take this blessing deep into my heart."

Handsome, understanding, and kind, Stealth would be such an affectionate Mate. But not for her. Aubrey didn't feel that way about him.

"We're not… like Mates, are we?"

He grinned indulgently.

"No. We're not."

Then focused on her meaningfully.

"But you know this, do you not?"

Aubrey regarded him, her gaze heavy with awareness. She knew what he was talking about. There were only three Lio Nels who had captured her attention since her arrival on Lio HomeWorld.

She nodded slowly. Stealth flopped into a relaxed posture.

"I am your friend. Shumal are not Mates to those they protect."

"Can they be anybody?"

"Potentially. Abah-Sah knows who is correct for each Honored Nessa in her Calling."

Stealth looked down, vulnerability shadowing his expression until he visibly cleared it. When he spoke, his voice was matter-of-fact.

"Are you unhappy with me?"

He looked at her, his eyebrows furrowed, ears low. He sprawled next to her, leaning on his elbow and hip on his side, facing her. His tail swished lazily.

The decorative metal ring beneath the thick tuft at the end of his tail flashed silver with his tail's sinuous motion. He picked up a piece of vegetation off the ground and started toying with it while he peeked up at her. Waiting.

I can't change what happened. The only thing I have control over is what I do now.

She'd come to Lio HomeWorld fully aware of her role as a potential Mate. She became an Honored Nessa and loved the advantages and gifts it gave her. If Aubrey had to pay the price of facing her deepest fear in order to live here, she would.

And she would not allow this to ruin her friendship with Stealth, either.

"We're good."

Aubrey pushed him over, making him laugh. Suddenly, she sensed the familiar, exciting buzz announcing a new presence.

Léandre.

Her guardian. Her obsession. Her sexy beast.

Léandre would scent her. And Stealth.

Stealth is in serious danger!

Chapter 4
Daniel

Daniel stepped into Capital Maituri's spacious Arrivals Lounge, the air cool and fragrant as he absorbed the clean, organic lines of the space.

The Lounge's decor resembled huge, artfully placed, overlapping palm fronds in shades of cream and gold. Slashes of colorful growing things with scented flowers climbed the walls up and across the ceiling.

Soft, diffused light beamed from opaque window-like spaces between the layered fronds.

Other newly arrived Honored Nels waited with him for their Pride-Choice Ceremony, which would happen straight away, one at a time. It was their official welcome into Lio HomeWorld as Citizens.

Lio and Honored lounged on curvy, low-slung, cushioned benches and chairs throughout the spacious room. Other travelers went through exits among the frond tips to be on their way.

Daniel rubbed the puzzling ache over his heart. Despite it, strength filled him, ready to embark on this new adventure in his life. It was his mom's greatest hope for him to be here and find happiness.

Sorely missing her, he wished he could share this experience with her. He remembered her eyes sparkling with humor as she took joy in their constant banter. Then he thought of his strong, loving dad. The old familiar pang of their loss ached like a dull bruise.

He glanced over, noticing Stanton Buey giving him a nasty sneer while staying far away. Daniel had stopped the bully's verbal jabs with one strategic punch to his pretty face.

Fucker.

He turned his back on the Honored Nel, consciously blocking the dark energy coming at him.

He sent a thought to whatever Higher Power was out there.

Please don't let me choose the same Pride he chooses.

Outside of a few asshole Honored Nels, Daniel's training with the Lio was all he'd dreamed of. During the often boring journey from Space-Port Haddou to Lio HomeWorld, his discovering the Technological Advancement Sector of the Lio Inter-Comms, led by a Lio Nel named Jovian, was his saving grace.

Daniel dove into the minutiae of new concepts and Tech possibilities, like a starving man at a buffet, wanting to learn everything. And Jovian fed him through the audio-only Deep Space Inter-Comms, always patient while explaining things in his low, rich voice.

Jovian seemed just as happy as Daniel to speak with someone who understood complicated technical problems and enjoyed conceptualizing through them. He hoped to meet Jovian in person one day.

Mentally shaking himself, Daniel gazed around. Stanton was gone and the group of new Honored Nels had steadily diminished during his thoughts as they were led one-by-one to an elaborately curtained entryway in the far-back of the Arrivals room by an imposing Lio Abassa priestess.

Her graceful fluid movements combined with her floaty, resplendent deep-purple and sheer-white garments made it seem like she flowed from place-to-place. Her coloring was like most Lio Nessas, golden except for the front of her body and lower face, which were snowy

Kassie Keegan

white. She had a lovely triple drape of chains down her middle and up across her ribs on each side.

She carried a gnarled wooden staff topped by radiant violet stones embedded in twists appearing like plant roots. Small ornaments wound around the top, wafting a fragrant vapor soothing to his senses.

Like all Lio Nessas, she had no mane on her head, only velvety fur. Simple but elegant glittering chains draped her head with a petite purple teardrop jewel resting high on her forehead. A larger plum-colored jeweled pendant shimmered at her neck. An elaborately crafted knife and sheath strapped to her thigh, glowing with violet accents.

Daniel sensed the power of her presence from across the room, triggering the sensory gift he'd had since childhood, exponentially enhanced after he became an Honored Nel. Her vibe was interesting and unique, like a low-level electric hum resonating up his hands and arms into his chest.

He usually used his gift with circuits and machinery, applying it to find problems. He could track energy flow to its source and pinpoint blockages and damage for repair. It was part of what made him so skilled with machines and Tech.

The Lio Nessa priestess ushered another Honored Nel to the curtained entryway. She paused with the Nel, her hand on his shoulder speaking with him.

I wonder if I can follow her intriguing flow to its source.

Daniel focused his senses and plucked the string of her energy to create a Resonance he could trace. The instant he plucked, she stopped speaking, turning to regard Daniel, giving him the full power of her mahogany gaze. They were unlike any eyes he had ever seen before.

He dropped deep into the depths of a vast sea of peaceful turbulence. Strong, slow, inexorable, unrelenting, rousing waves rolled through him, pulling him further and deeper into the endless ocean of an ancient consciousness.

Emotion overwhelmed him.

Love, compassion, and strength wielded by intelligence so great his mind would have burst had he not released the string he plucked.

He emotionally drowned.

Daniel's eyes locked with hers, wide in distress. He couldn't seem to take a breath, his thoughts strangely distant.

The priestess lowered her head, closing her eyes briefly, giving him what he needed to break the connection long enough for him to gasp some air. Sweat beaded and dripped along his face and neck, his stomach churning, shocked to his core by their moment of spiritual fusion.

She sent the Honored Nel through the PrideChoice entrance, before calmly approaching him, her expression a combination of interest and concern.

"How are you, Daniel?"

Flashes of relentless, loving waves continued to roll through his emotions. Daniel stuttered a bit as he fought to catch his breath.

"You kn-know my name?"

"Of course. I know of each Honored Nel making their PrideChoice this day."

She paused, her eyes kindly taking in his appearance from head-to-toe.

"You are Daniel Shaw, only son of Lauren and Lukas Shaw of SpacePort Arata. Student of Abassa Itakah, my acolyte. I am Ha-Abassa Sarina. Pleased to meet you."

She bowed in the Lio tradition, slightly tilting forward at the waist, head tilted to the side in a gesture of respect.

"Pleased to meet you, too."

He unsteadily tried to emulate her gesture, his knees strangely weak.

I think I'm going to fall over. I need to sit down.

Ha-Abassa Sarina asked soothingly.

Kassie Keegan

"May we share air?"

She wanted to touch foreheads in a formal greeting. Still stunned and intimidated by the depths of power and emotion he continued to drown in, he nodded despite his uncertainty.

Ha-Abassa Sarina approached him carefully, watchfully, ears pricked forward, her tail slinking evenly from side-to-side. She spoke, her low, feminine tone a calming balm to his turbulent mind.

"I did not know you were such a strong Energy Rider, Daniel. I would not have been open so wide had I known."

She placed her hand gently behind his neck and brought her silky furred forehead to his. He felt the barest hint of the jewel on his skin above where their foreheads touched. She had a unique, spicy scent.

Daniel didn't reciprocate her grasp. He could barely move, much less lift his arm, as waves of calm moved lushly through him, bringing him a consuming peace. He felt light-as-air, weightless, carefree, centered. His heartbeat thrummed steadily, his breaths becoming deep and regular, muscles relaxing as his eyes closed.

Tremendous strength filled him within the relaxation, which was a strange juxtaposition. He got his equilibrium back, opening his eyes as she pulled away.

The Lio Nessa's entire demeanor softened, ears high and alert, tail tip flicking lazily, as her lips upturned into a gentle smile, her mahogany eyes now easy to gaze into.

"How are you, Daniel?"

He thought for a minute, taking an assessment of his mental and physical state. Wonder and bewilderment swirled inside him, but he felt physically fine.

"I'm good."

"Yes, you are."

"What happened?"

"You skimmed the nature of Abah-Sah."

"Abah-Sah?"

"Yes. Priestesses of Abah-Sah, like me, are Abassa. Priests are Abassan. As a Leader of the Abassani, I am Ha-Abassa. Using the title honors our Creator, Abah-Sah, who I connect with and serve. When you plucked at my Source, you followed my Connection to Abah-Sah."

Daniel sighed, his mind full.

"This is a lot. I haven't even been here an entire day span and I've got so much weirdness going on."

He wanted to laugh, but resisted. Hysterical laughter was not a great look for him.

The Ha-Abassa tilted her head to the side, giving him a musically thoughtful hum as she regarded him.

"You have received a special blessing. Take time to recover and relax. Ask your questions when you are ready for answers. Until then, know you are most welcomed to Lio HomeWorld."

She released his neck and dipped her head respectfully toward him again as she stepped back.

"All will be well. Listen with all your senses, hear with your heart, and act with confidence. I'll bring you to your PrideChoice shortly."

Daniel grabbed his hydro-pack and sat down to wait while reliving the brief and amazing experience. He rubbed the constant warm ache in his chest, hot, but not burning. Buried deep.

He felt altered, but how wasn't clear.

I have a lot to think about.

After all the strange things already happening to him in his short time here, he wondered…

What will happen next?

Chapter 5
Léandre

Léandre smelled distress and tears in Aubrey's deliciously sweet scent. And overwhelming arousal.

I have to get to her!

She was Shaktah, an Honored Nessa female whose fear-scent attractor was so strong as to be almost irresistible to Lio Nels. He would never tell her how many males he fought regularly to keep them from scaring her when she triggered their beast-natures.

He stayed near Aubrey as much as he could, often invisibly. He didn't want to crowd her or limit her personal growth, but Aubrey was his to protect, and when she was ready, he intended to be hers.

He'd accepted Stealth into Aubrey's close circle because he hadn't sensed lust from him toward her.

The lusciousness of the scent heavy around her spoke to him on a bone-deep level.

Is Aubrey Called to Mate?

If so, Léandre must prove himself worthy to be Claimed.

First, defeat the rival.

Kassie Keegan

Being mute, Léandre could not physically growl like his Brethren, but it resonated within his spirit.

He turned and leaped onto Stealth with all the swiftness and strength he had. In the blink of an eye, his hand satisfyingly gripped the Lio Nel's throat, his body subduing his opponent.

Léandre's rival did not fight him at all, simply lying back in submission. His utter lack of combativeness kept Léandre's claws sheathed, soothing his initial drive to defend.

Stealth tried to speak.

He enjoyed the male's struggle.

Maybe this will teach you the lesson you need to learn.

Tightening his grip a fraction more, Léandre got in Stealth's face, breathing his air, making sure Stealth took in the scent of his aggression, his tail swishing angrily.

"Stop it! Léandre, stop it!"

Léandre turned to Aubrey, his lips pulled back in a mask of anger, showing fangs, his ears back and down. He knew his eyes glowed a luminescent gold lit from within with his emotions, but he made no sound.

Aubrey's stormy blue eyes plead with him, but she didn't move from her startled pose, sitting on the ground, legs bent and spread.

"Don't hurt him, please."

Her hands extended out to him in supplication.

How delicious.

Her curvy figure was on full display despite her overalls, the glistening sheen of her bare golden-tan neck and arms shimmering at him, her long, dark hair in wild disarray.

His attention caught, Léandre relaxed, but his grip on the Lio Nel did not.

Absolutely luscious.

Stealth tried to speak again, still struggling.

Léandre glanced at him, then back to Aubrey, snared by her scent and beauty. Her pleading.

Abah-Sah help me. I will belong to this female. I will serve her with every part of my body and soul.

Aubrey pleaded prettily.

"Allow him to talk. Come on, let up."

He deigned to look down at his adversary, thinking about it.

Her tone firmed.

"Now, Léandre."

Stealth got a few words out, despite Léandre's grip around his neck.

"Sh'mal. Um, 'er Sh'mal!"

Léandre's ear flicked in Aubrey's direction as she sighed with annoyance.

Reluctantly, he pulled his hand away, but kept Stealth subdued. The male coughed and swallowed, husking through his bruised throat.

"Shumal. I'm her Shumal."

Shumal?

Léandre swung his gaze to Aubrey.

Our time has finally come.

He would prove his worthiness, his beast-nature demanded it. Her Shumal would Witness, as he should.

Releasing his hold on Stealth, Léandre dismissed him as he continued to focus on his treasured Honored Nessa.

Pausing, he removed a small disc-like disruptor field generator from his belt, placing it on the ground. He activated it, ensuring privacy within its sound and scent dampening. A distinctive wavering distortion encircled them so no one could see them.

Léandre inhaled as he crawled on hands and knees toward Aubrey, opening his mouth to let the delightful scent of her rich arousal coat his tongue. He would sniff out where her Shumal had touched his beloved and over-mark it.

She will know who is worthy of her attention.

Aubrey became alarmed, surprised, as he steadily stalked her. She braced herself back on her arms while he crept into the space between her legs, gradually pushing them outward to make room for himself, intently watching her.

Sitting up between her legs, Léandre reached up, making sure his wrists were in sight, removing his Bandels wrist-cuffs, laying them aside, his gaze never leaving hers.

Aubrey gasped.

"Léandre, what are you doing?"

He didn't activate their holo-comm to explain, letting his actions speak for him. His fingertips grazed her cheek.

She didn't flinch.

He brushed the inside of his wrists across her neck, then cupped the back of her head.

No protest.

Léandre stroked down to grab the long hair at her nape in a firm, gentle grip.

She relaxed into his grip.

Holding her still as he smoothed his jaw along her silky, golden flesh, he covered her with his Mark, drowning the Shumal's scent beneath his own, one side, then the other.

His mouth watered.

Léandre buried his face in the crook of her neck and rested there. He wanted Aubrey comfortable with his intimate closeness, but would push her limits now that she was Called to Mate. To do so before now would have been cruel.

Devotion filled him as she shivered with reaction to his embrace.

He knew Aubrey feared intimacy, her fear-scent part of what made her irresistible to the Lio Nels, sparking males to Rut and females into Breeding Heat. She scented of female sexual prey.

My beautiful Shaktah.

However, Léandre desired her for much more than a trophy. He adored who she was, even her occasional foul moods interested him.

I will not have my Mate be afraid.

He firmly controlled his beast-nature, waiting.

Aubrey breathed steadily, held in his grip. Her fear-scent did not bloom, but her arousal most definitely did.

His breath chuffed across her sweat slicked skin, fascinating him when he saw her flesh pebble. Léandre deliberately blew on her to see what would happen. She shuddered, and he filed that nugget away to explore later, at length.

I need to taste her!

Léandre ruthlessly tightened his control.

I can survive on this until the MateDance.

He pulled back to see her face. She panted, her shimmering blue eyes heavy-lidded, cheeks flushed, blush-pink lips open invitingly.

Léandre used his grip to tilt her head further back, taking in everything. Her expression, the glow in her eyes, the invitation of her body, her delicious scent.

Tasty Mate.

Kassie Keegan

He leaned in to the divot at the base of her throat and gave a tiny test lick, his chest rumbling in reaction to her exquisite taste. Diving in for a deeper taste, he dragged the slightly rough center of his tongue over her collarbone, up the side of her neck to behind her ear in an achingly slow slide.

Aubrey claims all my senses.

His cock extruded from his sheath uncontrollably, his nectar dripping. He wore only a simple Shendyt around his hips, grateful for the lack of constriction. Léandre's chest rumbled with excitement.

The subtle sound of soil shifting as Stealth changed position caught his attention, causing him to glance over his shoulder.

Stealth sat up, leaning back on a hand, one knee raised with his other arm casually draped over it. He watched avidly, completely relaxed, tail flicking with interest.

Léandre narrowed his eyes at the male before ignoring him, then swept the perimeter, examining their surroundings, ensuring their privacy behind the disruptor field in the deep shadows of the Transport above them.

We are secure.

Turning back to his delicious Mate, Léandre swiped the tip of his tongue out to gather all hints of her flavor from his lips. Aubrey's gaze tracked his tongue, so he did it again, his shaft engorging even more as she enjoyed his play.

I will devote myself to lapping your cream day-in and day-out.

As her Honored Nessa beast-nature answered the Call to Mate, she would be insatiable.

My female will be satisfied, I will make sure of it.

Léandre leaned over her, smelling more of her Shumal's scent.

Unacceptable.

He released her mane and slid his hand slowly along its length to her shoulder, bending to pinpoint the strongest scent.

Hmm. The inviting mound of her breast is my target.

Léandre peeked up at her, seeing arousal and anticipation widen the pupils of her eyes. Slow-blinking, he reveled in their connection and affection as his fingers leisurely trailed down her torso.

Taking his time, he enjoying her hitched breathing and the rhythmic movement of her chest as she rapidly inhaled and exhaled, coming ever closer to her nipple where the precious point poked out at him impudently.

He cupped the side of her breast, plumping it, bringing the peak near his mouth as he bent. Staring into her eyes, he breathed heat over her nipple. She melted at the warmth through the layers of her clothes.

Léandre gave Aubrey a broad smile, showing off his fangs.

Yes, my delight. I will serve you well. Imagine this on your naked flesh.

He carefully nipped the very tip, making her yelp in surprise.

"Oh!"

He licked the fabric directly over her sensitive peak.

She tossed back her head, her bent knees spreading even wider in invitation, her hips rolling, seeking stimulation.

Abah-Sah, what a sensuous treat she is.

Léandre leaned in closer, ready to suckle, when Stealth growled low in warning. He sighed and pulled back, ear twitching in Stealth's direction, acknowledging the boundary he'd established as her Shumal guardian.

Staying close, he did not touch Aubrey as she recovered.

She panted through the lingering zings of pleasure from his play, gazing at him with amazement. She looked down at her breast, examining the damp spot he'd made directly over her hard nipple, then flicked her gaze back to him.

He mouthed, 'yes,' silently as she tracked his lips, then he salaciously licked his upper lip, making her gasp.

We have so much more to share, my beauty.

Her Shumal had released Aubrey from being locked into her Call to Mate but would not allow Léandre to over-mark with his tongue between her legs, stroking her to orgasm.

However, Léandre wanted Aubrey to fixate on his mouth, to begin a craving that would break down her walls and entice her to her Mates. Moving closer, bracing on one hand, he slid the thick furred end of his tail up her arm to her shoulder, rubbing her flesh delicately, watching as her gaze followed the caress.

He trailed his tuft down along her arm to her wrist, wrapping it with his tail, bringing her hand to his mouth, stopping where she could feel the heat of his breath, but not quite touch his lips.

He lifted a hand beside hers, making a loose fist with his thumb up.

She looked at their hands quizzically.

He shook her arm with his tail, showing she should do the same with her hand.

Understanding, she imitated his hand position.

Rumbling with pleasure, he chuffed, so she peered at his face again. He brought his hand to his mouth and delicately licked the tip of his own thumb, repetitively and at length.

Aubrey's eyelids dropped as she watched.

Oh, she loves it!

Her arousal scent announced it plainly, as did her fully blown pupils and avid gaze following his every move.

He stopped licking, the tip of his tongue peeking from between his lips as he paused again.

Aubrey gasped as he leisurely stroked his other hand down her torso, toward her core.

His gaze focused on her face as he nestled his fist tightly against her humid center, his knuckles pushing into her with steady pressure while his extended thumb pressed her clit.

Aubrey's eyes widened in a shock of pleasure, then rolled back and fluttered closed.

Oh, yes, my delight. Time to entice you to your Mates. This is only a taste of the bliss we will bring you.

Bringing her tail-captured hand close, he laved her thumb with excruciating slowness from bottom to top.

Her eyes snapped open, staring as his tongue danced over her flesh again with rapacious hunger. He tantalized the tip of her thumb with tiny flicks he matched with presses of his thumb over her tender bud.

Aubrey moaned hungrily.

Enchanting. Give me more, love.

Léandre licked her thumb faster, matching the rhythm on her clit. She ground into his fist, getting the contact she craved. Groaning, eyes closing, she dropped her head back. He didn't like that.

She needs to know the source of her pleasure.

With lightning-fast speed, he grasped her mane at the nape, bringing her head up. Her glazed eyes opened as she gasped breathlessly.

"Léandre. I need."

Yes, my delight. I provide.

He sucked her thumb into his mouth and suckled with deliberate precision while rubbing her clit in perfect unison.

Kassie Keegan

Ecstasy chased across Aubrey's expression, shuddering through her as she came for him. Her hips bucked, back arching as she groaned long and low in gorgeous release.

Aubrey owns me.

Her scent overwhelmed him.

I will be hers or be Bereft. There is nothing else for me.

Léandre released her mane, sitting back on his haunches as he grasped his aching erection under his Shendyt. His beast-nature demanded she know he would provide all the nectar she and their Honored Nel Mate needed.

He stroked his cock for her, his gaze latched on her face. Gaping at him, Aubrey's cheeks flushed deeper as she understood what he did from his arm movements.

Giving her all of his sensuality, Léandre showed every emotion, hiding nothing, baring himself to her as she had done for him.

We are equal in passion.

He grimaced with agonized, blazing carnality as he crouched forward, braced on one arm. Breathing deeply with exertion, tensing-and-releasing, he joyfully spilled his nectar on the ground before her in tribute, his pleasure-scent joining hers.

He hung his head as he recovered, chest heaving, Aubrey's small hand petting his long, braided mane. He lifted his head and licked the inside of her wrist.

Sitting up, Léandre let go of her arm with his tail, crossing his arms to grasp her opposite forearms with his hands. Bringing their wrists together, he slowly slid his palms along hers until their fingertips barely touched, then released her.

Glancing down, he grabbed his Bandels as he stood, putting them on. He picked up and deactivated the disruptor field generator, placing it back on his belt.

Savage Planet Embrace

Léandre paused, gazing down affectionately at his splayed Mate.

I hope I've made my intentions clear, but I want no doubt.

Eyes blazing with feeling, he opened their holo-comm connection.

LÉANDRE:

I Declare for you, Aubrey.

She blinked up at him, clearly gripped by a torrent of conflicting emotions. He was determined to love her through her fears and doubts.

Next, he intently focused on Stealth, communicating silently. When her Shumal nodded, reassuring him she would be comforted and cared for, he knew it was time to go.

He and his Brethren, Ferrand and Jovian, needed to prepare.

With a last heated look at his beautifully disheveled female, Léandre slow-blinked at Aubrey, then sauntered away, tail waving with contentment.

Chapter 6
Aubrey

Léandre walked away from Aubrey, his tail swinging in lazy arcs from the slit in the back of his Shendyt, the fabric swishing across his strong thighs, most of his golden-furred, muscular, drool-worthy form on bold display. His long, braided mane of multi-hued hair bounced with his stride.

She looked at him with fresh eyes.

All these years, Léandre had been her mentor and protector, her friend and companion. Sure, they'd shared her first kiss, but he hadn't pressed for more or made her feel uncomfortable.

Right now, she felt much more than uncomfortable. Aubrey was downright bothered. Incensed.

She stared at the thick, almost clear fluid he'd pumped on the ground between her legs. Her brow wrinkled, confusion sweeping through her as her mouth watered at the arousing scent.

She'd worked hard to process that her friendship with Stealth would remain unchanged, but with Léandre, everything was different now.

Everything.

I don't like it. Too much change, too fast.

Aubrey turned to Stealth with a frown.

He had been patiently waiting for her attention with an enormous smile, fangs on full display in his amusement.

"Fucking hot!"

"Stealth! My life explodes and you are making jokes!"

"I'm not joking! That scene was *blazing* hot! Besides, I think it was more like your body exploded. With pleasure."

She picked up a handful of soil and flung it at him. He leaped out of the way, shaking off any lingering bits clinging to his fur.

"I thought you were some sort of Protector."

He reared back indignantly.

"You were not in danger!"

His expression became mischievous.

"Your Mates may entice you to them, Aubrey. I'm not keeping them away from you or you away from them. A Shumal's purpose is to make sure it doesn't go further than you want it to. It was blatantly obvious you wanted the lovely interlude with Léandre."

Aubrey pointedly ignored Stealth, peering blankly at the sleek Transport her attention had been so captured by earlier, her thoughts consuming her.

I have so much to consider.

Stealth spoke, dragging her attention back to him.

"Did he Declare for you?"

Sighing, Aubrey stood up, brushing off her butt. She stilled, gazing down at Léandre's fragrant nectar, remembering. He was gorgeous when he came, his pleasured soul bared to her gaze.

Such a beast! I want him.

But not only him.

Kassie Keegan

She desired her glowing, unknown Honored Nel, too. And, since she was being *really* honest with herself, Aubrey craved two other intriguing Lio Nel males. In Lio culture, they came in a bunch, all or nothing.

Her time of coasting was over. She would have to make choices.

"Yup. He Declared."

She regarded Stealth with resignation and ruefulness warring in her heart. He tickled her under the chin, smiling.

"Hey, it's good."

She smiled back.

His ears flicked and his eyes gleamed, his expression and posture turning playful.

"Let's not make it easy for Léandre, Jovian, or the Commander. We wouldn't want them to get lazy, now would we?"

He offered her his creamy furred elbow. Aubrey laced her arm through Stealth's.

"No, we wouldn't!"

As they walked back to the Capital Maituri Grand Palace together, she looked forward to tomorrow's festivities with fear and anticipation.

Everything has changed.

Chapter 7
Daniel

A flash of heated pleasure skittered up Daniel's spine, exploding in his mind, immobilizing him in tingling breathlessness. That was the second time in minutes, this one stronger than the last.

He opened his eyes, sitting upright in the same spot, body clenched, drink in hand despite the fugue-state mental climaxes he'd experienced. He peeked down at himself, shaft hard and jutting noticeably. Again.

Great. Another boner. My cock is a dick.

Daniel adjusted his Chalel forward, thankfully his hard-on subsiding. He was getting used to horny weirdness on Lio HomeWorld.

Thank Creator for this cape-thing!

Putting his hydro-pack on the leaf-like table next to him, he glanced up to see sweet little Sawyer at the entrance to the PrideChoice. He was a good guy, shy, and quiet. Serious. Small and cute.

Daniel felt protective of him. They'd protected each other's backs against Stanton Buey and his bully friends.

He perceived a fuzziness in Sawyer's energy he recognized as emotional damage. The same fuzziness he sensed in Jensen Buey. It didn't excuse the way Jensen abandoned their friendship, but it was a hidden awareness Daniel paid attention to.

Kassie Keegan

Sawyer nodded as Ha-Abassa Sarina spoke to him. She shared air with him, petting his shoulder reassuringly as he slipped off his sandals. Daniel attentively tracked Sawyer as he paused, then stepped through the entryway, completely disappearing.

Ah! A dampening field!

No one could see or hear what happened past the barrier.

I wonder if my senses can perceive energy flow beyond it.

Certainly not at this distance. But he would have his chance to know soon.

An Abassa priestess snagged Sawyer's sandals and swept through an entrance with an air of purpose. He'd been absently watching this happen with others for quite some time.

Daniel felt fresh and ready after mentally checking out for a while and getting mysterious hard-ons. Glancing around the room, he realized was the last Honored Nel waiting.

He knew only a little of what to expect when he stepped into the Pride-Choice. Lio preferred experiential learning, encouraging people to understand through experience.

Honored decided for themselves how to select their Prime, and therefore, the Pride they would join. Plus, each Pride had centers of instruction, they called Liani, or a City under its care and each had a different way of doing things. There were no restrictions or time limit.

Lio created the PrideChoice Ceremony to keep Primes from killing each other over the Honored Mates their Prides needed. They no longer fought. Instead, Primes were the ones chosen by the Honored in a sacred PrideChoice Ceremony.

Primes were pinnacle males in Lio society, closer to their beast-natures, very protective, and aggressive. Each PrideHome had a single Prime Ambassador who fought for his place in the Pride.

The Prime's role transformed after the Cataclysm. The Prime Ambassador became a Protector of Honored families within the Pride, and counseled the Lio Nessa, called High Nessa, who ruled the Pride.

Daniel waited patiently, ready and eager, but not anxious.

I trust my senses. I trust myself.

Anticipation, a light buzz under his skin.

My mom wanted this for me. I want this for me, and here I am. Me, out of all the Space Rats out there. This is a miracle!

Ha-Abassa Sarina gracefully waved at him in a come-hither motion, tail meandering side-to-side contentedly, kindness in her face and demeanor.

Finally, showtime.

Getting up, Daniel made his way to her. He slipped off his sandals feeling the soft woven fabric beneath his feet, which was still a new sensation for him. Space Rats didn't go without foot coverings unless they wanted their feet shredded on rough composite flooring.

He peered down and clenched his toes on the thick, colorful fibers.

I love this.

Ha-Abassa Sarina spoke soothingly.

"Daniel, it is time for your PrideChoice."

He looked up at her as she continued.

"There is no wrong decision. It is simply a step forward in your personal journey."

She touched their foreheads together, and they shared air.

"Be blessed. Enter when you are ready. Your Prime will guide you from there."

She rubbed Daniel's shoulder in support and turned to leave.

"Wait! I mean, what do I tell them when I choose?"

Kassie Keegan

"Whatever you want to, my dear. This moment is unique to you. It matters not what others do."

Got it.

He nodded, facing the entrance, then walked through.

Chapter 8
Daniel

The soothing ceremonial space, softly shadowed with a similar organic feel to the Arrivals Lounge, resembled layered palm fronds with warm, dim sunlight shining through. The room was long and high, with a deeply shadowed area close to the peaked ceiling where Daniel sensed people watching.

Elaborately designed, colorful fabrics and sheers swathed decorated entryways. A Prime Lio Nel stood tall in each entry. All with luxurious manes and strong, virile bodies.

Some seemed more relaxed than others. They all wore the traditional Lio Shendyt, which was lengths of fabric artfully draped in a skirt-like garment with a belt at their waist. Their muscular upper-bodies were bare, with cuffs covering the insides of their wrists.

Dozens of Primes watched him, an electric stillness to the atmosphere.

Daniel swallowed, nerves creeping in. Then he detected the faintest hint of musk in the room, recognizing the scent from passing brothels on SpacePort Arata.

Something sexual happened.

He hoped Sawyer was all right.

I'm going to find out.

Nervousness gone, Daniel opened his senses to the energy of the room. He perceived the burning vitality of watchers above, then each Prime's vibrant hum buzzed through him as he focused on them.

The room's Resonance tasted of power, and patience flavored by anticipation. And...

What is it?

After a moment, Daniel realized what he sensed.

Joy. There is happiness in this place.

It made him smile.

Should I say something?

"Hello."

He got closed-mouth grins and nods of acknowledgment.

At his greeting, some Primes relaxed back against their entryways. All watched him closely. They assessed him as much as he considered them.

Daniel walked the length of the hall, senses open. Dampening Fields faintly buzzed behind each Prime, but he discerned faint energy signatures beyond some of them.

Sawyer is here.

Pacing to the end, he pivoted, his eyes locked onto a Lio Nel standing close to him. He'd searched for Sawyer's unique vibrance and, amazingly, found it blazing brightly behind a Prime with an impressive dark mane and long braided beard with a shock of white down the center.

The Prime stood with his hands braced on each side of the entry in a position of readiness.

Ready for what?

Daniel wasn't sure.

He detected Sawyer so distinctly because he was connected to the

Kassie Keegan

Prime's tail, half of which was hidden beyond the dampening field. He also perceived Sawyer being cuddled by another.

Daniel's protective instincts flared. Striding to the Lio Nel, he spoke without preamble.

"I am Sawyer's friend. I need to know if he's okay."

The Prime lifted an eyebrow, his eyes steady and intense, but otherwise his only movement was a subtle, slow motion of his half-visible tail.

Daniel didn't flinch under the male's unrelenting, golden stare. He wanted to know if his friend was safe.

After some time, the male's gaze warmed. The Prime gave a slight bow forward of his head.

"I am Rukhan, Prime of Bon'Torzal Pride, led by High Nessa Haziqa. We are from the Dark Realm, Masters of Liani Discipline. It is good to make your acquaintance, Daniel Shaw."

"You know who I am?"

"Yes, of course. They announced you."

Of course.

Daniel peered down ruefully for a moment.

Dark Realm. Oh, Sawyer, please be okay.

His gaze shot back up to the Prime.

"I need to know."

Daniel kept his eyes focused and steady.

"Please."

Prime Rukhan's eyes gleamed with pleasure at his 'please.'

"To reveal which Prime and Pride an Honored has chosen could influence others to choose the same. An instinct to be with someone familiar in a new place. It is forbidden to tell you who Sawyer chose. But if precious Sawyer were mine, I would guide and care for him. I would

Savage Planet Embrace

see that his specific needs were met. *All* his needs. As would any Prime here. Does this reassure you?"

The deep, dark well of sexual power emanating from the male engulfed Daniel's senses.

Prime Rukhan languidly, salaciously raked his gaze up-and-down over him, licking his lips lingeringly with a long tongue, gazing at Daniel invitingly.

"I can meet *your* needs, too."

Yes, you could.

Needs Daniel didn't even know he had and wasn't very comfortable with, either. This male's virility blazed so potently Daniel felt a flash of fear at the shadowy depths of it.

Way too much for me.

"Thank you, no. It's just… um, no."

"I like your protectiveness and loyalty, Daniel."

Low growls of approval surrounded them.

"Why did you approach me about Sawyer?"

Do I reveal my gift to all these Primes? Can I hide what I can do from them for long, anyway?

"I sensed my friend."

Curiosity lit Prime Rukhan's eyes, but he showed superb control and didn't ask questions. Instead, he again bowed his head in respect for Daniel's choice, and his answer.

Prime Rukhan told him that Sawyer would be cared for in a roundabout way. Daniel could either trust him or not. Despite his discomfort with the Lio Nel's overt sexuality, there wasn't anything about the primal male he'd sensed as untrustworthy.

Daniel now had a boundary.

Kassie Keegan

It's a good start. I'll meet each Prime to get a feel for them.

He moved to the next Prime.

"Hello, I'm Daniel. Nice to meet you. What is your name?"

His mom had drilled manners into him and they stood him in good stead here as the Lio responded respectfully.

He met Prime after Prime, gathering an impression of their character. He asked polite getting-to-know-you questions and listened attentively to the answers.

He learned some interesting things, like Primes had to be accepted by the Pride and deemed worthy prior to fighting a Challenge to be Pride Ambassador.

He discovered they were called 'Prize' males before winning a Challenge to become 'Prime.' Only a small percentage of Lio Nels matured into Prize males.

As he spoke with them, some Primes had intimidating rampant sexuality, some had aggressive energy he didn't connect with. Some were mysterious but compelling, and some downright repelled him.

Three stood out most positively.

Prime Pinnok of the Bon'Leval Pride had a soothing, easy manner and was in charge of Liani Tech, which Daniel loved.

Prime Vicarro of the Bon'Salel Pride lead the Abassani, where priestesses and priests of Abah-Sah Trained. His fur shimmered golden-blond with a long white mane braided thickly and elaborately back from his face. The seething, yet peaceful ocean of turbulent understanding he sensed in Prime Vicarro called to the moment of connection he'd had with Ha-Abassa Sarina earlier.

And then there was Prime Cassian of the Bon'Fiel Pride, which lead Liani Combat, making Daniel hesitate despite his instant rapport with the Lio Nel.

"Combat. Prime Cassian, I am not a Master of fighting. I don't like violence, but I don't avoid it either. I'm not sure I'd be right for your Pride."

Towering over Daniel, Prime Cassian stood loose, relaxed, pure male, comfortable in his own skin, exuding strength and health. His untamed, golden-brown mane with darker tips was pushed back from his face with an ornately designed band across his forehead, his thick golden beard and mustache as wild as his mane.

A pelt of longer golden-brown hair, different from the velvety-looking fur covering most of his body, arrowed down from his broad chest over his abdomen to under his Shendyt.

He wore an ornate band around his bulging right biceps and heavily decorated wrist-cuffs, which were thicker on the inside of his wrists. Like almost all Lio, a wide, silvery ring adorned his tail near the tuft. A chunky silver ring graced the top edge of his right ear.

Prime Cassian regarded Daniel with piercing light-green eyes, a dark-blue rim surrounding the irises in a striking contrast of color. His face was among the most lion-like he'd seen, with a long, flat feline nose. He spoke in deep, rich tones.

"We all start somewhere. Plus, there are many ways to combat. Not all of them are physical."

Daniel thought for a moment, agreeing with a slow nod. The Prime grinned.

"Fighting is fucking great, though."

Daniel grinned back, remembering his satisfaction from punching the asshole Stanton in the face.

"I believe this, too."

Interesting perspective. Sounds challenging in a new way.

"What do I need to know about you, Prime Cassian?"

Kassie Keegan

Prime Cassian's knowing gaze showed awareness of the complexity of Daniel's simple question. By asking it this way, Daniel could assess what the male thought was most important about himself.

"I am devoted to my people and my Pride. I pour myself into their Protection and Provision. All Primes are thus."

He paused thoughtfully.

"I think you want to know what makes me different from other Primes. To answer this, I am the newest Prime on Lio HomeWorld."

Daniel looked closer at the scars marking Prime Cassian's right shoulder, left arm, and both thighs. The large, slightly raised scars created pale golden skin grooves in his fur. Lio wore Challenge scars proudly, not healing them completely, although they had the technology to do so.

Prime Cassian moved his shoulder down for Daniel to see easily, his tail swaying happily.

"I am young."

Daniel was surprised because Prime Cassian didn't appear young. He seemed strong and mature. The Prime gave a lopsided, closed-mouth grin.

"We Lio have good genes. See?"

He shook out his wild mane, preening with a broader grin, now showing the tips of his huge, thick fangs, making Daniel laugh.

"I will be this way until I go to the Fade, as will you as an Honored Nel."

Daniel thought briefly of his mom.

Staying healthy until the very end sounds good.

Sounding rueful, Prime Cassian's gaze remained direct.

"I have not been Chosen by an Honored as yet, though I have presented at PrideChoice Ceremonies."

Is he trying to discourage me from choosing him?

"You would be my first PrideChoice, Daniel."

Prime Cassian sighed, gazing away for a moment, his ears turning back slightly.

"I think I will make mistakes."

I like his honesty and vulnerability.

Tension rose in the Prime's posture, his ears flattening more as his eyes lifted to assess Daniel's reaction to his words.

"If it matters to you, I am not a Lio HomeWorld native. I was born Pargen'Fiel of Lio Fleet Kahlina in Galaxy Sunastrana near your planet Earth."

Daniel's bond of connection strengthened even more.

Prime Cassian is a 'Space Rat,' too!

Daniel smiled, remembering his happiness arriving earlier.

"I was born on SpacePort Arata. Today, I stepped foot on my first planet."

Prime Cassian's ears perked forward, his eyes holding a wealth of understanding about what today meant for Daniel.

"Welcome to Lio HomeWorld. May you find happiness here."

Prime Cassian exuded warmth, his energy flowing sharp, open, and clear. Daniel felt seen and safe. This male would challenge him, but he sensed his boundaries would be understood and respected.

I've made my PrideChoice.

"I'm Choosing you and your Pride, Prime Cassian."

The Prime's light-green eyes glowed silvery with joy, his broad smile showing huge fangs as he growled low with approval, its Resonance vibrating deep within his chest.

"Daniel Shaw, as Prime Ambassador, in honor of High Nessa Katohna, Guide of Liani Combat, I welcome you to the Bon'Fiel Pride."

Kassie Keegan

Growls of approval surrounded them, along with the stamping of feet in the Lio form of applause.

Daniel laughed, very happy with his choice.

I look forward to whatever is next!

Sobering, he had a flash of memory taking him back to his dad's lovingly fierce, bone-crushing hugs.

I wish...

Daniel gazed at Prime Cassian with momentary longing. Catching the look, Prime Cassian paused in concern.

"What do you need, Daniel?"

Dare I say it? I should start by being honest with these people who are my new family.

"I'd like a hug."

Prime Cassian immediately folded Daniel into a glorious embrace, holding him close to his bulk. The Prime dipped his head and snuffled Daniel's hair, scenting him, making Daniel grin at the subtle push-pull of breath.

He hugged fiercely back, enjoying the feel of velvety fur and long, soft hair, learning the masculine scent of his Prime, relaxing into the friendly, warm, enveloping hug he'd needed.

Prime Cassian drew back and shared air with him, then moved away and held out his hand. Daniel took it and walked with his Prime beyond the dampening field into the unknown.

Chapter 9
Aubrey

A rms linked, Aubrey and Stealth strolled into the Grand Palace's Bon'Fiel PrideHall Common Room.

Aubrey's dear friend Destiny Dean Coron'Rial glanced up from her newest sketch, staring. Her usual warm greeting frozen on her lips as she narrowed her eyes, her gaze darting from Aubrey to Stealth. Dots of heat blushed Destiny's pale-gold cheeks.

Oh crap, she's enraged!

Stealth stopped, immobile until Destiny rose to leave, grabbing her tablet and sketches. When she stood up, he gave Aubrey's hand a small squeeze before disentangling from her. Moving swiftly to Destiny, he took her further back into the Common Room near the windows, tail agitated, posture alert.

They spoke quietly and intently, Stealth bending to examine Destiny closely at one point. It didn't seem like a pleasant exchange.

Anxiety spiked in Aubrey. They had been growing closer, but she only now realized how close as the tenor of Destiny's unhappiness swept through her.

Scuffling and shushed sounds surrounded her, but it wasn't significant enough to grab Aubrey's attention. Her focus concentrated on the serious conversation of two of the most important people in her life.

Stealth cupped Destiny's cheek while they spoke, bringing her in for a hug. After more words, Destiny struggled to get away, her copper-colored hair flashing in the sun. He held on and brought her closer, speaking urgently. Revelation showed in her expression, then determination.

Blushing wildly at his next words, Destiny finally relaxed into Stealth, dropping her papers, and returning his embrace. They stayed there for a long moment.

Did they make up? Will I keep my friends?

Peering over Stealth's shoulder, Destiny's intent, smoky-gray gaze captured Aubrey with its unique, piercing quality. She assessed her on a spiritual level. Aubrey opened herself up, wanting Destiny to see the truth.

Stealth is my friend, not my lover.

Destiny understood. Aubrey saw it in her eyes, sensed the change in her friend's emotional hum. She relaxed some, seeing Destiny turn to Stealth, trust in her gaze.

Aubrey's eyes widened at the sweet, gentle kiss Stealth gave Destiny, her eyes burning with the memory of Léandre sharing her first kiss.

Is it Destiny's first?

Thinking about how attached Destiny was to Prime Cassian and his Zumiel LifeMate, Travar, she thought perhaps not.

Their next kiss was not-so-sweet. Aubrey gasped, scorched by the searing sexuality sizzling between them.

Stealth is right. This 'watching' thing is hot!

She blindly glanced away, not seeing anything around her while trying to catch her breath and collect herself. Peeking back, she saw Destiny bend to pick up her papers. Stealth's arm cuddled Destiny close as they crossed the room to her. Aubrey still felt worried.

"Are you okay?"

Destiny nodded, giving Aubrey a lopsided grin.

"Yes. I'm good. Stealth explained things."

Relief swept through Aubrey.

Thank Abah-Sah!

"Oh! Good!"

She hugged Destiny, needing the reassurance. Destiny hugged her back one-armed while her papers crinkled between their bodies, then pulled away, chuckling while looking around them. Aubrey's gaze swept the room, seeing Pride Mates either lying down, as if taking a nap, or staring at them, grinning broadly.

How strange.

Destiny regained Aubrey's attention with a comment as they turned to stroll together out of the Common Room.

"Now tell me all about this 'Calling' experience…"

Stealth escorted them, then left them alone in one of the communal Bathing Chambers. They floated in the huge, warm pool, Aubrey's voice echoing lightly as she explained it all.

She sensed Stealth stayed nearby, turning others away so she and Destiny could have some time together to talk. She told her friend all of it, even the most embarrassing things. The soothing water eased the sharp edge of Aubrey's worry and she relaxed more and more through the telling.

Destiny didn't flinch at any detail, not even the ones about Stealth. She listened intently, asking a few questions, nodding now and again thoughtfully. After they were dry and in fresh robes, Destiny hugged Aubrey close, speaking low and fervently.

Kassie Keegan

"Thank you."

Aubrey sensed the weight of Destiny's feelings.

"Why?"

Destiny smiled.

"Because you never lie."

"Of course I don't!"

They gathered their belongings, and Destiny twined their arms together as they walked toward the Bon'Fiel Common Room. Stealth silently followed behind them, ears, posture, and tail showing his contented mood. Destiny leaned her head against Aubrey's.

"You are a great friend, Aubrey."

Stealth growled quietly in agreement.

Aubrey murmured.

"Same."

"Time to talk with Twylah about our outfits for tomorrow. We need to bring a few males to their knees!"

Stealth growled deeper with what sounded like anticipation.

Chapter 10
Daniel

Prime Cassian lead Daniel through the entryway into a large, dimly lit room. Colorful fabrics draped the ceiling and walls, very much like the room full of entryways they walked from.

There were piles of cozy blankets and multi-hued cushions of all shapes and sizes on one side, a low table in the middle, and another fabric-draped entry on the opposite side.

Daniel sensed three new presences, but could see only one.

He got only a glimpse of the Lio Nel waiting in the room before Prime Cassian grabbed him in an enthusiastic growly hug, rubbing their cheeks together. He gave the new Lio Nel a sensuous lick up his neck, leaving no doubt they were lovers. Their vibrant Connection showed brilliantly to Daniel as they embraced.

Prime Cassian pivoted, the new fellow still clasped close, and happily made introductions.

"Daniel Shaw Bon'Fiel, this is my Zumiel, Travar Pon'Pomol Bon'Fiel."

"Zumiel?"

"Zumiel are the LifeMates of Prize Lio Nels. They help us control our beast-natures so we don't go completely feral. We try to find them in our youth, though every male is different."

Kassie Keegan

Prime Cassian's Zumiel pulled out of their hug, turning to walk to Daniel. He raised his arms widely out to the sides as he spoke, grinning broadly, not hiding his long, elegant fangs in the slightest.

"You have chosen the best Pride in all of Lio HomeWorld, Daniel!"

Travar's energy exuded warmth, as much a part of him as the fur on his body. Humor colored his tone.

"Of course, I'm not biased at all!"

Lowering his arms, Travar swiveled, giving a flirty glance to Prime Cassian, who chuckled, blowing him a kiss.

Travar wore a simple, soft-looking purple Shendyt and a thick silvery necklace with curved shell-like pendants spaced out along its lower length, ending just over his belly button. Beautiful wrist-cuffs, narrow on the outside and long on the inside, adorned his wrists.

He had clear, pale-gold eyes with a dark rim surrounding the irises. There were whiskery wisps above his plush lips and longer but close-cropped golden fur on his cheeks and chin. Travar had dark-gold fur everywhere except for the center of his body, from neck to abdomen, which was a snowy white.

His dense, dark, curly mane was braided with shiny purple beads away from his face, draping halfway down his back. Daniel hadn't seen a mane like it. Travar bowed.

"Welcome to Bon'Fiel Pride."

Daniel bowed back.

"Thank you. It's nice to meet you."

His eyes strayed back to Travar's thick, curly mane.

"Do you want to touch it?"

His gaze flew to Travar's, whose eyes held warmth and humor.

"Is it allowed?"

Travar chuckled.

"Yes, because I allow it. Come, let's make a proper introduction."

Travar stepped close, clasping Daniel by his nape, pressing their foreheads lightly together. Daniel searched for Travar's nape under the thick, soft mane, but his fingers tangled in the curly mass. He gave up and gently grasped Travar's neck along with a handful of mane.

Travar had a soothing spice to his scent, distinctive from Prime Cassian's, but similar. They linked in his senses.

He relaxed as they shared air, flowing naturally into a loose embrace, with them resting their heads on each other's shoulder, arms wrapped around each other.

Daniel toyed with a curl, satisfying his curiosity about its texture. Travar spoke softly.

"Thank you for trusting Cassian. You will not regret it."

He pulled away to see Travar's face.

"You love him a lot, don't you?"

"Oh, yes. And he loves me. Trust and Devotion."

Travar had the confidence of a well cared-for Mate. Daniel wanted that for himself, not with these males specifically, but wanted the experience of loving and being loved.

He enjoyed their open affection. Human men could be reticent to share their feelings, but it was not so with Lio Nels. You knew where you stood in their esteem, their fondness or disdain was quite clear.

Distracted, Daniel glanced toward where he sensed the other silent presences.

Are they going to show themselves?

Travar brought his attention back.

"Cassian 'Found and Bound' me as soon as we matured. I didn't fight him hard."

Kassie Keegan

Smiling fondly in reminiscence, Travar peered over at Prime Cassian, his eyes glowing with affection. The Prime watched them, satisfaction buzzing through his Resonance.

Bemused, Daniel again glanced back toward the quiet watchers as Travar continued.

"We have been together all our lives. Prize males are aggressive, difficult, and unfocused until they find their Zumiel. But Cassian has always been level-headed, thinking with his brain and not his hormones."

Travar laughed, giving Daniel another glimpse of his elegant fangs.

"The Abassani say we are Fated Mates, born on the same day in the same Fleet. Our Honored grandparents were all rescued from the same disaster on the same day, too. A Space Pleasure Cruise explosion!"

Travar sighed.

"Many year spans later, their Lio Nessa daughters became our mothers. There is one other born for us, but he is discovering his destiny. I say no one can fight destiny and win. She has her way with us all."

Travar shared an amused, secret-filled glance with Prime Cassian.

I love a mystery!

Still, distraction nipped at him.

Who the hell is hiding in the room?

He couldn't relax until he knew.

"Daniel."

He glanced at Prime Cassian, realizing he'd been watching him closely.

"Why do you look over there?"

"Someone is there."

"Someone?"

"Yeah. Two someones."

Savage Planet Embrace

Prime Cassian unexpectedly boomed a laugh. Travar grinned broadly.

They know people are there.

"Come on out, Raaida and Rahimi! You do not fool our Pride Mate!"

Two shadows separated themselves from the darkened walls where he sensed them.

"May I present the twins Raaida and Rahimi, our Lio Nessa Protectors."

The identical, elegant, lithe female Lio Nessas bowed deeply to him.

Their clothing was leather-like straps gathered strategically to cover their most private areas, otherwise leaving most of their lean, muscular bodies visible. They had tiny knives strapped everywhere, along with two large knives each.

Raaida and Rahimi were beautiful and deadly. Daniel returned their bow, speaking politely.

"Nice to meet you."

They raised, then the twins intently stared at him, unmoving. He scrutinized them back, the room falling quiet, the only sound coming from the faint shush of an air current fluttering fabric. Daniel followed their lead, staying silent, and still, keeping his attention on the badass Lio Nessas.

He didn't sense aggression from them, but he wasn't taking any chances, so he waited for a cue from someone in the room. However, no one moved or spoke. After some time, he saw one of the Lio Nessas give a small grin and nudge the other with her shoulder.

"Told you."

"It wasn't long enough!"

"Yes, it was!"

The nudger walked close enough for him to scent her unique fragrance.

"I am Raaida."

Kassie Keegan

She regarded him, her eyes a pale-blue, her gaze direct.

"Welcome to Bon'Fiel Pride. You are under my protection."

Putting her hand over her heart, Raaida growled roughly in pledge. As she moved back, her sister stepped forward, her scent identical to her sister's.

He thought perhaps Lio, with their amazing sense of smell, couldn't tell them apart. Despite their similarities, their energy patterns flowed distinctively to Daniel, ensuring he would never confuse them.

"Welcome Daniel Shaw Bon'Fiel. I am Rahimi. You are under my protection."

Rahimi put her hand over her heart and growled long and low. Daniel nodded his appreciation.

"Thank you."

Raaida spoke up.

"We are surprised and proud you sensed us. Most cannot."

Rahimi chimed in.

"And you are comfortable with silence."

He would be honest with these people who were his new family.

"No, I was *un*comfortable with the silence."

They flashed fang-filled grins. Prime Cassian gave Daniel a pat on the back, helping him relax even more.

"Yes, but you didn't show it."

Something grabbed Daniel's attention from their conversation. He turned to Prime Cassian, his brow wrinkling in thought.

"We need protection?"

Travar stepped forward.

"Lio are close to our beast-natures. In our Prides and Cities there are pleasant Lio and unpleasant Lio, like there are pleasant Earthers and unpleasant Earthers. Plus, there are true wild beasts who roam the spaces in-between."

Daniel considered.

"But it's for more than wild animals, isn't it?"

Travar answered, stark and simple.

"Yes."

Daniel thought about the asshole Stanton.

They certainly let some jerks in.

His forehead creased with worry.

What if there are more of them than nice people?

Travar spoke sharply.

"Whatever you are worrying about, stop."

Daniel peered up at Travar, surprised.

Is he reading my mind?

No, more like reading his body language. The Lio were masters at it.

"I'll try."

Prime Cassian touched his arm lightly, and Daniel focused on him.

"Raaida and Rahimi work with Commander Ferrand to protect all our Pride, most especially you, a gifted Honored Nel. You are a treasure. This is not a euphemism, we protect our treasures."

Fabric surrounding the entry fluttered as a regal Lio Nessa breezed in, an elaborate band across her velvety forehead, ears high, long tail swishing in delight. Dressed in flowing, floaty robes, the Lio Nessa approached him in warm greeting, hands outstretched.

Kassie Keegan

Daniel reached out to her instinctively, her energy a glow he wanted to touch. They clasped hands as their foreheads rested softly together. He knew who this was without words.

My Pride Leader.

She pulled away to gaze into his eyes, bowing her head slightly, and introduced herself.

"I am Katohna, High Nessa of Bon'Fiel Pride. You are welcome among us, Daniel Shaw Bon'Fiel."

Her cordial greeting made the backs of his eyes burn. He thought about his mom.

You'd like these people, Mom.

Daniel cleared his throat, but his voice still rasped deep with emotion.

"Thank you, High Nessa Katohna. This means so much to me."

"I imagine it has been quite a day span for you! How about we feed you and you rest? The next day span will be here soon enough."

"Sounds wonderful!"

High Nessa Katohna lead him toward the center of the room.

"We stay here until we introduce you to the Prides. They will broadcast the celebration all over Lio HomeWorld and to all Lio Colonies and Fleets across the Known Galaxies."

"Each Chosen Prime will present their new Honored to the other Prides, eventually ending with a homecoming welcome for the Honored with their new Pride."

"Bon'Fiel Pride will cheer you to the rafters when you finally get to them! We're glad you chose us!"

Her enthusiasm was infectious.

"I'm glad, too!"

Wait. Did she say introductions to all the Prides? And it's broadcast?

"So I meet… everyone on live holo-vids?"

High Nessa Katohna petted the side of his face when she saw his hesitation.

"Not *everyone*, but most of the unmated from each Pride will be there to mix and meet. It's a joyful time for all! There will be food and drink, song and dance, and hopefully many MateDances."

Prime Cassian and Travar agreed, the twins' eyes sparkling with anticipation. Daniel was surprised.

"MateDances. You mean, I could meet my Mates at this greet-thing? Already?"

High Nessa Katohna smiled.

"Of course! You might even MateDance!"

Daniel's face warmed because he'd only ever danced in his room. Alone.

High Nessa Katohna looked at him with understanding, squeezing his shoulders reassuringly.

"If you were overwhelmed this day span, as most feel, the next span will be even more so. We stay here in a calm space so you can relax your first night on Lio HomeWorld."

The High Nessa led them all to the low table as Prime Cassian tossed over cushions to sit on before joining them. Raiida and Rahimi melted back into the shadows, then returned with plates of food.

As Daniel sat, a wave of tiredness washed over him.

So much change in one day!

He was peopled out, making him glad there were only a few in the room with him now.

They ate and drank their fill, talking with each other in relaxed camaraderie about inconsequential everyday things, providing undemanding insight into their world. He enjoyed the way they interacted, including him, but not requiring him to take part beyond his capacity. Daniel felt bone-tired.

Prime Cassian sat near Travar on the opposite side of the table, tails wound together, touching frequently. Now and again, their tail rings clinked, colliding.

After the meal, Prime Cassian took him to the small but well-appointed grooming room. He gave Daniel a soft, short sarong to wear and showed him the elegantly curved Mistaray. Strangely, it looked like a single giant free-standing white tusk suspended over a dip in the floor.

Daniel grew up using a portable and efficient Solaray to laser-wash grime away. Squandering water to bathe was a punishable crime on SpacePorts. It also had the added benefit of whisking away waste, although a Lio Solaray kept scents intact.

"I don't think I'm ready for the Mist thing yet."

"That's fine, Daniel. Use the Solaray right over there."

Prime Cassian showed where the button was, speaking over his shoulder as he left the room.

"Come out when you are refreshed and prepared to rest."

Daniel activated the Solaray. It was a different shade of blue than he was used to, but he felt better, even if it was only because it was familiar when everything else was foreign.

He put on the sarong and looked at himself in the mirrored wall. Same brown eyes, wavy brown hair, and light-gold skin. Identical outside appearance, but he felt changed inside. Hopeful and new. And so tired.

I need to sleep!

He walked into the main room. They'd pushed the cushions into a nice nest for sleeping, the Lio piled on the cushions to rest, a heap of boneless feline relaxation, limbs and tails every which way.

He kept apart from the others, his skin too sensitive to be touched. Daniel could barely tolerate the sarong he wore or the super soft blanket he wrapped himself in. His extreme sensitivity got worse as the night went on, making him toss and turn.

His shaft throbbed uncomfortably hard, yet he couldn't bear the touch of his own hand when he tried to adjust, longing for another's caress.

He thought of the flower he'd scented when he first stepped foot on Lio HomeWorld. He remembered the scent and burned.

Chapter 11
Daniel

Daniel faced the huge, elaborately decorated Introduction Entrance of Capital Maituri's Grand Room. The doors before him loomed tall and wide, white, with layered palm fronds etched into their shiny surface. Rhythmic drum-based music and muted conversation sounded on the other side.

High Nessa Katohna and Prime Cassian stood on either side of him. Travar, along with Raiida, Rahimi, and the vibrant Lio Nessa, Twylah, were behind him.

I wonder if I'll meet my Mates today? High Nessa said it could happen.

Daniel chaffed in his nice, new clothes as he waited, his skin supersensitive. Only now, he felt hot, too, like he had a fever but wasn't sick.

Trying not to fidget, he occupied himself by sniffing the ribbon he grabbed from his pocket. The scent soothed him enough to get through the awful greet-thing. He closed his eyes and shook his head at how baffling his behavior had been earlier that morning.

Savage Planet Embrace

The Bon'Fiel styling crew descended after his small group had a quiet, relaxed First Meal. Six Lio entered the room, wearing harnesses strapped across their lean bodies with tools and devices holstered or hanging from the straps.

The Lio Nessas had swaths of gauzy fabric covering the tops of their breasts and short skirts, split in the back for their tails. The Lio Nels wore Shendyts, with large decorative belts. All wore sandals.

His companions rose, letting the crew get to work. Slower to understand what was happening, Daniel was a bit confused.

Prime Cassian stood still and relaxed, arms extended out from his sides as a Lio Nessa stylist began fluffing his fur, trimming here and there with laser shears. He noticed Daniel's attention and gave him a warm grin.

"We do this for big events. You get used to it."

Yipping when his stylist nipped him on the shoulder playfully, Prime Cassian growled a short chuff of rebuke at her and focused forward regally dismissive, which made her ears lower and flick, but she kept grinning as she worked.

The entire room became filled with purpose and affection. They styled everyone in a tidal wave of efficiency.

A bold Lio Nessa swept into the room, heading directly to Daniel. Magenta wisps of fabric artistically wound around her body with randomly spaced ribbons attached. She had magenta outlines accentuating her shimmering golden eyes, examining him up-and-down with an air of intent. Raising her hand to her chin thoughtfully, her tail whipped back-and-forth with determination.

"Bring me his Chalel!"

Her sudden feminine roar surprised Daniel, and he didn't school his features to hide it. The Lio Nessa's eyes twinkled with humor, waving dismissively as she circled him.

"Oh, cutie, you get used to it."

Kassie Keegan

Daniel glanced over at Prime Cassian, who had said the same thing.

He made a 'Did you hear this?' motion with his hands at the stylist who had nipped him. The Lio Nessa laughed heartily as she blew a puff of air at his face with one of her tools.

Prime Cassian growled in rebuke again, which was again completely ignored because there was no true aggression from him even as he grumped.

"You are a menace!"

This is what big families are like, what I'd wondered about and longed for in my lonely bunk on SpacePort Arata.

Enjoying the peaceful thread of Connection among the Pride members, Daniel took a deep breath, getting his emotions under control. Looking up, he realized the shouting Lio Nessa stood before him, absorbed by his expressions. She spoke kindly, with a soft smile.

"Time for a proper introduction. I am Twylah Bon'Fiel."

She tilted her head to him, and he tilted his head respectfully back.

"I'm Daniel Shaw."

"Daniel Shaw Bon'Fiel, you mean?"

Warmth filled him at the reminder.

"Yes, you're right. It's my name now."

"Say it then! You are ours. Let no one forget it. Most of all, know it *yourself.*"

He grinned.

"I am Daniel Shaw Bon'Fiel. Nice to meet you, Twylah Bon'Fiel."

He held back his natural inclination to shake hands. Something humans had been doing for millennia, but wasn't the norm on Lio HomeWorld. Twylah approached him.

"May we share air?"

Daniel agreed, and she stepped forward. They gently clasped each other's napes as they made acquaintance. Abruptly, buzzing awareness zinged through him.

Creator, the scent! It's here, on this Lio Nessa.

Releasing Twylah's nape, Daniel grasped her waist lightly, bringing her closer to sniff her fur. She stood stock-still, but relaxed, despite how strange he acted. Burying his nose in her neck, he took a deep breath.

No, that's not it. Nice, but not my flower. I can't stop until I find the source of the scent.

Lifting his head on another breath, he realized the colorful ribbons with unique patterns tied at random in Twylah's outfit held distinct fragrances. He aimed for her shoulder and there it was!

This one! This is it!

Again, he sniffed at the ribbon on her shoulder, his eyes rolling back with pleasure.

Oh, yes. This is the one. I have to have this ribbon.

Focusing on it avariciously, Daniel wanted to rip it off of Twylah's garment.

Stop. Breathe. This isn't like you. Think.

Daniel forced himself to step away, clenching his fists to keep from grabbing the strip of fabric he couldn't tear his eyes from.

I want this scented ribbon more than I've wanted anything, and I can't have it.

At the thought, bestial anger rose within Daniel, unlike he'd experienced before. He growled.

Suddenly, Prime Cassian stood firmly between him and his prize, prompting Daniel to growl again, deeper.

With lightning speed, Prime Cassian grabbed the back of Daniel's head, growling fiercely, grazing his scalp with pricking claws. He pressed their foreheads together, forcing Daniel to share air with him.

Kassie Keegan

Prime Cassian's strong, fiery male scent broke the spiral of aggression he'd fallen into when he sniffed the ribbon.

What the fuck was that?

Seeing Daniel gain control, Prime Cassian let him go, but stayed close, hands loose on Daniel's shoulders. He spoke calmly.

"What are you feeling?"

"I need the ribbon, Prime Cassian. I feel like I could *kill* for it. I can't... What is happening?"

"Calm. Why do you want this specific one?"

"The flower. It's the flower I first scented when I stepped onto Lio HomeWorld. I need it. What kind is it?"

I have to know.

Prime Cassian ignored Daniel's question.

"You seem to be out of sorts today. Are you okay?"

"No. I think I'm sick. My skin feels weird and I'm hot."

And my achy cock won't stop throbbing.

Daniel breathed deeply, getting a big whiff of Prime male and a delicate hint of the scent he loved more than any other. His eyes strayed to where he thought Twylah might be behind Prime Cassian's bulk.

Perhaps if I ask nicely, she will give me what I want.

He certainly would not make it past Prime Cassian with force.

"Twylah?"

"Yes, Daniel?"

"May I have the wonderful-smelling ribbon on your shoulder?"

"You want to keep it?"

If I say 'No,' will it make her more inclined to offer it to me? It would be a lie, though. I will never *let it go.*

"Yes, I will keep it for forever. Will you still give it to me?"

The precious ribbon appeared, grasped in a feminine feline hand over Prime Cassian's shoulder. Daniel snatched it, causing Prime Cassian to firm his hold on his shoulders.

He brought it immediately to his nose, instantly soothed by the blessed scent, his spirit and body settling. Prime Cassian's grip on him relaxed.

"Better now?"

"Yes. I'm sorry. I don't know what happened there."

"I'm here for you, Daniel. We all are."

Prime Cassian moved back, and he saw the room for the first time since his ribbon obsession over took him. The expressions on their faces ranged from wonder to excitement, some grinning with delight. There was none of the condemnation he expected.

Daniel lifted the strip of fabric back to his nose, feeling its soothing power over his senses.

"What kind of flower is this?"

Twylah stepped forward, her vibrant energy glowing even brighter as she scrutinized him affectionately.

"A very special one. You may keep the ribbon for forever as you wished."

Sweeping her gaze around the room, she clapped her hands.

"Back to work! We must be ready!"

Prime Cassian returned to his Lio Nessa stylist. Moving closer to Daniel, Twylah waggled her fingers in his face for attention.

"I design garments. There's a fancy word for who I am and what I do, but do you care, my dear?"

She smirked.

"No, you don't, and neither do I. All you need to know is I will dress you in garments causing all the unmated Honored Nessas to cream their thighs. Some of the Mated ones, too."

"Um."

"Excellent. I need your cooperation."

"Um."

"Ah! Here's your Chalel! Lovely designs. Delightful! I can work with this."

"Okay."

Twylah whirled to one of her fellow Lio Nessas and began talking about outfit ideas. Daniel stood, sniffing his new favorite thing, relaxed and compliant.

He peered over to Prime Cassian, who was being dressed in a beautiful, draped fabric Shendyt. His Prime's expression became questioning. Daniel shrugged.

"You get used to it, right?"

Prime Cassian grinned a terrifying, fang-filled grin. Nodding, he pointed at Daniel with both hands.

"Exactly."

Daniel opened his eyes.

He felt good. He knew he looked attractive in his dark-brown, buttery-soft leather trousers and vest, his green and gold Chalel draped over one shoulder.

A Master Designer, Twylah dressed him in deceptively simple garments, enhancing his attributes, subtly enticing the eye.

His trousers were in separate pieces that fit him perfectly, molding to him in all the right places while still giving him room to move. The leg sections attached on the out-facing side to a decorative metal belt at his waist.

There was a loincloth section reaching down to mid-thigh made of the same leather, draped front and back. The trousers had some gaps, especially over his flanks, so he knew he flashed skin as he moved.

Daniel felt daring.

His one-piece vest fit him beautifully. It attached at his sides by intricately woven strips of leather with a deep V showing off his chest and back, leaving his arms exposed. The cut emphasized his broad shoulders. He wore barely there sandals on his feet.

Daniel took another sniff of the ribbon, turning to his High Nessa.

"Any advice?"

The regal female scrutinized him, affection lighting her features.

"Be yourself and find joy, Daniel. Trust your senses and instincts. You are Bon'Fiel. We are proud you chose us."

High Nessa Katohna bent, giving him a gentle rub, her velvety fur a sweet caress against his cheek.

"We choose you, too."

She faced the doors again, waiting patiently for their introduction. Emotion burst inside Daniel in a potent jumble as he, too, faced forward, feeling a comforting hand pet down his back. Travar.

In this moment, he felt both powerful and vulnerable.

Within this new Pride Family, I can do, or be, anything.

Chapter 12
Daniel

The heavy doors opened smoothly, revealing a huge oval room made of light.

Capital Maituri's Grand Room featured towering ceilings, elegantly curved walls, and smooth, shiny floors glowing with soft white in flowing lines, drawing the eye. The brilliant blue sky shone through a grid pattern spanning the center of the ceiling.

Along the walls were three huge buffets interspersed among large rounded nooks filled with over-sized low-slung couches stacked with many comfortable-looking cushions. Above each nook fluttered a unique banner.

Three elevated oval stages dominated the middle of the room.

Music stopped, allowing the din of conversation to overtake the room. Lio and Honored were everywhere, strolling, chatting, and lounging on angular seats and settees throughout the space.

Most of them now looked at him.

Oh, shit, that's a lot of people.

Smoothing his expression, Daniel stood proudly.

I own my life. This is my Choice, my Pride, and I am proud to be here.

An elegant Lio Nessa sparsely dressed in swatches of shimmery gold fabric with draped chains and jewels, stood to the side of the door, intoning in a loud resonant voice that carried throughout the room.

"Announcing…"

Conversation stopped.

"Daniel Shaw Bon'Fiel!"

He didn't recognize the sound that swelled around the room at first, but then he realized many of the Lio stomped their feet in applause. Joyful roars and supportive human shouts began in the purple and gold nook to his right, others throughout the enormous space joining in.

Their powerful, joyful energy crashed upon him in a breathtaking wave. He took it all in, savoring the moment.

A bright blast of emotional energy came from Prime Cassian, prompting Daniel to look at him. His Prime stood stoically pleased, utterly controlled, not a flick of tail or ear showing the depths of Prime Cassian's feelings. But Daniel knew.

His Prime looked at him, his face and body still, his eyes shimmering. He spoke deeply, meaningfully.

"Thank you, Daniel."

Prime Cassian nodded formally, his hand sweeping out toward the room gallantly.

"You may lead us in."

Daniel took his cues from Prime Cassian and, imitating his proud, formal demeanor, strode forward into the room. Eventually, the cheers and stomping died down into a more toned-down burble of conversation on all sides.

A stunningly beautiful Lio Nessa glided to them. Gold outlined her eyes, brightened her lips, covered her nipples, and shone along the rims of her ears.

Kassie Keegan

She dripped with jewels. Her only clothes were a small shimmery gold drape of fabric between her legs and a long flowing cape attached to her shoulders by golden chains. Tiny chains secured her sandals, wrapping around her lower legs like glittering ribbons of gold.

When the regal Lio Nessa stopped in front of Daniel, the announcer introduced her with quiet authority.

"Oriela Coron'Rial, Lio Crown High Nessa, Ruler of Lio HomeWorld, treasured granddaughter of Lio High Nessa Vicari of Pride Bon'Rial."

She swept her hand out to Daniel.

"This is Daniel Shaw Bon'Fiel, Honored Nel of Lio High Nessa Katohna Bon'Fiel, treasured daughter of Lio High Nessa Akelah Bon'Fiel."

The announcer curled her hand toward Prime Cassian.

"First PrideChoice of Prime Cassian Pargen'Fiel Bon'Fiel, treasured son of Charlotte Pargen'Fiel of Lio Fleet Khalina in Galaxy Sunastrana, Prime grandson of Prime Mezere Pargen'Fiel, beloved of Katherine Bennett Pargen'Fiel."

Clasping her hands together, the announcer turned to Daniel with an air of expectation.

To him, it all sounded like, 'Blah, blah Lio. Ruler, blah-blah. Daughter, name. Name, *Daniel*. More meaningless names. Daughter, blah-blah, treasured granddaughter. Blahdy-blah, Prime son, blah, Katherine, blah.'

Still, he'd listened intently. Although most of the announcer's words were insignificant to him, he heard the way she said them and understood the emphasis she made on family ties.

Seems like family connections are important here. I didn't hear my folks mentioned.

Daniel and those with him bowed respectfully, but it bothered him. He wanted his parents' names with him on Lio HomeWorld, even if they could not physically be there. Before anyone could speak, he turned to the announcing Lio Nessa, speaking quietly.

"Ma'am."

Her eyebrows rose in surprise.

"Yes?"

"Please make note I am the treasured son of Lauren and Lukas Shaw of SpacePort Arata in Galaxy Avecorastrana."

They looked at each other for a long moment. He didn't sense aggression in her energy, but he'd surprised her, making her assess him deeper and speculate about him.

Yeah, you can wonder. And while you do that, respect my parents.

"Noted, Daniel Shaw Bon'Fiel, First PrideChoice of Prime Cassian Bon'Fiel Pargen'Fiel, treasured son of Lauren and Lukas Shaw of SpacePort Arata in Galaxy Avecorastrana."

This time, the announcer Lio Nessa bowed to him. He nodded and bowed, then turned back to the beautiful ruler of the entire World he lived on, and wanted to be a part of.

Calm, stay calm.

He swallowed, waiting to see what would happen next.

Crown High Nessa Oriela assessed him with cool gray eyes, as sharp as diamonds. He sensed the shrewdness and depth of her perception, wondering if she had a gift like he had. She spoke in beautiful, resonant tones.

"How interesting you are, Daniel Shaw Bon'Fiel, treasured son of Lauren and Lukas and, I dare say, even more deeply appreciated by Bon'Fiel Pride after your uncommon, bold display."

Stomps, roars, and shouts came from his right and scattered throughout the room, but he kept his attention on the most important person in his World, the dangerous and beautiful Crown High Nessa. His Bon'Fiel escorts stayed a silent bulwark of support.

Crown High Nessa Oriela flicked her gaze to the announcer Lio Nessa, who responded by going close to her.

Kassie Keegan

I am so fucked.

Daniel silently, respectfully, bowed again to the announcer, staying tight and controlled. The Crown High Nessa waved her hand and three other elegant Lio Nessas came forward, escorted by three handsome, hulking Lio Nels. She gestured at the newcomers.

"These are some of my Harem Mates."

One of the Lio Nessas was a tiny thing, who was very pregnant.

Daniel's control cracked as he looked at her cute bulge of a belly. She grinned widely back at him, showing adorable little fangs. He gave her a warm smile, enjoying the content buzz of her sweet energy.

"You look happy."

"I am."

The sweet Lio Nessa nuzzled Crown High Nessa Oriela, who petted her tummy with affection. Daniel calmed, sensing the swell of loving energy among the Crown High Nessa's Mates.

A hard-as-nails leader who loved her family as intensely as the Crown High Nessa did wouldn't harm him for loving his family, too.

One of her Lio Nels enfolded the little Lio Nessa into his protective arms as Crown High Nessa Oriela turned back to him.

"Will you share air with me?"

Gasps sounded throughout the room at her request. He agreed, recognizing the tremendous honor from the reactions of those around him.

She took his nape in a firm, decisive grip, placing her bejeweled, softly-furred brow against his. The faceted jewels on her forehead were hard, but warm from her body. She gave a hint of claw in her hold, but he stayed relaxed, gripping the back of her nape gently but firmly.

Warm vitality flowed smoothly through them in an easy arc from where their palms and foreheads connected, chased by a sensation of coolness in its wake.

Savage Planet Embrace

The regal Lio Nessa had a woodsy scent and a sharp, unforgettable energy pattern that felt honest, strong, and true. He respected this being, her affection warming him. She pulled away with a soft smile.

"Welcome to Lio HomeWorld, Daniel Shaw Bon'Fiel, treasured son of Lauren and Lukas Shaw of SpacePort Arata in Galaxy Avecorastrana!"

She kissed him on his brow where they'd touched.

Again, the room erupted in stomps and roars as she and her entourage sauntered away to speak with others. Rhythmic music resumed, and most returned to their conversations.

High Nessa Katohna pivoted, regarding Daniel, her mouth pursed, eyebrows high, then glanced meaningfully at Prime Cassian.

"Very… interesting!"

"Yes, it was."

Prime Cassian angled close to their quiet Protectors.

"Raaida and Rahimi, be invisible, but do not leave him. Claws will be out."

The Lio Nessas nodded, giving Daniel a reassuring pet on each shoulder before melting into the crowd. High Nessa Katohna led them forward, ready to introduce him to the Prides.

Daniel took a surreptitious sniff of the ribbon, soothed by its scent, then leaned toward Prime Cassian as they walked in measured strides to the edge of the huge circular room.

"Am I in trouble? Did I do something wrong for the Pride?"

Prime Cassian reassured him.

"No, Daniel. You were authentic and perfect, which is why your blessing will anger the status-seekers among us. You are competition."

"Status-seekers?"

Travar nodded at an acquaintance they passed as he answered.

Kassie Keegan

"Yes."

"I call them assholes."

Travar looked at him, astonished.

"This is an insult?"

"Well, yeah. It is."

He looked flabbergasted.

"But ass is delicious."

Daniel barked a laugh, but no one joined him.

He gaped at his Lio companions, all of whom, including High Nessa Katohna and Twylah, nodded in agreement with Travar. Prime Cassian licked his lips.

"I wouldn't know!"

Travar grinned.

"Ah. There's no rush to such pleasures."

Daniel blushed to the roots of his hair in a raging wash of color. Prime Cassian tilted his head toward him, smiling.

"We've embarrassed you with our honesty. We must do it frequently to get this beautiful color!"

His companions chuckled, then Travar spoke up, excitedly.

"Let's have our own word for them! The Honored Nessas made me consume a bite of 'muffin' once. I think she called it a 'banina muffin.' It was disgusting! We can call status-seekers 'Muffins.'"

Daniel compressed his lips so he wouldn't laugh out-loud again, disbelief and humor coloring his words.

"You want to call assholes 'Muffins?'"

Travar protested.

"No! That would insult tasty ass! We can call status-seekers 'Muffins' because they are too sweet and insubstantial. Plus, mean people leave a foul taste."

Daniel laughed.

This is great!

"Got it. Gold-diggers and jerks are 'Muffins.'"

Travar looked at him blankly.

"We do not dig the gold here. Mimetic Mineral is the chief export of Lio HomeWorld, however."

Daniel grinned wider.

"Got it."

Prime Cassian pushed Daniel to the left with his tail, urging him to follow High Nessa Katohna.

"Now we mingle and show you off!"

Sarcasm dripped from Daniel's words.

"Oh, joy."

Prime Cassian gestured for his attention.

"See what you can learn from those you meet. I look forward to your insight."

"You want to know what *I* think about people?"

"Very much so."

Daniel turned to his High Nessa, who glanced back at him, agreeing.

Okay! This is a game-changer.

It switched his perspective. No longer a bug under their microscope, they would be in *his* sights.

Maybe this can be fun!

Chapter 13
Commander Ferrand

Commander Ferrand Bon'Fiel observed Bon'Fiel Pride's newest Honored Nel with great interest and complete focus.

He was a beauty with wavy brown hair, close-cropped on the sides and back, and longer on the top. He sported a trim beard and mustache, lightly covered with human fur across his chest and down his torso.

Ferrand got glimpses of pale golden skin through slashes in his trousers as they introduced him to each Pride. The Honored Nel nodded respectfully, his body moving with solid, masculine grace.

Twylah designed those garments to torture me.

Bon'Fiel Pride would be the last Pride they presented him to. He and his Coalition Brethren would welcome Daniel quite warmly.

He peered over at his Brother of the Heart, Léandre, who stood back and to the side of where Aubrey lingered.

Léandre, like Ferrand, admired Daniel, and took obvious delight in Aubrey's rapt expression as she worked her position in the room to keep eyes on Daniel. Léandre had already Declared for her. He and Jovian would do so soon.

He sought Jovian, who was in his usual corner, tucked into the curve of their Pride's assigned area for the Presentation. But instead of being buried in his tablet working on projects, his focus locked on the new Bon'Fiel Honored Nel, too.

Oh, yes, Daniel is the One.

Ferrand quietly commed his Second-in-Command. Sec. Com. Savani took care of things at Bon'Fiel PrideHome while he was with Katohna and Cassian in the Capital.

His private holo-comm gave a slight shimmer beside his right eye. He activated it with a specific squint of his eye, chose his Sec. Com. with an extended glance at her contact symbol on the tiny shimmering screen, and waited for the connection.

"Commander."

"Savani, we will stay longer than expected."

There was a long, thoughtful pause.

"It's the Bon'Fiel Honored Nel, isn't it?"

"Most definitely."

His savvy Sec. Com. paused again.

"I'm watching the feeds. No one in the Known Galaxies is going to know what to make of him. And those not viewing today will pull it up once word gets around."

He scrutinized Daniel, then turned to observe a fully entranced Aubrey. Ferrand felt predatory, heavily influenced by his beast-nature, which he usually had no problem controlling. For him, it was definitive confirmation.

Aubrey is finally Called to Mate.

Sec. Com. Savani asked point-blank.

"Will you Dance and Declare?"

Ferrand growled low, prompting uncomfortable glances, and subtle and not-so-subtle movement away from where he stood casually against the wall, arms crossed. Sec. Com. Savani sounded amused.

"I'd say, 'yes.' You're not fooling anybody. We all know you have a hard-on for Aubrey, and not because she's Shaktah."

She's my *Shaktah.*

Lio Nessas needing help to conceive coveted Aubrey's scent-covered blankets and used clothing. She was utterly blind to it, simply accepting the always-new clothes and linens.

In so many ways, Aubrey innocently trusted. In many other ways, she did not. Her sweetness of character drew Ferrand deeper than her scent ever would. Aubrey needed the depths of love he had to give, and in return, she brought life and color into his regimented existence.

He stated a stark truth.

"I love her."

"Does she know?"

"She knows. She hasn't been prepared to hear it. Makes it too real and she's afraid. Our Honored Nel changes things."

There was another long pause.

"Is she ready now?"

Ferrand gazed at his caring, strong yet vulnerable, beloved Honored Nessa. One of Aubrey's favorite Earther sayings came to his mind.

"Ready or not…"

Sec. Com. Savani finished the phrase, having heard it often from her Honored Nessa friends.

"Here you come?"

"It's my hope, Savani. My sincerest hope."

Ferrand wanted a complete family, craving deep connection with his Lio and Honored Mates. He hoped Aubrey and their Honored Nel would heal his heart, and the hearts of his Coalition Brethren, Léandre and Jovian.

Kassie Keegan

Sec. Com. Savani reassured him.

"We're good here, Boss. Thanks for letting me know."

"You're going to get everyone in the PrideHome to the feeds, aren't you?"

"Abah-Sah knows, yes! We won't miss a second. Make your move, Commander. We cheer you!"

He sighed before voicing his deepest fear, next to losing Léandre and Jovian.

"They could refuse. We could become Bereft."

"Not a chance, sir. For Abah-Sah's sake, Léandre instructs other Nels how to MateDance! Combined with your beefcake and Jovian's intellect, you're undeniable!"

"Beefcake? You've been learning Earther slang from Vivian again, haven't you?"

"Yes, sir!"

He could hear her crunching.

"Snacks? Already?"

She spoke with her mouth full, slurring her s-sounds.

"Oh, yeth! We are ready! Go get 'em, thir!"

Roars and stomping resounded in the background. His eyes pricked with emotion at their display of support.

I thank Abah-Sah every day for being adopted into such a loving Pride.

Ferrand growled.

"I'll make my move when *I'm* ready."

She swallowed, chuckling.

"Yes, sir! Enjoy!"

He grinned to himself as his Sec. Com. disconnected, the shimmer near his eye dissipating. Standing straight, Ferrand stalked over to Jovian.

Ready or not…

Chapter 14
Jovian

Jovian Bon'Fiel, adopted from the Disgraced and Disbanded Bon'Ocal Pride, flicked his thick, wavy golden mane over to the side in a practiced move. A habit since childhood, the wild waves covered the chink in his ear.

He briefly flashed back to when Commander Varushka Bon'Tecol sliced his ear from behind, Klavdiya Bon'Tecol in front, watching in stone-faced judgment. They'd healed the mark open as a reminder to him and others of what had happened.

As if I could ever forget.

Jovian shook his head, a physical reaction to his disturbing thoughts. To observers, it would be just another strange thing he did. He'd given up caring what those outside his friends and Pride thought ages ago.

His eyes locked onto Daniel Shaw Bon'Fiel.

You chose well.

Bon'Fiel Pride was a generous, loving, boisterous lot. He was thankful they adopted him into their midst when he needed them most.

They will do the same for you, Daniel.

Kassie Keegan

Jovian swung his gaze over to Aubrey, who couldn't take her eyes off of Daniel, either. He grinned.

She had not once been interested in an Honored Nel.

Léandre is correct, she is Called to Mate.

Anticipation swelled within him.

And so are we.

He'd returned to the Bon'Fiel Pride and his Coalition Brethren, Ferrand and Léandre, from his last Prowl just before Aubrey first arrived on Lio HomeWorld. Her damage matched his damage. Her rage echoed his, and they'd bonded as they healed.

Aubrey fascinated him with her unexpected perspectives, her quick wit, and keen mind. Jovian deeply loved Aubrey, knowing she loved him, too, despite her fears. She'd bonded with his Coalition the instant they met and had looked at no others.

Blazing heat rippled up his spine as he allowed himself to think of her sexually for the briefest moment. Jovian viciously controlled those thoughts, locking them down ruthlessly.

He did not want to meet their Honored Nel Mate with an extruded shaft bulging through his Shendyt. Didn't want to scare or surprise Aubrey with a side of him she hadn't seen before. There would be time enough to introduce her and their Mates to all he'd learned about sensual pleasure, but not yet.

He returned his gaze to Daniel, who seemed like he was meeting an old friend, an Honored Nel recently announced to the Bon'Torzal Pride. Prime Rukhan kept the small, pretty Honored Nel close.

The Prime had a possessive air about him, which was unusual. Jovian made a note to watch this social development in his tablet. He'd spent a lot of time with Prime Rukhan and hadn't sensed this specific thread of Connection with an Honored Nel before.

Interesting.

Most Honored Nels were smaller than Lio Nel males, but Daniel's thick, muscular form made his friend seem even more delicate by comparison. They both had glossy brown curls on their heads, Daniel's much shorter. But where Daniel showed hints of intriguing fur on his face and body, his friend was smooth.

After their initial hug, which caused Prime Rukhan's tail to writhe with interest, Daniel and his friend spoke animatedly for several minutes before they parted with a handshake, a peculiar Earther gesture.

Daniel was happy, which made Jovian happy. He wanted his Honored Nel to be content. And the male was most definitely *his*. He'd known it the moment he'd heard Daniel's voice across the room, standing up to the Crown High Nessa in defense of his family line.

During their extensive talks through the Lio-Intercoms, Daniel's smooth tenor tones and humble genius intrigued Jovian, capturing his attention, sparking his sexual interest, making him burn. And here Daniel was, better than Jovian ever imagined.

Defending his family.

Fascinating Aubrey and his Coalition.

Being decidedly delicious.

This was a male worth pursuing. An Honored Nel worthy to Mate-Dance with. Jovian's grin deepened, exuding anticipation, his ears high and alert, his tail sweeping with excitement.

Leaning against the far wall, watching the spectacle, Ferrand glanced back at Jovian, catching Jovian's attention as he stood to make his way over through the crowd. He reduced his tablet, stashing it away in his ever-present tech-bag strapped to his thigh. He spoke their thoughts out-loud when Ferrand was close.

"It's *him*."

Ferrand leaned on the wall next to him, crossing his arms.

"Definitely."

Ferrand glanced around subtly, seeking Léandre's new position in the room. Jovian nudged Ferrand's shoulder toward the shadows behind Aubrey.

Léandre stood in the semi-darkness, arms down, watching both Aubrey and Daniel, completely unashamed of the enormous bulge his raging hard-on displayed. He had no shame in him about his responses, feeling no need to be anything other than who and what he was. Jovian loved that about him.

Ferrand snorted as he glanced at Léandre.

"I see *he* approves of Daniel."

"I know *I* approve."

Ferrand looked at him intently. Jovian gazed back in mutual understanding. Things would not be the same after tonight.

Am I ready for the change?

Jovian nodded his head, completely committed to their path. Ferrand growled his approval, accepting his Brethren's reassurance. Affection for Ferrand warmed him.

He is such a caretaker.

Ferrand looked at Aubrey with desire banked in his gaze. Then he flicked his heated glance to Daniel.

"Good. We meet, we MateDance, we MateBond, and become Claimed."

A decisive caretaker.

"Commander Ferrand declares it so!"

Ferrand grinned, anticipation shining in his eyes.

"I do, indeed."

Daniel had only traversed halfway across the vast Grand PrideHall. They had plenty of time to watch and wait. Jovian settled comfortably beside Ferrand, lounging against his Brethren's arm and shoulder, his heart full of hope.

Chapter 15
Daniel

Daniel gave a huge grin seeing Sawyer, not at all surprised he was with Prime Rukhan, the Prime who had so sexually intimidated him. Nodding respectfully, the hulking Lio Nel smiled indulgently as Sawyer launched himself into a hug with Daniel.

Beaming with health and happiness, Sawyer gave Daniel the first big smile he'd ever seen on Sawyer's face as they caught up. He would leave for the Dark Realm the next day, but they could comm each other whenever they wanted. They promised to talk again as they shook hands in farewell.

Daniel hoped this goodbye wasn't their last.

Seeing Sawyer reminded him of how they'd initially become friends. Daniel walked away, lost in the tainted memory of meeting nasty Stanton and losing his friend, Jensen.

Jensen froze, all the light and life draining from his eyes as he spotted a newly-boosted Honored Nel across the expanse of SpacePort Haddou's huge, busy Cafeteria.

Kassie Keegan

Daniel stopped eating, paying close attention to the stranger. The good-looking guy had mean eyes, scanning the room with an air of superiority. Jensen swung to face Daniel, leaning in as he murmured in a lifeless voice.

"I'm sorry. I thought I was free, but I never will be."

Jensen got up and walked away.

Daniel's eyes went back to the newcomer as the Honored Nel's gaze sharpened and narrowed on Jensen's retreating back, then slid speculatively to him.

He sat stone-faced, staring back blankly. He'd learned while growing up to never show emotions to an enemy. Vulnerability only made you a bigger target.

The new guy sauntered over to Daniel's table with a couple of other Honored Nels.

If this jerk spooked Jensen, I need to be careful of him.

Daniel closely tracked their approach. The man braced his hands on the table and took a big dramatic sniff.

I'll take the bait.

"What are you doing?"

The outwardly handsome, inwardly ugly man kept his eyes on Daniel.

"You hang out with trash, so you must stink."

Time for introductions.

"Who the fuck are you?"

The guy gave him a sideways grin.

"I'm Stanton Buey."

Buey... Jensen's family.

Stanton noted the recognition.

"Ah, I see you know my asshole cousin."

Before Daniel could answer, small and quiet, unsmiling but kind Sawyer Tate interrupted with unexpected boldness.

"You appear to be the biggest asshole in this place."

Stanton turned toward Sawyer, who sat diagonally across from Daniel.

"Who do you think you are? Talking to *me* this way, you tiny freak?"

The guy looked like he was going to take a swing at Sawyer.

Daniel didn't like violence, but this was too much. Bullies only understood power and pain. Either they gave pain to you or you gave it to them. He wasn't taking it from this jerk, and there was no way in Creation he would stand by and let him abuse sweet Sawyer.

Standing up, Daniel punched Stanton right in his big, fat mouth, knocking him flat. Looking down at his sprawled opponent, he shook out the sting in his fist.

"I'm Daniel. Fuck off."

After his friends helped him get up, Stanton impatiently brushed them off, glaring with spiteful hatred. Daniel had met dangerous people like him before. He would need to keep his guard up.

Assholes are everywhere, it seems, even among the Honored.

Daniel gestured for Sawyer to get up and they exited together. Outside the Cafeteria, without a word, they shook hands in respect and mutual understanding, then went their separate ways. They would casually, and quietly, watch each other's backs.

He'd felt hurt when, soon after, Jensen left for Lio HomeWorld. He never directly spoke to Daniel again, despite Daniel's efforts to reconnect.

Kassie Keegan

I wonder if I will ever know what happened to Jensen.

Daniel could probably ask his new Pride Family at some point, but for now, he squared his shoulders and pressed on. He would not let shadows from the past or fear of the future darken his day.

Seeing Sawyer again was a highlight.

Most of the Lio he met were genuinely friendly, some were neutral. Some were outwardly nice but had seething energy, and some were simply dismissive. He enjoyed meeting other Honored, too, many unmated like him. A few, he wanted to meet again and get to know better.

Listening with all his senses, especially his newly awakened ones, Daniel made careful mental notes, and whispered his observations to High Nessa Katohna, Prime Cassian, Travar, and Twylah.

After some time, he became tired. Raiida appeared at his elbow with a drink and snack of some sort of filling fruit, then slinked back silently into the crush. When he was done, Rahimi slickly brushed by and collected his empty drink and plate, before disappearing as smoothly. They were quietly taking care of him. It was nice.

However, Daniel gradually became twitchy and unsettled. Now-and-then, he'd get the faintest hint of the flower he loved. He had to take deep sniffs of the ribbon to control the possessiveness rising within him.

Periodically, silence descended as they formally introduced other new Honored Nel Pride members, who began their tour around the room to meet the Prides of Lio HomeWorld.

They would end their circle with their new Pride. Roars and shouts would momentarily halt conversation in the room, catching everyone's attention with joyous welcome.

I look forward to my grand finale.

The room grew quiet as they announced another Honored Nel. Stanton Buey stood framed by the Introduction Entrance, preening during his announcement as they presented him for the Bon'Rocinal Pride. It did not surprise Daniel the bully chose a Prime who repelled him at his PrideChoice.

Among the most beautiful Lio Nels Daniel had ever seen, Prime Bellisio's energy clanged against his senses uncomfortably. At the PrideChoice Ceremony, Daniel could barely get through the niceties before gratefully moving on.

Crown High Nessa Oriel greeted Stanton and his companions, but did not linger.

High Nessa Katohna and Prime Cassian noticed his concentrated attention. Daniel wasn't sure what his expression conveyed that sharpened their focus on Stanton Buey, but he was glad they didn't need a long explanation.

"That guy is one of the ugliest Muffins I've ever met."

His comment caught the attention of Travar and Twylah, too, who pivoted to note who he spoke of. They didn't laugh or joke. Travar commented quietly to Daniel.

"Not surprising. He chose an ugly Muffin Prime."

No more needed to be said as they swiveled to greet friendly people from the Bon'Terral Pride.

Then the music changed, and everyone turned to the elevated ovals in the center of the room. On the one closest to his side of the room, three Lio Nels stood in a matched posture, arms outstretched toward the crowd. They'd removed their wrist-cuffs and put them on the edge of the stage.

Daniel leaned close to Travar.

"What's happening?"

"You are witnessing a MateDance."

Oh, yes!

"Why did they take their wrist-cuffs off?"

Kassie Keegan

Travar raised his arms. The intricately engraved cuffs he wore were narrow at the back of his wrists and long on the inside of them, longer than most he'd seen, flexing with the movement of his wrist.

"The Bandels? Do you know why we wear these?"

Daniel thought back to his instruction by Abassa Itakah on SpacePort Haddou.

"To show you are in a Coalition committed to finding Honored Mates."

"Yes. But do you know *why*?"

"No."

"We Lio are scent-driven beings. The glands at our wrists mark heavily. We reserve this level of scent-marking for our Mates. We rub faces with our Pride and those we feel affection for, but *this* we save for Mates."

Travar lowered his arms as they turned to watch the Dancers.

The Lio Nels moved slowly and sinuously, their concentration centered on an Honored Nel with long brown hair braided back from his face. The guy watched stoically, his gaze hot like green fire.

Travar spoke low.

"He's making them work for it."

Their companions growled in agreement.

Daniel scanned the room, noting the crowd around him and how many Lio Nels had Bandels and how many didn't. He leaned toward Travar, his gaze returning to the MateDance.

"So the Lio Nels not wearing Bandels..."

Travar sidled closer to Daniel, while he, too, kept watching the spectacle.

"Do you know how possessive Honored Nessas are? They are twice as territorial as Lio Nessas and viciously protective of their Claim. It is a product of human-nature combining with Lio beast-nature."

"I didn't know."

"Males in a Lio Harem do not wear Bandels, as it does not enrage their Lio Nessas for them to scent-mark other females. A Lio Harem often has three or more females with five or more males to love and breed. The combined scents of their Mates comforts them."

Makes sense.

"Honored Nessas are much more possessive. Many of them do not realize this trait themselves until they are Called to Mate. They cannot abide their Mates' scents strongly on someone they have not Claimed for their own."

"Honored Nels, like me, don't need Bandels?"

Travar gave him a glancing, carnal grin.

"No, my dear. You scent-mark in a special way. She will crave your cream-scent on her and your Mates. She will demand it!"

Daniel flushed, heat scorching him. His achy shaft pulsed into full hard-on at the thought of a needy Mate craving him and his 'cream.'"

Cream-scent. That's new.

He eased his Chalel forward over his shoulder to cover himself just as the watching Honored Nel jumped on the stage with the Lio Nels and danced for a cute, curly-haired blond Honored Nessa. Transfixed, she showed the most predatory expression he'd seen on a woman's face.

She became more savage as she jumped onto the stage and leaped onto her Honored Nel, the man taking her weight easily. Wrapping her legs around him, she reached out to her Lio Nels. They surrounded their Honored Mates, rubbing themselves sinuously against them, touching everywhere they could. Low growls rumbled from them and throughout the crowd.

Standing below the stage, a Prime Lio Nel bellowed a roar, turning the writhing MateDancers' attention to him. The Prime gathered the Lio Nels' Bandels, motioning to them. They jumped down, following him, their Honored Nessa still clasped tightly to her guy.

Kassie Keegan

Daniel felt a wave of joy overlaid with sexual tension rush through the entire room. As it passed over the far side, four concentrated streams of blazing energy hit him like a blast, making him gasp.

Then, in a blink, they were gone.

His attention sharpened, searching the gathering, unsure of what he sought. He again caught the faintest flavors of four focused energies before they disappeared.

Sighing, Daniel comforted himself with a sniff of his ribbon as the Mate-Dancers entered an alcove. He leaned close to Travar.

"What's going to happen next?"

"You mean, are they going to go fuck now?"

Daniel gave Travar a pointed glance.

"That wasn't what I asked."

Utterly still, Travar stared at Daniel, who gazed back at him. After some time, Daniel broke.

"Okay. You win. Are they going to go fuck?"

Travar grinned knowingly.

"Be honest. We are not shy about our needs here."

"Yeah, I'm beginning to understand that."

"The answer is no. They are in a tenuous time when an Honored Nessa must be assured of her choice. Her Pride will protect her as she decides. When it is time for MateBonding, her Honored Nel will sense her readiness to Mate, and her Coalition will prepare a private place for them. She will Claim them and the MateBond will be complete, her Mates Declared, Claimed, and Sealed."

"Thanks for telling me. I couldn't get Abassa Itakah to explain."

"She wasn't being mean to you. It wasn't time for you to know yet."

"And now is?"

Travar affectionately grabbed Daniel's arm close, hugging it as they walked further around the room.

"Yes, my dear Daniel. Now, you need to know."

Travar squeezed his arm again, then released it, walking ahead, his tail sweeping in jaunty arcs.

Chapter 16
Daniel

An intimidating Lio Nessa approached Daniel and his companions, her garments adorned with draped fabric leaves in all colors of green, fluttering as she moved. She showed a tight, faintly annoyed expression. Her ears tilted slightly back, her tail giving little irritated flicks at the tip.

Three unsmiling Lio Nels strode with her, one with his hand casually on a knife sheathed at his waist, his gaze riveted on Prime Cassian.

Most Lio wore knives somewhere on their bodies. Some, like his twin Protectors, geared up with many knives, but none kept their hands on the hilt. It was an aggressive posture aimed at Prime Cassian, who focused on the male with vigilant attention, his eyes glowing silvery green.

Tension flowed through the energy of Daniel's friends. Sweeping his gaze over them, outwardly no one showed anything but relaxed confidence. He restrained his need to sniff the ribbon, not wanting to show a hint of weakness when his Pride was on alert.

The new Lio Nessa spoke sharply.

"High Nessa Katohna Bon'Fiel, Prime Cassian."

Savage Planet Embrace

The two groups, including Daniel, bowed briefly, respectfully to each other, but didn't drop their eyes. His Pride Leader replied smoothly.

"High Nessa Klavdiya Bon'Tecol. Greetings. Greetings Olinder and Luguerin."

Two of the Lio Nels nodded back at High Nessa Katohna. They did not introduce the antagonistic Lio Nel.

High Nessa Klavdiya pursed her mouth, stepping closer to Daniel with an assessing look. High Nessa Katohna, on his other side, matched her move perfectly. Actively ignoring the mirrored movement, she scrutinized him, her voice and demeanor haughty.

"Bon'Tecol guides Lio HomeWorld's Liani Transport, which is quite prestigious."

The now-smug Lio Nessa scanned Daniel head-to-toe.

"We are also in cooperation with Bon'Retal, Bon'Sotil, and Bon'Rocinal Prides to guide Liani Defense after an unfortunate incident with a Disgraced Pride that brought corruption to our attention."

She looked at him with false kindness while Daniel regarded her blankly. Her words were not for him. They aimed at his companions.

She takes digs at my Pride Mates.

Daniel sensed the barbs, but didn't understand how they were supposed to sting.

This Lio Nessa is a bitch!

His eyes narrowed as she continued.

"Bon'Fiel Pride is so very *lenient*, sheltering all sorts of riff-raff, but we Bon'Tecol believe in higher standards."

Did she call me riff-raff? What is riff-raff, anyway?

"We must root out all corruption, don't you agree, Daniel?"

This is some sort of trap.

Kassie Keegan

Daniel felt the intensity of High Nessa Klavdiya's regard as she studied him, trying to make him uncomfortable, to see if he could withstand her social pressure.

Fuck you, lady.

"I know nothing about it, High Nessa. Nor do I want to."

"We shall see, Daniel Shaw Bon'Fiel."

She gave his shoulder a gentle pet which looked outwardly like a show of support, but the hidden slight scrape of her claws sent a different message. A subtle threat.

High Nessa Katohna chuffed at the gesture, removing the pretentious Lio Nessa's hand from him in a lightning-fast sweep. High Nessa Klavdiya licked her arm where High Nessa Katohna touched her, then flicked an amused glance in his Pride Leader's direction.

Daniel stayed still, keeping his expression neutral as countless undercurrents flowed through the aggressive introduction. Travar shifted to behind Daniel's back in an unmistakable show of support and protection.

Twylah smoothly glided forward beside High Nessa Katohna. Utterly bored, she partially angled away, looking down at her hand where she casually trimmed a claw with a tiny lethal knife, her threat as clear as the unnamed Lio Nel's.

The silently hostile third Lio Nel now gave Prime Cassian a sneering, up-and-down scan. Prime Cassian rumbled briefly deep in his chest, but didn't move a muscle at the non-verbal Challenge. High Nessa Katohna's gaze narrowed on the threatening Lio Nel.

"I see you are accompanied by Second-in-Command Tozzo this day span."

Sec. Com. Tozzo's confrontational attention broke from Prime Cassian to make a required nod-and-bow to High Nessa Katohna, severing the high tension between the males. Daniel respected her social mastery.

High Nessa Katohna pivoted back to High Nessa Klavdiya, asking with mild curiosity.

"Where are Prime Agawahl and his Coalition? Your Harem Mate Yann? Your newest Honored Lio Nel? I didn't see him introduced as yet."

High Nessa Klavdiya sniffed, turning away to peruse the crowd.

"Unlike you, I do not keep my Prime, my Harem Mates, or our Honored on a tight leash. I'm surprised you don't move your PrideHome to the Dark Realm, Katohna, with the way you bind your Pride to you."

Dark Realm. That's where Sawyer is going. This bitch is acting like it's a bad thing.

High Nessa Katohna's eyebrows lifted, but otherwise she didn't react or respond.

A powerful Prime Lio Nel with a jovial demeanor, strode up behind Sec. Com. Tozzo, his attention caught by High Nessa Klavdiya's comment. This new Prime spoke as he pounded Sec. Com. Tozzo on the back with a heavy hand in friendly violence.

"Bon'Fiel Pride is most welcome in the Dark Realm!"

The boisterous greeting forced Sec. Com. Tozzo finally to take his hand off his knife.

Masterfully done!

The friendly Prime's primary color was golden-brown, from his mane to his fur, eyes, and garments comprising a draped fabric Shendyt and long flowing cape.

Sec. Com. Tozzo wore a sour expression, not even attempting politeness. High Nessa Klavdiya stared at the new Prime, her cold amber eyes saying he was a bug to be crushed. She didn't intimidate the Prime at all. In fact, he stepped closer to her, prompting Sec. Com. Tozzo to growl and step between them.

High Nessa Katohna grasped Daniel's arm, pulling him a few steps away, so they could watch what happened from a safer distance as the new Prime spoke.

"I hear your derision toward my Realm. How uncharacteristically intemperate of you, Klavdiya."

He flicked a fluttering piece of fabric on her dress with a casual claw, causing a slight snag to mar it. Sec. Com. Tozzo growled aggressively, gently pushing High Nessa Klavdiya steps further behind him. The verbally sparring Prime Lio Nel ignored him.

"Prime Cassian snatching such a prize from your clutches must anger you to no end."

Does he mean me?

"Come off it, Mahkar. Why act so proud and offended? You, your people, and the Dark Realm Prides are a bunch of freaks cavorting in the Forest!"

Daniel blinked.

What? I have questions.

Sec. Com. Tozzo and Prime Mahkar stood chest-to-chest, arms down by their sides, ears aggressively lowered, tails whipping back-and-forth angrily. The Second-in-Command's growl grew louder when Prime Mahkar moved them both one step closer to High Nessa Klavdiya, showing he was the stronger of the two. Prime Mahkar spoke derisively.

"Don't stand there pretending your Harem Mate Yann and Prime Agawahl aren't buried dick-deep in your new Honored Nel as we speak. Breaking him in, right? More important to have him trained for Bon'Tecol cock than to be introduced to potential Mates, which benefits all of Lio HomeWorld."

High Nessa Klavdiya's face flashed with rage, her fur on end giving her a fluffed appearance. She hissed.

"You dare!"

He leaned closer.

"Don't spew your hypocrisy in my hearing and expect to go unscathed, Klavdiya."

She yowled in anger, ears lying flat, pulling her arms back, claws extended to make a swipe at Prime Mahkar.

A regal Lio Nessa appeared to float toward them. The delicate, sheer aqua-colored fabric of her garments billowed out with her measured movements, her hands holding a metallic cylinder.

Three lethal-looking Lio Nels followed behind her. One, with an elaborately braided beard and mustache, had his hand purposefully on his knife as they approached. She spoke in low, beautiful, musical tones.

"What is this? Why such a spectacle High Nessa Klavdiya? Calm yourself."

The Lio Nessa's words had an immediate effect. High Nessa Klavdiya dragged in a breath, forcing her features into a falsely serene countenance, the lie told plainly by her undisciplined angry tail.

"He..."

"Shh. I heard. All in the Known Galaxies heard."

Daniel stiffened, again remembering the celebration was broadcast. High Nessa Klavdiya's expression became stone-hard as she stared at Prime Mahkar.

Cooly unruffled, Prime Mahkar stepped back out of Sec. Com. Tozzo's space, gazing at High Nessa Klavdiya benignly as he spoke.

"You think because I am 'sexually depraved,' according to your standards, that I have no morals. I defend the lifestyles of my fellow Lio because I want to make my own choices."

He waited for a beat.

"The problem here, Klavdiya, is you pretend to be something you are not. It doesn't matter to me what you and your Pride do. You can fuck each other with bird feathers, for all I care. In my Realm, we do what we want, without subjugation or shame."

Prime Mahkar paused again, his expression becoming a sensual invitation.

"Unless you *like* subjugation, Klavdiya. Then, you will most definitely like it in my freaky Forest. Consider yourself invited for education."

Prime Mahkar gazed at her with meaningful intensity, then slowly licked his lips with his long tongue in a blazingly sexual gesture.

High Nessa Klavdiya glared at him, trying to give him the same haughty look she had earlier, but Daniel sensed the flash of heat coursing through her energy at Prime Mahkar's words.

"No, Mahkar. No."

Without saying more, High Nessa Klavdiya wheeled and walked away to a nook in the back of the room, her head held high, her tail low, and unmoving. Her Lio Nels followed quietly.

Humor shimmered in the newly arrived High Nessa's gaze.

"Well, Mahkar, you sure know how to make an introduction."

She swiveled to Daniel.

"I am Sarafene, High Nessa of Bon'Sotil Pride. This hothead is Prime Mahkar Bon'Nopal. He and High Nessa Samitah guide Liani Frolic of the Dark Realm."

They all bowed in respectful greeting.

High Nessa Katohna introduced the High Nessa's companions as Sarafene's Harem Mates, Stern and Marini, and Commander Kaushil, who now had his hand near, but not on, his knife.

High Nessa Sarafene gave Daniel a friendly look, her piercing blue eyes missing nothing.

"Welcome To Lio HomeWorld, Daniel Shaw Bon'Fiel. May you be enlightened here."

Savage Planet Embrace

Although exuding warmth and kindness, curiously, High Nessa Sarafene's energy burned cold and steady, even during her fellow High Nessa's upset. No spikes of joy or irritation, no ripples of reaction at all. The difference between her vibrant outward demeanor and her cool, almost still inner flow intrigued Daniel.

"Greetings High Nessa Sarafene. Which Liani does the Bon'Sotil Pride guide?"

"My Pride guides Liani Metallurgy, producing Mimetic Mineral Shield Discs and refining the materials our Prides use for bladed weapons."

"I noticed most Lio wear a knife."

"At maturity, all Lio train with a Rav Knife, the only weapon capable of penetrating our Shields. Projectiles and energy weapons are useless against it without shield disruptors like disruptor dots."

"Do I get a Rav Knife?"

High Nessa Sarafene raised her eyebrow.

"Do you need one?"

Would Daniel demean his Pride's abilities to protect an Honored Nel in front of all the Known Galaxies through the feeds if he said, 'Yes?'

Will I ever get one if I say, 'No?'

He answered carefully.

"I want to earn one."

The High Nessa gave him a small, slow smile, her feminine fangs flashing.

"Deftly stated, Daniel. I look forward to seeing how you settle in. You are welcome to talk with me anytime."

"Thank you, High Nessa Sarafene. I appreciate the offer!"

She stepped to High Nessa Katohna, sharing affectionate rubs of their cheeks. Pivoting to Daniel, High Nessa Sarafene briefly petted him right where the rude High Nessa stroked him with her claws, then she turned to Prime Cassian, walking a step closer to stroke across his cheek with gentle fingers.

"Your family must be so proud of you, Cassian! First clawing your way to Bon'Fiel Prime, a Pride protecting a Shaktah, no less."

High Nessa Sarafene nodded toward Daniel.

"Then this beauty chooses you as FirstChoice."

Prime Cassian gave her a gratified smile.

"My Pride Family and Fleet cheer me. From Prowl to Prime, they have supported me. I am dedicated and determined to give my best to Bon'Fiel, honoring Prime Bastian. He was one of a kind."

High Nessa Sarafene looked down, sadness blanketing her at the mention of the Bon'Fiel Pride's former Prime. She took a deep breath, looking back at Prime Cassian, regarding him reassuringly.

"You will make a mark of your own."

She gave them a friendly, regal nod as she, her Mates, and her Commander flowed back into the crush.

Daniel, his companions, and Prime Mahkar stood quietly for a time after the contrasting encounters with the two Lio Nessas.

Talk about social whiplash!

Glancing at Travar, Daniel sensed flares of attention bouncing back-and-forth between him and Prime Cassian, but observed no overt sign of communication.

Interesting.

Prime Cassian tilted his head questioningly.

"Some thoughts, Daniel?"

"I really like High Nessa Sarafene with her soothing voice, but the High Nessa dressed in green is definitely a Muffin."

Prime Cassian, Travar, and Twylah started laughing. Their friend Prime Mahkar looked at them, confused.

"Ugh, muffins are disgusting! Do you remember the gathering when all the Honored Nessas insisted we try them?"

Daniel's companions roared their laughter even louder, leaning against each other in their mirth. Prime Cassian cracked up the hardest. High Nessa Katohna kept some dignity, but stood grinning.

It was another spectacle.

Travar gasped an explanation while doubled up, holding his belly. Prime Mahkar's voice boomed over their amusement.

"But ass is delicious!"

Daniel blushed again and rolled his eyes at them. Turning away from their silliness, he spotted a stunningly beautiful blue-flowering tree with a warm golden glow at its center, near the back wall. He took a deep sniff of the ribbon that soothed him.

I need a break.

Chapter 17
Aubrey

Aubrey kept her eyes on her handsome, glowing man as they introduced him around the room, making sure not to lose sight of him. She wanted to learn everything she could about this stranger who was *hers*.

Her Honored Nel was kind and friendly, but guarded. Daniel looked people directly in the eyes and thought before he spoke. He seemed an excellent judge of character, status not impressing him.

His gentle but firm manner commanded respect. He was already comfortable with many of the most powerful people in her Pride and on Lio HomeWorld.

Aubrey's chest tightened at his sweetness with Crown Nessa Nour. Daniel wanted kids, she could tell.

Oh, Abah-Sah. Why? Why can't I let him go?

Her heart and body warred with her fears, the beast-nature within Aubrey driving her to Claim him for her Coalition.

I want him.

The little cut-outs on the back and sides of his trousers made her crazed with the need to touch the creamy gold flesh flashing at her. She wanted to stroke those arms, pet those flanks, taste those lips.

Can a woman combust from arousal?

She'd been sensitive and achy since she first discovered Daniel. If she hadn't worn the amazing, moisture-absorbing panties Twylah gave her, she would be drenched to her knees.

It was always the same with these formal events. All the unmated Honored Nessas were rounded up as Twylah and some of her crew swept in, pulling back each Honored Nessa's hair with a uniquely patterned ribbon. They took the ribbons back when it was time for hair-styling.

For this Ceremony, Twylah had the Honored wearing white toga-like drapes of fabric with gold belts and accents. There was usually a theme and, because Twylah was a Master Clothier, everyone dressed in a style flattering to them.

Aubrey didn't care what she wore, as long as she finally got to meet her mystery man.

She felt desirable, basking in the memory of Ferrand's expression when she walked out with the rest of the Pride. It was then she decided she liked how everything had changed and began reveling in her new sexual awareness.

He and Stealth had been waiting to escort them. Cooly-controlled Commander Ferrand actually growled long and low as he inspected her with a slow, sensual sweep. Then his eyes locked with hers as they luxuriated together in their sizzling attraction.

How will you taste, my Commander? What will your heavy weight feel like, driving into me?

When Ferrand took a step toward her, his nostrils flaring with deep, dragging breaths, Stealth gently grasped her arm and led her away to the Palace's Grand Room. She saw Ferrand clench his fists then relax them, carefully keeping the crowd between him and Aubrey. But he hadn't stopped watching.

Jovian's gaze feasted on her as he stood in the alcove given to the Bon'-Fiel Pride for the event. When he'd first seen her, he'd inhaled a shud-

Kassie Keegan

dering breath and licked his lips, the heat in his eyes scorching her, piling on the arousal sparked by her mystery man and stoked by Ferrand.

Abah-Sah, Jovian is so gorgeous. I want to bury my hands in those waves while he licks me.

He did not approach her, but his eyes didn't leave her, skating over her body, breathing fast and deep. Jovian was such a controlled male, she enjoyed seeing he was as affected as she was.

Can I make him lose control? What will his face look like in pleasure?

Later, after the event was in full swing, she found Léandre in the shadows, watching her, waiting for her to notice him. He leaned against the wall, uncaring of anyone else, his concentration only on Aubrey. One hand covered his heart, the other cupped his hard shaft, which jutted prominently under his Shendyt.

As she watched, he rubbed his fingers achingly slow across his nipple, face contorting in pleasure, then he covered his heart again, his eyes intently focused on her face. Léandre's actions communicated clearly to her.

"My pleasure is yours. My heart is yours."

Next, he moved his lower hand sensuously over the bulge of his erection, closing his eyes in abandon at the sensation.

Sexy beast.

Léandre opened his glowing golden eyes, continuing to pet himself, staring at Aubrey with heat and affection.

"My body is yours."

He moved his hands out to her in a here-I-am gesture.

"Take me, I'm yours."

Under his delicious spell, Aubrey stepped toward him.

Mine.

Stealth grasped her arm, speaking kindly but firmly.

"Not yet, Aubrey. Not yet."

She didn't resist, knowing it wasn't time.

It will be.

Soon.

Léandre lowered his arms and stood watching her. Forcing herself to step away from him, Aubrey could only take a couple of steps, thinking one word over and over as she stared at her sexy beast.

"Mine."

"Yes, Aubrey. He's yours. All yours. Only yours."

Okay.

She allowed Stealth to soothe her.

"You want to meet your Honored Nel, don't you?"

She agreed, moving forward, but halted again. Turning back to Léandre, her attention still captured by him. She scanned his beautiful, scarred face and body, yearning.

Léandre's expression changed, relaxing from sexual intent to loving affection. He'd heard Stealth. Nodding reassuringly, he made a 'go' motion with his chin, releasing her from his spell.

Aubrey took a deep, bracing breath and did something she hadn't done before. She blew him a kiss. He grinned widely, acting like he caught the kiss in mid-air, placing it on his heart, his hand back where it had been when she first saw him.

Butterflies took flight in her belly.

Oh, how I want him!

She pivoted, burning, but in control, a savage edge creeping into her thoughts and feelings.

These males are mine.

Kassie Keegan

The MateDance she witnessed only made her more fierce. If Tassy could Claim Kurt and her Coalition, Aubrey could Claim hers, too.

What if some other female came sniffing around my males?

A low growl rumbled from her chest.

Stealth stayed close, but no longer touched her, remaining in her sightline. Aubrey didn't want anyone sneaking up on her while she stalked.

She had a peripheral awareness of how non-threatening, Mated Bon'Fiel Lio Nels surrounded her, maintaining a loose perimeter of space between her and everyone else. Every now and again, one would break off to control someone, replaced immediately by another Mated male, but she didn't care about any of it.

Pausing her Prowl, Aubrey laid Claiming eyes on each of her Mates. Léandre shadowed her on the edges, Ferrand and Jovian stood over among the Pride. They all watched her closely, postures alert.

She focused back on Daniel, her prey, enjoying the rush, the anticipation, the hunt. Aubrey would wait and watch some more before making her move.

Chapter 18
Daniel

Living on SpacePort Arata gave Daniel few opportunities to see growing things like plants and trees, only the very wealthy having access to SpacePort Gardens. He'd enjoyed the flourishing green places on SpacePort Haddou while being genetically boosted, and looked forward to exploring Lio HomeWorld's verdant, wide-open spaces.

However, he'd seen nothing like this immense tree that drew him like a moth to a flame. It was not rooted in soil, the exposed roots in varying shades of green, with tendrils resting on the floor solidly.

The bush-like tree had green branches, some smooth, some with huge, wickedly sharp thorns. A few vines draped among the branches, its leaves dark green, long, and narrow, with sharp tips.

Most of the branches bloomed with enormous, delicately gleaming, velvety azure-blue flowers with orange-yellow centers. There were golden sparkles fizzing from some centers. Earthy and fresh, the flowers emitted a soft, inviting scent, drawing him near.

The warm golden glow in the tree's heart was even more irresistible to Daniel, calling to the energy flow within him like a siren's song. It was a gold shimmer ensconced in the center of the branches, contained in some sort of clear vessel.

Savage Planet Embrace

He couldn't figure out what it was, so he strolled closer. As he did, a powerful, but non-aggressive vibrancy spoke to him through his gift. He received a verbal impression expressed directly in his mind.

"You are Seen."

Another impression whispered softly to him without actual words. Daniel experienced it as more of a feeling.

Welcome.

Daniel approached with slow, measured steps.

This is not a regular tree! But what, or better yet, who is it?

Friendliness and enthusiasm exuded from this being of living color and light.

Cautiously walking closer, he studied the glow at the tree's heart and its small container. It was thin, round, see-through and made of plastic.

Then, astonishingly, a knowing came to him that the container was a pudding cup, although he'd never tasted pudding or seen a cup like this.

I want to touch this amazing being so much!

Daniel held back, examining the sharp thorns cautiously. They could rip him to shreds.

A reply came softly through his senses.

"You may."

Still, he hesitated until the thorny branches fell back gracefully in invitation. He focused his thoughts toward the tree-being.

Thank you.

He sensed its pleasure at his gratitude and fascination.

Daniel gently touched one silken flower petal, so delicate as to be almost imperceptible. He relaxed, letting go of the tension from meeting crowds of strangers, and buried his face in the soul-stirring, dainty fragrance of the gorgeous glowing flower.

Invigorating!

Hearing a squeak, Daniel lifted his face, peering way up to where a tiny creature stared at him, bent low on a branch above his head.

The little squeaker was the most endearing thing, with two coal-black beads for eyes, and a narrow, elongated snout with a tiny, twitching pink nose. It had a woolly reddish-brown coat and a long, striped tail wrapped firmly around a branch. Its ears stood high with red wispy tufts at the top.

Is this some type of HomeWorld squirrel? Do Lio eat squirrel? They better not eat this one!

"Hello, little fella. Be careful you don't become a snack!"

The critter scrutinized him, unmoving except for his adorable, quivery nose. Its eyes blinked.

"I'm Daniel, little guy. You are cute! Don't be afraid, we can be friends."

As if he understood and accepted Daniel's words, the precious creature gave a high-pitched purr, sat up, and preened his small face with tiny hands, each sporting three little dexterous fingers.

Contentment eased through him. Lio HomeWorld was vibrantly alive in all the ways he'd dreamed of.

I am so happy to be here.

He placed his palm on the smooth green bark of the amazing tree, his energy tenderly flowing toward the beautiful living being.

The scent he loved wafted over him in a wave so strong his knees weakened. Daniel's eyes closed, his mouth watered, and his head tilted back in delight as the unique and seductive fragrance of his flower drenched his senses. His heart beat faster and his shaft hardened.

He heard the faint sound of steps. Whipping his head up, his eyes snapped open.

Savage Planet Embrace

A lovely Honored Nessa stood on the other side of the tree. She had long, dark-brown hair loosely flowing over her shoulders and supple bare arms with soft, golden skin beckoning him to touch. Her eyes were a clear, bright-blue, sparkling with invitation and attraction for *him*.

She wore white fabric draped across one shoulder, secured at the waist by a golden leaf-like belt, ending at her knees in a V-shape at the hem. She barely glanced at the pretty tree. Her complete focus was on Daniel, scanning his features, inspecting him up-and-down, eating him with her eyes.

He did the same to her.

Lifting the ribbon up to his nose for comparison, he smelled her fragrance stronger than the ribbon or flowers surrounding them.

She is my flower!

His beautiful Honored Nessa glimpsed his hand.

"My ribbon!"

Everything in me longs for this woman.

Savage possessiveness rose within him, a need to Claim and be Claimed, a ferocious, fathomless well of desire for this stranger with the scent that owned him. Daniel would kill to have her writhing beneath him, could almost taste her pleasure.

This ribbon is mine, just like you are mine.

Holding still, he used his grip on the tree as a physical anchor while his world flew apart and re-formed, with her at its center.

Keep Control, don't scare her. Say something!

He asked, wonder in his tone.

"Who are you?"

"I'm Aubrey. And you are Daniel."

Aubrey. Gorgeous name.

They stood gazing at each other, desire, confusion, and wonder ripping through him as he devoured her appearance and scent. Aubrey stepped closer.

"This may be bizarre, but I think I sensed you when I came here."

He thought of all the strange experiences he'd had since arriving on Lio HomeWorld.

"If you're bizarre, I am, too."

She peeked shyly down, then up again in helpless captivation.

"You glow."

"I do?"

"Yes. It's lovely."

Daniel eyed his arms and torso, not seeing it, but after all his weird stuff, he didn't doubt her.

"I don't see it. But I know you intrigue me more than any person I have ever met, and I met you a minute ago."

Aubrey came as close as she could, blocked the tree branches between them.

"I've been watching you since they introduced you."

Daniel's heart pounded.

She's as fascinated by me as I am by her.

Placing her hand on the opposite side of the tree trunk to brace herself, Aubrey leaned forward, looking at his lips, inviting a kiss. She whispered.

"I can't help myself, Daniel. I want…"

"Oh, yes."

He leaned forward, a breath away from her lips.

"Aubrey, may I?"

She sighed her answer.

"Yes."

He kissed her with a slow, sweet press, unmoving as he absorbed their sizzling chemistry, then he caressed her lips with a gentle sweep, before pulling slightly away to make sure of his welcome.

Aubrey panted, her face tilted toward him, eyes narrowed in enjoyment. Her pupils were large and dark with desire, swallowing the irises of her eyes.

Oh, yes. She's with me.

His lips met hers again in a deeper tasting glide. Their tongues touched softly, then lushly, taking in each other's flavor, adjusting their angles for better contact, mouths flowing with ease as hunger built between them.

Her incredible scent swamped him, his erection throbbing, heartbeat racing.

Exhilarating! I'm addicted.

Their energies connected, intertwining, pulsing together in a tingling rush.

I never want to be without this. Without her.

Aubrey grasped his nape, touching him with tender passion. Daniel caressed her cheek as they deepened their kiss, energy bursting from him, seeking her.

Vibrance flowed in a loop from him to her and back again through their lips, their stroking hands, and through the smooth tree trunk they both braced upon. The branches between them dug into his abdomen as he strained to get closer to her. Their Connection amplified, burning into his soul as it surged in an endless river of heat, with her as its source.

A long, purring squeak sounded above them. The tree shuddered, making leaves and flowers rustle as if a breeze blew over them. They broke apart gasping heaving breaths, their gazes locked, hands dropping to the branches separating them.

Aubrey is my Mate!

Another shudder shook the tree they still braced upon, flowers and leaves fluttering more intensely. Suddenly, a turquoise sparkle burst from some blooms and the golden glow at the tree's center exploded in blinding brightness, then diminished to a gentle luminescence.

Daniel thought to the being, concerned.

Are you well?

He sensed an answer from the quiet one.

Thank you for this gift.

The energy in the tree's heart answered contentedly.

"We will not forget."

Daniel's distraction made Aubrey curious.

"What?"

"I sense thankfulness."

She appeared thoughtful and gave the tree trunk a loving stroke.

"You feel it, too?"

"Yes, it's amazing."

She gazed affectionately at a blossom with a new turquoise shimmer, tenderly touching the bloom.

"How you bless us…"

A flowering branch slowly moved in a gentle caress along her arm. Daniel peered up, seeing only the tip of the little creature's tail, but its lazy, relaxed movement reassured him it was fine.

Daniel looked back at his lovely Mate, filled with wonder. They stood gazing at each other for long moments, no words needed. Then she grinned.

"Nice to meet you, Daniel."

He grinned back, his chest tight with joy.

She's worth crossing Galaxies for.

"*Very* nice to meet you, Aubrey."

Her grin grew into a full-blown smile.

"Shall we talk now or make out more?"

"I like both!"

"Okay, then!"

Leaning in for another kiss, Aubrey looked past Daniel's shoulder, her face dropping into disappointment.

"We might have to wait a bit. There are many people who want to meet you."

"Your Pride?"

"Yup."

"Anything you want."

Daniel would follow Aubrey anywhere. They moved in unison to hold hands and walk beyond the branch separating them.

His companions, along with a bunch of other males, formed a perimeter surrounding him and Aubrey. Even Raiida and Rahimi were there, including a Lio Nel with incredibly long, white-blond hair in a thick braid, all of them facing outward protectively.

Did they circle us while we kissed?

Glancing around, Daniel noticed waves of movement in the crowd as people moved about. The low hum of conversation became punctuated by growls and roars of pleasure, sounding like Lio were mounting right there, in the hall, no one paying particular attention.

Kassie Keegan

Does this happen all the time?

They were so open about their needs and desires here.

Can I be like them?

He wasn't sure.

A reverential feeling dominated the atmosphere. Even the music stopped. As Daniel and Aubrey took it all in, Prime Cassian pivoted to them, before Daniel became too uncomfortable.

"Daniel, I see you have met Aubrey Newton Bon'Fiel, Honored Nessa of High Nessa Katohna Bon'Fiel, treasured daughter of Nancy and Pete Newton of SpacePort Omori in Galaxy Anelastrana, PrideChoice of Prime Bastian Bon'Fiel Lon'Fiel of Lio Glevoni."

Grinning, Daniel and Aubrey bowed to each other without releasing hands at the formal introduction. He kept his eyes on her flushed face, while Aubrey's gaze kept flicking away and back to him, as helpless as he was to stop staring.

Then, a detail from her introduction caught his notice.

"SpacePort Omori? Isn't it a Pirate outpost?"

"Yes, mostly. We weren't supposed to be there long. Things changed when my dad disappeared."

Daniel's eyes widened at the unexpected similarity.

"Yeah. For me and my mom, too. I'm glad you got out."

"Me, too."

She looked thoughtful.

"Your dad, too?"

He nodded. Aubrey surveyed him again, this time taking in the smallest details of his appearance, as he did the same to her. Her sweet curves enticed him. He ached to hold her, his mouth watering for another taste of her lips.

She grinned teasingly when she spied the edge of his cape.

"Space Rat, huh?"

"That's me!"

"Me, too!"

They laughed together, enjoying their similarities.

I want to learn everything about you.

Daniel realized something else.

"Wait, Bon'Fiel?"

Prime Cassian answered.

"Yes. She is Shaktah under Bon'Fiel Pride protection, as you are in our care. It is pleasing you have such a connection."

Prime Cassian understated his happiness. Daniel sensed his deep joy in what had happened. The rest of their companions relaxed into less protective postures, and people around them began speaking in low tones as the music resumed playing.

Daniel's gaze returned to Aubrey, who stepped closer to him, eyes flirting.

"Pleasing. Yes."

He smiled at her.

"This means we live in the same place, right?"

She nodded as Prime Cassian spoke.

"You have also made the acquaintance of Priti Sawat Azure."

Daniel looked at him, confused.

"Priti…"

"Priti is the golden life-force, an ageless ancient. Sawat is the living tree-like being who protects it. Each Sawat is unique and speaks only to their

Kassie Keegan

Priti. This is Priti Sawat Azure because their blooms are azure-blue. They have existed on Lio HomeWorld for millennia."

A haunting, resonant, echoing hum lilted through the hall from the heart of the tree-being.

"*Greetings.*"

The Priti's audible "voice" had the same strong, humming tenor as one source he had heard and communicated with in his mind earlier.

Didn't I sense two voices? Does no one else hear them both? Curious.

A worrisome thought struck him.

Did I screw up touching it? First the Crown Nessa, now this.

Daniel's face tightened with distress. He didn't want to shame his new Pride, or his flower, with his ignorance.

The Priti spoke in his mind.

"*Calm.*"

Then the quiet Sawat.

Good.

Concerned, Aubrey came closer to him, stroking his arm with her fingertips. His flesh burned where she caressed him.

"It's okay. Priti Sawat Azure loves us. They knew you didn't know. They wanted to see and experience you. I did, too."

She touched her lips in memory.

"I couldn't resist you."

He sighed, his eyes bouncing between hers searchingly. Choosing to trust Aubrey and let the new being reassure him, he relaxed. Turning while keeping Aubrey's hand, he bowed low to Priti Sawat Azure.

"It was wonderful and weird to meet you. I hope we meet again."

They answered in sonorous tones, branches adjusting position with a whisper-flutter of leaves and petals.

"We will."

"Take care, little guy!"

He got a faint chitter in response. Daniel swiveled to glare at Prime Cassian.

"No one eats the squirrel!"

Prime Cassian's eyebrows twitched in amusement.

"That is a Dharmik. We do not eat the sacred creatures bound to Priti Sawat."

That reassured Daniel.

"I hope you are not like this with every animal you meet. It will make hunting difficult."

"I don't know. I don't think so. I've not been around many animals."

He gave his attention back to Aubrey, gently touching her bottom lip with his thumb, enthralled by its soft plumpness. He remembered what she'd said earlier.

"I can't resist you, either."

At this, she let go of his hand and clasped his arm, which he bent so she could nestle in close, his heart clenching at the contact. They stood staring into each other's eyes with wonder.

Aubrey is amazing.

"Does it ever get less weird here?"

She gave an enchanting giggle and squeezed his arm.

"Nope. It's usually weird. You get used to it."

Aubrey shrugged, which made Daniel laugh, thinking about his experience getting ready earlier. Prime Cassian motioned for their attention.

Kassie Keegan

"Time for you to meet your Bon'Fiel Pride Mates, Daniel."

"Okay."

He didn't move, continuing to stare love-struck at Aubrey.

"Daniel, Aubrey, you have to walk to get there."

They answered in unison, gazing into each other's eyes.

"Okay."

They still didn't move. Prime Cassian slid in behind them, putting his hands on their backs, propelling them forward.

"This way."

Travar laughed.

"This is going to be good!"

Daniel agreed.

Yes. Very good.

Chapter 19
Aubrey

"Over here."

Prime Cassian guided them toward their Pride, the crowd talking again in a loud din of eager conversation.

Aubrey's hands and arm tingled at her points of contact with Daniel. It was an innocent touch, but ignited her entire body.

What would happen with a more sexual touch?

She shivered.

Daniel is so unexpected! So much more. We have so much in common. Am I dreaming? If I am, I'm not ready to wake up.

Prime Cassian chuffed as he urged them toward the large nook where their Pride gathered. Neither of them was willing to untangle their arms. High Nessa Katohna matched her pace to theirs, walking beside them with Travar and Stealth following closely behind Prime Cassian.

Aubrey focused on Daniel's lips, remembering his flavor, wanting more. She licked her lips, and he stumbled slightly, making her eyes flash up to his. He acted as spellbound as she felt. And as needy.

Prime Cassian stopped pushing when Daniel stumbled, affably chiding, amusement coloring his tone.

Kassie Keegan

"Steady, Daniel! Aubrey, don't kill the male before we introduce him. If you keep looking at him like that, you may cause all the blood to leave his head."

She was confused.

"What?"

Leave it to Travar to answer with embarrassing detail.

"You make his dick so hard, all the blood rushes from his head. Daniel can probably cut stone with it."

Aubrey's eyes slid down Daniel's body to his large, noticeable bulge.

Adjusting his cape forward, he hid her pretty view. Disappointment filled her. Daniel sounded rueful.

"Yeah, thanks for pointing it out."

Travar chuckled kindly, smacking him on the back of his shoulder.

"I'm here to support you, Daniel. And bring attention to hard-ons."

"Creator help me..."

Those closest to them snickered as Prime Cassian urged them to walk again.

She enjoyed Daniel's blush, feeling flushed, too. They were equally matched in their attraction, which reassured her. However, he began avoiding her eyes, something she didn't want.

"Don't be embarrassed. I like how you are with me."

He studied her, his brown eyes so deep she could drown in them. Aubrey could no more stop her words than she could hold back the Ocean's tide...

"You give me a Lady Boner."

Daniel full-on stumbled, making Prime Cassian pause again with an exasperated chuff as he started belly-laughing. Enchanted, she laughed with him. Prime Cassian lifted his hands in frustration.

"Now she's broken him!"

Daniel wrapped her in a big hug as they laughed, cuddling her close, his arms holding her tenderly. Sliding her arms around his waist, she laid her head on his warm, solid chest under his chin. They rocked slightly side-to-side with shifts of weight, chuckles mellowing to soft grins as they embraced, uncaring what happened around them.

She loved his scent, feeling the hum of contentment flow through them both. Aware of the warm press of his bulge on her belly, she felt no unease about it.

"I like it. I like *you*."

His embarrassment faded away, leaving only warmth in its wake.

Their Pride Mates didn't mean to distress Daniel, they were just open and honest about sexuality.

He has a lot to learn and I will help him.

Daniel spoke with wonder, sliding a lock of hair from her cheek with a gentle finger.

"You fascinate me."

He bent to kiss her again as she lifted, closing her eyes, so ready for another taste. And kissed the back of a velvety furred hand.

Startled, Aubrey opened her eyes to see Prime Cassian's hand floating between their faces. Prime Cassian chuckled.

"No. Now is not the time for kisses."

Daniel's frustrated voice came from the other side of Prime Cassian's hand.

"Says who?"

Prime Cassian kept his hand there a moment longer, then dropped it. Stealth laughed.

"Oof, cock-blocked. Well, kiss-blocked."

Daniel pulled away from Aubrey, wiped his mouth with one hand before turning to glare at Stealth.

"Who are *you*?"

Stealth gave him a huge, fang-filled grin.

"I'm Stealth Pon'Salel of Lio Fleet Kahlina."

Daniel bowed his head in greeting when an instant of realization paused his movement.

"Wait, Lio Fleet Kahlina is the same as Prime Cassian's, right? You are both from there?"

Stealth's grin softened as he nodded. Travar piped up.

"And me, too."

Daniel squinted at Travar, who sent a loving glance to Prime Cassian, then settled his gaze steadily on Stealth. Stealth returned the look before turning back to Daniel.

"As Aubrey's Shumal, I am your walking, talking cock-block."

There was a gasp in the crowd of avid listeners nearby. If the kiss wasn't enough of a signal, Stealth's comment made things clear to everyone. Aubrey had a Shumal, meaning she was Called to Mate, and staked her Claim on Daniel.

Aubrey flushed a little as Stealth revealed her private business to the masses. It was going to come out, eventually. Might as well get it all out. Her actions with Daniel spoke much louder than Stealth's statements. Daniel had questions.

"Shumal?"

"Yes, Aubrey's Guide and Protector during the MateDance."

He seemed concerned, lines appearing between his brows as his eyebrows drew in.

"Aubrey needs protection? Not from me!"

She could feel him tensing, and she glared at Stealth.

"You're upsetting him."

Stealth raised his eyebrow at her, then returned his attention to Daniel.

"Do you think Aubrey is worth protecting?"

"Definitely."

"Will you be with her every moment?"

"I want to be, but probably not."

"There you have it."

Daniel's eyes narrowed on Stealth, his muscles coiling under her hands.

"And *you* are doing this 'every moment' protecting?"

High Nessa Katohna stepped closer to explain, taking Daniel's attention away from Stealth.

"As Abah-Sah wills, each Honored Nessa has a Protector when she is Called, someone not a Mate."

She paused for emphasis, making sure he understood what she said.

"Mates are close to their beast-natures during the MateDance and can be… very focused on the Claiming. It is comforting for an Honored Nessa, without fangs or claws to protect herself, to have an advocate when she is overwhelmed, and it all seems out-of-control. Can you understand this?"

Daniel thought for long moments, the storm clouds of his upset fading away as he relaxed, refocusing on Aubrey.

"You need protecting?"

She didn't want to alarm him, but after all the incidents, she didn't want him blindsided either.

"Yeah, probably."

"Do you feel overwhelmed?"

Kassie Keegan

Yes. Yes, I do!

She nodded.

"Don't you?"

"Hmm."

He might not admit it, but yes, he does.

Daniel draped her hand back into the crook of his arm, pivoting them to face Stealth.

"It's good to meet you Stealth Pon'Salel of Lio Fleet Kahlina. Thank you for protecting Aubrey."

They bowed their heads respectfully to one another, then Stealth pointed his finger at Daniel.

"There will be no fucking until you are Claimed by Aubrey."

Daniel's face stayed neutral, although his eyes widened, and his eyebrows raised. He blinked once slowly, then cleared his throat.

"Okay."

Stealth looked satisfied with the boundaries he'd drawn. Prime Cassian turned them around and pushed them to keep going toward his gathered Pride. Daniel muttered back to Prime Cassian.

"I didn't enjoy kissing your hand."

Prime Cassian snorted as a flirty Travar chimed in from behind them.

"I do."

Stealth jumped in.

"Yes, but you also enjoy kissing his..."

High Nessa Katohna broke in, laughing.

"Enough! Give poor Daniel a break. I think his blush might start a fire."

Aubrey studied her sweet, blushing man's face. His pale golden skin tinged a delightful pink, his brown eyes warm and full of humor.

I want to know everything about this man.

"I like your blush."

He gave her a heated look, causing her to blush, too.

"I like *you*."

They tried to slow and turn to each other again, but Prime kept gentle, firm hands on their backs, continuing to propel them forward, growling.

"No, you don't. Introductions, then making out."

Aubrey agreed.

"Excellent plan."

Daniel grinned.

Chapter 20
Daniel

The trajectory of Daniel's life's choices led him to this beautiful moment, greeting his new Pride with Aubrey on his arm.

He glanced over at her again, her smooth golden skin enticing him. Her gorgeous blue eyes sparkled with intelligence and humor, her gentle curves making his palms itch to explore. The memory of her soft lips kept his shaft hard.

I might never lose this hard-on.

She sent him another heated glance from those gorgeous eyes.

I want to always remember this.

Prime Cassian's insistent prodding finally got them where a large group gathered. Everyone quieted, the music stopping as they approached. Daniel blanked his expression, unsure of what came next.

Feeling savagely protective, he carefully pried Aubrey's hands from his arm so he could anchor it firmly around her, curling her close to his body. She melted into his side, wrapping her arm around his waist.

His heart ached as she accepted his protectiveness, her nearness and scent soothing him.

High Nessa Katohna stepped forward.

"I present our newest Bon'Fiel Pride Mate, Daniel Shaw Bon'Fiel!"

A simple introduction, after all the fanciness of his previous ones.

His new Pride exploded in celebration, Lio and Honored roaring and shouting, stomping their feet, clapping, and whooping. Daniel beamed at their enthusiasm.

Beside him, Prime Cassian silently raised his arm. When he made a fist, everything stopped, none moving or making a sound. As one, they bowed low to him and Aubrey. They paused and raised up as one, too.

Then, the Pride placed hands over their hearts, growling low. Daniel remembered Raiida and Rahimi doing the same as they pledged protection on his first night.

This is more than a welcome. It's for me to know Aubrey is safe in their care. It's a pledge to me, too.

Daniel wanted to acknowledge their gesture.

Lightly squeezing Aubrey, he pulled out of their embrace, trailing his hand down her arm as he did so, snagging her hand in his. He brought it to his lips for a gallant kiss on the back of her hand, something he'd seen in ancient storybooks. Aubrey shivered as he whispered to her.

"You are my sweet flower."

Turning to his Pride, Daniel didn't release Aubrey's hand as he bowed low, pausing for a measured span, then rose. Mirroring their pledge, he placed his free hand on his heart.

He didn't growl, instead, he gave a shout of joy, pouring all his excitement for a new life into it, giving it to his brand-new Pride Family.

His Pride joined him, roaring again, accompanied by scores of others around the room until the walls and ceiling of the enormous space shook at the sound. When the shouts ended, it left them gasping and laughing, including Aubrey, who'd shouted her happiness as loudly as the rest.

Kassie Keegan

Many came to meet Daniel, saying their names in introduction. He knew he wouldn't remember them all, but said, 'Hello'. They didn't touch him or Aubrey, only approaching from the front.

High Nessa Katohna and Stealth stood at Aubrey's side, Prime Cassian and Travar stayed by him, the twins at their backs. Their positions allowed him to relax his protectiveness toward Aubrey and enjoy meeting his new Pride Mates.

They know I need their buffer. Creator, I love these people.

Twylah strode up with three Honored Nessas dressed similarly to Aubrey in outfits of draped white fabric with gold accents. Aubrey released Daniel's hand to run and meet them, hugging as they squealed together in feminine celebration. After they settled down, they stayed in a loose circle, their arms entwined amicably.

It's sweet seeing her with her friends like this.

It gave him insight into who she was outside of their sensually charged connection. He liked what he saw.

A curvaceous blond spoke in a hushed tone.

"Give us some deets! Does he taste as yummy as he looks?"

Aubrey grinned, flushed, and nodded.

"Yes!"

This time, the blond didn't whisper.

"You really said, 'You give me a…'"

Her friends said the rest in unison at the top of their lungs.

"Lady Boner!"

They all shrieked in laughter, Aubrey joining in laughing as hard as her friends and many of those around them.

"Abah-Sah, yes! It just came out!"

The blond was insistent.

"I think it's great! I intend to say it as much as possible from now on!"

"Me, too!"

"Me, three!"

They giggled some more and settled down to radiant smiles. A copper-haired Honored Nessa with light-gold skin swiveled toward him.

"Let's meet him!"

They walked to Daniel, a palette of feminine loveliness with complimentary coloring in all shapes and heights.

The red-headed beauty with intent silver-gray eyes assessed him as they drew near, her vibrancy shining like a beacon so bright, she momentarily blinded Daniel's senses to everyone except Aubrey, whose energy linked firmly to his.

She has a powerful gift!

Tall and full-figured, her white and gold garment accentuated the shape of her breasts while covering them completely, the skirt a long, split drape of fabric, front and back, from the waist down, exposing the naked flesh of her hips and thighs as she walked.

Travar gave an unexpected growl. When Daniel glanced at him, he saw the red-head riveted both him and Prime Cassian.

Interesting.

She broke off from the rest, stepping forward to offer her hand to Daniel. He took her hand in a firm but gentle grip. After two customary polite pumps of the handshake she didn't release his hand. Instead she asked him rapid-fire questions that he answered as fast as she dished them out.

"Hi! I'm Destiny.

"Nice to meet you! I'm Daniel."

"How do you like it here?"

"I love it!"

Kassie Keegan

"What do you think of Aubrey?"

"She's fascinating and beautiful."

"Are you a criminal evading authorities?"

"No."

"Are you a drug-abuser?"

"No!"

"Are you a womanizer?"

"No! Why are…"

Prime Cassian interrupted the inquisition by grasping their hands and pulling them apart.

"Enough, Destiny."

He rubbed her hand across the fur on his chest, over-marking Daniel's scent on her hand where they'd touched. Destiny flushed at the gesture, her attention completely captured by Prime Cassian. He reached his other hand out and seductively stroked the exposed curve of her hip.

"You look beautiful."

She kept her eyes steady, but her cheeks pinked more.

"Thank you, Prime Cassian."

He bent, her hand still caught by his, his hand still caressing her flesh, and rubbed his cheek softly, sensually across hers. He whispered in her ear.

"Cassian."

Destiny shivered, her voice breathy.

"Thank you, Cassian."

"Good."

He pulled back, taking his hand off her hip, then leaned in, and gave a gallant kiss to the back of her hand, like Daniel had done for Aubrey. Destiny gasped at the romantic gesture.

Daniel couldn't resist a comment.

"I saw what you did there. You stole my move."

Prime Cassian and Destiny continued to gaze at each other, her hand tenderly in his grasp, as he answered Daniel.

"It was genius. Honoring and honorable. I know something good when I see it."

Prime Cassian's thumb stroking over Destiny's hand made Daniel believe the last part was about knowing Destiny was a good thing too.

"You may have single-handedly renewed such romantic gestures throughout the Known Galaxies."

Daniel shrugged, looking over at Aubrey standing across from him with her friends. He enjoyed romance with his lady, looking forward to finding out what she liked and showering her with it.

He hadn't minded Destiny's questions. She was being protective. And she seemed like a very focused individual, so Prime Cassian's ability to break her focus had been a sight to see.

Twylah stepped forward, clearing her throat, prompting Prime Cassian to release Destiny's hand. Aubrey went to Daniel's side, both reaching out to each other, as if they had been doing it for years, needing the contact. They stood together holding hands, dreamily looking into each other's eyes.

Twylah interrupted.

"Let's make introductions! Daniel Shaw Bon'Fiel, I am pleased to formally introduce Destiny Dean Coron'Rial of Capital Maituri, natural-born Honored Nessa of Marion and Matthew Dean. Under the protection of the Crown Family, she resides with the Bon'Fiel Pride as she pleases. She is a renowned artist, known for capturing an essence, not just an appearance."

Kassie Keegan

She is definitely gifted!

This time, they bowed to one another.

"Again, nice to meet you, Destiny."

He glanced over at Travar, who stared at her with intense golden-eyed attention, caressing every inch he could see of her with his roving eyes, not hiding his regard in the slightest.

She has to be the 'destiny' he hinted at after my PrideChoice!

Destiny enjoyed Travar's scrutiny, turning her back a little so he could see more of her ass, causing another one of his growly breaths. She smiled to herself at the sound, pretending to ignore him and Prime Cassian.

One glance at how Stealth helplessly watched Destiny confirmed his suspicions. Stealth discovered Destiny as a Mate. He was the missing part of Prime Cassian's and Travar's Coalition.

Twylah stepped over to an Honored Nessa with reddish-brown curls. She was the shortest of the four friends, tiny and compact, with an extreme hourglass figure emphasized by her belted outfit. She had dark-brown eyes and lovely freckles that looked like a dusting of golden shimmer on her skin.

"This is Talia Mullins. Natural-born Honored Nessa of the famed Honored doctors Claire and Jared Mullins of SpacePort Vardar in Galaxy Sunastrana. She is a Medical Instructor at Liani Health and Liani Science, working closely with Liani Savor on natural cures. She resides with Bon'Fiel Pride as she pleases."

Talia was friendly, but reserved as she greeted him. They bowed to each other.

"Nice to meet you, Talia. Natural-born?"

His eyes bounced between Destiny and Talia, who answered.

"It means our parents were boosted but haven't found their Coalition. They married despite it, and had Honored children who are natural-born, not boosted."

Daniel hadn't considered the possibility of not finding his Coalition. After meeting Aubrey, he could understand how two Honored would still marry and have kids. Destiny spoke up.

"Usually families of such unions have tons of children. How many siblings do you have, Talia?"

"Four. There's five of us all together."

Destiny nodded.

"See? There's five. I am an only child. My mom died when I was a baby. My dad died a few years later. Capital Maituri Prides raised me pretty much, and I get to Prowl like the males if I want. I love Bon'Fiel Pride, Daniel. I think you will, too."

It was a nice thing for her to say. He peeked down at Aubrey.

Yes. I will like it there. She is there.

He now knew these other people's talents, but he didn't know Aubrey's, and she was his most important person.

"What do you do?"

"I fix things. Anything that runs, I can fix. What do you do?"

Daniel grinned broadly.

"I build things. I can build almost anything that runs."

Excitement rose in her expression.

We are made for each other! I can build it; she can fix it.

The blond didn't wait for introductions. She busted into their renewed gazing to get his attention. Grabbing his available hand, she raised it, giving him a fist bump despite his hand being awkwardly open.

"Love-sick, much? Hiya, I'm Viv."

Viv had long, blond hair piled in a wild mass on the top of her head. Her hazel eyes exuded warmth as she gave him a big, bright smile.

Kassie Keegan

Everything about her was overblown, her figure, her hair, her smile, her gestures, her personality, all of it.

She stepped back and gestured to Twylah, who seemed somewhat miffed.

"Do your thing, Twylah."

"May I introduce Vivian Warner Bon'Fiel, natural-born Honored Nessa of Honored Caroline and Jack Warner of Lio Alestia in Galaxy Corastrana. She chose Bon'Fiel Pride by Prime Bastian, Prime Cassian's predecessor. She is a respected Surveillance expert."

Vivian made a V gesture with her fingers and motioned from her eyes to his eyes, whispering under her breath.

"Always watching."

He pressed his lips together, trying not to laugh at her antics during her formal introduction, and nodded with false gravitas.

"Yeah! Thanks, Twylah! My folks didn't get their magical Coalition either, and there's ten of us kids. They are definitely torqued up all the time. Sheesh, so uptight! My advice? Grab it when you can, Dan!"

Good advice, Viv. Advice I intend to take.

"Noted."

This time he reached out his hand, fist ready. She bumped it with a wide grin.

"All right!"

Viv peered back over her shoulder.

"Could we get this show on the road? I am *dying* to see what happens next. Get up here, Jovian, *please*!"

Chapter 21
Daniel

Excitement burst through Daniel.

"I know a Jovian on Lio HomeWorld! We became friends on the Technological Advancement Inter-Comms!"

Aubrey's attention sharpened on him.

"You know Jovian?"

"There might be more than one, but yes. The guy I know is seriously Tech savvy."

Aubrey gestured over to a Lio Nel sauntering toward them.

"I'm sure he's the one."

He approached from among the Pride, his fur a golden yellow, lighter and brighter than typical Lio coloring, his mane beautifully layered waves of gold. His facial hair was the palest of golds, while the center of his body was a bright-white. He stood about the same height as Daniel, just a bit taller.

He wore a Shendyt and an elaborate belt with a sheathed Rav Knife attached, and a double pocket tech-bag strapped to his thigh. Decorative chains criss-crossed his chest, dangling across his belly, drawing Daniel's eyes to his core muscles, which bunched and released with his sinuous, unhurried walk. He wore Bandels, and an ornately chiseled band around the biceps of his left arm.

The Lio Nel's tail swished in lazy arcs, the thick ring near his tuft flashing, his posture alert, but relaxed. As he drew near, Daniel noticed his eyes were a piercing bright-blue with unusual golden centers.

Peering into Jovian's eyes, their vibrancies snapped into connection. The Lio Nel's energy had a flavor Daniel recognized, having tasted it briefly as pleasure swept the room after the MateDance he'd witnessed.

It revealed Jovian was not nearly as relaxed as he seemed. The boiling sexuality within him spoke to Daniel on a bone-deep level, Calling to him.

Creator, don't let me get an erection again!

Daniel had seen many beautiful Lio Nels, but none drew him like Jovian did.

I want to know you.

The compelling Lio Nel stopped in front of Daniel and Aubrey, regarding both of them with heated awareness. High Nessa Katohna spoke.

"This is adopted son Jovian Bon'Fiel, Chosen through Combat by Bastian Bon'Fiel and beloved of our Pride. I believe you have met. He is our Tech Master and Leader of the Technological Advancement Sector of Lio HomeWorld Inter-Coms."

They bowed to each other, Jovian softly smiling.

"We have indeed met. I've been waiting for you, Daniel."

The Lio Nel's deep, rich voice was definitely one he recognized.

"Waiting for *me*? I was hoping to meet *you* here!"

"And here I am."

Embracing Daniel in a big hug, Jovian's hot, firm muscles pressed against him through the vest, the softness of his fur stroking over Daniel's bare arms, the spice of his scent making Daniel's mouth water.

Jovian rubbed his cheeks gently across both sides of his in a deeply affectionate gesture. When he stepped back, Jovian turned, opening his arms to Aubrey, who came in for an enthusiastic hug of her own.

Does she have a Coalition? Is Jovian in it?

The spark between them was apparent in the sensuous rub of their bodies.

Can it be that one of the beings I most respect in the Known Galaxies is connected to the woman I most want?

Jovian swung Aubrey around in his arms, so she faced Daniel. He saw she'd fallen into the same deep sexual well he sensed in Jovian, her breathing fast, pupils wide-open with arousal.

Standing behind her, he wrapped one of his arms across her front from her waist, angled up to her shoulder where he toyed with a lock of hair. Both of them surveyed Daniel, their mutual desire for him clear, despite the claim Jovian staked on Aubrey.

Daniel tore his eyes away and gave the vicinity a sweep, noticing the surrounding crowd waited quietly.

It seems like everyone waits to see what I will do.

He returned his gaze to the cuddling couple, feeling calm and wondering about it.

Why don't I want to rip his head off? I did with other Nels who even hinted at coming near Aubrey.

He realized a reason.

She welcomes Jovian's embrace.

Then another reason.

I know Jovian from countless hours of conversation and I really like him.

Kassie Keegan

Even before he'd seen how beautiful Jovian was, Daniel had a foundation of trust with him.

I want both Aubrey and Jovian. And they want me!

He blinked.

My life has gotten very interesting in the span of moments.

The tenor of a new sexy voice behind him captured his attention.

"Hello, Daniel."

He spun to it, his gaze devouring the tall, handsome Lio Nel standing before him, stacked with muscles... everywhere.

The male's fur was deep-gold with a creamy white torso. Long facial hair, the same cream color as his chest, was braided and fastened with beads on each side of his lips and down the center of his beard. The Lio Nel's eyes were an amazing pale-green, full of warmth, and fully focused on Daniel.

His mane was all colors of gold, red, and brown, pulled up into a messy top knot. There were additional random braids and beads in his mane.

He wore an elaborate belt, a sheathed Rav Knife, a velvety-looking purple and red Shendyt, and a short purple cape with red trim over one shoulder attached by a decorative chain crossing his chest. Additional chains dangled tantalizingly across his chest and abs.

The Lio Nel's Bandels were different, following the length of his forearm from the inside of his wrist to his elbow, where sharp-bladed tips extended past it. They looked deadly, yet he sensed no danger to Aubrey or himself. What Daniel sensed knocked him off center.

Longing hit him like a blast of heat from this gorgeous, towering Lio Nel. Caring, protectiveness, and need swept over Daniel in a heated wave. He couldn't speak through the riot of his senses as High Nessa Katohna made introductions.

"I introduce adopted son Commander Ferrand Bon'Durel Bon'Fiel, Chosen by me, High Nessa Katohna, upon tragic circumstances when he was young. Ferrand is now the respected Commander of our Pride leading Bon'Fiel Pride Security."

Commander!

He believed it. Every inch of this male commanded attention. Commander Ferrand asked in a deep, rich rasp.

"May we share air?"

He agreed. Commander Ferrand's huge hand covered the back of Daniel's head as he bent forward to touch their foreheads together. Daniel didn't even try to reach up, so caught up in the torrent of honeyed energy rushing through him. Sizzling sparks at their contact points made Daniel lose his battle with his dick.

And there it is! I'm hard.

The male's scent intoxicated him. He wanted to bathe in its rich, masculine flavor. Daniel panted. Commander Ferrand inhaled deeply, his mouth open slightly. He breathed air in, held it, then released it over the back of his tongue, tasting Daniel's scent, growling resonantly, making Daniel's lower regions throb and ache.

Say something.

He sounded breathless.

"Nice to meet you, Commander Ferrand."

Commander Ferrand lifted his head, staying close, breathing his air while they drowned in each other's eyes. Bending, he rubbed both sides of Daniel's cheeks with his velvety soft ones before nuzzling in close to his neck. The Commander gave a tiny lick under his ear and Daniel felt more than heard his whisper.

"You may call me Ferrand."

He shivered as Ferrand's heated breath teased over his sensitive flesh. The huge Lio Nel hummed his satisfaction at the reaction, giving one more tiny lick under Daniel's ear before pulling all the way back and away.

Kassie Keegan

Ferrand went to Aubrey, bent, and rubbed his cheeks against hers, just as he had done to Daniel. He licked her under her ear, making her shudder, too. Then he stood behind Jovian, who held Aubrey through it all.

She panted as she looked at Daniel, eyes wide. He realized he panted watching *them*, then sudden awareness slammed him.

There is another.

A male approached from the side, stalking from across the huge room. Daniel felt devastating focus from the individual, knowing he would never forget meeting the person exuding such a force of personality. He pivoted and froze.

The Lio Nel was utterly compelling, moving with stalking grace, his entire being concentrated on him with glowing, golden-eyed intensity. Daniel stood utterly still. He was being hunted.

The intriguing stranger had coloring similar to Ferrand's, his long mane pulled back from his face into a braid down his back. His snowy white facial hair was long above his lips and trimmed to a soft-looking V below his chin. He wasn't as tall as Ferrand, having a more compact build.

A scar sliced across the bridge of his nose, but it was the thick, jagged silvery scar across his throat that drew attention, a heinous mark in his deep-gold and bright-white fur. Scars also marked one of his thighs.

The stalking male wore a velvety red Shendyt with an elaborately engraved belt and Bandels. His sheathed Rav Knife hung below his belt, decorative chains draping across his taut belly, some dangling across his thighs.

The male's focus didn't waver as he strode toward Daniel with feline grace, sporting a very large bulge.

I think he likes me.

High Nessa Katohna spoke.

"Commander Ferrand and Jovian's Coalition Brethren, Léandre, approaches."

Confirmed!

Aubrey had a Lio Nel Coalition, which meant *he* had a Coalition because he was not letting her go, ever.

Creator, this Lio Nel is sexy when he stalks.

High Nessa began making introductions.

"The beast storming at you like an animal is my adopted son, Léandre Bon'Durel Bon'Fiel, Chosen by me with his Pride Mate Ferrand, upon tragic circumstances when he was young. Léandre is a MateDance Instructor when he likes the Lio and Honored who need instructing. He is mute."

Daniel dragged his eyes away from Léandre to glance at High Nessa Katohna in surprise.

Why is he mute when it's something that could be corrected?

"He cannot speak by choice. Léandre has his reasons. Although, I believe you will find he communicates quite well."

Léandre kept moving toward him, with a prominent hard-on. An erection Daniel answered with his own still-raging one. It was intimidating and exhilarating.

How can I slow this guy down?

Léandre was close.

What's he going to do when he gets to me? Fuck me or beat me up?

Falling back on his human manners, Daniel unthinkingly stuck out his right hand for a handshake, stopping Léandre in his tracks, mere steps away. He stared down at Daniel's offered hand, up to his eyes, over to Daniel's prominent bulge, and back to his eyes.

Léandre threw his pretty Bandels off his wrists to the floor with a metallic clang, taking Daniel's outstretched hand with the wrong hand for a handshake, grasping it reverently as if Daniel gave him a priceless treasure. He'd made a strategic error in communication, signaling surrender instead of a polite greeting.

Kassie Keegan

Léandre brought their fronts fully together, face-to-face, chest-to-chest, cock-to-cock. He rubbed his cheeks over Daniel's in a sensual caress, but didn't stop there. He brushed his face over Daniel's neck and shoulders, drenching him in the masculine musk of his scent-mark.

Keeping hold of Daniel's hand, he spun him in a smooth move. The large, hard shaft under his Shendyt pressed insistently against the crease of Daniel's rear, Daniel's arm stretched across his chest and ribs, held in Léandre's firm grasp, caging him back against the Lio Nel.

Daniel gasped, gazing over at Aubrey, whom Jovian held in a similar grip. Léandre chuffed a breath over his neck, his other hand coming out to caress Daniel's arm soothingly before lowering to hold his hip. Daniel blazed hot, shivering at the long lick Léandre gave his neck.

Léandre's energy burned like turbulent flame, roiling and seething, turning to ash any hesitation Daniel had with what was happening, even if it was in front of his brand-new Pride or in feeds across the Known Galaxies.

Léandre banged on the floor with the flashing metal band near his tuft, causing a loud crack. Music started immediately in a rhythmic, tribal pulse.

Beginning a subtle sway to the beat of the music, Léandre's body guided Daniel's back-and-forth, side-to-side, until Daniel relaxed into the swaying motion. He gripped Daniel's hip, guiding him in a step to the side, a pace back, and a slide left, all the while undulating their bodies.

Releasing Daniel, he grabbed both of Daniel's hands so he could show him arm movements, too. Hands on hips, next lifting out, then up.

Daniel's concentration on what Léandre guided him through made him blind to his surroundings. The moves and motions repeated, and he memorized them without deliberate intent.

Léandre brought Daniel's hands down his body, roaming the contours of his front, coming close, but not touching Daniel's raging hardness. Daniel glimpsed motion in his peripheral vision and glanced over.

Jovian moved Aubrey through the same movements, and she was as avidly captivated by the Dance. Commander Ferrand echoed the moves with them, making Daniel shiver with realization.

I am in a MateDance.

He had a decision to make, continue or stop, because this was for forever with these people. It was forever for *him*.

Searching his feelings, Daniel mentally pulled back to think as Léandre continued to guide his movements. He felt a soul-stirring connection with Aubrey and these three Lio Nels. They had obviously chosen him.

This is fast. But why wait?

Daniel had already completely changed his life, his very DNA, so he could taste the life offered to him now. He knew, down to his bones, Aubrey was the woman he wanted, and this was his chance for the family he desired.

Would he trust his instincts and risk it all to join his life to strangers?

I've waited long enough. Time to live. Time to love.

Daniel released his reservations, letting his body take over. Léandre no longer guided him. Instead, they moved effortlessly together. Léandre acknowledged the change with a low, satisfied purr and a lick to Daniel's neck. Then he gripped Daniel's hips, stopping them.

Jovian, Aubrey, and Ferrand stopped. Léandre and Jovian let Daniel and Aubrey go, then walked toward the nearest elevated stage.

Ferrand stooped to pick up Léandre's abandoned Bandels and followed them. Jovian and Ferrand removed their Bandels, putting them on the edge with Léandre's pair.

Jumping onstage, Jovian and Ferrand positioned themselves behind Léandre, beginning their MateDance moves to the tribal beat. A deep stance, a step to the side, a pace back, a slide left, always undulating. Hands on hips, next lifting out, then up, dragging their hands down their torsos.

Kassie Keegan

They watched Daniel, asking him without words to join them, to become Coalition. To dedicate himself, with them, to loving and caring for an Honored Nessa, Aubrey.

I want this life they offer me. I want them.

He jumped on the stage, taking his place beside Léandre for the MateDance.

Their eyes were only for Aubrey now. She would either Claim them or not. Aubrey drew closer to where they Danced, a predatory, feral expression upon her, which kept Daniel hard, and made him Dance more fluidly for her.

Yes, look at all this. Us. All for you, Aubrey. Come and take us.

She gave a low feminine growl, pacing back-and-forth gracefully, watching her males present for her. She rubbed her crossed arms in a self-soothing gesture. The music sped up almost imperceptibly, rising toward a crescendo.

Aubrey broke, leaping on the stage, turning her back on Léandre, plastering herself against his front. She grabbed his braid as she Danced with him, desire coloring every motion.

Léandre caressed her waist and licked her neck, completely focused on his feral Mate. Aubrey was a female ignited by her males. Unpredictable and mesmerizing, incandescent with passion.

She pushed away from Léandre and sashayed to Ferrand, turning her back to burrow into him. He growled in savage enjoyment, his masculine bulk emphasizing her femininity.

He towered over her, yet their movements were in sync, flowing smoothly. Ferrand put his huge hand across her belly, holding her firmly to him, making them both growl in need. Aubrey gave him a sizzling look as she pulled away from him and sought Jovian.

Jovian's arms were out toward her in welcome. When she spun and crushed her sweet behind into him, his arms curled up around her shoulders, anchoring her to him. He rubbed the insides of his wrists on the sides of her neck while they danced. She took part in the scent-claim, rolling her neck to make it easier for him to Mark her flesh.

Her hands grasped his flanks as they moved in unison. When she leaned forward, he let her go with a gentle, gliding touch of his fingers down her arms as she walked to Daniel.

She stood watching him for a moment, the naked need in her expression an echo of his blazing desire for her.

Come to me. Be mine. Make me yours.

When she spoke, he wondered if she could read his mind.

"Mine."

She swiveled and eased back, crushing into him, making them both groan in pained pleasure. Reaching up and back, she grabbed the nape of his neck, her back arched. He gripped her hips, helping her grind her ass into his hard length as they moved.

They danced in a cataract of joy and need. His heart bursting with happiness, Daniel bent to speak in her ear.

"I give you everything I am."

She stopped. He stopped. Their Coalition stopped. The music stopped.

Aubrey spun around, reaching up to stroke his hair, bringing their faces close.

"All I've ever wanted."

She kissed him, and there was only her in his world. Her leg lifted over his hip, straining to get closer. Daniel bent his knees and scooped her up so she wrapped her legs around him, his hard shaft lushly nestled against her humid cloth-covered core.

This is it. I'm hers.

Chapter 22
Daniel

Their Coalition surrounded them, growling, petting, and licking, stoking the blaze of heat between Daniel and Aubrey as they passionately kissed.

Prime Cassian's powerful roar got their attention, pulling Daniel away from the kiss to blink glaze-eyed at his Prime. Aubrey ignored everything and everyone except Daniel, feasting on any exposed flesh she could get her mouth on. Licking up his neck, nipping his ear, kissing his shoulder, starved for him.

He needed to get her somewhere safe and private to explore their passion.

Prime Cassian gathered the Bandels, gesturing toward an alcove his Pride cleared a path to.

Ah, right. We get to go somewhere and not-fuck.

Whatever. As long as he was with his Mates, he'd go anywhere.

Aubrey clutched firmly to him as Daniel slid off the stage, easily handling her weight, absolutely loving the jolt it gave his erection pressed to her heat. She groaned.

He moved swiftly to the small room Prime Cassian motioned him into, sensing his Coalition with him. When Daniel got into the nook, he went

Savage Planet Embrace

to the closest wall, slamming his back against it, bracing himself as Aubrey ground into his hardness in a frenzy for pleasure.

They kissed again, devouring each other.

Ferrand made a gentle tsk at Daniel's ear while easing behind him, his bulge pressing into his lower back, a muscled, heated buffer from the hard wall. Ferrand's huge hands held Daniel's hips steady for Aubrey.

Léandre supported Aubrey's thigh and back on one side, Jovian supporting her on her other. They gave her freedom of movement as she deliciously rubbed their bodies together.

I won't last much longer.

Aubrey arched her back, grinding on him. One of her hands grabbed Léandre's braided mane, her other buried in Jovian's golden curls. She trusted them to brace her as she sought her peak.

She released with a beautiful feminine groan, as if from the depths of her soul. Her hips pumped rhythmically, triggering blazing bliss to pulse out of him with a matching deep groan. Aubrey collapsed against Daniel, both panting. Jovian delightedly drew out a comment.

"Gorgeous."

Ferrand growled in agreement, stroking Daniel's hips in comfort and affection. Then he grabbed Aubrey from Daniel's arms, taking her to a large comfortable cushion with a high padded back, stacked with pillows. It was huge, big enough for ten Lio.

While cuddling Aubrey close, Ferrand paused, allowing Léandre to release the clasp of his cape. It slid to the floor in a silken swath, then he removed Ferrand's belt and Knife, dropping them on top of the cape. Ferrand kicked off his sandals, then comfortably settled on the cushions with Aubrey facing forward in his lap.

He crossed his muscular arms over her, making loving comfort noises as she continued to catch her breath, senseless to her surroundings.

Stroking Daniel's cheek, Léandre caught his attention.

He held out his hand, showing Daniel a small, white absorbent cloth. It had the same texture as the neon yellow insta-dry cloths he'd grown up using on SpacePort Arata.

Reaching inside Daniel's trousers, Léandre matter-of-factly wiped him and his clothing, making him gasp with post-orgasm sensitivity. Léandre put his clothes back to rights just as straightforward. Daniel felt comfortable and cared for.

"Thanks."

Léandre licked his neck in answer before rubbing the dry, scented cloth along his own abdomen, drenching his fur in Daniel's musk.

This must be what wearing cream-scent is. Fucking hot!

Tucking the cloth into his Shendyt, Léandre kept it. Unfastening Daniel's Chalel, he skimmed it off, along with his vest, handing them to Raiida, who hung the clothing on pegs near the opaque Shielded entry.

Léandre and Jovian removed their belts, Knives, and decorative chains, passing them over to Rahimi, who also picked up Ferrand's garments, hanging it all on pegs.

Léandre motioned for Daniel to take off his sandals as they slid theirs off. Stealth moved to Aubrey and smoothly slipped off her sandals. They were much more comfortable.

Suddenly, all that happened swamped Daniel.

"My legs feel like rubber."

Concerned, Léandre led him to sit beside Ferrand. He went to a small table of refreshments and got a couple of juice hydro-packs, handing one to him before settling in on the other side of Ferrand. Léandre's motions and his expression insisted Daniel drink.

As he sipped the refreshing fruity beverage, Daniel surveyed the nook. They were in a cozy room with a dampening field across the entrance. Stealth, Rahimi, and Raaida were with them.

Jovian gathered something from his tech-bag, attaching a small device to the entryway. A new wash of rainbow color overlaid the haze of the dampening field.

"No Surveillance is getting through this. Whatever we say is for us."

Daniel motioned his hydro-pack to where Stealth took up position on a large pillow on the floor at the foot of their cushion. The twins sat near the entry at a table with a couple of chairs.

"And them."

Jovian joined Daniel on the enormous cushion, taking the spot beside him. He grabbed Daniel's empty hydro-pack, putting it aside as Léandre gave him a fresh one, then snuggled up close.

"We want them here. They make Aubrey feel safe."

"She doesn't feel safe?"

"No, she doesn't. We will talk with her about why."

Raiida stood up, striding to them as Rahimi leaned forward in her chair, her tone and demeanor serious.

"We will keep your Rav Knives secure. Hand over your tech-bag, too, Jovian. We know where your true weapons are."

Jovian smirked as he complied. Raiida carried Jovian's tech-bag over to the pegs before resuming her seat as Rahimi advised them without pause.

"You must lower all your defenses to your Mates, males. Honored Nessas are extremely sensitive. Do not hide who you are. Even if it hurts. They will sense it, and reject the Call."

Rahimi let her words settle for a few moments, then continued.

"When Aubrey's awareness returns, she will seek reassurance she is making her best choice in Mates. She needs to get to know Daniel. Accept the changes in her relationships."

I want those things, too.

Kassie Keegan

"She will feel vulnerable and lusty. You may satisfy her and yourselves as much as you like with your garments on. If you cannot control your beast-natures, we will help you do so. Do you understand Coalition Brethren of Aubrey Newton Bon'Fiel?"

They all agreed with nods and rumbles.

"Good."

Raiida and Rahimi pulled out some sort of game with colorful sticks and beads, and played. Stealth sat gazing at the Coalition with a happy, lovey-dovey expression on his face. He wasn't even pretending not to observe them. Amusement swept through Daniel.

"You're going to sit there and watch everything."

"Oh, yes. It's glorious seeing it all unfold."

"You're getting off on this, aren't you?"

"Not currently. Maybe later. It's so romantic."

Stealth sighed, put his head on his hand, and regarded them avidly, his tail swishing with happiness. Jovian leaned in close to Daniel.

"Ignore him. Stealth is Aubrey's Shumal. He is necessary. What she needs, she gets. Agreed?"

He nodded.

"See? Easy!"

Jovian motioned to his juice.

"Drink, my heart, we want you healthy."

Jovian snuggled closer, wrapping an arm around Daniel's ribs. Ferrand's huge hand stroked over the back of his head, and Léandre's tail possessively wrapped around his ankle. Daniel's heart exploded into a thousand pieces at the care these males showed him.

I'm falling in love.

Chapter 23
Aubrey

Aubrey drifted, eyes closed, held in her Commander's embrace, warm and comfortable. She lay on his big, firm body, his beefy arms crossed over her in a heated mountain of flesh. She felt and heard the low, soothing rumble of his contented purr and she, too, was content.

Masculine voices murmured nearby. Her Mates. A barely there caress on her neck roused her enough to open her eyes.

Léandre scrutinized her with care and concern, the intensity of his gaze like a physical touch. He snuggled up beside them, his face close to hers, pressed against her hip and thigh, his tail lying across her legs.

He softly petted her neck and shoulder, his bright golden gaze following his stroke on her skin. His ears perked as he visually swept the full length of her form. When his gaze returned to look into Aubrey's eyes, his brow furrowed. He tilted his head questioningly, in his way of asking if she was okay.

She stayed relaxed, smiling tenderly, enjoying his care. She nodded.

Yes, I'm good.

Ferrand lowered his arms some while Léandre brought a juice hydro-pack to her lips. She drank deeply, feeling settled and alert. Happily, her most possessively protective Mate was quite calm. With the MateDance, Léandre Declared for Daniel as clearly as he Declared for her.

Aubrey's gut tightened at the thought of conflict among her Mates, which Léandre saw. He rubbed her worried forehead with a gentle finger, his expression wondering, asking about her tension. She whispered.

"Daniel."

He stared behind her to the other side of Ferrand with heated intent, licked his lips, then swept her with the same fiery gaze, licking his lips again.

Léandre definitely wants us.

His tail draped across her legs.

He's so possessive, he's probably somehow wrapped around Daniel.

Aubrey had to touch him. The instant she tried to move, Ferrand lowered his arms all the way down, Léandre adjusting to make room for his massive upper arm. Ferrand helped her turn to face Léandre, one big hand anchoring her hip, while the other rubbed her back in slow, lazy circles.

Ferrand's thick, hard shaft nestled against her rear, but there was no urgency or concern about it as she concentrated on another Mate. She fondled Léandre's long, silky, white facial hair as he angled in for a kiss.

I want you, Léandre.

Aubrey recognized deep in her consciousness that even in her mind, she was too scared to use the 'L' word.

Léandre started leisurely with a tender press then pushed lushly into her, seeking her tongue with his own. His unique flavor burst through her senses, his kiss a feast of taste and touch. His scent drenched her with potent male arousal, a strong undertone of Daniel's unique fragrance on Léandre, which pleased her.

Their tongues stroked. He was careful to rub softly with his rough center. His tongue was longer and could wrap around hers in a curling caress that made her roll her hips toward him. Ferrand rumbled his approval.

She grasped Léandre's cheeks as she became more aggressive, Claiming this male for her own.

Mine.

She explored him, sucking his textured tongue, licking his powerful fangs, reveling in the heat. She slowly pulled away to make sure Léandre knew who he belonged to.

"Mine."

He gazed at her, lips swollen from their kisses, eyes heavy-lidded, pleasure in every line of his face. He gave her a slow-blink of affection before rubbing his cheek on hers. Daniel's voice was deeper than she remembered.

"Creator, that's arousing."

She wanted to see him. Aubrey lovingly stroked Léandre's cheek, then rolled toward Daniel. Ferrand helped her turn easily, readjusting her position with a pleasured moan as her rear stroked over his bulge from one side to the other.

Daniel faced her, Jovian cuddled up to his back like a second skin. Jovian's arm reached over his hip, his hand palming Daniel's hardness over his clothes, while his hips pumped against Daniel with small measured digs. Jovian watched her with sizzling intent as he commented.

"Yes, it *is* arousing."

Sliding close behind her, Léandre lifted his leg over Ferrand's, his thigh under her butt, curling her legs forward. She knew he was grinding on Ferrand from the little clench-and-release of his leg muscles. Ferrand's hand kept her hip anchored and steady even as he continued to pulse his cock gently against her.

Kassie Keegan

Léandre's warm breath flowed over her neck, breathing her scent across his tongue, his mouth partly open as he tasted it. Daniel watched Léandre, transfixed by a gesture that was most likely new to him. He whispered to himself as he eyed Léandre with an avid gaze.

"Fangs."

Daniel's fascination caught Jovian's notice. Jovian licked his neck, making him shudder, then breathed questions over the delicately sensitive skin he teased, causing Daniel to shiver more.

"Have you ever kissed a Lio?"

"No."

"Do you want to know what Léandre tastes like?"

Another deep shudder.

Léandre is yummy, Daniel.

Aubrey licked her lips, catching Daniel's attention, so he now stared at her lips hungrily.

"Yes."

She came closer to Daniel, and he leaned to her, cupping her cheek as their mouths met in a sensual tasting. His tongue moved soft and nimble, different from her Lio. She craved both kinds of kiss. Daniel grunted with discovery.

He can taste Léandre.

Her brain and body melted at being the conduit for Daniel's first taste of his Lio Mate. Heat exploded in her, her hips grinding, seeking something to press against.

Ferrand's huge hand settled firmly and perfectly on her seam over her clothes, giving her the pressure she needed. Jovian's deep voice stoked the fire of their kiss.

"Léandre gave Aubrey her first kiss."

They moaned at his words.

"Aubrey took Léandre's first kiss."

She pulled away from a panting Daniel to see Jovian, while Daniel stared at Léandre, whose flavor mingled with hers. Jovian continued his revelations.

"Aubrey shared Ferrand's first kiss."

She gasped, turning to peer up at her Commander. Handsome Ferrand gazed at her lovingly as he sat up slightly, jostling his hand cupped so beautifully over her core, readjusting Aubrey. Her neck arched toward him as he bent forward.

His lips captured her gasp of pleasure as he kissed her long and slow, his agile tongue touching hers with careful attention. He sweetly caressed her neck and shoulders with his free hand, his other hand still wonderfully trapped between her legs.

She felt the hum of his entire being focused on their delicious kiss, her heart burning with affection as she writhed on his hand in excitement. He gave her a lingering lick, pulling away. She whispered.

"First?"

Ferrand smiled softly and nodded as he resettled. Jovian made a musical sound of desire deep in his chest, capturing her attention.

"Hmm, so inviting. Time to taste again, Daniel."

He and Aubrey kissed, this time sharing Ferrand's flavor with sensual glee, grinding with their Lio Mates in mutual enjoyment. Jovian pulled them apart with a grip on Daniel's hair, tilting his face up to the side, showing Aubrey his profile.

Daniel relaxed in the hold, his kiss-swollen lips slightly open, panting with arousal as Jovian spoke.

"I will take your first Lio kiss for my own, Daniel."

Jovian licked his cheek up to the corner of his mouth while studying her with his piercing blue eyes, their golden centers burning brightly as he tasted Daniel's flesh. Aubrey and Daniel shivered.

Jovian's hand moved from Daniel's swollen bulge, grazing his fingertips up over his torso to lightly grasp his neck. Nuzzling the side of Daniel's face, Jovian held him still, his gaze locked on her as he controlled their Mate.

She wanted them. Their power and sensuality, their strength and submission. She loved them together, reveled in their pleasure.

Mine! My Mates. Show me more!

She writhed with need, her body moving in luscious counterpoint with Léandre and Ferrand as they watched Jovian seduce Daniel, which seduced them as well.

Jovian glanced with heated awareness at Ferrand, then Léandre, and back to her. He gave Daniel a sweet kiss on his cheek.

"Daniel, have you ever fucked?"

Arousal zinged through Aubrey at Jovian's crude words. Daniel husked, answering.

"No."

Something relaxed within her at Daniel's response, even as her need spiraled.

He's a virgin, like me! It's kind of reassuring.

She wondered if this was Jovian's reason for doing and saying these things. To reassure her.

It would be like him.

"Have you *been* fucked, Daniel?"

"No."

Daniel's eyes were heavy and dark with excitement, his lips open and hungry. Held by his hair, gripped gently at the throat, his rear pressed firmly against Jovian. Bulge visibly hard beneath his clothes, body shivering, a vision of pleasured abandon.

How I want this man!

"Aubrey is a virgin."

Maybe Daniel needs the same reassurance.

As Daniel reached a hand out to her, she grabbed it. The vital hum of their connection tightened their hold on each other, their tie deeper than a physical touch, enslaved to mutual passion. Jovian continued.

"Léandre is a virgin."

Léandre nodded on her shoulder before he licked it with tiny tasting swipes of the soft tip of his tongue. She kept watching Daniel and Jovian, thinking back to when Léandre found her after being released from her Call.

"How did you know how to…"

It was Ferrand who answered, amusement coloring his voice.

"Léandre watches, studying everyone and everything, Aubrey. Lio are not shy about pleasure. One can learn if they want to. We Lio even have instructional vids!"

She laughed, peering back up at him.

"Hey! How come I didn't get to see anything like that?"

Ferrand's reply dripped with anticipation.

"You will have a more experiential introduction to your Mates."

Jovian continued his revelations.

"Ferrand is a virgin."

Surprise lit Aubrey's eyes, prompting him to question her.

"Surprised? Why?"

He bent to kiss her forehead.

"Neither Léandre nor I desire any female but *you*. We have always been yours. We wait to share all our sexual pleasures with you, Jovian, and our chosen Honored Nel Mate."

Kassie Keegan

It shouldn't surprise her. Ferrand was controlled and careful. Focused. He hadn't ever shown interest in any Honored except her.

The same with Léandre. She had taken it for granted, but no longer. She felt special. Adored. Her heart crammed with emotion, her breathing heavy.

She and Ferrand turned together to look at Daniel, aroused and surrendered in Jovian's grip. Ferrand stroked over Daniel's hair.

"And now we have this beauty. I study everything, too."

She glanced at Ferrand as he swept his gaze over Daniel with a wealth of knowledge in his eyes.

"I look forward to putting my learning to the test."

Jovian put Daniel into profile again, grabbing Aubrey's attention. He released Daniel's neck and sensually brought two of his fingers to Daniel's mouth.

"Open your mouth."

He opened. Jovian slid the fingers shallowly over his tongue.

"Suck."

Daniel's mouth closed, and he sucked, his cheeks hollowing. He surrendered as Jovian pushed his fingers deeper, then lazily pulled them out. All her Lio Mates moaned at the sight. She ground into Ferrand's still-trapped hand.

Licking the tip of one of his own fingers, a tiny sound escaped Jovian at Daniel's flavor. He rotated Daniel's head so he could see what happened next.

Jovian offered his fingers to Léandre, who leaned forward over Aubrey's shoulder to lick the side of one in a lewdly suggestive display. He then held out his fingers to Ferrand, who slowly, sensually laved the underside while gazing into Jovian's eyes.

Jovian slow-blinked back as Ferrand gave his fingertips a final sweet kiss. He brought his fingers to her.

"Open your mouth."

She opened with anticipation. Jovian slid his fingers over her tongue.

Closing her eyes, Aubrey focused on the flavors and textures. She could taste all her Mates on him. It made her grind hard against Ferrand's hand at her core. Both Ferrand and Léandre matched her movements with their own rolling surges.

His fingers were smooth, masculine skin on the underside, very different from the soft velvet of his fur. His retracted claws sported bluntly sharp tips that could still hurt if he wasn't careful. He dragged his fingers over her tongue as she blinked her eyes open.

He and Daniel avidly watched her, both of them panting with arousal. Jovian gave her chin a loving stroke with his thumb, then offered his fingers to Daniel.

"Open."

He opened.

"Suck."

He sucked with a groan, his eyes closing in exquisite enjoyment.

"Deeper."

He took Jovian's fingers deeper. Aubrey could tell by the way his jaw worked Daniel was licking, too. Jovian's voice was a heavy rasp of need as he penetrated Daniel's mouth with his fingers.

"Yes, Daniel. Good. All the flavors of your Mates. Tantalizing, yes?"

Blissfully, he continued to lick and suck, humming his agreement.

"I love your soft, velvety mouth. I am obsessed with it."

She licked her own lips in memory of the tasty flavors Daniel now enjoyed. Jovian stared at her while he worked Daniel. Growling deep, he pulled his fingers out, causing Daniel's eyes to snap open.

"Look at my mouth."

Jovian opened wide. There were four teeth in the middle, with blunt ends like a human's, but smaller. Next to those on either side were human-sized sharp teeth, then big lion fangs. Smaller fangs were on the bottom.

"You have no fangs."

He raised Aubrey and Daniel's still-clasped hands and licked their entwined fingers with the center of his textured tongue, making them both shiver.

Abah-Sah, his tongue is so long and hot.

She pressed harder on Ferrand's hand between her thighs as Jovian soothed his rough swipe with the velvety soft tip.

"Our mouths have differences."

He kissed their linked hands before releasing them, so they dropped on Ferrand's thigh.

Jovian opened his grip on Daniel's hair and pressed him back, lifting over him, his tail curved high. He gave Daniel his weight by careful degrees, aligning their bodies with care, alert for any sign of fear or discomfort. There was none.

"Your mouths are a delicious playground for Lio. So soft. So sweet."

Daniel's free arm came up over Jovian's shoulder.

"I want to live and die in your mouth."

He dove deep, taking Daniel's kiss.

Aubrey loved watching them. She witnessed Daniel's enjoyment, something she couldn't see while kissing him herself. She experienced Jovian's utter concentration and marveled at his sensual skill.

They pumped their hips together. She felt the build of tension in the hum of her connection with all her males.

Abah-Sah! Yes!

She ground harder into Ferrand's perfect hand. Léandre panted and ground his cock against Ferrand's thigh, Ferrand growling as he undulated smoothly against the side of her rear.

Daniel and Jovian peaked, breaking away from their kiss, Daniel groaning in aching abandon as Jovian roared his climax.

Her lovers' crest buffeted her with vibrant heat.

She, Léandre, and Ferrand joined them, surging into pulsing pinnacles of their own. She and Ferrand gasped their pleasure while Léandre chuffed rough, deep breaths.

Aubrey and Daniel's hands remained clasped together through it all.

Ferrand began a rumbling, contented purr as Jovian whispered to Daniel.

"So handsome as you come, my heart. So generous."

He kissed Daniel's cheek, then regarded her as he spoke, making sure she knew his next words were for her as well.

"You will have everything we can give you. You will take it all."

He bent and nuzzled Daniel's neck, swiping a lick.

"Your flavor is exotic and unique, my heart. I can't wait to savor your cream. To give you my nectar."

He peered at Aubrey again.

"I am so hungry for you!"

She shivered, despite being boneless with relaxation after her second mind-blowing orgasm with her Mates.

Jovian lifted off Daniel, reaching over to a stack of insta-dry cloths, taking one. He deftly, thoroughly cleaned Daniel. Next, he rubbed the fragrant cloth across his abdomen, deeply satisfied with his scent-claim. Daniel watched him do it with heavy-lidded eyes.

Aubrey loved it. She craved more of their combined scents.

Kassie Keegan

Jovian tucked the cloth into his Shendyt before grabbing a new one. He tossed it to Léandre, who discreetly used it inside his garments. Ferrand eased Aubrey off of him, sliding her closer to Daniel. Léandre handed the same cloth to Ferrand, who also used it to refresh himself under his Shendyt.

She and Daniel curled up together in each other's arms, her head cuddled beneath his chin, resting on his chest. Her arm draped over Daniel's ribs with her leg over his hip.

Ferrand slid a long narrow pillow under Daniel's head to his murmured thanks. Aubrey vaguely knew that Jovian cleaned up with the same insta-dry, then tucked the pleasure-scented fabric into Daniel's trousers.

She could smell the combined scents of her males, which comforted her as she drifted into rest, well-satisfied, surrounded by her Mates, secure in Daniel's embrace.

Chapter 24
Daniel

Supremely content, Daniel snuggled Aubrey tight.

She fit him so well. He wanted to know her inside and out, looking forward to discovering her hopes and dreams, to revel in her strength, and to support her when she needed it.

Affection welled up for their Lio Mates, who accepted him with open arms and open hearts, sharing their pleasure generously.

He was drunk on her scent mixed with their Coalition. It felt necessary. His precious flower held close, safe and sated, surrounded by their Mates, relaxed him. He sighed and dozed off.

Daniel woke softly.

Delicate, gentle fingers touched his hair and face. His eyes opened to Aubrey's warm, beautiful blue ones. He greeted her.

"Hi."

She smiled sweetly.

Kassie Keegan

"Hi, there."

"Are you okay?"

"I was going to ask you the same question."

A warm, furred body eased up behind him and settled in. Daniel knew in an instant it was Léandre, his Mates' energies tuned to his senses clearly. He would never confuse them.

Léandre stroked down his arm, leaving a tingling wake. Ferrand reclined on the other side of Aubrey, petting down her back, nudging them to sit up.

"Time for refreshment, beauties."

They sat up. Jovian gave them hydro-packs, then dropped onto the far side of Ferrand. Daniel didn't see them drinking and was concerned.

"Aren't you thirsty, too?"

Jovian's eyes warmed.

"We snacked while you rested. Are you hungry?"

They shook their heads. The drink tasted good, and he finished it quickly. Léandre whisked the hydro-pack away when he was done doing the same for Aubrey.

He sensed a waiting among his Lio Mates. For what, he wasn't sure. Aubrey turned her back to Daniel, settling into him. He adjusted to accommodate her, snuggling her close, both facing Ferrand and Jovian as Aubrey spoke.

"First kisses? I knew those were mine, but yours, too? You didn't tell me."

Léandre leaned over him to give her a kiss on her shoulder, making her smile, Then he settled back, caressing both of them idly with soft pets, his touches possessive and cherishing. Ferrand answered for both Léandre and himself.

"We want no one else, Aubrey, but we don't wish to pressure you, either. You are careful. Cautious. You don't trust easily."

Ferrand shrugged.

"We don't trust easily, either. But considering Daniel's arrival, and our change in relationship, we need to talk and understand each other. Create a solid foundation."

Daniel felt a kinship with them. He, too, had trust issues. Ferrand continued his forthright honesty.

"We have to be open if our family is to thrive. It won't be easy because it makes us vulnerable. But we must do it now, while we are clear-headed."

Daniel's mind was heavy.

"Why don't you trust, Ferrand?"

"My original Pride, and Léandre's, was the Bon'Durel Pride. A sinkhole destroyed our PrideHome when we were both young. We lost most of our Pride within minutes."

He paused and swallowed.

"Léandre, my best friend then, and always, was in a Land Transport with me and my family visiting Telledea when we heard the news. Our Transport malfunctioned and crashed, knocking me out, on our way to help our Pride."

Léandre's petting stopped, and he tensed, a stillness looming within his vibrance. Daniel sensed currents of a dark, opaque, seething chasm of mixed emotions. He gave Léandre's leg a reassuring caress. Léandre responded by wrapping his tail around Daniel's ankle possessively.

Ferrand glanced at Léandre, who stayed tensely frozen behind Daniel as their story was told. He lightly touched Léandre's scar.

"My family died from the crash. Léandre's family had already died in the Sinkhole, but we didn't know it yet. It was a double tragedy. He got this injury. I woke to find him lying on me, and my only brother, Faha-

Ian, covered with blood. He was already gone, but I didn't realize it until later."

He closed his eyes briefly before looking up again. Grief clear in the contours of his expression.

"We don't know exactly how it happened. My Shield mostly protected me. I had a serious concussion, and not a single scratch on me."

Jovian cuddled close to Ferrand's side and laid his head on his arm.

"We think a Mimetic Mineral piece of the ship broke off on impact, causing shrapnel to shred through Léandre's and Fahalan's Shields. It's the only thing that could have penetrated and cut them so viciously. I staunched Léandre's bleeding and dragged him and my brother behind a boulder. I was small then. It was a struggle."

He glanced away, caught up in his memories.

"It was just in time. The ship exploded. I couldn't save my mothers and fathers. It haunts me."

Ferrand studied Léandre, his eyes brimming with pain and questions.

"Was there more I could have done? What if I woke up quicker, moved faster, was stronger? Could I have saved them?"

Aubrey cupped Ferrand's cheek in her palm, turning his face so he focused on her. She shook her head slowly, leaning up to give him a gentle kiss of comfort and compassion.

He accepted her gentleness, closing his eyes, breathing her scent in with a deep breath, visibly relaxing. Ferrand opened his eyes as Aubrey pulled away.

"Thank you, love."

She nodded, but didn't speak. He suspected she couldn't speak. Daniel had a lump in his throat, too, from Ferrand's telling of events. Léandre remained a solid, stiff presence behind Daniel, his energy curiously still. Ferrand took another bracing breath.

"Léandre's vocal cords suffered damage. His voice gone. He refuses to be healed."

He looked at Aubrey, then at Daniel, shadows in his eyes.

"He fights and panics if we even talk about giving him a voice."

Léandre tried to pull away, but Daniel gripped his leg tighter and trapped his tail between his ankles.

"He says it's not 'his' voice. He won't be anything other than who he truly is."

Ferrand gazed at him, complex emotions flashing in his expression.

"I respect Léandre and his choices."

Léandre chuffed his breath in response.

"Bon'Durel hearts shattered. Lio respected, memorialized, then dispersed the remaining Bon'Durels. Survivors were adopted into other Prides on Lio HomeWorld or left to join Lio Fleet Pon'Durel Prides and Lio Colony Lon'Durel Prides. The Mineral Mines are now overseen by a group of several Prides."

He touched a silvery metal ring pierced through the top rim of his right ear. It was something both he and Léandre had.

"Before the last Bon'Durel left, all of us survivors took this ring to remember our lost Pride."

He stopped and gazed at Léandre, Aubrey and Daniel turning to look, too.

"We have been together all our lives and would have it no other way."

Ferrand scratched Léandre behind his ear affectionately, a gesture Léandre leaned into with enjoyment, relaxing.

"When Jovian came to Bon'Fiel Pride by right of combat, he was our missing piece. The three of us are all protective and possessive of what we choose because we know firsthand what it is to lose everything we love. We chose Bon'Fiel Pride as much as they accept and loved us. We are careful who we give our affections to because we don't want to lose them and be hurt again."

Léandre touched his and Aubrey's shoulders to get their attention. He vulnerably peered at them. Aubrey sounded concerned.

"You seem worried, Léandre. Why?"

He sat up on his knees and moved to the side so they could see him easily. Léandre touched his lips first, then his scar, his eyes dark with emotion. He leaned forward, past Aubrey and Daniel, resting his hands over Ferrand and Jovian's hearts. He held there for a moment before pulling away, putting his hands over Aubrey and Daniel's hearts.

Léandre sat back and placed his hands on his own heart and looked at all of them one-by-one. Aubrey reassured him.

"You communicate well, Léandre. With or without your Tech."

As one, Jovian, Ferrand, Aubrey, and Daniel moved close to Léandre, each placing a hand on his hands stacked over his heart.

High Nessa Katohna had been right. Léandre communicated clearly without his voice. Not once had he needed to use his comm with Daniel, yet they understood each other quite well. Daniel felt compelled to speak.

"Let your worry go."

Léandre gazed at each of their faces, devotion and longing shining in his eyes. He nodded, accepting their words, accepting their affection.

Daniel perceived his internal release as a cooling wave crashing against his senses. Léandre's straightforward nature and unwavering commitment to his Mates shone brightly, overshadowing the curious blankness he sensed in Léandre earlier.

Chapter 25
Aubrey

A ubrey enjoyed snuggles with her Mates. Ferrand's bulk was on one side with Jovian, while Daniel and Léandre were on the other. She thought about what she'd learned about Ferrand and Léandre, and the depths of the tragedy they experienced.

She knew her Lio Nels had painful pasts, but they hadn't ever spoken about it. She knew of two Pride losses near the same time, long before she arrived at Lio HomeWorld, but hadn't researched them.

Aubrey, experienced with grief, briefly recalled her mother. But the door burst wide-open in a flood, making her shiver, a chill wave of buried fear washing over her.

Gasping, Daniel growled low in his throat, his body tensing. Her gaze flew to him in surprise. Ferrand and Jovian joined his growl with menacing rumbles of their own. Léandre's tail unwrapped from Daniel's ankle to wrap around her forearm.

Daniel's intense gaze captured hers, a resonant shot of vibrance racing through her humming senses. She couldn't look away from him.

He stared at her with ferocious focus, his nostrils flaring. Slowly and carefully, he pushed a strand of hair off her face, tucking it behind her ear, his gentleness a stark contrast to his fierce expression. She didn't flinch or pull away, as she might have in the past.

She trusted Daniel as he showed her a new side of himself. He'd been protective before, but not at this level.

"Aubrey, honey, my sweet flower. What were you just thinking about? Because the scent of fear coming off you so strongly makes me want to rip something to shreds."

She sensed no aggression from him toward her. He aimed it at what made her afraid. Aubrey had been facing her fears alone and knew she could continue doing so, but she still liked his protectiveness.

This shocked her into breaking Daniel's spell on her gaze. She peered down at her hands gripped tightly together, her forearm wrapped possessively with Léandre's tail.

I'm not ready for this.

Swallowing the lump in her throat, she scanned the small room.

Raiida and Rahimi stood, hands on their Rav Knives, their tails whipping in agitation, their lithe bodies tense and alert, eyes on her.

Poised to pounce in a crouch at the end of the cushion, Stealth's eyes riveted to her, his expression one of deadly intent to protect. Gone was his happy-go-lucky friendliness. This was a battle-ready Warrior's stance.

Oh, crap!

She looked at Léandre, knowing from experience he was prepared to attack and defend. Ferrand reclined, his face cold and sharp, his eyes scanning for danger as the focused hum of his attention centered on her and her movements, despite his eyes being elsewhere.

Jovian contemplated her calmly and thoughtfully, as alert as they all were, but with a seemingly less aggressive demeanor. He did not fool her. His mind worked on twenty things at once, trying to pinpoint the source of her fear, planning on how to defeat it.

Daniel's fingers on her chin tenderly urged her to look at him again.

"Please, honey. I can't take your distress. It upsets me in a way I have no words for. I don't know what to do with all these feelings."

That makes two of us!

Aubrey breathed slow and deep, closing her eyes. She focused inside herself, finding her center of calm.

I've got to tell them, but I need more time to be ready.

"I promise to tell you. I need a moment first to collect my thoughts. My feelings. Can you give me some time?"

Daniel nodded slowly, the lines between his eyes becoming pronounced with his concern.

"Of course."

Jovian rested more comfortably against a still-tense and alert Ferrand as he made a suggestion.

"Tell us where you are from, Daniel. What was your life like before you became Honored?"

Léandre flopped beside Daniel to listen, seemingly at complete ease, but he didn't fool her any more than Jovian had. He was on high-alert, his tail still gently wrapping her forearm.

"Oh! Sure."

Daniel settled, putting his arm around Aubrey's shoulders, stroking her arm idly. She was grateful for her reprieve.

"I grew up on SpacePort Arata in Galaxy Avecorastrana."

Daniel gestured toward his Chalel hanging on the peg near where a now-relaxed Raiida sat. Rahimi and Stealth also eased into their previous postures, but both their faces serious. All three listened to their conversation with undisguised attention.

"A SpacePort Rat."

Kassie Keegan

He grinned down at Aubrey, who grinned back.

We are both SpacePort Rats.

He looked up.

"My mom was my rock most of my life. She's the one who encouraged me to apply to the L.I.O."

He looked shy, making what he said sound like a confession.

"I loved the Lio StoryVids. Those stories were my favorites. Mom knew it."

Excitement raced through her.

Aubrey adored the Lio StoryVids they filmed on planets across the Known Galaxies. There were six long-running series so far. She sat up higher as she asked enthusiastically.

"Which ones were your favorites?"

Daniel's beautiful brown eyes sparkled at her, his eyes crinkling.

"I became hooked with *Lio Declared*."

"Oh, I love that one! With Miriam and Logan? Now I'm addicted to *Lio Brawl*."

"Me, too! I can't wait to find out what happens to Octavia and Eric on planet Duelz. Do you think he will have to fight?"

"Yes! If Octavia doesn't take on the whole Cartel herself. She is such a badass! We binge watch it when it comes through the feeds. Join us."

His expression made her pause her excitement at sharing her enthusiasm for the StoryVid.

"What is it?"

"I would love to watch shows with you and your friends, Aubrey."

He's been lonely.

She remembered her desperate loneliness on SpacePort Omori as every day she struggled to survive and keep her and her mom safe.

Coming to Lio HomeWorld changed everything for the better.

Her memories must have altered her scent again because Daniel's nostrils flared as he inhaled, his face and body tensing, but he managed not to growl. She gave him a small smile.

"I remembered being lonely growing up."

Understanding warmed his eyes.

"Yes. It's hard to make friends on a SpacePort. Usually, everyone there is on their way to somewhere else, and they have no time or interest in people who live there."

She nodded as he continued.

"I had a few friends over the years, but most got out to other places. I made friends with Sawyer on SpacePort Haddou where I became Honored."

"He's the one you greeted earlier?"

His eyes twinkled at her.

"You really were watching me that whole time, weren't you?"

Ferrand spoke up.

"We all were, Daniel."

He laughed, then sobered.

"I had another friend, too, but his asshole cousin ruined it. I'm not sure how. His cousin arrived on SpacePort Haddou to become Honored and that was it. My friend didn't speak to me again. I think it might have been to protect me."

He paused, gazing at her with open vulnerability.

"Still hurt."

Kassie Keegan

Shaking his head, Daniel snorted a laugh.

"Travar came up with a creative way to say 'asshole' because Lio strongly insist ass tastes delicious."

Jovian grinned.

"Because it does!"

Daniel and Aubrey looked at Jovian with wide eyes as he licked his lips, his grin turning carnal. They turned back to each other, eyes even wider, their cheeks pink. Daniel cleared his throat.

"Yes. Well, apparently Lio despise muffins."

She burst out laughing at Ferrand's and Jovian's sick expressions, glancing at Léandre, who shivered with disgust at the mention.

"Oh, Abah-Sah! I remember that fiasco when Dawn from Bon'Clazol Pride brought banana nut muffins to an Honored Presentation."

Aubrey giggled as she explained.

"They were tasty muffins to *me*, but the Lio hated them. It was amusing to watch Lio one-by-one taste a muffin, hate it, then hide their disgust so they could get more Lio to try them and share the misery. "

She laughed harder.

"Even after they knew it would be gross, Lio, who hadn't eaten the muffins, couldn't help but experience the texture and flavor for themselves. It was 'curiosity killed the cat' in action. We laughed all night watching them!"

Daniel chuckled, shaking his head at the scene she described. Their Lio Mates smiled with them, eyes, ears, and postures relaxed. Ferrand and Jovian's tails curled at the ends with lazy motions. Léandre's tail still lovingly wrapped around her forearm, moving easily with her as she told her story.

Daniel piped in.

"Travar decided 'Muffin' was a better word for an asshole because everyone disliked them. So now, that's what we call jerks and status-seekers!"

She laughed harder, wiping her tears of mirth with the heels of her palms.

"Oh, Abah-Sah! That's hilarious! You can say it right to their face and they have no clue."

"Yes!"

Ferrand was curious.

"Who was the 'Muffin' you created this term for, Daniel?"

She could feel the hum of Ferrand's protective instincts on high-alert. They all listened intently.

"Oh. It's that Stanton guy. The Honored Nel who chose the Bon'Rocinal Pride."

She had no memory of the male, as she'd focused entirely on Daniel, but Ferrand grunted understanding. He would probably research the male at his first opportunity, considering him a security risk for his Mate.

Jovian shifted, his expression tightening at the mention of that Pride. It made her curious.

"You okay, Jovian?"

Jovian regarded her with a slight sideways grin that did not match his eyes, and nodded. She remained unconvinced, determined to ask him about it later. Daniel continued.

"So yeah, your invitation to watch StoryVids is sweet. I look forward to it."

"Good!"

She gave Daniel a kiss in a soft meeting of lips filled with understanding and affection. They lingered. After, she gazed at Daniel warmly.

"Tell me about growing up on SpacePort Arata."

Kassie Keegan

"My mom and dad are Lauren and Lukas Shaw."

Daniel quieted.

"Dad disappeared when I was fifteen."

Memories swamped her as Daniel shared his life with them.

"He wouldn't ever leave us willingly. I was already working with him on the Docks, building and repairing Space Transport Engines when he was called to a remote section of the SpacePort for a private engine repair."

He shook his head.

"He never came back, and no one had any information about the Transport. Someone wiped the SpacePort memory drives. I hacked them all and there was nothing."

He peered down, sad. She took one of his hands in her own, prompting him to gaze at her with shadowed eyes.

"We believe someone took him. I hope he is still alive somewhere. And if he isn't, that he didn't suffer."

Léandre rubbed his cheek on Daniel's shoulder, comforting him. Ferrand petted his hair with a soft stroke, Jovian's tail trailing along his arm. Daniel looked at them, smiling faintly at their gestures.

"I continued on the Docks while Mom worked on the SpacePort's heating and air functions. She was tiny and could crawl into small spaces to make repairs. She hid there, too, when she needed to. Being an unclaimed woman on a SpacePort is a dangerous thing. You know this, don't you, Aubrey?"

So, so well, Daniel.

"Anyway, we survived this way for years, hoping Dad would return. We never made enough Galactic Credits to get Off-Port. But then, Mom was in the wrong place at the wrong time and got exposed to a shipment of irradiated ore."

He shook his head sorrowfully.

"She died slowly. I worked every shift I could while she slept, so I could have time with her when she was awake. All my extra G-Creds went to treatment, but we couldn't afford complete healing."

He pressed his lips together as if he didn't want to say the next words, but said them anyway.

"We could have gotten a cure for Mom if I indentured myself to the SpacePort. But it meant they would have taken me to the brothel immediately, and we would never see each other again."

Ferrand and Jovian growled.

"She told me she would rather die. With Dad gone and being without me, she would die of a broken heart even if her body healed. So, no. I only considered it briefly when I was desperate to save her. Instead, she insisted we fill out the forms for the L.I.O. together. Here I am, because of her."

This time, his Mates growled with approval.

"You know what? She never lost her sense of humor. She could find something to joke about, no matter how dark it got. I love that about her."

Daniel gave a bittersweet smile, his mind on his memories, his scent heavy with the tang of sadness.

"I've been thinking about her a lot since I came here. Mom and Dad dreamed of making it to a Colony and here I am, on Lio HomeWorld. I know they would be happy I made it. This is a dream come true."

He scanned everyone in the room, ending with Aubrey, touching her face with gentle fingers.

"*You* are a dream come true."

Oh, Daniel. You melt my heart!

He turned to each of his Lio Mates, looking at them with affection.

"You all are."

Kassie Keegan

She understood how much it meant to them, too.

He is such a worthy man. Strong, devoted, hard-working, and affectionate. A wonderful choice.

She took a deep breath.

I guess it's my turn.

Chapter 26
Aubrey

"My dad is Pete Newton. He was a Mechanical Technician on a Galactic Pleasure Cruiser when he met my mom, Nancy. She worked as an entertainer, singing and dancing in the evenings and serving food and drinks during the day. She moved to working in the Cruiser kitchens when she got pregnant with me."

Aubrey petted the soft fur at the end of Léandre's tail, still wrapped around her forearm. It gave her a comforting repetitive motion while she talked about difficult things.

"When I was born, Mom went back to singing and dancing and Dad became my caregiver. They strapped me to the front of him and he carried me everywhere. Dad told me I rarely fussed. He worked long hours and still cared for me. When I started walking, he made a portable pen for me. My toys were things he fashioned from spare pieces of equipment."

She smiled, remembering some of the whimsical items her dad created for her as she was growing up.

"He said I was a skilled Mech Tech. Even as a toddler, I could fix things. It's easy for me."

Time to be really real.

Kassie Keegan

"Machines hum for me. It's like they tell me where they need help and where I can fix them."

Aubrey peered up to see their reactions to her revelation, but no one seemed surprised. Daniel smiled. She paused in wonder at it, prompting him to comment.

"Please continue, Aubrey. I understand the way you perceive things."

She eyed him as she spoke.

"People can hum for me, too. You're the only one who glows."

Daniel smiled wider, making her pause again with curiosity.

"Just more we have in common. Please tell us your story."

Wonder tingled up her spine.

We are so perfectly matched.

He motioned for her to keep going.

This is not the reaction I expected.

"Mom was sad. She missed me, missed my dad. Wanted more time with us. Dad missed her, too. When I was around seven years old, they had enough of Cruiser life and decided to make a change, trying to settle down on a Colony World. They made a mistake, though."

She looked down.

"They thought telling the Captain they wanted to leave at the end of their current term would give him time to find people to replace them. Then they could start their journey to a Colony from SpacePort Bazzini, where their Cruises stationed."

She shook her head.

"The Captain was angry and malicious. He ended their contracts immediately and sent them by Freighter Transport directly off the Cruiser to the nearest SpacePort."

She peered up at Daniel.

"SpacePort Omori."

He shook his head, grave with understanding, his voice deep with emotion.

"The infamous Pirate outpost."

"Yes."

His expression became grim.

"He sent you there to die, didn't he?"

She nodded. Ferrand sounded too casual while asking his question.

"What was the Captain's name, Aubrey?"

She looked at him knowingly. Ferrand would see the man dead in a second, but it wasn't necessary.

"Prime Bastian made sure he paid for his actions long ago. He called it the 'Captain's reward.'"

Ferrand growled his satisfaction, relaxing.

Aubrey remembered the Prime she'd Chosen years ago, thinking about how comforted she felt in his presence. She missed him terribly. Her Mates shifted.

They must scent my unhappiness again.

She took a deep breath.

"SpacePort Omori is dangerous and expensive. Most people end up enslaved or indentured, like Daniel mentioned."

She cupped Daniel's face.

"I'm glad you and your mom made the choices you did, Daniel. They brought you here. To me. To *us*. I'm sorry she suffered, but I'm glad you're here."

He turned his head, kissing the center of her palm, then took her hand in his, holding it while she talked.

"Dad was determined to protect us and find a way out. It took most of their saved Galactic Credits to secure safe quarters deep in the bowels of the Dock mechanics. The smells of mech fluid and oil remind me of safety to this day. It was a small place, but it served our needs. Mom made it as colorful and lively as she could."

Aubrey gave a faint smile as she thought of her vivacious mother when she was happy. Then her smile disappeared.

"Dad worked the Docks. He helped Mom find work in a club that didn't require sex service. He was a vicious fighter, who pulled no punches. He fought a lot those first weeks."

Aubrey's eyes prickled with the start of tears, and she blinked them back.

"Mom cried all the time, sorry she'd wanted more. They were worse off than they'd been on the Cruiser. Dad worked harder and longer, becoming more determined to get us out."

Daniel squeezed her hand.

"I began working the Docks with Dad, dressed like a boy. I kept my hair short, wore only work coveralls, and rarely spoke. Dad called me 'son' all the time, saying I was younger than I was to stave off questions about my size."

Léandre stroked her back comfortingly.

"It didn't matter how old I was, I could do the job. I had a reputation for fixing things, so people left me alone. I took standard Vid School classes at night for as long as I could stay awake."

She shook her head.

"It went on like that for years. We were so *close* to getting out. We had the G-Creds and scheduled Transport to Vedah when Dad disappeared without a trace."

She focused on Daniel, who looked at her with deep understanding and compassion.

He truly understands. He's been through it.

"We missed our flight Off-Port searching for him. We know he was either taken or killed. No way would he leave us there. But we'd paid the fees. No 'take-backsies' on SpacePort Omori. A deal is a deal, and we missed it."

The tremendous weight of that terrible time crushed down on her.

"Mom lost her shit, gone to grief. Hardly able to get out of bed. I worked as much as I could, even at night. Thankfully, Mom still had rights to our home under the Dock, so we had a place to live."

Growls rumbled throughout the room, the unfairness of it incensing her companions. The same aggression rose in her heart at the injustices.

My story won't get better.

"After a few month spans, Mom got up and started moving, even though she was only a shadow of who she'd been before my dad disappeared. She got her old job back, but this time she didn't have Dad's protection."

She took a deep breath, letting it out slowly.

"That's when human club owner Brad stepped in. Pretty, pretty Brad. Abah-Sah, was he handsome on the outside and such a snake on the inside. He offered Mom his 'protection.'"

Aubrey made air quotes, lifting her arm with Léandre's tail still wrapped around it.

"His protection included exclusive sexual rights, of course. But Mom decided being at the mercy of one calculating abuser was better than being used by dozens. She kept him away from our home as much as she could, which was fine with him. Brad had no interest in her runt of a son, or in her life beyond what she did for him."

She closed her eyes in sorrow at her mom's terrible choices, remembering her mother's tears, her desolation. Her pain. How some days her mom could barely walk after a night with Brad, her bruises terrible to see. Aubrey experienced it all without comment, helping as much as she could.

This, and all the ugliness she witnessed in the hallways of the SpacePort, and her later experience with Brad, made sex seem like a terrible thing.

I probably wouldn't have any sexual feelings if I hadn't become an Honored Nessa.

Her Lio-enhanced beast-nature demanded she choose a Coalition and Bond sexually and emotionally. With her Mates, Aubrey learned about pleasure, embracing it with all her might.

Her Mates gave her loving strokes of comfort. Squeezing Daniel's hand again, she centered herself with the hum of his compassion and care.

What a stark contrast my life is to my mom's.

She opened her eyes.

"I stayed a boy, but when I reached puberty age and no big changes happened, the vultures became suspicious. I went to work, kept my head down, and talked as little as possible. I studied at night, and when I could, viewed the Lio StoryVids, dreaming of new worlds where I could be who I truly am."

She looked at Daniel.

"Those StoryVids kept me sane. It was a lonely way to grow up, but I still had hope there was something better out there. Like you did."

Daniel lifted her hand and kissed it gallantly. Her heart pounded like it had the first time, loving the romantic gesture.

"Mom sent applications to the L.I.O. for both of us. She had to work months and make all kinds of concessions to Brad to get them sent. I think one of them was to allow Brad to make her pregnant."

She tried to pull her hand out of Daniel's grip, but he gently tightened it, not letting go.

"Her pregnancy was a nightmare. Mom was sick practically the whole time. After the first four months, Brad refused to pay for more medical care. He said she was getting too expensive. She couldn't work while she was so sick, which he blamed her for. He said she was lucky he paid for food, which he barely did. She wasted away, day by day."

A tear rolled down her cheek. The room was completely still.

"Mom went into premature labor. No one would answer my comms, no doctor would come to our aid. They knew we couldn't pay and Brad wouldn't."

More tears fell.

"I delivered my brother by myself. I gave his tiny, lifeless body to my mother, who named him Paul. She knew she was dying. I couldn't stop the bleeding. So much blood…"

Aubrey swallowed a sob and kept talking, needing the story finished.

"Mom told me to hide the evidence she and Paul had died. I could send them to space from a chute at the Dock. She wanted to buy me time to collect what I needed to stowaway or get a job as a Mech Tech on a Transport off Omori. It's still dangerous, but a single male travels much easier."

She peered up, barely able to see through the shimmer of her tears. It was Léandre's eyes she stared into. Daniel held her hand, Ferrand stroked her knee, and Jovian's tail petted her thigh.

"She looked at me with love as she died, saying no matter what regrets she had in life, having me wasn't one of them. I was her greatest joy, and I should seek my happiness."

Léandre tried to save his loved-ones, too. She saw his understanding of her pain in his golden eyes. Swinging her gaze to Ferrand, she saw his familiarity with grief and loss in the swirl of his emotions.

"I loved her and I couldn't save her or my brother."

She sighed, tears dripping.

Kassie Keegan

"I did what she told me to do, but I didn't expect Brad to barge in on me before work hours a few day spans later. I scored a job as a Mech Tech on a Raider vessel, leaving soon after repairs were complete, which must have gotten back to him. He knew I wouldn't leave without my mother, so he already suspected she was gone."

Aubrey swallowed the knot forming in her throat, memory taking her back in time, to her tiny home on SpacePort Omori under the Dock.

"Nancy! Get your lazy, skinny ass up!"

Pound, pound, pound.

"I need some sexy candy sitting around while I make a new deal. I know you can do it. No one cares about your fat belly, with a face like yours. Get the fuck up!"

Pound, pound, pound.

Aubrey stood frozen, her nutrition bar halfway to her mouth. She wasn't ready for work yet, and especially not ready to engage with Brad. Her panicked gaze went to her concealing work coveralls hanging by the door. She was in her thermals, which clearly revealed her feminine shape.

Her mom hadn't given Brad Entry Permissions, but she heard the telltale scrapes at the entryway mech as he hacked the entry. He'd be inside soon.

Not enough time to put on the coveralls.

Tossing her food to the table, she ran to the bedroom to grab one of her dad's old shirts, her mom having kept all of his things. She had just dropped it over her head when the door shushed open.

Brad barged in, shouting.

Savage Planet Embrace

"Abassan Blue Balls, Nancy! Get your ass out here!"

Brad stood framed by the bedroom entryway, in all his pretty-boy glory, dressed beautifully in clean, silky clothes. Not a hair out of place. His shrewd eyes took in the scene with one glance.

"Where's Nancy, runt?"

Aubrey was in a shit-ton of trouble. Brad might be pretty, but he was also strong, and a nasty fighter. You didn't succeed on SpacePort Omori without being vicious.

Her Transport out of this hell wasn't until tomorrow. If she could escape him, she could hide easily until then. Her mind raced with all the ways she might get away and survive. If she made it past him.

"Where's your cunt mother, boy!"

Her eyes narrowed, but she didn't speak. It was the biggest indicator she wasn't a male. Through the years Aubrey had said only a few sentences to Brad, ever. She shook her head.

Brad's expression turned calculating. He leaned against the entryway, relaxing, enjoying himself as he toyed with her.

"Yeah. Thought so. I heard you got a transpo gig. No way you'd be leaving without your bitch mother. They don't take bitches who aren't working on their backs. And she can't do that while she's breeding my bastard. She's too sick."

His face showed sneering satisfaction.

I'm dead. This fucking monster knows about the job.

Aubrey's thoughts were desperate, but she kept stone-cold. Not even by a flick of her eyelash would she give anything away to this scum.

There were grooming tools on the small table near the bed. She could grab something and use it as a weapon when he attacked her. And he would attack. It was inevitable.

"She got out, huh? Well, too bad for you, boy. She signed herself over to me and I had plans to make some serious G-Creds on her skinny ass when she finished whelping my kid. Guess I'll have to make money on *your* ass. But not before I have it myself."

Brad stood to his full, imposing height.

"Bend over nice and easy, son. You give it up good for me and I'll make sure you get the small dicks. At first."

Aubrey didn't move or change her expression, simply waiting for her chance. She had one shot to make it work, and wouldn't waste it being distracted by his threats of rape and sexual slavery.

"Of course, you have to take *my* dick."

Brad stroked himself through his clothes, his erection filling. He was not small.

"I get to bust your cherry ass wide-open. Might keep you a while. I'm getting my contract paid in Newton flesh one way or another. Might as well be your holes servicing me."

Fucking monster.

Aubrey's chest ached with anguish at her memories. She hadn't been fast enough to get away. Shaking her head, she brought herself out of the memory.

"Brad attacked me when he realized Mom was missing. He said he'd take his fee out of Newton flesh whether it was me or my mother. He intended to rape me, then put me in a brothel."

She shook her head again.

"I fought as hard as I could, but he was, of course, stronger. Imagine his surprise when he discovered I was a girl. He shouted with delight! He said he'd get a spawn off his fresh, new piece."

She shuddered with revulsion.

"That's when Abassa Itakah arrived with a Lio Warrior contingent. She didn't need the Warriors, though."

This time Aubrey shuddered at the memory of feminine roars of rage. Wet, ripping sounds accompanied by Brad's shrieks of pain, followed immediately by the distinct smell of blood.

"Brad left the door open. Abassa Itakah took one look at the scene and ripped Brad to shreds right in front of me. There's no remorse for the pain he suffered as he died."

She breathed deep and steady, her tears dwindling as she reached the end of her tale.

"Abah-Sah sent Abassa Itakah to collect me for the L.I.O. program just in time. She cleaned me up and took me out of there. I became Honored on SpacePort Lina, then came to Lio HomeWorld. Without a word to any other Prime, I chose Prime Bastian in my PrideChoice. I walked straight to him to be folded in his arms."

She smiled faintly at the memory of that first glorious hug.

"From the moment I saw him, I knew he was safe. It was all I wanted. Prime Bastian and Bon'Fiel Pride taught me how to defend myself against stronger opponents. It was slow, but I made friends. Found a place among these people, with a job I love."

Her companions were back on high-alert, but controlled themselves enough to stay locked in their casual positions. She sensed the seething hum of their anger at her experiences.

She scratched each of her Lio Mates behind an ear for a moment, leaving them with more relaxed expressions on their faces.

"My Lio found me."

She sniffed away the last of her tears.

"I miss Prime Bastian. He was such a wonderful male. A father figure when I most needed one. I don't know why he went to the Fade so fast, and left us so unexpectedly. I hadn't sensed the Fade in him."

She paused, thinking about how devastated she'd been, losing another father. She shook off the sad thoughts. Prime Bastian would want her joy, not her sadness.

"Prime Cassian is a wonderful male, too. Smart and strong. I believe his successor would please Prime Bastian."

She turned to Daniel.

"I watched you take your first step on Lio HomeWorld, Daniel. It reminded me of my own first steps. I love having shared it with you before I even knew who you were."

He smiled softly at her, his voice deep.

"I love it, too, Aubrey."

She searched around for something to wipe her eyes. Léandre handed her a clean insta-dry cloth. After she wiped her tears, he took the cloth, laying it aside. Leaning close, he comfortingly rubbed his velvety cheeks against hers.

"Thanks."

She scanned the room, absorbing her companions' support and compassion.

"Thank you all."

Ferrand spoke deep and gravelly with emotion.

"You don't have to thank us. We are your Mates and allies. Your pain is our pain. You are beloved."

"Oh! You are going to make me cry again!"

Ferrand moved, sliding lower on the cushions, angling his back and shoulder so Jovian sat slightly beyond his far shoulder. He spread his legs, drawing Aubrey up and across his lap to straddle his thigh closest to Jovian. Once she settled, Ferrand guided Daniel to straddle his other thigh, tucking Daniel's knee beside and slightly behind Aubrey's knee between his legs.

Savage Planet Embrace

He drew them down to his softly-furred, firmly-muscled chest, tucked together under his chin, wrapping his arms around them in an enormous bear hug while they faced each other.

"My Mates have endured so much. You are safe now, with your Lio, who love and protect you."

Ferrand squeezed them a little tighter.

Aww, he is so sweet! I suppose this is more a lion hug than a bear hug.

She giggled at her thought, her face smooshed to Ferrand's chest.

I think I'm giddy after the stress of my story.

Daniel sounded muffled.

"What?"

It made her giggle harder.

"We are in a big lion hug, not a bear hug."

He chuckled as he sat up from the embrace, bringing her up with him. He petted Ferrand's chest.

"Thanks for the hug, Ferrand."

He turned her to face him.

"Thanks for your truth, Aubrey."

He kissed her sweetly in an undemanding tasting, full of comfort and affection.

Oh, I love this man.

Her thoughts startled her into pulling out of the kiss to gaze at him with wonder, realization settling within her.

I love him. I can say it in my heart now.

She looked at Léandre, Ferrand, then Jovian.

I love all of them.

Kassie Keegan

She felt released through sharing her pain, able to start fresh. A new beginning with the Mates she Claimed. But there was still one more story to be told.

She stared at Jovian with expectation. Daniel put his arms around her, his chin resting on her shoulder as they straddled Ferrand's thighs.

Time to spill, Jovian.

Chapter 27
Jovian

Léandre affectionately pulled Jovian's chin fur, hinting for him to speak. Jovian gave him a rueful grin, moving over to Ferrand's side so he could face his Mates.

Settling comfortably, Léandre faced him with his arms crossed over Ferrand's chest and abdomen, his chin on his arms as they all prepared to listen to Jovian tell his story.

"Before I start, we need Daniel to understand one last thing about you, Aubrey."

He focused on Daniel, seriousness weighing his gaze.

"Aubrey is Shaktah. We now understand better why."

Daniel took his words to heart. Love for his resilient Honored Mates filled him, making Jovian's chest ache with the breadth of his feelings for them. He was grateful they trusted by sharing their pain and vulnerability.

Jovian could do no less. Even though, deep in his heart-of-hearts, he expected them to reject him as so many others had.

"Aubrey's scent is a mixture of innocent sweetness combined with potent fear. An alluring combination for animalistic predators. Which is who we Lio are when our intellect slips the leash off our beast-nature."

Kassie Keegan

Daniel became thoughtful.

He's felt his beast-nature rise within him.

"Aubrey's scent can trigger a male to Rut and a female into Breeding Heat."

She gasped in surprise, staring at Jovian with wide eyes.

"Hasn't someone explained this to you?"

How can this be?

"Well."

She cleared her throat.

"The females used unclear terms like 'scent attractor' and 'scent assist' when describing why I smell so good to Lio. I didn't understand exactly what the big deal was and didn't care. I just want to live my life."

She had an expression of revelation on her face as things fell into place for her.

"Wait. That's why all the fresh ribbons in my hair and always-new clothes, sheets, and blankets. They want my scent! You all knew this the whole time?"

She glanced around to see the Lio agreeing.

"What are the females doing? Using my clothes to get laid?"

Jovian's eyebrows went up, but she was indeed correct. He confirmed with a rueful expression.

"This is so, Aubrey."

"Huh. I'm not sure what to think of this. I mean, isn't it weird?"

Ferrand answered.

"Not for Lio. We are scent-driven beings. You bless these families with your scent. Many young have been born because of you, despite your innocence to it."

He stroked her cheek, his expression full of affection.

"Lio are very sexual. You are not interested, so you've been intentionally blind to much of this part of Lio life. Lio understand and accept this about you. But that's changed now."

Ferrand's eyes blazed with desire, his hand now stroking languidly across her throat and upper chest, causing her lids to lower with arousal. Aubrey rolled her hips in tiny pulses against Ferrand's thigh.

She's heating up again.

Jovian's shaft engorged in its sheath. They would taste pleasure at least once more before leaving this space. Ferrand continued gently.

"You are Claiming Mates and becoming more aware as you experience Awakening. These truths must be made clear to you during your Mate-Dance. Some may try to entice you away from us, Aubrey."

Ferrand spoke confidently, sure of her commitment to them as her Coalition. His huge, gentle fingers now lavished attention to her bare shoulder and arm. She shivered at his touch, her nipples peaking in her bodice.

Jovian licked his lips in anticipation of tasting her flesh, bringing her pleasure, and devouring her cream. He swept his gaze over Daniel as his anticipation doubled. Two juicy Mates to gorge his dormant appetites upon.

I've waited this long. I can wait until they are ready.

He glanced at Léandre.

Léandre will be a hedonist when he lets go. He will have no limits as long as it brings pleasure.

He considered his beloved Commander Ferrand. Ferrand's sexual tastes were still somewhat of a mystery to Jovian. He would enjoy discovering them.

Ferrand continued his tender seduction of Aubrey.

"Who is it you want, Aubrey?"

Kassie Keegan

She answered breathlessly, her voice light-as-air.

"You. My Mates."

Ferrand crushed her breasts to his chest, moving subtly as he gave her a deep, sensuous kiss. Daniel pressed his torso along her back, giving Aubrey's shoulder tiny kisses while he watched them kiss. Aubrey and Daniel ground on Ferrand's thighs.

Jovian reveled in Daniel's fascination, enjoying the rise of tension in the room. Léandre leaned back as Ferrand sat up higher, stroking Daniel with soft, lingering touches up-and-down his bare arms.

Jovian smiled as their arousal scents bloomed.

Ferrand pulled away from a panting Aubrey, moving to Daniel, who he treated to a blistering kiss, Daniel's second with a Lio. Aubrey was just as fascinated watching Daniel receive Ferrand's attention.

They are perfect Mates for each other, and for us.

Ferrand pulled away from Daniel and casually laid back again. This time, his large, engorged cock was prominently displayed, their eyes drinking in the sight of him spread out like a Lio feast before them.

Yes, sweet Mates, this is what you get when you answer the Call to Mate.

Ferrand relaxed, enjoying their admiration, reveling in anticipation. Aubrey couldn't resist petting Ferrand's erection through his purple Shendyt, taking full measure of her Mate's endowment.

Chuffing his pleasure, Ferrand covered her hand with his, undulating against her. His other hand lifted hers to his mouth for a kiss on the back of her hand, imitating Daniel's signature move. They smiled at each other.

Jovian growled low to get their attention. He allowed his desire for them to rise, showing them all of it, holding nothing back. Fierce need pierced their expressions, making them pulse harder against Ferrand's thighs. Ferrand purred his enjoyment.

This is as good a time as any to tell them.

Arousal distracted them.

Maybe I can gloss over some details.

Léandre settled back down on Ferrand's chest to listen. Aubrey and Daniel's attention remained sharp on him.

I may underestimate their interest in my story.

His heart-of-hearts warmed.

Maybe they won't put me aside.

"We are all three adopted by the Bon'Fiel Pride. High Nessa Katohna brought in Ferrand and Léandre, but I have a different story."

Jovian's thoughts turned dark, bitterness threading its way into his memories. He became caught up in them, trapped until Aubrey spoke.

"I remember your seething anger at the world, Jovian. It matched my own when I first arrived. You told me the bare bones of what happened, and I accepted it, just like you accepted me and my anger. We understand each other without words. Now, I need the words."

I give my Mate what she needs.

He looked down as he spoke.

"My time with Bon'Fiel Pride starts shortly after what happened to Ferrand and Léandre."

He paused for a deep breath.

"My birth Pride, The Bon'Ocal Pride, is Disgraced."

He flicked his right ear, bringing their eyes to it.

"Every member of my Pride is Marked, the shaming cut sealed open. They stripped our name of honor and erased it."

He flipped his mane over the ear with a practiced move.

"Liani Defense educated Lio on how to protect from invaders. They accused our Liani of corruption, saying there were deliberate vulnerabilities our Pride benefited from here, and on Lio Colony Worlds."

He looked up at Aubrey, seeing her compassion.

"My family was part of the Bon'Ocal Defense Team on their way to Capital Maituri with our Pride Leadership to fight our case when there was a 'malfunction.'"

He grimaced.

"Everyone died. Another sad tragedy stacked upon all the others."

He gazed away, his attention deep in the past.

"With no Leadership and no Defense, the Pride Judges found the Bon'Ocal Pride guilty and had us Disgraced and Disbanded. Everyone, even us young, were Marked. The Bon'Rocinal Pride made the cuts. Prime Bellisio took enjoyment in it."

Daniel growled, getting Jovian's attention, his face tight with anger.

"This is the Prime asshole Stanton chose. I am not surprised."

Jovian nodded distractedly, turning his gaze to stare blankly to the side, his mind far away from them as he shared his memories.

The moment so strong in his memory, he again felt the sharp sting of the slice to his ear, experienced the blood running hot and fresh down his neck. Tasted the bitterness and confusion of all of it happening when he had also lost his loving parents.

"My Pride's will to fight died with our Pride Leadership. They accepted Judgment, then left Lio HomeWorld."

He tensed.

"Because they accused my family specifically of being spies for conspirators, the Pride Judges made an example of me and my brother, Griffon. I barely had ten year spans, my brother had only twelve. We were too young to be sent Off-World alone and, because of who our parents were, many Prides hesitated to adopt us."

He returned his heavy gaze to his Mates.

"They were preparing to exile us to a barren island in the Ocean, but Prime Bastian Bon'Fiel fought for our lives. Literally. It was a vicious battle with Prime Agawahl Bon'Tecol. Prime Bastian shed much blood to Choose me and my brother for Bon'Fiel Pride. I will forever remember his fierce defense."

Daniel put pieces together as Jovian mentioned names.

"Wait. I met the Bon'Tecol High Nessa. So mean-spirited. She said Bon'-Fiel needed to root out corruption. Prime Mahkar didn't let her get away with it, though. She was one of the first people we called 'Muffin.' Was she taking a shot at *you*, Jovian?"

"Maybe. She takes digs at Bon'Fiel whenever she can because Bon'Tecol lost the fight to exile me and my brother."

Daniel bristled.

"What a bitch!"

Daniel seethed with anger. Jovian didn't want that.

"Relax, Daniel. She doesn't matter. No one matters except us. Here, together. Right now."

Daniel breathed deep, visibly calming.

Good Mate.

"Bon'Fiel Pride saved my life. They loved me and helped me find my skills."

He paused.

"However, the Dark Realm Prides helped me keep my soul."

A ripple of awareness flowed through the room.

"Bon'Fiel gave me freedom to Prowl as much as I needed. I went from Liani to Liani, as most male Lio do on their Prowl, trying to find the field of study I was most called to. I discovered Tech and dug in deep."

Jovian looked at Ferrand, then Léandre.

"Ferrand and Léandre Bonded to me. They were my Brethren, my Coalition since we first met. My brother Griffon went to Liani Prime when he presented as a Prize Lio male, but he could not forgive or forget what happened here on Lio HomeWorld."

Jovian had a firm conviction.

"Bon'Ocal Pride was innocent. I am not the only one who believes it."

Ferrand petted his back.

"Griffon left as soon as he could. He found his Zumiel Kinari Pon'Panal on Lio Fleet Khalina, near Earth. They work on the Security Force together."

He sat up and stared down, not looking at anyone while he spoke.

"When Griffon left, I lost my way. I traveled to the Dark Realm Forest. I believed I was going to die of grief. Despite my connection with Ferrand, Léandre, and Bon'Fiel Pride, I saw no reason for my existence."

He paused again, the only sound Ferrand's big hand petting loving strokes down Jovian's back.

"The Dark Realm Primes took me. By day, they required my lessons at Liani Tech with the Bon'Leval Pride. By night, they showed me how to transform my rage and find solace in sexual fulfillment. I learned how to give up control, how to have self-control, and how to guide someone else's pleasure. I reveled in their tutelage."

He peered up at his Mates, looking at each one, his gaze open, revealing the darkness within him. He would not hide it from them.

Ferrand stopped stroking when Jovian pulled himself forward, squaring his shoulders. His movement revealing his most physically vulnerable areas while he revealed his deepest vulnerabilities.

They must see and know me in all my colors, dark to light. If they keep me, they keep the real *me.*

"You held yourselves pure for your Mates. I am not pure in any sense.

I'm not innocent. I have done everything and had everything done to me. And I loved it! Every moment!"

Time to face the ultimate rejection.

Jovian watched them with a guarded gaze, waiting for them to pull back. For their expressions to change. For the rejection to begin.

They regarded him steadily, each Mate's expression serious.

Without a word, Aubrey put her hand over Jovian's heart. Daniel covered her hand, and Léandre covered Daniel's. Ferrand's huge hand covered them all.

He stared down at their hands stacked over his heavily beating heart. He scented no anger. Felt no silent withdrawal. Sensed no rejection.

It's like they are shielding my heart.

Jovian put both his hands over theirs, clutching them close, crushed by the weight of emotion flowing through him. He gasped with it, overwhelmed, his eyes burning with tears he let fall.

They petted and caressed him, showing without words their affection and support. Gentle fingers stroked the curve of his ear where it was split and healed open, a Mark of Shame. His eyes, shimmering with tears, shot up at the touch.

It was Aubrey who delicately grasped the curve where it split, her voice soft with compassion.

"I believe you."

He gasped, his gaze wheeling around the room, seeing everyone nod in agreement, even Stealth and the twins.

It's more than I hoped!

Jovian leaned back and roared with a release of pain and joy, clutching his Mates' hands to his heart. After, he dropped his grip on their hands, melting forward onto Ferrand's chest, into his Mates' embrace.

Kassie Keegan

Aubrey lay on his back, a warm feminine weight pressing him into Ferrand's silky pelt. Ferrand's hand lay heavy and still on Jovian's hip. Daniel's distinctive masculine fingers carded soothingly through his mane.

Léandre pinged his holo-comm asking him to communicate. Jovian opened a channel with a thought and a crinkle of his eye, realizing it was an open channel shared by all his Mates.

Aubrey sat up, urging Jovian to sit up, too, so he could see them. Daniel had a wondering expression on his face. Léandre's comm began when Jovian looked at him.

> LÉANDRE:
> You seem to think we are not like you. That you are damaged or unworthy.

Léandre dried Jovian's tears with an insta-dry cloth, setting it aside with Aubrey's cloth from earlier.

> LÉANDRE:
> We are all damaged.

Léandre stroked his hand over the scar showing vividly through the fur across his throat.

> LÉANDRE:
> We are all worthy of the life we seek together. Everyone confronts pain and grief differently.

His Mates agreed with nods.

> LÉANDRE:
> You are ours, Jovian. Accept this.

Jovian scanned their faces, seeing their possessiveness of him, his heart blazing with happiness.

> LÉANDRE:
> Do not run from us.

Savage Planet Embrace

He looked at Léandre in surprise, whose glowing, golden gaze watched him, steady and focused.

LÉANDRE:

> We do not release what is ours. Remember this. Where you go, we go.

Jovian studied their determined faces. Léandre made it clear Jovian would not be hiding his emotions from his Mates.

A swell of well-being began in his heart, sweeping through his mind and body, leaving calm in its wake. A mischievous grin bloomed.

If he wasn't going to the Dark Realm to drown his rage when he needed, he would have to work it out by fucking his Mates at Bon'Fiel PrideHome. Anticipation rose in him.

I can do this!

LÉANDRE:

> Do you accept?

Jovian's grin widened as he agreed.

They do not know what this means. But I will enjoy showing them!

Léandre closed the holo-comm, gave Jovian a tug on his beard, then settled back with an air of expectation.

Chapter 28
Jovian

There was one part of himself Jovian saved to share only with his Mates.

Jovian met Léandre's steady, carnal gaze as it roved him from mane to tail, resting at his tuft intently. Léandre's eyes flicked back to Jovian's meaningfully.

Does he know?

His eyes narrowed on Léandre.

How could he know?

Léandre lifted an eyebrow in challenge, expressing, *'Does it matter?'*

No, it doesn't matter.

Jovian brought his tail forward.

"Aubrey, Daniel, do you know what this ring is called?"

He showed them the thick, intricately engraved ring below his tuft at the end of his tail. Daniel shook his head. Aubrey brightened as she answered.

"It's a Serc!"

"Yes! What is it for, Aubrey?"

She considered it, pursing her lips.

"I thought a Serc was for tail decoration, and defense if a Lio needed it when fighting."

Léandre and Ferrand shifted postures, anticipation rising. Their friends also watched attentively.

Of course they watch! I'm about to reveal my most vulnerable, hidden part of myself to my unsuspecting Honored Mates.

He held his tail at eye-level for Aubrey and Daniel, its tip flicking with excitement he didn't even try to control.

"You are correct, Aubrey, a Serc has those purposes. It also has another."

Jovian slid his Serc off the end of his tail. He burrowed into the thick hair of his tuft, pulling the hair backward toward his tail. He then put the Serc back in place at the end of his tail so it secured the hair back out of the way, exposing the naked tip for his Mates.

Their eyes riveted to the end of his tail.

"A Serc holds our tuft, so Lio may use their sabah unimpeded."

Her voice breathy, Aubrey spoke wonderingly.

"Sabah?"

"Yes. The cock in my tail."

Aubrey and Daniel gasped, their eyes flying to Jovian's face, then back to his tail tip.

Ferrand was a study of indulgent enjoyment as he used flicks of his tail tuft to caress Aubrey and Daniel under their chins.

Aubrey stared at Ferrand's tail, before swinging her gaze back to Jovian's, as if she'd not seen one before. Her expression became concerned, then collapsed into horror.

"Does this mean petting Lio tails is a sexual thing?"

She was obviously thinking about her innocent touches in the past, concerned she had made a cultural faux pax in her innocence, re-evaluating other's actions, too.

Jovian needed to stop her line of thinking immediately.

"No, my heart. Let this worry go. Lio are affectionate. Your sweet pets are understood as friendship and respect, nothing more. This part of us, our sabah, is deep inside our tail, some of it protected by the Serc. Our tuft protects the vulnerable end. Touching others with our tuft is simple affection."

She still looked worried. Jovian insisted she truly hear him.

"Believe me, Aubrey."

Aubrey regarded him for long moments as she considered what he'd said. Finally, her features relaxed.

Daniel's eyes hadn't left the tip of Jovian's tail, his gaze blazing with curiosity.

Yes, Daniel. We Lio offer so much to our Mates.

Jovian allowed his arousal to rise, focusing on his sabah, enjoying his Mates' attention. The blunt, exposed end of his tail had a dip in the center that gradually showed a protrusion. By increments, his sabah revealed itself.

First, the flexible tip became a pointed crown flowing into a long, narrow column of golden flesh with tiny darker-gold nubs in a distinctive pattern. It was as thick as his tail and longer than his hand.

Instead of an opening in the crown, there was a flexible tip he could control like a finger. He moved the tip to show them. The possibilities for bringing them pleasure with his sabah were unlimited.

He savored his Mates' reactions as his sabah came alive for them. Jovian's cock emerged from its sheath, too, the scene electrifying him as he revealed the last hidden part of himself.

Aubrey and Daniel's breathing came fast and deep, their unconscious pulses against Ferrand's thighs a subtle, but clear sign of their arousal. Jovian whispered to them.

"This is the one thing I kept for myself. For my Coalition. For my Mates."

His breathing became labored as Daniel licked his lips.

Oh, Abah-Sah! To have those lips on my sabah!

Gasping, his gaze flew to Aubrey as she leisurely grasped his tail below his Serc, husking his name.

"Jovian."

She brought it closer to her and Daniel.

"Does this mean you are a virgin here?"

He nodded, absolutely entranced.

Daniel put his hand over Aubrey's as they guided Jovian's tail with his hard, pulsing, erect, and vulnerable sabah between them. He was exposed, ripped-open for his Mates physically and emotionally. They could damage him in ways he would not recover from, but Jovian didn't pull back.

These are my Mates. I want all of them. They must have all of me.

Aubrey and Daniel watched each other as they softly kissed his sabah, one on each side, making him growl at the gentle caresses. Daniel spoke to Jovian while gazing into Aubrey's eyes.

"So, this means we can take your virginity here? That our mouths, the ones you want to live and die in, can be the first to lick and suck your sabah. That yours can be our first sabah?"

His breathing was now so labored he chuffed with each breath.

Aubrey and Daniel turned, their eyes sweeping over him, waiting while their eyes roved, taking in his abandoned response.

Kassie Keegan

Léandre moved, mounting Ferrand's leg behind Daniel, pressing into him, his hands on Daniel's hips. Daniel's eyes blinked heavily at the feel of Léandre against him.

Ferrand's hands lay on Aubrey and Daniel's thighs, one on each side. Aubrey ground down into Ferrand's thigh.

Jovian's hips moved sinuously as he answered, his voice a husky whisper.

"Yes. You are taking my last virginity as you have your first taste."

Their eyes gleamed at his admission. Aubrey and Daniel turned to each other and smiled slow, sexy smiles, communicating wordlessly. They were perfectly angled in profile for him to watch as they leaned toward each other, his sabah between them, their mouths open to take him.

He groaned at the pleasure of their soft, velvety mouths surrounding both sides of his sabah, his eyes wide-open, almost unblinking, watching his fantasy come to life.

They moaned at Jovian's flavor, pushing forward to deepen their caress, tongues bathing his sabah, vibrations from their soft moans sensitizing him. Then they deepened their kiss with his sabah between them, tasting each other as they enjoyed his sabah.

The dip, glide, and slide of their lips and tongues as they kissed and licked was as delicious as Jovian dreamed it would be.

Under his Shendyt, his untouched cock released nectar in a rush that made him roar with pleasure, his head thrown back. His arms supported his body as it arched in carnal ecstasy, drawn out by gentle sweeps of their tongues laving his sabah.

It took a long moment for Jovian to regain his senses. When he recovered enough to see again, all his Mates peered at him, panting and needy.

I'm not done, and neither are they.

He grabbed Aubrey and laid back, straddling her legs around his hips, placing her core against his still-hard length, right where they both needed. She cried out in delight at the pressure, bracing her hands on his chest, gazing down at him with helpless arousal. He encouraged her roughly.

"Take your pleasure, my heart."

She ground herself on him as he moved in counterpoint.

Oh, yes. Own it. Own me.

Soft, warm velvet danced over Jovian's sabah. He swung his gaze up to see Daniel continuing to lick him while watching them. Ferrand had pulled Daniel up onto his hips, very much like Jovian had done to Aubrey, leaning him forward, pressing their cocks together.

Léandre embraced Daniel from behind, his hands guiding Daniel in a slow back-and-forth grind, pleasuring them all.

Léandre leaned forward over Daniel's shoulder as Ferrand sat up. Daniel glanced over at Léandre, who brought his long tongue out and gave Jovian's sabah a lick. Léandre's golden eyes glowed with sensuality as he tasted Jovian.

Jovian growled, enraptured by what his Coalition did to him, Aubrey's attention just as transfixed.

Daniel turned his head for Léandre's passionate kiss, their first. Léandre's hands roamed Daniel's body as their kiss deepened, their bodies rubbing together in a dance of passion.

Jovian and Aubrey's bodies flowed together with the same rhythm as their Mates as they watched.

Léandre and Daniel slowly ended their kiss, then turned toward Ferrand, Jovian's sabah in front of all their faces.

Jovian peered up at Aubrey, who looked down at him. She sensed his build-up in her special way. His eyes widened, Hers dark with concentration, their hips flowing effortlessly together.

Jovian moaned as the flexible, soft tips of Ferrand's and Léandre's tongues joined Daniel's thicker, velvety one on his sabah. They licked, tasted, and enjoyed him, growling at his flavor.

He drowned in ecstasy, his body shaking with the power of his release, reveling in the sound, scent, and movement of his Mates joining him in bliss.

Aubrey collapsed forward onto his chest and shoulder, panting. He enfolded her in his arms, utter contentment washing through him, eyes closed, a deep purr rumbling his chest. Soothed, she relaxed bonelessly against him, her pleasure-scent and those of his Mates Marking his soul.

Jovian eased his sabah back into the sheath of his tail. One of his Mates pushed his Serc further down to release the hair at his tail tip, smoothed his tuft, then put his Serc back into place.

Rousing himself enough to turn his head, Jovian open his eyes to gaze at his Coalition Mates, while his female snuggled satisfied and safe in his arms.

It must have been Léandre who put his tail back in order, because Ferrand cleaned Daniel with an insta-dry cloth. When he was done, Ferrand gave Daniel a gentle kiss before dragging the cream-scented cloth across his abdomen, taking Daniel's pleasure-scent for his own, as Léandre and Jovian had done.

Daniel had fully scent-marked them all as Brethren.

Ferrand tucked the cloth inside his Shendyt. He would keep the scrap of fabric forever. Just as he and Léandre would with their own pieces of cream-scented cloth, a memento of being Marked by their beloved Honored Nel.

Jovian felt ready for a new future, one he'd hoped for, but didn't believe he could have until this moment, his past no longer a looming barrier to the intimacy he craved.

They accepted him. *All* of him.

Chapter 29
Commander Ferrand

A buzz of satisfaction welled within Ferrand from the Bonding he and his Mates experienced. He hadn't seen Jovian so content, or Léandre so relaxed.

Léandre helped Daniel sit up and swing his leg over and off Ferrand's hips. Ferrand petted Jovian on the shoulder to rouse him, his caretaking instincts wide-awake.

Time to clean up. Our Mates needed food, too.

Jovian sat up, aiding Aubrey, who still straddled his hips, back onto her haunches. His purrs slowed, finally easing quiet as he gave her a gentle kiss of comfort and care. Ferrand sighed at the sight, enjoying his Brethren's attentiveness for Aubrey and Daniel.

I love them. They warm my heart.

Ferrand grabbed an insta-dry, quickly dipping inside Daniel's coverings to give him a thorough swipe with the fresh cloth, making Daniel catch his breath. He used the same cloth to clean himself.

Finished, he tossed it to Léandre, who did the same. Léandre passed the insta-dry over to Jovian, who used it under his Shendyt.

When Jovian was done, he took the dry, scent-drenched cloth, folded it in quarters, then slowly, sensually, slid the fabric inside the bodice of Aubrey's dress. Stealth stood up, growling with menace.

Jovian calmly glanced over at Stealth, then back to Aubrey, who watched his hand.

"Only a moment, Stealth. I'm putting our scent where it belongs. Next to her heart."

Jovian slid his fingers out of her bodice as lingeringly as he'd inserted them. Aubrey's nostrils flared at the combined scents of her Mates, smiling a soft, secret smile.

She liked it, prompting another wave of satisfaction to flow through Ferrand. He got up and assisted Aubrey from the cushion onto her feet. As she stood, he folded her into a hug, enjoying her feminine curves against him.

Such a brave, sweet Mate. I will reward your trust with so much love and pleasure.

Daniel and Léandre rose, putting their clothes in place. When Jovian straightened up, Rahimi spoke.

"Are you ready for the Solaray?"

She would activate the Solaray laser that cleaned them and took away waste, but would not remove the scents they had Marked each other with. Everyone agreed, and she activated the Solaray, which lasted but a moment.

Aubrey shook her silky brown hair out into a shimmering fall and smoothed her skirt.

Rahimi returned their Bandels, chains, belts, and Rav Knives. Daniel and Ferrand donned their Chalels, and everyone put on their sandals.

Suddenly Jovian growled, his eyes focused on the entry still covered by its dual dampening fields. Raiida and Rahimi moved swiftly to him, taking in his dilated eyes and aggressive posture.

Jovian's beast-nature overwhelms him.

Ferrand knew it sometimes happened after Mates initially Bonded. If a Lio Nel felt overly protective, the moment the dampening field opened, exposing their Mates to others, could trigger an aggressive drive to protect their Mates.

Raiida and Rahimi tensed, utterly focused on Jovian. Stealth gently guided Aubrey to the side as she studied Jovian, distress bleeding into her expression. Daniel asked, in concern.

"What's happening? What's upsetting Jovian?"

Ferrand answered calmly as he angled himself between Jovian and his Honored Mates. Léandre went to Jovian's other side.

"Jovian is feeling protective at the thought of opening the entrance, right Jovian?"

Jovian glanced at him, looked back at the entry, and growled his agreement. Ferrand heard Daniel's worry.

"What can we do for him?"

Good question.

Jovian prized his control. He would be unhappy if he went deeply into his beast-nature, ferally and irrationally protective, to the point of being restrained. It would taint Jovian's memory of their satisfying interlude while Bonding.

An idea struck Ferrand.

"Jovian, look at me."

Ferrand waited until Jovian's blue and gold eyes were on him.

"Do you have our Mate Tribute Rings in your tech-bag?"

Jovian nodded.

"May I get them?"

He saw the logical part of Jovian understood Ferrand's intent, but his beast-nature was so close, all he could do was growl his assent.

Kassie Keegan

Ferrand grabbed Jovian's tech-bag, rummaging and finding the colorful fabric wrapped around strong, simple hoops their Coalition had chosen as Mate Tributes. The rings would adorn their left ears, matching the ones in Ferrand's and Léandre's right ears as Tribute to their lost Pride.

Jovian's next growl was a long aggressive rumble, prompting Raiida and Rahimi to grasp him by the shoulders and put him on his knees, Raiida's hand on the nape of his neck.

Despite his growls, Jovian did not resist. The battle to conquer his beast-nature raged in his eyes as he made no effort to escape their hold.

Ferrand turned to Aubrey and Daniel, who followed Jovian's distress with worried eyes. Stealth stood beside Aubrey, his face calm, serious, and assessing. Ferrand approved of Stealth's caution.

"Stealth, in order to settle, Jovian must be soothed by their scents and Claimed with their Mate Tribute Rings. Please allow this."

Aubrey's Shumal could take her away in a heartbeat, fully in his rights as her Protector during the MateDance to remove her from a dangerous situation. This was his role. Raiida and Rahimi would abide by his decision and assist decisively by submitting his entire Coalition, if necessary.

It was Ferrand's task to make sure it wasn't necessary.

Stealth considered, watching with narrowed eyes as Jovian battled his beast-nature on his knees with no resistance to the twins' hold.

"He may have her scent with her consent. One lunge and she's gone."

Stealth turned to Aubrey.

"Are you afraid of Jovian?"

"Not in the slightest!"

This was gratifyingly true, as not a hint of fear-scent came from her or Daniel.

"Excellent. You may approach Jovian and stand in front of him."

She did so, boldly. Daniel went with her, standing beside her. They held hands, peering down at Jovian.

Stealth stayed close behind Aubrey, not touching, on high-alert.

Jovian bent and cuddled his cheek on Aubrey's thigh, his face aimed toward her core, inhaling her delicious scent. His gentleness, even while in the grip of his beast-nature, was reassuring. Jovian's posture relaxed in the twins' grip. Aubrey languidly caressed Jovian's face and mane with her free hand as he rested against her thigh and scented her.

Raising his head, Jovian turned, placing his other cheek on Daniel's thigh, breathing deeply. Daniel stroked with lingering touches along Jovian's neck and shoulder as his tension eased.

Léandre kneeled gracefully beside Jovian, peering up at his Mates, his heart in his eyes.

Time to join them.

Ferrand handed the Tribute Ring-filled cloth to Rahimi as he kneeled on the other side of Jovian.

Jovian returned to Aubrey, again immersed in her scent.

Rahimi stepped behind the Lio Nels on their knees, facing their Honored Mates. A soft tinkle of metal on metal announced she unwrapped the Mate Tribute Rings. Jovian sat back at the sound, gazing up at his Honored Mates, drunk on their scents, calmed.

Rahimi spoke.

"Aubrey and Daniel. These Rings are Mate Tribute Rings, Marking these Lio Nels as Claimed Mates. It declares you will take them into your hearts and into your bodies as Mates. If you do not complete the Mate-Bond, they will become Bereft, never answering the Call to Mate again."

She paused to let that settle in before continuing.

"Do you seek to Claim Commander Ferrand Bon'Durel Bon'Fiel, Léandre Bon'Durel Bon'Fiel, and Jovian Bon'Ocal Bon'Fiel for your own?"

Aubrey and Daniel nodded consent.

"You must *say* it."

Their voices rang, confident and clear, in unison.

"Yes."

Ferrand's heart swelled with love.

"May I place these Mate Tribute Rings to lay your Claim upon these Lio Nels as Mates, Aubrey Newton Bon'Fiel and Daniel Shaw Bon'Fiel?"

Aubrey answered eagerly.

"Yes, please."

Daniel answered solemnly.

"You may."

Jovian gazed at Aubrey, his eyes fervent and focused.

"I Declare for you, Aubrey. I am grateful Daniel is my Coalition Brethren."

Rahimi placed the Rings in Raiida's hand. Taking two Mate Tribute Rings, Raiida placed their openings to the upper curve of Jovian's left ear, and firmly secured them.

Jovian's eyes closed, his entire body shuddering as she placed the rings. When he opened his eyes, his beast-nature was under control and Jovian's cool intellect shone once again.

"Thank you. I panicked at the thought of you, my precious Honored, out there. Vulnerable and exposed. I've never felt like that. Not even in my deepest rage."

His eyes lowered, shame visibly worming its way into him.

Daniel and Aubrey both reached out, one hand cupping his cheeks on each side. They raised his face up, bringing Jovian's eyes up to theirs, his gaze bouncing between them, absorbing their kind, loving expressions. Aubrey chided him.

"Oh, Jovian. You need us. You love our scent. You want us for Mates. Where is the shame in this?"

Daniel's voice was clear.

"Do not hide your needs."

Jovian studied them, then nodded. Wonder and love colored his words.

"No shame, Mates."

Aubrey and Daniel lowered their hands, turning to watch as Rahimi took two more Mate Tribute Rings, stepping behind Léandre to secure them into his ear. Léandre's breathing deepened, his eyes glowing with pride at being Claimed, giving them a beautiful smile unlike Ferrand had ever seen before.

Daniel and Aubrey smiled back at Léandre, their joy reflecting his as they caressed his cheeks.

Rahimi stepped behind Ferrand, clinks sounding as she took the last two Rings. He loved his Honored Mates with his eyes as Rahimi pressed the Mate Tribute Rings into the curve of his left ear, Claiming him for them. He reached a hand to each Mate, immediately grasped by theirs.

"I Declare for you, Aubrey. I am yours for all of my days. Daniel, it pleases my soul to be in Coalition with you."

They tightened their grip on his hands, then caressed his cheeks. He closed his eyes, reveling in their combined touch.

Such delight.

Ferrand opened his eyes as Daniel faced Aubrey, her hand now in his.

"I feel like I need to say I Declare for you, too, Aubrey."

Daniel kissed her hand in his special way. Aubrey looked supremely happy, which made his chest ache with happiness, too. Daniel glowed with contentment.

This is as it should be.

Kassie Keegan

He stood, as did his Coalition Brethren, pulling Aubrey and Daniel into his embrace. Jovian and Ferrand cuddled close, joining him in holding their Mates before they left their little sanctuary, and faced the Prides.

They were scent-marked and Mate Claimed. There was no doubt their Coalition had been accepted. Now it was up to Aubrey to answer her Call to Mate and bring their MateBond to fruition.

Ferrand was confident it would happen soon.

Chapter 30
Léandre

Satisfaction dug deep as Léandre and his Mates slowly pulled away from their embrace before opening the privacy nook's entry to Capital Maituri's Grand Room.

Raiida walked over to Aubrey, giving Daniel a reassuring pet down his back in passing, granting a nod to Stealth as she approached. She grasped Aubrey's shoulders, turning her to face her squarely. Aubrey seemed confused. Raiida tilted her head.

"How are you feeling, my friend?"

Aubrey smiled gently.

"Oh! I'm good!"

She grasped Raiida's forearms in a familiar hold, one Léandre had seen them in often. Raiida's eyes narrowed watchfully as her tail stroked along Aubrey's arm in another familiar gesture.

Normally, Aubrey would reach over and pet Raiida's tuft, enjoying its soft touch, understanding the sweet affection communicated by the Lio Nessa. This time, Aubrey hesitated, her body tensing with indecision. Raiida spoke in her usual direct tones.

"Aubrey, discovering the joys of your Mates doesn't mean you stop loving your friends."

Rahimi came up behind Raiida, wrapping her arms around Raiida's waist, resting her chin on her sister's shoulder, peering at Aubrey. She joked, but her eyes were serious.

"Don't get weird about it. We like your pets. If you stop, it will hurt our feelings."

Aubrey was thoughtful. Then she smiled, petting Raiida's tuft in her usual manner, making both Raiida and Rahimi relax. Rahimi found her humor again.

"See, it's not so hard, is it?"

Aubrey gasped as she caught the bawdy double meaning, reaching over to push Rahimi's shoulder, which barely moved. The twins laughed huskily as revelation dawned in Aubrey's eyes.

"Does this mean…"

Raiida and Rahimi gazed at her expectantly.

"… Lio Nessas have…"

Now the twins had wide, fang-filled grins while Aubrey blinked at them in surprise. Rahimi's words dripped with humor.

"She's going to make it weird."

Raiida laughed, not taking her eyes off a stunned Aubrey.

"She so *is*. This will be fun!"

Rahimi became affectionately serious.

"Sabahs are private. Intimate. Sharing sabah is the ultimate act of trust."

Raiida continued.

"Some Lio never reveal it."

Aubrey glanced over at Jovian, still cuddled by Ferrand, facing outward with Ferrand's hands on his hips. Daniel glanced over at Jovian, too.

Aubrey and Daniel now had a deeper understanding of the trust Jovian gave them, and why the vulnerability overwhelmed his beast-nature.

Daniel went to Jovian and pressed close to his side, laying his head on Jovian's shoulder, wrapping his arm around his waist. Jovian held him, burying his face in Daniel's mane, breathing in his scent, his eyes on Aubrey. Aubrey made to go to Jovian, too, but Raiida held her.

"Keep your knowledge of sabah private, please. Let your friends discover with their Mates, as you have."

"I will."

Aubrey walked over to tuck herself into Jovian's other side. Léandre approached the beautiful group.

My family.

Aubrey and Daniel lifted their arms to him in welcome, hands stroking his back as he pressed into Jovian's torso, fitting his Honored loves comfortably under his arms and into his sides.

He rested his forehead on Jovian's as they shared air heavily scented with their Mates' pleasure. Léandre's spirit settled in their profound moment of connection.

The center of my Universe is right here.

They stayed that way for long moments, the room quiet, then Léandre stepped away to collect himself to face the Prides. His Mates did the same.

Raiida returned Jovian's tech-bag, then moved to stand alertly by the entry. Daniel appeared confused.

"I know Aubrey needs protection, but you guys look like you're getting ready for battle. What are you expecting when we go out?"

Stealth walked over to stand with Daniel.

"A Challenge. Honored Nessas are highly prized, Shaktah even more so. There are two distinct occasions when an Honored Nessa chooses a Pride. During the PrideChoice Ceremony and during the MateDance."

He looked at Aubrey.

Kassie Keegan

"An Honored Nessa chooses where she wants to establish her family with her Mates. If her chosen Coalition has connection to a different Pride Family than the one she lives in, she can move to the new Pride."

Stealth looked at Léandre and his Brethren.

"Because all of Aubrey's Mates are Bon'Fiel, those who seek to Challenge could cry foul, saying Bon'Fiel Pride didn't give her the opportunity to meet other open Coalitions from other Prides. Which isn't the case, as Aubrey has frequently attended Presentation Ceremonies, witnessed by all in the Galactic feeds. But it doesn't mean there might not be trouble."

Daniel straightened, a determined light in his eyes as he, too, 'prepared for battle.' Ferrand stood firm, stoically back in his Commander role, Jovian calmly control as he disengaged his augmented dampening field.

Daniel faced Aubrey, sweetly sliding a strand of hair off her cheek before offering his hand, which she took with a smile. They pivoted to face the entry.

Raiida and Rahimi stood closest to the entrance, and would step out first when the last dampening field disengaged. As Security Leads, they put themselves between their charges and unexpected danger.

Aubrey and Daniel would exit next, Stealth beside Aubrey. Léandre, Ferrand, and Jovian exited last, behind their Honored Mates, on high-alert, ready to protect.

Few Lio or Honored were as dangerous as those in their MateDance before their Honored Nessa answered her Call to Mate and Claimed them forever. Challengers would be dealt with decisively.

Léandre expected at least one Challenge from the Bon'Rocinal Pride. He touched the scar across the bridge of his nose as he remembered his confrontation with Sinitzyn, Cybulski, and Divov Bon'Rocinal many year spans ago.

Aubrey had newly settled into her place in the Bon'Fiel Pride, working as a Mech Tech.

Léandre stayed close to Aubrey wherever she was when he wasn't instructing a MateDance lesson or doing other Pride business. He had stealthily found a shaded spot beneath another broken Transport nearby, content simply being near her, wondering when he could approach her with the food he brought.

She enjoyed their picnic meals together. He lived for them. It often lead to him asking questions about the job, then her explaining the intricacies of the work she loved.

He loved listening to her. They would spend the rest of the afternoon with her speaking and him handing her tools.

Often she asked him about Lio HomeWorld or about his MateDance lessons and he would holo-comm her his answers. Léandre hoped for another delightful day with her.

Unaware of his presence, Aubrey's concentration focused deep in the repair of a small Land Transport on a grassy hillside outside Telledea on the Northern Peninsula. Her fellow Mech Tech Team members were working on a massive engine rebuild in the hangar a distance away.

Abruptly, he scented Bon'Rocinal brothers approaching sneakily downwind. Aubrey didn't notice, the rumble of the imbalanced engine she tried to engage obscuring any sound they made.

The Bon'Rocinal Lio Nels were so focused on her, they didn't detect him. Léandre held back, not sure of their intent. It could be friendly. Lio enjoyed being stealthy. Sneaking up on each other was fun.

His eyes narrowed, body tensing as the Lio Nels positioned themselves at Aubrey's back, spread out to deter escape, trapping her against the bulk of the Transport.

The engine sputtered off again as she reached for a tool next to her. Sinitzyn, who stood in the middle, spoke first.

Kassie Keegan

"Hello, pretty."

Aubrey startled, swiftly turning, taking in the situation and its implications with lightning-fast judgment. She picked up her heaviest tool, casually bringing it in front of her in a defensive posture. She belied her defensiveness with a mild, friendly tone.

"Hello, gentlemen. Taking a walk on this fine afternoon, are we?"

The brothers smirked at each other. This time Cybulski spoke.

"We are not men, pretty."

Divov sneered his comment as he leered at her.

"We are not gentle, either."

Aubrey didn't bat an eye or move an inch.

"Please be on your way. I need to get back to work."

Unsurprisingly, Sinitzyn moved a step closer, ignoring Aubrey.

"Anyone who scents as sweet as you do needs a Coalition We have come to serve your needs."

Divov and Cybulski edged closer, closing in on her while licking their chops.

"What I *need* is to repair this engine. Serve that need and shoo!"

Aubrey made a threatening sweep of her heavy tool as she said "shoo." Her fear-scent bloomed strong despite her bravado. The brothers very much enjoyed her fear. Léandre did not.

Their looks of anticipation and unsheathed cocks bulging beneath their Shendyts sealed their fates.

Fools. You think to ForceBond Aubrey? I will fuck you up to save your lives. If you survive the lesson.

Léandre would make sure these ill-mannered, undisciplined youths never approached a female this way again, learning he was much more than a MateDance Instructor. He kept downwind as he silently stalked them, thumbing disruptor dots hidden on the inside of his belt into his palm.

With strategically placed disruptor dots, Léandre had Divov down with a dislocated kneecap, a dislocated shoulder, and a broken arm before his brothers even registered his presence.

Feeling and hearing Divov's ulna and radius crack against his thigh satisfied him. Divov writhed on the ground, no longer a threat.

Léandre kept his Rav Knife sheathed and his Shield disengaged. He would win this Mate Challenge honorably.

No need to make this quick. They wouldn't suffer enough to learn the lesson.

Sinitzyn and Cybulski spun with growls of rage, alerted by the cracks of bone and the meaty thump of Divov's body hitting the ground, followed by his subsequent screams of pain once he could get enough breath to let them out.

Aubrey's Mech Tech Team would hear the screams and run to her aid as fast as they could, but the confrontation would be over before they got to her.

Sinitzyn and Cybulski shielded up, unsheathing their Rav Knives and separating, trying to divide Léandre's attention, dismissing Aubrey behind them.

Dishonorable worm-spawn.

Aubrey's voice rang out.

"Jerk-offs, if this is a Challenge, you better drop your Shields or you're cowards."

They growled viciously, dropping their Shields.

Clever Aubrey, evening the fight.

Without hesitation, she decisively took out Cybulski with one blow on the back of his head with her tool.

Fucking beautiful!

Kassie Keegan

Aubrey stood over the fallen Lio Nel, tool gripped tightly, chest heaving, looking feral.

A female worthy of respect.

Pride at her fierceness ripped through Léandre as he stared at Sinitzyn with a hunter's focus.

Well, well. She's not as defenseless as you thought, huh, weakling?

Sinitzyn glanced at his brother lying still on the ground, turning to look at Aubrey with death in his eyes. When he re-engaged his Shield, showing an undisciplined rough texture, Léandre stopped playing.

His claws would not penetrate the Shield, but he could use his weight, momentum, leverage, and experience to unbalance Sinitzyn and submit him. He leaped upon his opponent.

Sinitzyn went for the kill, aiming at Léandre's throat, but missed. It was easy for him to dodge the unskilled strike, but Sinitzyn made a wild, shallow cut, slicing his forehead and nose as he subdued the Lio Nel. Léandre had Sinitzyn disarmed and submitted with his arms secure behind his back when Aubrey's Mech Tech Team swarmed in.

They witnessed Sinitzyn's Shield still activated, shaming Sinitzyn. Any Lio who could not control their Shield during a Challenge pelt-to-pelt was a Disgrace. The Mech Tech Team commed Telledea Security, who took the brothers away.

Léandre remembered Aubrey's gentleness as she staunched the blood dripping down his face, her Team Leader sealing the cuts, leaving the scars as was tradition after a Challenge fight. It was then Aubrey gave him his first kiss, a moment he would treasure all his days.

Long after the brothers physically healed, the Disgrace hadn't left them. Sinitzyn, Cybulski, and Divov were Censured for their actions by the Judge Elite, making it clear Lio would castigate any such aggression toward Aubrey, or any other Honored Nessa under Lio Protection in the Known Galaxies.

Still, Bon'Fiel Pride quietly ensured Aubrey was never truly alone when she was off Bon'Fiel land. She knew nothing about it, moving on from the confrontation, continuing to thrive. Her resilience humbled him.

Aubrey gave him a sweet, brief touch on his arm, rousing Léandre from his thoughts. He chuffed affectionately at her as Raiida disengaged the dampening field.

Time to greet the Prides.

Chapter 31
Léandre

Groups of people in animated conversations appeared when the dampening field silently dropped.

Seductively potent scents whooshed from their alcove, gaining everyone's attention, a few Lio falling to their knees, the scents so intoxicating. Their acute response didn't surprise Léandre. He and his Mates were well-satisfied during their interlude.

Katohna, Cassian, and Travar made their way over to them, Katohna giving them a delighted smile as she looked them over. Cassian blinked and tried to stay stoic, but failed, his happiness clear in the curve of his lips and the glow in his eyes.

Cassian's front broke as he gave them a huge, fang-filled smile. Travar didn't even try to hide his pleasure at seeing and scenting them, grinning broadly.

His High Nessa and his Prime opened their arms for congratulatory hugs, Aubrey hugging Katohna while Daniel embraced Cassian. Katohna spoke with Aubrey as they hugged.

"Are you pleased, Aubrey?"

She answered shyly, but proudly with a blazing blush.

"Well pleased, High Nessa."

Katohna gave a husky chuckle.

"Wonderful!"

Releasing Daniel from his hug, Cassian affectionately smoothed over his curly mane, Travar petting Daniel's back, leaning close.

"You pleased as well?"

Daniel swept his gaze over to Aubrey, then back at Léandre and his Coalition, quietly happy, making Léandre's heart clench.

"Very much so, Travar."

Katohna grasped her Commander's arm in a Warrior's clasp, wrist-to-wrist, as they shared air. They pulled back, gazing into each other's eyes without words, their mutual love and respect massively clear.

Jovian came out of Cassian's congratulatory embrace, switching with Ferrand, sharing air with his High Nessa. Léandre was proud of his Mates and Pride Family. His Mates were his heart, when they were cared for, he was happy.

Cassian surprised Léandre by grabbing him and Ferrand together into his enthusiastic hug, making them all laugh, Léandre's chuckle a repeated chuff of air as he smiled. Cassian happily shouted.

"Scent-marked and Mate Claimed!"

Many others echoed his shout. Grinning, Jovian went to Aubrey and Daniel as Katohna came over to Léandre to share air.

Léandre loved Katohna. She was a magnificent Pride Leader and friend. She'd seen him and loved him when he had been invisible to everyone except Ferrand and Jovian. Peering into her golden eyes, he poured care for her into his expression. She smiled at him, scratching behind his ear, whispering.

"Mutual."

Ferrand moved forward, his arms outstretched to the sides, gathering up Aubrey and Daniel, facing them toward the banquet tables.

Kassie Keegan

"Enough congratulations and chit-chat. My Mates need refreshment."

No one argued with him. Katohna, Cassian, and Travar stood aside for Ferrand to sweep his Mates to the food. Lio expected attentiveness, especially during the MateDance, but Ferrand would always be this attuned to their needs. Caring for those he loved was as much a part of him as his right arm.

Jovian glanced at Léandre and slow-blinked affectionately, then followed Ferrand and their entourage, with Stealth and the twins close behind. Léandre lingered back. He wanted a clear picture of the Prides' genuine reactions to their MateBonding. To do this, he needed to ease back to the edges and observe.

Aubrey's friends had a different plan. Vivian grabbed him around the waist and cuddled up under his arm.

"No, you don't. You come join the feast with us, Léandre."

Shy Talia came to his other side, tucking up under his opposite arm, her ease with him a measure of deep trust. Talia's voice was soft.

"Yes, Léandre. No watching from the shadows tonight. You are a Guest of Honor."

He peered quizzically down at the females so unexpectedly hugging him. Destiny came in from behind, wrapping her arms around his chest in a tight squeeze before releasing him.

"Don't fight it. Celebrate with us. Relax. We've got you."

Léandre made a visual perimeter sweep. Bon'Fiel Pride members surrounded him and his Mates in seemingly random clusters, making him feel cared for and honored. He should have expected nothing less than his Pride protecting them.

Vivian squeezed him, prompting Léandre to look at her as she grinned up at him, chuckling as she joked.

"Always watching, remember?"

Talia smiled her shy smile at him, and he couldn't resist. Nodding, Léandre agreed to go, expecting them to step back, but again, they surprised him. They kept close, walking with him while tucked under his arms. When they got to her, he saw Aubrey scanning the room distractedly.

"Ah! There you are!"

She was looking for me?

His stomach flipped at the realization. Vivian, Talia, and Destiny melted away as Aubrey captured his attention, walking to him with a smile.

"Here, take a bite of this. It's your favorite."

He opened his mouth to take the tidbit she offered him from her fingers. It was indeed his favorite kind of meat. Buvol, lightly seasoned, and rare. Wonder filled him.

She knows my favorite food.

Aubrey must have been paying attention to him like he paid attention to her all these year spans. She fed him more bites from her own plate.

Does she even know what a Claim she stakes upon me? The honor she gives me, feeding me like this in front of all the Known Galaxies?

He decided Aubrey was simply being her lovely, generous self, making it clear he was important. He'd been holding a sliver of doubt in his heart, worried Aubrey and Daniel would not accept him equally among their esteemed Mates.

Ferrand is Commander. Jovian, a renowned inventor and Tech genius. What am I? A mute MateDance Instructor. And part-time spy, not that anyone knows. There is no comparison.

Daniel handed Léandre a hydro-pack.

"Hey, we are hanging out over here while I learn about some of this new food."

Grabbing his hand, they strolled with Aubrey to his Coalition Brethren and a small group they were chatting with, including Aubrey's friends.

Kassie Keegan

Daniel kept Léandre's hand as he resumed his conversation, obviously enjoying his touch. He stood there between his oblivious Mates as he fell apart inside, piece-by-piece.

There is no comparison with my Brethren because my Mates do not compare us. I am equal in their hearts and minds.

He took a deep breath.

They accept me fully as Mate.

Daniel squeezed his hand, and Aubrey petted his back. Neither one looked at him while he internally broke and re-formed.

Maybe they are more aware of my emotions than I thought.

Aubrey pulled his braid, making his gaze fly to hers.

"Have a drink, Léandre. This is only the beginning."

She kissed him gently, her lovely blue eyes sparkling with humor and affection, before sauntering to the banquet table for more food. He could tell by the way she walked, she knew his eyes were on her luscious rear. Daniel watched, too.

"What a view."

Léandre chuffed agreement and drank his hydro-pack in two gulps, suddenly very thirsty. Daniel took his empty hydro-pack, then pressed his lips gently to Léandre's in a matching caress to Aubrey's kiss.

"Stay close. We like it that way."

Léandre nodded while his heart broke open, overflowing with love. His gaze followed Daniel with heated admiration. Ferrand came from behind, pressing Léandre back against his bulk with an enormous arm across his chest.

Jovian strolled up to Léandre, giving him an affectionate grooming swipe up his neck, then returned to Daniel's side, pointing out a delicacy for him to taste. Aubrey motioned Léandre and Ferrand to come over, her eyes twinkling with mischief.

Abah-Sah, she is beautiful!

"Hey guys! Dawn brought muffins! Want one?"

Both he and Ferrand shuddered with disgust, but Ferrand dropped his arm and they prowled toward her. They would eat the disgustingly sweet, cursed muffins if she wanted them to.

Léandre felt lighter after releasing his buried insecurity. It was an unnecessary barrier to his MateBond and he would tolerate none of those, not even from within himself.

He picked up one of the blighted confections, which appeared diseased with strange blue dots, snagging a morsel in his claws. He brought it to Aubrey's lips.

Taking it with a hearty laugh, she chewed and swallowed, then delicately licked a few remaining crumbs from his fingertips and claw tips. When she was done, humor and love were a heady blend in her smile.

"Hmm. Delicious."

He blinked slowly as his answering smile bloomed for her.

Chapter 32
Aubrey

Aubrey enjoyed herself, energized and happy, a sweet hum buzzing. Ignoring her fears.

Idly walking from group to group, casually talking with her Pride Family and friends, Aubrey caught a pointed sneer from a conceited Lio Nessa toward her Mates Léandre and Jovian.

"The Bon'Fiel are outrageous, allowing an Honored Shaktah to Mate-Bond with a mute waste-of-space and a Disgraced outcast! Can you imagine? What's next? A cave-dweller or a Pirate?"

The nasty Lio Nessa's companions laughed meanly with her.

In days past, Aubrey may have ignored her, but now she refused to, aggressive protectiveness burning through her.

No one will slander my Mates!

Stealth whispered caution.

"Careful, Aubrey."

She ignored Stealth, walking directly up into the Lio Nessa's space. Aubrey was livid, all of her senses alive and alert.

The Lio Nessa must not have realized she was within hearing, because the female seemed genuinely surprised. Her ears went back, her tail stilling mid-motion.

I'm Challenging this bitch! You don't get to spew your hatred at my family without consequences.

"Who are you to judge my choice of Mates?"

The arrogant Lio Nessa shook off her surprise, becoming amused, her ears perking up.

"Silly Shaktah, I am uniquely qualified to judge as a member of the Judge Council Elite."

She didn't care who this Lio Nessa was. Her senses were vibrating, so hyper-alert she could feel air currents in the room.

Stealth stood three steps behind her on the right. Léandre stalked closer, stopping three steps behind her on the left, Jovian flanking Léandre. Ferrand and Daniel walked up directly behind her, a few paces back.

She sensed the non-threatening, shifting flow of people around her as they noticed the confrontation. Neither Bon'Fiel Pride, Stealth, nor her Mates would interfere because Aubrey was the Challenger. She needed to win this fight on her own, and she was determined to do so.

This Judge better keep her mouth shut.

Three brothers who'd tried to attack her in her first days on Lio Home-World drifted up in a show of support for the Lio Nessa she Challenged.

They are trying to scare me, like they did before.

Those days were long past. She would not be intimidated by them, or the Lio Nessa.

"Elite Judge? You don't seem to be an expert judge of character to *me*. Keep your nasty comments to yourself."

The Lio Nessa pressed a claw into Aubrey's chest above her bodice, aggression in her gaze and posture. The surrounding crowd gasped at the touch.

Kassie Keegan

The Lio Nessa's claw pricked her, but she controlled the tingle of her Shield from engaging in defense, suspecting this female was related to the Lio Nels. She wanted Aubrey to activate her Shield to somehow twist it into a defense of her Disgraced relatives.

Not going to happen.

Aubrey was much too well-trained and controlled.

The Lio Nessa dug her claw in deeper, a drop of blood welling up and trickling down to Aubrey's white bodice. Her words dripped with provocation.

"Or else... what?"

"Or else I'll make you eat those words."

Aubrey's energy hummed so acutely she perceived the smallest changes in the Lio Nessa's posture and position, sensing the moment she decided to use her tail's Serc in a blindsiding blow. With a lightning-fast move, Aubrey captured the Lio Nessa's tail as she tried to land the strike, utterly shocking the Lio Nessa, whose expression turned almost comical.

When the Lio Nessa jerked her tail away, Aubrey eased her grip enough for the tail to slide through her hand, but grabbed hold of the Serc in her fist as the Lio Nessa's tail tip continued its momentum down and away. Growling, the Lio Nessa showed fang when Aubrey held up her Serc.

"Nasty way to fight, Judge Elite."

"Give it back!"

"Oh, no. I'm keeping this. Let it remind you to keep your mouth shut about me and mine, Judge Elite."

When the Lio Nessa went for a full swipe at her, claws extended, Aubrey was ready. She blocked the blow with her forearm, sliding her hand to the Lio Nessa's wrist to control it. At the same time, Aubrey stepped forward, hooking her heel behind the Lio Nessa's, then pushed her backward with all her might, her other fist still clasping the Serc.

Savage Planet Embrace

The Lio Nessa lay on the floor on her back, blinking up at Aubrey when she released her wrist. Bending, she slapped the Lio Nessa's face with an open hand across her mouth.

Stepping back from her defeated opponent, Aubrey knew she made her point, even as she gained a new enemy. This Lio Nessa was not her or her Pride's friend, anyway.

The brothers sidled closer, fangs exposed, deep growls coming from them. One of them reached for his Rav Knife, and Léandre and Stealth moved forward. The brothers' eyes focused on Léandre, who'd unsheathed his Rav Knife.

But it was Léandre's activated Shield that taunted them, showing only across his upper chest and shoulder in the exact undisciplined rough pattern one brother had used that long-ago day when he'd threatened Aubrey. They understood his reminder of their shame, growling in anger.

The Lio Nessa leaped back to her feet with a yowl, her hand on the hilt of her Knife. She paused, blinking, when she realized what she was doing. Aubrey had bested the Lio Nessa with no claws or blade. To pull her Knife now showed cowardice, and it would ruin her.

Léandre slid in close behind Aubrey, his arms circling her with his Rav Knife in front, the long sharp edge facing their enemies. His other hand held a vertical defensive position, hinting at the depth of his Combat Training. Clearly, he tolerated no more aggression toward his Mate. Aubrey had won the Challenge.

Growls reverberated from the Bon'Fiel Pride behind them. High Nessa Katohna strode forward, her expression incredulous.

"You dare threaten a Challenge Victor? An Honored Nessa Shaktah on the eve of her MateDance, after insulting her Coalition in her presence. What did you think would happen Judge Council Elite Hulin?"

Judge Hulin took her hand off the hilt of her Rav Knife, raising to her full height, facing High Nessa Katohna. She motioned for the Lio Nel behind her to release his blade. Léandre lowered his arms, sheathing his Rav Knife, moving to stand beside Aubrey.

Aubrey didn't trust Judge Council Elite Hulin for a second, keeping her gaze intently on the Lio Nessa she still considered a threat. The Judge spoke with demand.

"I want my Serc back."

High Nessa Katohna lifted her eyebrow.

"You don't always get what you want. Aubrey took it fairly when you attempted to strike her."

Aubrey heard a curious ripping sound, but didn't look back. She scented Prime Cassian coming close behind her. He spoke in her ear.

"Show me the Serc."

She lifted it up in her palm, eyes on the enemy Lio Nessa. Prime Cassian reached around her with a finger-width length of rough-edged, purple and gold fabric hanging from his fist.

He must have sliced the cloth from his cape with a claw.

Prime Cassian threaded the fabric through the Serc.

"May I?"

Aubrey consented with a wordless nod. He lifted the Serc by the fabric and tied the ends behind her neck in a long makeshift necklace dangling over her belly.

"My grandmother Kat is going to be very proud when she hears about this! Well done, little Warrior."

Aubrey's interest piqued about Prime Cassian's family, but she kept her focus on the Judge, answering simply.

"Thank you."

He kissed the top of her head before standing back. The Judge observed the entire process, anger blazing, shaking her head.

"You can't do that."

High Nessa Katohna answered with finality.

"It's done."

"You will regret this, Katohna!"

High Nessa Katohna looked away, bored.

"Yeah, yeah. Enough threats, Hulin."

Judge Hulin growled low and long, prompting High Nessa Katohna to step close, ears high, tail still and curved up aggressively. She didn't put her hand on her weapon or tense, holding herself in a relaxed readiness. High Nessa Katohna didn't raise her voice when she spoke. She didn't have to.

"Hulin, ever since we were young, you've never been satisfied. You are critical of others who show excellence. You became a Judge Elite through social climbing, but you have forever been someone who judged others harshly. And I dare say, unfairly."

Judge Hulin showed fang. High Nessa Katohna's tone deepened with threat, her ears turning slightly back, her tail swaying.

"Keep your judgment off my people. Next time, you answer to *me*. I guarantee you'll lose more than a Serc when you do."

Their gazes locked. Then someone in the crowd behind Aubrey stage-whispered.

"Muffin."

As the word repeated throughout the crowd, Judge Hulin stared past Aubrey. Bon'Fiel Pride repeated it over and over, louder and louder.

"Muffin. Muffin. Muffin!"

It became a shout, the Pride's attitude making it clearly an insult, offending Elite Judge Hulin, but she couldn't exactly pinpoint why. Those around her had the same confused expressions.

Kassie Keegan

The Judge swiveled and left with a growled huff, followed closely by her Bon'Rocinal Pride members and friends. Something flew past Aubrey to hit one of the mean brothers in the back, exploding in a burst of crumbs and blueberry chunks.

The male spun, hissing at them as the chant dissolved into belly laughs. His brothers grabbed him and dragged him away as another muffin-bomb hit him in the face. Bon'Fiel Pride Mates howled with laughter. Dawn, Aubrey's friend and avid muffin-baker, loudly complained, exasperated.

"Stop throwing those! Okay. Looks like it's time to try cupcakes."

There were groans from the Lio and cheers from the Honored.

High Nessa Katohna went to Aubrey, placing a gentle hand on her cheek to get her attention, but she ignored her until the ugly Judge and her group were no longer in sight. Aubrey finally turned to blink up at her High Nessa, who watched her with proud concern.

"How are you feeling?"

Aubrey laughed.

"Pretty damn rage-beast!"

High Nessa Katohna smiled indulgently.

"Time to bring our festivities to a close. This has been an exciting day. Say, 'rest well,' to your Coalition. You need to calm and sleep."

High Nessa was correct. Tiredness crashed over Aubrey after the rush of her Challenge.

I need to rest and think.

High Nessa Katohna leaned toward Prime Cassian, whispering.

"We won't make it back. Prepare the room here. My guess is tonight, maybe tomorrow. Make sure he's ready."

Prime Cassian nodded, rubbing his chin thoughtfully.

Aubrey walked to Léandre, who hugged her close. They were soon joined by Daniel and Jovian at her sides with Ferrand at her back, who reached around to complete the group hug. She sighed.

"Rest well."

They released her with sweet kisses and lingering touches. She turned to say, 'rest well,' to Prime Cassian and Travar as her Mates commented in low murmurs to each other, Daniel sounding breathless.

"My flower is a fucking Warrior!"

Her Mates growled in agreement as Ferrand spoke with amazement.

"I almost came again from watching her."

Deeper growls made her glance over her shoulder at them. They all had expressions of mixed desire and wonder while gazing at her.

Fist clasped around her Serc prize, Aubrey sported a wide, satisfied grin as Stealth escorted her and her friends to their sleeping area.

Chapter 33
Aubrey

Aubrey's eyes snapped open, feeling restless, like her skin was too full. She'd tossed and turned for hours. Dreams plagued her, stealing her rest.

She wore a golden, light-as-air, silky, flowing gown Twylah brought her. It didn't bind her anywhere, but it was still almost too much to bear. Sitting up on the soft, cushioned bed in her private sleeping nook, she threw her pillows to the side in frustration.

Honored often wanted to rest alone instead of in piles like the Lio did. The Bon'Fiel Pride quarters at Capital Maituri Palace accommodated their Honored with small sleeping nooks connected to a Common Room where small-group socializing and dining occurred.

Stealth wanted to sleep across her threshold, but she wouldn't have it, insisting she was safe in her nook.

Maybe I need a snack.

She walked to the Common Room, waking Stealth, who slept on one of the couches. Technically, not on her threshold, but close enough. He smiled softly at her.

"Can't sleep?"

She shook her head.

"What do you need?"

She rubbed her arms.

What do *I* need?

Suddenly, food wasn't appealing. She needed something physical to do.

"I think I want a swim."

Stealth stood up, ready to escort her. He took her to the Bathing Chambers, letting her choose the one she wanted. He inspected the room before settling himself comfortably on the floor on the other side of the entrance to give her privacy.

"Take your time, Aubrey. There's no rush."

"Thanks, Stealth. You are a great friend."

His tail waved at her around the threshold of the entry, making her chuckle.

Skimming out of her gown, she hung it on a hook, then waded into the warm pool. Instead of relaxing deep into the water and floating, as she usually did, she paced the shallows, plagued by her thoughts.

Aubrey had not been one hundred percent revealing to her Mates, and she wrestled with that fact.

If I cannot be honest, I am not a worthy Mate.

She paced faster, feeling trapped by the room, but mostly by her thoughts.

I need more room!

She left the pool, dried off with a large insta-dry cloth, dropped the gown over her head, then restlessly paced around the pool. The space stifled her.

It's not enough.

She stopped pacing.

I'm *not enough.*

Kassie Keegan

The stark thought struck her hard, making her need to run. She looked around in a panic. Shadow played across a somewhat concealed curve in the wall she hadn't seen before.

What's this? It must be backdoor access to the Bathing Chambers! How interesting!

Exploring somewhere new would be just the thing to distract her from her heavy thoughts. She wouldn't go far.

Aubrey followed the long hallway without a second thought, believing she would find her way into another Bathing Chamber. She would sneak back around to Stealth and have a laugh at having finally snuck up on him, for once.

The hallway split and she followed the one she thought would curve up and around to Stealth. Then it split again, and again.

She became tired, her thoughts even more distracted, her skin now burning as if a fire baked her from inside. She considered turning around, but couldn't remember if it had been the right or left hallway she last took.

I might as well continue forward.

She spotted a little, dimly lit room off to the side and investigated.

What is this place?

There was a small table and a couple of chairs with a couch and some cushions. It reminded her of her home under the SpacePort Dock. It was comforting.

I'll take a moment here to work out my thoughts. Running around in circles isn't doing me any good.

Aubrey sat on the couch, cuddling a cushion to her chest. She couldn't smell any recent occupants, so she didn't feel like she was trespassing.

Who could know all the secret passageways of a place like Capital Maituri's Grand Palace?

She knew why she was so unhappy and had to face it.

I don't want kids.

It's not that she didn't like young. She did. But she did not want to have them herself.

Seeing her mother suffer through her pregnancy, assisting the terrible birth of her still-born brother, watching her mom die, and dealing with her grief alone made her dead-set against making babies of her own. The thought of it filled her with dread, a chill sweat of terror breaking out across her skin.

The fact was that Lio expected young from their Honored Nessas, otherwise, she wouldn't even be here.

Aubrey had hoped to avoid the dilemma altogether, thinking that maybe, with time, her connection with Ferrand, Léandre, and Jovian would wane. Perhaps they would show an interest in another, allowing her to fade into obscurity, not hurting anyone with her personal deficiencies.

She'd ruthlessly tamped down on her needs until Daniel arrived. Aubrey had underestimated her response to the One who would Call her to Mate. Daniel Called to her even now.

From the moment she discovered him, Aubrey had been swept into a tidal wave of desire for her Mates. They fascinated her, so worthy of respect and care. So damaged and resilient. So generous. They deserved a female strong enough to fill their home with babies.

Ferrand and Léandre must crave young to carry on the line of their lost Pride. And Jovian surely needed to have young to assuage the pain of his own youth. She remembered Daniel's expression as he regarded Crown Nessa Nour and her swollen belly.

He hasn't said as much, but Daniel definitely wants children.

She should have talked it out with them while they were together in the alcove. Instead, she'd escaped into the pleasure they offered, and ignored her deepest fear.

Here, in the quiet night, alone with her thoughts, she would no longer run.

What to do?

She sat and faced herself in stark honesty. She wanted her Mates. She did not want young.

I must be honest with them. Let them choose.

She stared into space, absorbed in her musings.

What if they reject me? I will be forever alone because I will seek no others.

The thought made her sob, crying so hard her whole body shuddered as she mourned the possibility of losing them.

Eventually calming, she wiped away her tears, clarity settling within her. Aubrey would talk with her Mates. Be honest with them, like they'd been sincere with her, sharing herself and her fears. And she would work it out with them, trusting them.

Even if it meant giving them up.

If she wasn't strong enough to give them young, she must be strong enough to let them go.

Aubrey took a deep breath and stood up, ready to find her way back to Stealth. He had surely discovered her absence by now. There would be hell to pay from him, too.

It was then she realized the open entry was sealed shut with a portion of wall perfectly, seamlessly matched to all the other walls.

I'm trapped!

She took another deep, centering breath.

If it closed, it can be opened.

She searched for the door mechanism meticulously, but found nothing. Her skin became more sensitive by the moment, burning like fire, needing her Mates.

What if they don't find me? What will they think?

Dread filled her.

They will think I don't want them.

She shook her head.

They will be broken and Bereft, and it's my fault.

Tears dripped as Aubrey stared hopelessly at the seamless wall.

Chapter 34
Daniel

Daniel was not okay.

He sat up in his cute, little sleeping sook, looking around. Rest eluded him. He scratched the back of his head, peering down at the sheer, golden sarong Twylah brought him to wear.

Daniel fingered the fabric. He'd never worn anything so fine and delicate. He liked it, his skin so tight and sensitive he didn't think he could tolerate wearing anything else.

His cock was hard, but he didn't want to touch it. What he wanted were his Mates.

He dreamed of smooth, golden feminine curves and firm muscles covered in velvety fur caressing his skin, pressing against his body, bringing fulfillment. Waking up alone was a deep disappointment.

He had said, 'rest well,' to Ferrand, Léandre, and Jovian in the Common Room with a group embrace before going in to sleep, exhaustion hitting him like an anvil.

His clothes were still on the floor from when he'd slipped them off, barely able to secure the sarong before falling on the cushion asleep. At least he'd hung his Chalel on the hook by the entry.

Now Daniel was wide-awake, his senses uncomfortably alert. His internal energy pattern felt rough, a constant low-level scratching at his awareness, like fine-grit sandpaper rubbing him raw from the inside out.

Needing something to do, he picked up his clothes and folded them neatly, laying them on the bed. The cloth Jovian had tucked into his belt was tangled in his trousers. He lifted it to his nose, dragging in a deep breath to gather as much of his Mates' scents into his lungs as he could. He released the breath gradually, reveling in the combined fragrance.

It soothed and excited him.

Rummaging in his clothes, he found the ribbon he loved and folded it with the fabric over his hand, taking another deep sniff.

This is even better!

It was good he had the fabric and ribbon, but he wanted the real thing.

Is there any reason I can't find my Lio Nels, at least?

He couldn't think of one.

I'm going to find them.

With that thought, Daniel went to the entry and dropped the privacy field. The Common Room was transformed. Curved couches pushed to the edges of the circular room. Sheer, colorful fabric draped the ceiling from the center of the room to the walls, creating a cozy, inviting atmosphere, the lighting warm and muted.

A huge round cushion took up most of the floor. Silky, shimmery, golden fabric, similar to the sarong he wore, covered the cushion. There were pillows of all shapes and sizes scattered across it in luxurious piles.

On the far side sat Prime Cassian, cross-legged, hands on his thighs, eyes closed in a meditative posture. His ears were high and alert, his tail tip waving slowly.

Kassie Keegan

Prime Cassian wore a similar sarong to Daniel's, but his was pure black. Without opening his eyes, Prime Cassian spoke in a low, reverential tone.

"Gather your Chalel, Daniel."

He blinked for a moment, then grabbed his Chalel off the hook. He stood in the entry, not sure what to do next. Prime Cassian took a deep breath and opened his glowing, pale-green eyes, his expression serene and kind.

"Drape your Chalel in the center and approach me."

Daniel did as instructed. As he stood peering down at his Prime, he was full of questions. It must have shown on his face because Prime Cassian motioned with his hand for him to sit beside him.

"Ask."

Daniel sat comfortably, gesturing to the room with a sweep of his hand,

"What is this?"

"We have prepared for your Call to Mate."

He had a moment of revelation. He'd heard the Lio speak of the Call to Mate, but he'd thought it was a euphemism for the entire Mating process.

"It's an actual 'Call?'"

"Yes. A spiritual Call to Mate."

His eyebrows pulled together as he tried to understand, Prime Cassian continuing to explain.

"We are all made of body, mind, and spirit."

He agreed.

"As we are of all three, none can be denied or we live life unfulfilled."

I've never thought about it this way before.

"You have committed to Aubrey and your Coalition, correct?"

"Yes."

"Your body has tasted fulfillment with your Mates."

Daniel's cock throbbed, his face flushing with memories of their time together.

"Yes."

"You and your Coalition Declared for Aubrey?"

He nodded.

"Now it is time for you to spiritually Call Aubrey to Mate."

Maybe this is why I feel like I have sandpaper under my skin.

"When she answers your Call, Aubrey will Claim you. After, she will Claim your Coalition Brethren. You and your Mates will join and your MateBond will be complete."

The thought of 'joining' made heat skitter down Daniel's spine and settle deep.

"Is this something you want?"

"Definitely!"

Prime Cassian smiled.

"To do this, you need one more hormonal boost from me, your Prime."

"How do we do that?"

Prime Cassian gazed at him warmly.

"You have choices, Daniel. I am your Prime. In this, I serve your needs and provide."

His senses buzzed. There was a lot he didn't understand here.

"I'm not sure what you mean, Prime Cassian. Please explain."

"I will be direct."

"Please."

"My Prime-level hormones will be the final catalyst for your Call to Mate, and Seal you to me as your Prime."

Daniel's eyes widened.

"How you get those hormones is up to you. But one thing is for sure, you will release when you get them."

"But…"

"The scent of your release will Bond me to you as your Prime."

"I thought we had already done the Choice thing."

"We have, but Mating is different."

Prime Cassian tilted his head and settled back on his arms.

"One reason is, without an anchor to your Prime, should you lose your Mates and become Bereft, your Pride would lose you, too. Our connection gives Bon'Fiel Pride hope you would live."

Daniel didn't even want to think about the possibility of losing one or all of his precious Mates.

"Another reason is this gives you your final hormone-boost as an Honored Nel Mate."

"I'm not done?"

Prime Cassian shook his head.

"Why wasn't I told?"

"You may not have ever found your Mates, Daniel. Many don't. Why be unsatisfied for what you cannot have?"

"Abassa Itakah said something like this to me, too."

"Being MateBonded means you crave your Mates. You need them forevermore to live your fullest life. There is no going back to how you were before the Call. It changes you."

He thought about this as Prime Cassian continued.

"You have an inkling of the longing Honored have for Mates they don't find. It is but a shadow to how they would feel to have completed their transition without loving Mates to soothe and satisfy their cravings."

Prime Cassian stretched out his legs and studied Daniel with thoughtfully narrowed eyes.

"Would knowing this have made a difference? Would you have changed your mind?"

He thought about it for a while, thinking through all he'd done to get where he was to find the wonderful Mates he had.

Would I change anything if it meant I would not have Aubrey, Ferrand, Léandre, or Jovian in my life?

He wished his father stayed and that his mother could have lived. She wanted his happiness with her whole heart. But she lived and died on her terms, and he respected her for it.

I would make the same choices, knowing all of it.

Daniel was confident when he answered.

"No. I wouldn't change my mind."

Prime Cassian smiled.

"Excellent."

"I don't like big surprises, is all."

Prime Cassian shrugged.

"This is our way. As Lio, we accept you. You must accept us, too. This is another reason we have this time together, Daniel, so you understand what is happening."

Prime Cassian petted Daniel's shoulder, his face becoming serious.

"You've had all this happen quickly. I understand this. Our Pride understands this, as does your Coalition."

Prime Cassian's worry for him shot through the flow of his energy.

Kassie Keegan

"Is it too much? Are you ready?"

Am I ready?

Everything *had* happened super-fast. He'd only stepped foot on his first planet day spans ago, and now he had Mates. He'd longed for the family within his grasp, wanting it with every fiber of his being.

He already loved and respected each of them. He didn't care if he had only known them briefly. They'd shared the depths of their hearts. They were good together, and he didn't want to wait, didn't want to stop.

"I don't know if anyone can be truly ready for this. It's overwhelming."

"It is."

Prime scrutinized him.

"So, we move forward?"

His cheeks heated as he agreed. Prime Cassian relaxed.

"This will be intimate. But you are in control of how intimate, so relax, if you can."

"We don't have to…"

"Fuck? No. Bon'Fiel Pride keeps fucking for your Mates. Everything else is available for your final boost."

Daniel's blush deepened.

"Neither fucking nor sucking are what you want with me, is it?"

He shook his head. He wanted those things with his Mates. Prime peered at him with kindness and compassion.

"There is no Mating without your final catalyst. Ferrand, Léandre, and Jovian understand this."

Prime Cassian's tuft trailed along Daniel's thigh.

"You are new here with our people. Lio are open with our sexuality and sharing pleasure is common. However, you should know that once a MateBond is complete, Lio desire only their Mates."

"Honored, too?"

"Yes. You will all spiritually and physically MateBond each other."

Prime Cassian's tone became wistful.

"There is nothing like the MateBond Lio Nels can have with their Honored Mates. We Lio Nels who are committed to a Coalition want it desperately."

"And Aubrey?"

"She understands, Daniel. She has a Shumal, remember?"

Yeah, I remember.

"Seeing you affected Aubrey so deeply, and caused her such intense arousal, she could barely move from the power of it. Stealth helped her survive the moment. As her Shumal, Stealth will see to her health, and protect her until the MateBond is complete."

And Stealth made it clear Aubrey's needs would be met until he stepped up as a Mate himself.

Well, I'm stepping up!

Thinking about his Mates made him think about Travar. And Destiny.

"What about Travar?"

He liked Travar and wanted to be great friends with him.

"I am a Prime. It is understood a Prime male belongs to his Pride. All Lio know this and respect the importance of my role in our Pride. Travar will not be angry with you, or anyone."

He knew he was prying now, but he really wanted to know how all this relationship stuff worked on Lio HomeWorld.

"And Destiny?"

Prime Cassian looked down and smoothed his sarong for a thoughtful moment before peering up at him. He didn't deny his longing for Destiny.

"Honored Nessas are quite possessive. It's a rare thing for a Prime to be Claimed as a Mate."

He shook his head.

"It is so rare that when it happens on Lio HomeWorld, the entire Pride changes their name from 'Bon' to 'Argen' to reflect the honor bestowed. If Destiny gave me such a gift, our Pride would be called Argen'Fiel for as long as I serve as Prime."

Prime Cassian's lips tightened for a moment.

"An Honored Nessa would have to share her Prime Mate's time and affection with the Pride. And accept the intimacies required when an Honored Nel is ready to Call a Mate."

Prime Cassian's face cleared.

"With Bon'Fiel, these intimacies are not extreme."

He reached his hand out to Daniel, who took it.

"Time to let go of your concerns."

He put Daniel's hand on his chest over his heart.

"We Nels seek our Mates. And our pleasure."

He stroked up Daniel's arm with soft fingers.

"How would you like to come?"

Prime Cassian gazed into his eyes with open interest.

Creator, he is a gorgeous male. I want to take a bite out of him.

He truly did. It surprised Daniel at how much he genuinely wanted to bite his Prime. Prime Cassian wondered at his consternation.

"What is it? Tell me."

"I really want to bite you!"

His Prime grinned.

"Well, all right! Let's get to it."

"Just like that?"

"Yes, just like that."

"Um, where?"

Prime Cassian flipped his thick mane out of the way, indicating a meaty muscle between his neck and shoulder.

Daniel didn't want an intimacy with Prime Cassian he hadn't first experienced with his Mates. He'd straddled Ferrand's hips.

He moved tentatively, settling over Prime Cassian's thighs, then he sat still, Prime's hands on his back. Lifting his hands to Prime Cassian's shoulders, Daniel looked at him, waiting for what was next.

"You're doing great. Still want a bite?"

He did, aggressiveness slamming him.

"I think I'm going to bite hard."

Prime Cassian's eyes gleamed with amusement.

"I'd be disappointed if you didn't."

Pulling more of his mane out of the way, he tilted his head to the side and waited. Daniel smelled Prime Cassian's rich, masculine scent, and his mouth watered. Prime's hands lowered to his hips, pulling him closer, bringing their cloth-covered cocks together.

Leaning in, Daniel bit deep, right on the meaty muscle. Flavor burst on his tongue in a heady rush, and he moaned, his scalp tingling. Zinging pleasure raced from his head to his toes, leaving goosebumps in its wake.

Prime Cassian reached inside the folds of Daniel's sarong, palming his cock. One tight squeeze had Daniel coming with a scream, his teeth clamped hard on Prime Cassian. His Prime shivered and growled, climaxing with him, the scent of his release intoxicating Daniel.

His peak went on and on, his body shuddering and shaking, until Daniel finally released his bite. After, he drifted in a relaxed haze.

Kassie Keegan

He came back to himself cuddled close to a purring Prime Cassian, his head tucked into his neck, comforted by the smooth vibration and his Prime's scent. His cheek rested where he had bitten Prime Cassian's shoulder. There was no blood.

Daniel floated, relaxed and content. Prime murmured to him.

"Beautiful. Simply beautiful."

He sighed.

"Are you ready for your Coalition?"

He responded dreamily.

"I want them."

"Good."

Prime Cassian moved one arm. There was a click, then an entry shushed open.

"He's intoxicated by the hormone-rush. Ride the wave, help him Call to her."

Ferrand sounded concerned.

"He screamed."

"Yes. The intensity of his response will bring a strong Call. He's fine, I promise."

Daniel stayed bonelessly relaxed as Ferrand lifted him, comfortably arranging him with Léandre and Jovian cuddled close.

Ah, this is bliss.

Chapter 35
Commander Ferrand

This is a nightmare! Ferrand bathed a writhing Daniel with a damp moisture-cloth. It had been hours. Sweat drenched their sarongs, Daniel's Chalel, and the thick cushion beneath them.

Aubrey had not answered Daniel's Call.

Daniel's skin burned with fever, and he spoke unintelligibly, often tensing to call her name then fall back into his writhing.

Ears back, Léandre petted Daniel's hair, tail flicking with agitation, hopelessness creeping into his eyes. It would be his turn next to share his nectar with Daniel to soothe him.

After the first hours, Ha-Abassa Sarina asked them to come for Daniel, rubbing their essence into his burning hot skin. It worked at first, bringing him a measure of relief. For Ferrand, it had been a mechanical act fraught with worry and utterly unfulfilling. He needed his Mates intact, happy, and whole.

On high-alert, Raiida and Rahimi guarded the entrance. Bon'Fiel Pride was concerned, protectively staying close to their troubled Pride Mates in the Bon'Fiel wing of the Palace, making sure they had what they needed.

Jovian, as usual, put his mind to what could be wrong. One ear constantly flicked in Daniel's direction to monitor him, his tail swaying energetically with upset and the speed of his thoughts.

"Can we stop the process?"

Ha-Abassa Sarina, Katohna, Cassian, and Travar huddled close by with Jovian, trying to figure out a solution. Katohna nodded at the possibility, but Ha-Abassa Sarina denied it.

"No. If you do, he can never MateBond completely with his Mates. He would live a half-life. Do not do it to him, or yourselves."

Compassionate, Ha-Abassa Sarina gently put her hand on Jovian's arm.

"Not every Honored Nessa answers the Call. If he survives the Heat, Daniel can live productively with you and your Coalition."

Having a moment of clarity, Daniel showed he was more aware of what happened around him than he appeared. Arching back, he glared fiercely at them.

"Don't stop anything! Aubrey answers! I feel her!"

His eyes closed as he curled in on himself with a belly cramp, moaning in deep pain. Ferrand gently massaged Daniel's clenched muscles, attempting to ease him. Léandre brought him a hydro-pack, helping him drink. Katohna had tears in her eyes.

"But Daniel, you suffer so."

He cried out in desperation.

"She suffers with me! *Find her*!"

Ferrand and Katohna gazed at each other helplessly.

Find her? She is safe with Stealth, right? It is Aubrey's choice to answer the Call or not.

Stealth had not answered his holo-comm, but it was to be expected when he comforted an Honored Nessa in distress. Then Stealth burst into the Common Room in a panic, startling everyone. Prime Cassian rose with a growl.

"Where's Aubrey?"

"She's missing! And her holo-comm tracker is off."

Ferrand's heart died, grief overwhelming him. He and every being in the room roared with anguish, including Daniel.

Cassian shook himself, then grabbed Ferrand's mane and shook him, bringing him out of his grief-spiral enough to focus his thoughts. His Prime did the same for Léandre and Jovian, then he fiercely turned to Aubrey's Shumal.

"How, Stealth?"

Ferrand respected Cassian's control, not piling blame on the poor male, who was already clearly devastated. He'd been an attentive protector. It must have been an extraordinary circumstance for Aubrey to be out of his sight, even for a moment.

"I took her to the Bathing Chambers when she couldn't sleep. I checked the room. It was sealed. Aubrey seemed troubled, Cassian. I worried she wouldn't be able to commit because she had doubts."

Léandre curled deeper into himself, his tail wrapping around his own leg, his ears flattening in sorrow.

He thinks she changed her mind because of him.

Ferrand pulled Léandre's braid so his grief-filled eyes focused on him.

"Stop. Daniel says she answers. Trust him."

Léandre nodded, ears easing up slowly, and gently licked Daniel's shoulder as he sat up toward his friends, leaning on one arm to look at them.

"We are connected. I feel Aubrey. She answers. We suffer together."

The clear implication that she was suffering alone, as terribly as Daniel, struck terror in Ferrand's heart. He could tell it did his companions as well. Stealth anxiously gave more details.

"A wall was opened. It had to be an Architect or someone with top clearance to open access to the Catacombs of the Palace from the Bathing Chambers."

The Catacombs!

A person could be lost for days in them. It was confusing on purpose so the Capital Elite could use hidden rooms for secret deals, assignations, and other private purposes.

"I waited on the other side of the open threshold, because it's the way Aubrey wants it at the Bathing Pools. She was gone but moments before I realized it was too quiet."

Stealth reached up and pulled his ears, his face a study in confused despair. Cassian and Travar went to him, taking his hands in their own and bringing them down. Travar hugged Stealth as he shook his head, defeated.

Ferrand would not see such a quality male brought so low.

"Stealth."

He turned to Ferrand, looking ready for harsh recrimination.

"This is someone's plan. There is no other explanation. You checked the room."

He nodded hesitantly.

"Aubrey is modest. She did not want you watching her bathe."

He shook his head.

"Aubrey is curious and independent. Under stress, she would seek distraction."

Stealth understood, nodding.

"It's not that she didn't trust you."

A tear slipped down Stealth's cheek.

"None of us expected this level of sabotage."

Everyone shook their heads.

"We don't know who to trust and we are surely being watched. Contacting our allied Prides will alert our enemies that Aubrey is vulnerable."

Ferrand's mind worked through moves and countermoves. He hated to ask Daniel, but he must.

"Daniel, focus. Is Aubrey being hurt by others?"

He moaned in pain, but Ferrand understood the sound wasn't from his physical discomfort, it came from the possibility of Aubrey's torture. Lying down, Daniel closed his eyes, his back arching stiffly as he began his mumbles again. Katohna shook her head in sorrow, ears low.

"We've lost him again."

Ha-Abassa Sarina shushed her with a slice of her hand, her eyes far-away, her attention focused internally. Daniel groaned, then relaxed onto his back, his voice rough and dry.

"She's alone. *So alone*. She longs for us. She's sorry. She weeps."

He curled in on himself again, sobbing almost silently, his body shuddering. Léandre curved around Daniel, giving him soothing strokes. Jovian and Ferrand wrapped their tails around his leg, needing contact with their suffering Mate.

She is probably sobbing exactly like this somewhere. Alone.

Ferrand steeled his resolve.

"We must find her on our own."

He closed his eyes for a moment and centered himself. When he opened them, he saw Léandre and Jovian had done the same, determination driving them.

We will find our Mate.

Jovian started the plan.

"Cassian, you have the most sensitive nose. If anyone can find a Shaktah in a Mating Heat, it's you."

He turned to Stealth.

"As her Shumal, I know you will find her no matter what our enemies have done. Do not give up."

Jovian peered down at Daniel and cupped his cheek, prompting him to open his eyes.

"We will not give up, either."

Sweat and tears streaked Daniel's face. Wiping his face clean on his arm, he rolled up and onto his elbow, attempting to get up while Léandre moved back. Ferrand laid his hand on Daniel's shoulder.

"We cannot go, Daniel. It's our purpose to be here when Aubrey answers the Call."

"But she can't!"

"I believe you. However, we cannot separate and wander the Palace in search of her. Are you in a condition to do so?"

His lips thinned.

"I would do it for *her*!"

Ferrand slid closer to Daniel, gathering him in his lap, looking into Daniel's pained, deep brown eyes.

"Yes. We would do anything for Aubrey. Die for her, right?"

More tears fell as Daniel agreed.

"Staying put and trusting others with her well-being will be the hardest thing we've ever done."

Ferrand stroked his thumb over a tear trail.

"They must bring Aubrey to us. We must stay together and be ready for her when she arrives. It's what she needs. For us to be here, strong and ready, for her. Can you do this?"

Painful resignation and quiet hope visibly warred in Daniel, even as he consented to wait with a sad nod. Ferrand cuddled him close to his chest as Léandre laid his head on Daniel's lap. Then Stealth revealed another problem.

"They jammed my holo-comms. They're still jammed."

Jovian leaped on him, angling Stealth's head away so he could see the tiny, mostly hidden holo-comm mechanism. Daniel shuddered with another wave of heat, speaking in a thin, reedy voice.

"Check the Quantum Scalometer."

Jovian reached for the tech-bag he'd discarded to the side hour spans ago, taking out a device, bring it close to Stealth.

"Diminished."

Daniel growled.

"Was he 'Pulsed?'"

"Yes."

"Boost him."

Jovian rotated Stealth's head forward to look into his eyes.

"I need to boost your holo-comm. When I do, it won't return to regular comm levels. You will be sensitive to ultra-sonic holo-comms. I can help you control it, but for now, you will be wide-open. Do you consent?"

Stealth's expression firmed.

"Don't tell me about it, do it!"

Jovian went back to his tech-bag and grabbed several items. He attached some things to Stealth's head behind his ear for a few moments before putting everything away.

Kassie Keegan

The shimmer of Jovian's holo-comm activated, then Stealth's activated. Stealth sucked in a ragged breath, releasing it gradually, obviously affected by what Jovian commed before he spoke out-loud.

"Remember what I said, Shumal. Now, keep your holo-comms open."

Stealth hugged Jovian close, then pivoted to Prime Cassian.

"Ready to hunt?"

"Always."

Cassian bent to Travar, giving him a slow lick up his neck, scratching behind his ear.

"Take care of them, Zumiel."

"Trust and Devotion, Cassian. You will find her!"

Travar tenderly pulled Stealth's ear, who gave him a shadow of a smile, quickly gone. Ha-Abassa Sarina went to Cassian and Stealth, laying her hands on each of their shoulders.

"Cassian, this is a Shaktah virgin in her Mating Heat. You will need to center. Be stronger than you have ever been. Most Primes will never face this kind of Challenge."

Prime Cassian's face tightened.

"Stealth. Accept the truth. Release your hesitations. Assist your Prime."

Stealth gazed at Cassian with mysterious eyes. Ha-Abassa Sarina grabbed a satchel, handing it to Stealth.

"There's a tranq, a stim, a med kit, a healer, and medical-grade hydro-packs inside. Use whatever you need to get her here as fast as you can."

Ha-Abassa Sarina detached the purple teardrop jewel hanging in the middle of her forehead, giving it to Cassian.

"This will open any hidden entry. May Abah-Sah guide you. Go!"

And they were gone, taking Ferrand's hopes and dreams with them.

Chapter 36
Aubrey

The rise and fall of Aubrey's pain seared her in a predictable rhythm. She could almost brace for the violent wave of unfulfilled arousal wracking her body, screaming when she couldn't bear it.

She lay on the couch, drenched with sweat and her juices. She wore no magic panties now. Her tears soaked the cushion under her head.

She thought constantly of her Mates. When Aubrey was in her calmer moments, she could remember the tiniest details of them.

The exact shade of red some strands in Léandre's mane revealed in sunlight. How Jovian's mouth tensed over his fangs as he puzzled through a problem. Ferrand's green eyes glowing when he admired something. The velvet glide of Daniel's lips on her own.

I'm so sorry, my loves.

Aubrey would have given up during the worst of it, if not for Daniel. She felt him with her, suffering, too.

I'm not truly alone.

She didn't remember at what point the indistinct hums that were a natural part of her had become actual messages she could understand, but she was grateful for it.

Kassie Keegan

Aubrey put her hands over her heart as she thought to Daniel.

"Thank you for not leaving me."

She sensed him.

"I will never leave you."

Then.

"They are coming."

"What?"

"They will find you."

Oh, thank Abah-Sah.

The next wave ripped through her, and she drowned with Daniel, writhing in the molten heat of unfulfillment. Aubrey fell into a fugue-state, barely moving, mumbling to Daniel when she could.

She was Fading.

She sensed Daniel's frantic Calls to her, and she answered. Love for Daniel. Devotion for Ferrand. Loyalty for Jovian. Faith in Léandre.

The air changed.

A cool current of air blew over Aubrey's moist, fevered skin like a benediction. It sharpened her awareness, bringing to her the distinct scents of Stealth and a delectable male, healthy and perfect, even before she heard their voices.

The primal male's voice was deep, rough, and breathless.

"I know this is it. It has to be."

Then Stealth.

"She's here."

A gentle touch caressed her hair, pushing it off her face. She smiled faintly, but didn't open her eyes or move. It was better when she stayed still. Even the fresh air was an irritant to her over-sensitive skin.

"Abah-Sah, help me. She smells so needy, so tempting. Savion, I… don't know if… Oh, Abah-Sah, help me."

"Stay over there, Cassian."

"Disengage holo-comms."

"Confirm, disengaged. Why Cassian?"

"I *cannot* leave her like this. What kind of male would leave a female to suffer like this? It is unconscionable."

Stealth spoke close to her ear.

"Aubrey, can you open your eyes, please?"

Stealth needs me to do something.

She didn't open her eyes, but she managed to speak, her voice ragged.

"Are you really real?"

"Open your eyes. See me, Aubrey."

Ah, right. Stealth wants me to open my eyes.

It seemed like such a difficult thing to do.

A hydro-pack pushed against her lips. She opened her mouth, but couldn't suck. Stealth squeezed the pouch, and she swallowed greedily. He brought another to her lips, and she drank it, too. Aubrey's belly cramps eased, allowing her to relax deeper into the cushions.

I'm comfortable enough. Now might be a good time to leave all the suffering behind.

"Aubrey, please."

Stealth's voice aimed at the other male.

"She's not coming out of it."

The primal male spoke, his rumbling tenor catching the barest thread of her interest.

"Give her the stim."

There was a long pause before he spoke again, as if the words were pulled out of him.

"But first, give me the tranq."

"Is it so bad?"

"She entices me more than I can bear. I need to fuck more than I need to breathe. She would take me and howl with pleasure."

He growled, his arousal clear, making her thighs clench.

"I wouldn't stop until we were both sated."

He growled long and low in pleasured abandon, as if he were already fucking her. Aubrey gushed at the sound of it.

"It would ruin our futures with our Mates, Savion. People we love and respect with all our hearts. Then we would both lose the lives we want and possibly lose our souls from the grief of it. Tranq me! Now!"

There were rustling noises, next a crack, and the distinctive hiss of an atomizer accompanied by deep sniffing.

"Thank you, Savion. It takes the edge off."

"Only the edge?"

"The barest edge. We have to get her up and get moving."

Stealth returned to her. She heard another crack and hiss. A cool, moist scent went up her nose. Instantly, a surge of energy burst through her system, her eyes popping open.

The perfect primal male waited across the room on his hands and knees, his tail curved up high and agitated, his mane wild. His face strained with arousal. He had his mouth slightly open with his huge fangs visible, savoring her scent across the back of his tongue.

Stealth was on his knees beside the couch she laid on.

At that moment, they were not friends. They were males. Healthy, sexual males who had thick cocks she needed.

The gorgeous beast's eyes glowed pale-green and he tensed tighter when their eyes locked.

"Oh, Abah-Sah, here she comes. Help me!"

Aubrey lifted on her elbow and bent her knees.

Oh, yes. He's the One. The most potent male. The best choice to fill me.

Aubrey leaped, and he caught her. She wrapped her legs tight around his waist, the fabric of her gown bunched between them as her core pressed solidly against his luscious abdomen.

She growled in triumph when he was in her clutches. Winding her arms around his neck, she buried her face deep into his thick mane, reveling in his rich, masculine scent.

Burrowing in, she licked her prize, savoring his potent flavor. He moaned, moving his body in sultry undulations with hers. Then Aubrey caught a hint of an even *more* enticing scent.

She sniffed along his neck, up to his jaw. She nipped his jaw, prompting him to growl, which made her thighs clasp him harder.

He slowly rotated his head for her, and there it was.

That scent, the one she loved.

The scent of the one she loved.

Her love.

Daniel.

His name burst from her lips in an anguished rush.

"Daniel! I *need* you!"

Aubrey's spirit reached out to the One she longed for, and he answered.

"Come to me."

The male holding her put his hand on the back of her head and directed her face to the strongest source of her love's scent. She buried her face in it and writhed with need.

Kassie Keegan

She couldn't hold back her scream.

"I *need* you!"

The male holding her moaned again, his anguish matching hers.

"Please, Savion."

"What can I do?"

"She's going to come and take me with her. Take me, so I don't take *her*. I know what this means for you. I didn't want it to be this way."

A deep breath, same strained voice.

"I treasure you."

Big swallow. Small groan.

"Travar and I have chosen you for our Coalition since we first Bonded, you know this. We've waited, knowing you needed the freedom to fly, and explore, and experience."

A long pause, sorrow in the male's voice.

"If I had more control, if I was stronger... You wouldn't be in this situation. I'm so sorry, Savion. Don't resent our Bond!"

The Lio Nel came close beside her.

"I will never resent this, Cassian. Your restraint thus far, with me, and with Aubrey, makes me adore you even more."

He rubbed his cheek against the cheek of the male in her arms.

"I accept, Cassian. I accept you and Travar."

He dropped below her. Rustles sounded. She sensed movement, felt the brush of fur near her thighs. Her primal male groaned as if he were dying, rolling his abdomen voluptuously, spiking her arousal.

The Lio Nel below her moaned in abandon, a sound that made her grind hard on the luscious male she clung to. The moan cut off abruptly with a long, steady push from the male's rippling abs. It was replaced by the subtle, succulent sounds of cock being sucked.

Her primal male pulled Aubrey's head back with one hand. She focused on his face, firm with command. He ground her core harder on him with his other hand on her rear.

"Come, Aubrey. Come screaming for your Mate."

He used his grip in her hair to bury her face in his shoulder over the perfect, heady scent.

"Yes, Savion. Right there. It's delicious. All for you. Take it!"

His voice, his words, the scent she loved, the motion of their bodies grinding, all built to a crashing climax. Her arms reached out for the One she craved and screamed his name.

"Daniel!"

The male bringing her relief shuddered and shouted.

"Savion, yes! I'm yours, yes!"

His growls went on and on as their peak held them in its grip for long, unrelenting moments, then released them.

She relaxed against the male, who fell back deeper on his haunches. Aubrey lost herself, drifting.

When she returned to awareness, the males were talking, but she couldn't be bothered to move.

"Come here."

Movement, brushes of fur.

"I treasure this gift, Savion."

Kisses.

"How are you?"

"Happy. A little fearful. Hopeful. Worried for Aubrey and her Mates."

"We'll take care of you later."

"There's no need…"

Kassie Keegan

A growl of disapproval.

"Stop. We will well-reward you, my Brethren. Now come close so I can get another taste."

More brushes of fur.

"Take her. She's calm and her Mates will tolerate you carrying her more easily."

They lifted her into Stealth's hold and she rolled comfortably onto his shoulder, her legs draped over one of his arms, her back supported by the other.

When she opened her eyes, Stealth's face was in profile, Prime Cassian's hand on his cheek, sharing air. Prime Cassian spoke, his words thick with gratitude.

"Thank you."

Aubrey wondered when Prime Cassian arrived.

"Hi, Prime Cassian!"

He and Stealth peered at her, relieved smiles on their faces.

"Can you take me to my Mates, please? I need them."

Prime Cassian gave her a kiss on her forehead as Stealth chuckled.

"Lead on!"

"On it!"

And they were on their way.

Chapter 37
Aubrey

Aubrey sensed her Mates were close.

Stealth moved with smooth feline grace despite his speed, so he didn't jostle her much, and her surroundings blurred because she couldn't focus her eyes well.

Being closer to her Mates made her anxious and restless. However, she tried not to move. She didn't want Stealth distracted and slowed down.

Faster, Stealth. Faster.

Her gown fluttered against her hyper-sensitive skin as they hustled, making her grit her teeth. Touch was uncomfortable.

She knew they passed Bon'Fiel Pride Mates in the halls, and she didn't care. The ones she needed, the ones she sought, were close. She could almost taste them. Aubrey panted, the hum within her resonating at an incredible level.

He knows I'm near.

She could feel Daniel's blistering joy.

And there he was, her beautiful man, leaning back on his elbows, wild-eyed and rough. He wore a sheer, golden sarong that only emphasized his gloriously thick, long, hard cock.

Kassie Keegan

He smelled utterly alluring, like her Lio Nels had drenched him in their scents.

She looked for her Lio Mates, saw them, and felt reassured.

Poised in low crouches, they were spaced out around the edges of a large circular cushion Daniel lay in the center of. Ferrand had both Raiida and Rahimi flanking him. Travar was close to Jovian, and High Nessa Katohna had a hand on Léandre's shoulder.

Aubrey leaped from Stealth's arms into a crouch.

The people near her Mates were acceptable, but there was something she violently disliked. She focused on the offending hand on Léandre and shouted her Claim.

"Mine!"

The word trailed off into an angry feminine growl. The hand moved hastily off her Lio Nel.

Good. I will not have to shed blood.

She scanned the room with a feral gaze, glancing at the priestess, who sat unmoving and calm, her expression oddly pleased. Aubrey sensed no threat.

Ha-Abassa Sarina is acceptable.

She stared at Prime Cassian steadily until he went to the entry and showed her the secure seal. She motioned him to stay there, in her sight. He dutifully sat, his posture alert but relaxed.

This is acceptable.

Stealth stood behind her. She didn't like it. She wanted everyone in her sight. Aubrey glared over her shoulder at him and growled viciously, her lips curled back from her teeth. He didn't move fast enough, so she hissed at him.

That got him moving!

She motioned with her chin to where she wanted him to be, tracking his movement with focused attention. She hummed in satisfaction when Stealth sat, eyes wide, posture non-threatening.

Acceptable.

She made one last visual sweep, laying Claiming eyes on each of her Lio Nels, their expressions reassuring her they accepted her Claim. She would have them when she was ready for them.

Ha-Abassa Sarina spoke formally.

"Aubrey Newton Bon'Fiel, do you lay Claim upon Daniel Shaw Bon'Fiel?"

She gazed at the lovely man she would Claim first. Daniel hadn't moved, which she liked, his body on full display.

Hers.

Hers to Mate.

Mine to Claim.

Aubrey growled her answer.

"I Claim him!"

Daniel shivered as she intently stalked him on hands and knees. He watched her every move, his gaze caressing her. She liked his attention, wanting it on her always.

I want to be the center of your world.

He would be at the center of her world, too.

She reached his legs first, sniffing over his flesh. Her Lio had touched him. She leaned closer to his thigh.

Mmm.

She recognized the scents of their pleasure.

They rubbed their nectar onto my male.

Kassie Keegan

Aubrey focused on Jovian, her golden beauty. She eyed him lingeringly, enjoying the flex of his muscles, the color of his fur, the strength of his stance as he restrained himself to her will. He tasted her scent, his tail wildly excited, yet he kept strict self-control.

You are being so good for me, aren't you?

Aubrey bent over Daniel's fragrant thigh. Jovian's eyes tracked down to her breasts, so she was sure her gown gaped wide.

He licked his lips helplessly.

When she opened her mouth, his eyes snapped there and followed with deepest pleasure as she slowly dragged her tongue along the delicious mix of flavors she sought to enjoy on Daniel's thigh.

She growled in approval and licked again, slower. Daniel panted as her tongue stroked. All her Mates groaned.

Aubrey smiled, reveling in her feminine power over them.

Jovian collapsed from his crouch to his knees, his shaft a visibly throbbing column of need under his sheer golden sarong. She growled low.

Aubrey would have Jovian's potency within her soon, but first, Daniel. Putting her hands on Daniel's legs, she skimmed them up under his sarong, fanning open the folds like unwrapping a present.

Daniel's cock was beautiful, a silky, smooth, thick, light-gold shaft of flesh pulsing with the beat of his heart. She petted its hard, velvety length from crown to base, his erection lifting at her touch as if trying to follow her hand. She caressed him again and again, fascinated, as he sensually moaned for her.

She watched him as she teased, his head falling back, his mouth slightly open, panting with pleasure. He enthralled her, and she wanted his eyes on her.

"Daniel."

He lowered his head to look at her, his eyes dazed.

"Watch."

This time, she licked his shaft from base to crown. They moaned together, he from her lick, she from his luscious flavor.

Daniel is mine!

She would Claim him.

This cock is mine!

She would have it.

It was time.

Aubrey grabbed the hem of her gown in the front, ripping it up the middle to under her breasts, flinging the ragged sides back and away, exposing her lower-body in its open slice.

She looked up, inspecting Ferrand across from her. He crouched low to the ground on all fours, his tail high and still as his eyes roved over her.

She put her hand on her belly, stroking it down over the patch of silky hair covering her mound to her soaked center, watching him track her hand, breathing irregularly.

He made small moaning noises in the back of his throat she was sure he wasn't aware of. Aubrey petted her clit while her gaze devoured him. She spoke in a soft whisper.

"Ferrand."

He tracked her hand as she lifted it to her mouth and licked her own fingers, enjoying her tangy flavor as they stared into each other's eyes. He growled so passionately he seemed angry, his claws extending fully, digging deep into the cushion and ripping. Ears back, his tail whipped fiercely in excitement.

Yet she knew he would control himself. She trusted him implicitly.

Aubrey's gaze traced the firm, striated muscles of her aggressively straining Mate with possessive eyes, delighting in his masculine strength.

Ferrand is a work of art.

Kassie Keegan

She would have Ferrand's beautiful brawn within her soon.

She turned her attention to Léandre, who crouched low on hands and knees, his mouth open, his nose wrinkling with the rhythm of his deep breaths. His tail snapped from side-to-side.

Her gaze caressed his strong, tight body, anticipation settling heavily in her core, enjoying his glowing golden gaze upon her.

She would take his fierce power within herself, too.

But first, my lovely Daniel.

Daniel watched her, his nostrils flaring, moaning for her, his hips writhing with the need.

"Please. Aubrey. Come to me. Please."

"You're mine, Daniel. I Claim you. I keep you."

"All yours, forever. Claim me."

Aubrey climbed up over his hips, her swollen, hot, wet, ready core settling directly on the underside of his hard cock, now pushed between her and his abdomen. They both shouted out at the press of their most private flesh finally touching intimately, grinding together in pained pleasure. She needed more.

How to get it?

She moaned her words.

"I need it. Help me."

Jovian guided them, his voice deepened by lust.

"Aubrey, lift up."

She braced herself on Daniel's chest, peering down at his erection, now glistening with her arousal.

"Daniel, raise your cock. Hold it steady for her."

He lifted his length straight up, holding it with one hand at the base in a sexy offering she was determined to have.

"Aubrey, take him inside you. Be fulfilled, my hearts."

She repositioned herself over his hard column, feeling his tip grazing her moist folds.

Focusing on Daniel's pleasure-dazed face, she made a few adjustments to get him right where she wanted him and then she slowly, achingly, lowered herself onto his thick shaft.

Daniel filled her as she let her weight push her tight, swollen sex onto him. She was so aroused the slide was smooth, but her eyes opened wider at the burn as his flesh dug deeper.

It didn't make her stop her Claim. She had already suffered much worse in her need for the cock she was taking. Triumph flared as she took all of him.

Aubrey gazed down at him, deep inside her, looking up at her with pleasured devotion. The man who had suffered with her, and stayed with her through it all, her Mate, Daniel, who she loved.

She bent to kiss him, pulling off his erection some to reach his lips, uttering a long, drawn out whisper.

"Mine."

The word pulsed with the depth of her feelings for him as their lips met. Daniel poured his soul into their kiss, reaching up to grasp her hair gently in one hand while his other caressed the flesh of her side and hip.

She reveled in the slow, sensuous dips and glides of their kiss, their tongues teasing and tasting. When she sat up, taking him deep again, she felt floaty.

Daniel spoke, serious and determined.

"Aubrey, does this feel good?"

It did, but she needed more. She wanted to come, but she wasn't sure what to do next. She knew there would be moving.

"Yes, but…"

Kassie Keegan

"You need more?"

Her answer was breathy.

"Yes!"

A feral grin unlike anything she'd seen bloomed on his face, his deep brown eyes hot and carnal. He gripped her hips firmly, making her gasp and relax in his hold, enjoying his strength.

"I Claim you too, Mate. I Claim the right to pleasure you. And make you scream."

Daniel pumped up hard into her.

Her eyes widened at the burst of glittering tingles racing through her. He pulled back and filled her again, giving her more prickling euphoria.

She wanted *more*. Her hips moved in counterpoint to his as they found an exhilarating rhythm together.

Aubrey glanced over at Léandre, who had his length in hand under his sarong, rapturous while watching his Mates join. He pumped his cock to their rhythm.

Sexy beast!

Jovian continued his guidance.

"Angle her hips slightly up and back. Yes, her ass higher, like that, Daniel. She can slide her clit along your shaft as you pump."

Each stroke blazed a long drag of delight. Aubrey dropped harder on Daniel as he rose higher. He pounded himself up into her faster, his face tight with concentration. She was close, and the power of her build-up scared her.

"Daniel!"

"Do it! I'm with you. We go together."

Their bliss-hazed gazes locked, the hum of their vibrant Connection resonating within her, rising with their crests. They went over, shouting their pleasure together.

Daniel arched hard into her as they peaked, caught there for long moments in fulfillment, until they were released. Aubrey felt utter satisfaction.

Ha-Abassa Sarina intoned.

"Daniel is Claimed. His Call is Answered."

It was all Aubrey's mind and body could take.

Straddling Daniel, still filled with his throbbing hardness, she tried to brace her arms against his chest as, in slow motion, she melted forward into unconsciousness. She had a vague awareness of violent roars, shouts, scraping noises, rips, and scrambling happening all around her and Daniel.

Ferrand sounded frantic.

"No! No! She's Fading. *No!*"

His anguish crushed her.

Aubrey tried to reassure Ferrand, sliding her hand toward him over Daniel's shoulder as she fell on top of him, but it was too late.

Darkness greeted her.

Chapter 38
Daniel

Daniel held Aubrey close as the room exploded into sound and movement.

He looked back over his shoulder at Ferrand, who seemed incensed with Raiida and Rahimi restraining him. He shredded the cushion with his claws, trying to get leverage away from them as they hooked themselves onto his bulk, keeping him in place through skill and combined strength.

Fuck, he is formidable!

Daniel realized Ferrand restrained himself even in his rage and fear because he didn't seek to harm the twins, only escape them. Ultimately, he allowed them to confine him, but his tail slid forward and twined around Aubrey's arm, which extended out to him.

Perhaps he could feel her pulse beating there because he stopped, relaxing into the twin's hold on him.

Jovian scrambled toward them, too, but Travar leaped onto his back, enfolding Jovian in a tight embrace with his arms and legs, rolling them onto their sides, facing Daniel and Aubrey. Travar whispered reassurances, while Jovian wrapped his tail around Aubrey's ankle.

Savage Planet Embrace

On Daniel's other side, Léandre also lay turned toward them, held firmly by High Nessa Katohna, her knee on his hip, her hand pressing the side of his head into the cushion.

He appeared relaxed in her hold, his eyes focused on Aubrey's face, which was turned toward him. Daniel realized he closely watched the breaths she took. Léandre's agitated tail moved in jerky waves.

Daniel tried to reassure his Lio Mates.

"Guys! Guys, she's okay. I feel her with us. Look, she's breathing, just exhausted. Give her a moment. It's okay."

Prime Cassian went beside them, checking his vitals as Stealth checked Aubrey's.

Ha-Abassa Sarina rose, gliding to Ferrand. She quietly touched the center of his forehead and tension left him. He relaxed forward onto his stomach, Raiida and Rahimi still blanketing him. His chin rested on his folded hands, eyes on Daniel and Aubrey, no longer tense or anxious.

She bent to Jovian, whose arms fell limp when she touched his shoulder. Travar relaxed his hold, but did not move away.

She dropped to her knees in front of Léandre, prompting High Nessa Katohna to do the same behind him. They clasped wrists together over Léandre's prostrate form. High Nessa kept her hand on Léandre's head, while Ha-Abassa touched his hip. Léandre shuddered violently once, then relaxed, his tail falling still.

She rose and moved to Daniel.

When Ha-Abassa Sarina placed her hand on his head, a blessed coolness eased him. His muscles unclenched one-by-one, although his shaft remained hard within Aubrey's warm, wet clasp. He had no urgency about it. He was hers to take as long as she needed.

When Ha-Abassa Sarina touched Aubrey's shoulder, she gave an unintelligible sound and relaxed deeper into Daniel's embrace as she, too, eased.

Kassie Keegan

Stealth had a healer-mech in his hand, taking it steadily from Aubrey's head to her feet. It would ease minor aches and abrasions and heal her from his taking her virginity.

Satisfaction settled within Daniel. She was as much his as he was hers, then tiredness overwhelmed him.

Ha-Abassa Sarina motioned to Prime Cassian and Stealth. Soon he had a cushion under his head and insta-dry cloths close at hand. She laid a gossamer sheer swath of golden fabric over them.

He was comfortable, his beloved flower safe in his arms, his body buried deeply in hers, and his Mates were near and relaxed. Daniel could finally rest.

He came awake as Aubrey made subtle movements showing she was waking up. He stroked his hands up-and-down her back as she roused.

She sat up blinking, golden fabric dropping liquidly off her shoulders with a silken hiss. She gasped a surprised yip, peering down at where they still joined. Her eyes flew to his in amazement and amusement because he was still hard within her.

He shook his head, as confounded as Aubrey.

"I didn't go down. And I was comfortable. I even slept!"

She snickered.

"Judging from how well I rested, I was comfortable, too!"

She braced herself as she pulled off him, making them both moan.

He grabbed an insta-dry cloth and gently cleaned her, enjoying caring for her in the quiet aftermath. She delicately cleaned him, too. He took the cloths, folded them together, and laid them aside.

Aubrey tenderly covered him, pulling the folds of his sarong down as he brought the ripped sections of her gown forward and overlapped them over her. Kissing her softly, he whispered lovingly against her lips.

"Mate."

Suddenly, her eyes shimmered with tears, and his heart froze.

Does she have regrets?

She spoke, sadness heavy in her tone.

"You may not want to keep me."

What?

He shook his head in confusion, then Ha-Abassa Sarina interrupted.

"Aubrey and Daniel."

Their little bubble popped. They were far from alone. Everyone sat up now in their places around the room, relaxed and refreshed.

Prime Cassian spoke matter-of-factly.

"A Nel, whether Lio or Honored, will be available to serve and pleasure his Mates as long, and as often, as they require, until he gives out from exhaustion. It is one of the grand benefits of becoming Honored."

A grand benefit, indeed!

"Lio Nessas and Honored Nessas have control over their fertility cycle. When an Earther becomes Honored she no longer menstruates. She decides when it's time for her to procreate and her body prepares."

Aubrey's face and posture closed down further.

"Sometimes, a Lio Nessa will need a hormone surge to get her there. This is how Shaktahs help. A Shaktah's scent can induce readiness in a female and entice continued service from an exhausted male."

Daniel watched Aubrey closely. She studied Jovian, Ferrand, and Léandre with desire. And fear.

Why?

Kassie Keegan

Daniel spoke distractedly.

"Thanks for explaining, Prime Cassian."

A pause, then Daniel tried again.

"Aubrey, what's..."

Ha-Abassa Sarina interrupted, her voice stern and formal.

"Aubrey and Daniel, you have suffered much to come this far. Every letter of the Protocols will be followed and fulfilled. I will not have this MateBond Challenged."

She gave Aubrey her attention.

"Aubrey Newton Bon'Fiel, you have Answered Daniel Shaw Bon'Fiel's Call to Mate and Claimed him as rightfully yours. But you have not formally laid Claim before me, your High Nessa, or your Prime to this Coalition of Lio Nels who have Declared themselves for you. Do you seek to Claim Ferrand, Léandre, and Jovian for your own?"

Their Lio Nel Mates froze, waiting for her answer like her words determined whether they lived or died. And, in a real way, they did.

Aubrey looked at Ha-Abassa Sarina, eyes shining with unshed tears.

"I want them."

They relaxed, but Aubrey's next words froze them again.

"They may not want *me*."

Growls of angry denial sounded around the room. Ha-Abassa Sarina spoke over them.

"Has someone enticed you away from this Coalition?"

"No!"

"Has this Coalition coerced you in any way?"

"No!"

"You seem fearful, Aubrey. Are you scared of your Coalition?"

"*No!* But I *am* scared."

It was Daniel who asked the big question.

"Why, Aubrey?"

"Because I do not want to have young."

It was like her words sucked the oxygen out of the room.

Everything stilled.

Ha-Abassa Sarina acted unfazed, the twins sat stoically neutral. Prime Cassian and Travar were both thoughtful. Stealth had an "a-ha" moment. High Nessa Katohna appeared most surprised.

"Why?"

Ferrand answered, his voice rough with emotion.

"We know why she would not want young."

Ferrand protected her, making sure Aubrey didn't have to talk about things that hurt her.

He narrowed his gaze at Léandre, Jovian, then Daniel, who looked back at him and nodded confirmation that nothing had changed for them. After what she'd seen and experienced, Daniel could understand her fears about having kids.

Why would she think we don't want her?

Ferrand asked for them all.

"What have we done to make you doubt our devotion?"

Aubrey gasped.

"Nothing! You are all beautiful and perfect for me."

She looked down at her tightly clasped hands.

"But… you should have a Mate who will fill your home with young. I was not honest with you about this. I do not deserve you."

Kassie Keegan

Tears fell in silvery trails down her cheeks. She was clearly expecting rejection. Jovian seemed confused, puzzling out her thought processes.

"When have we said we needed a home full of young?"

"Well, you've all lost Prides, and Daniel has dreamed of a family."

Daniel stroked his distressed Mate softly on the cheek, rubbing away some of her tears.

"Yes, I want a family. Which means *you*. You, Jovian, Ferrand, and Léandre. Kids were this shadowy possibility for the future, but I don't need it."

Hope broke into Aubrey's eyes, then faded.

"What if you change your mind later?"

Ferrand spoke simply.

"You must trust us, Aubrey. Remember the foundation we are building? We have Declared for you. We commit to you. Nothing you've said has changed that."

She swept her gaze over Ferrand, Jovian, and Léandre, landing on Daniel. They all agreed, confirming their commitment to her. Ferrand continued.

"Do you trust us to love and protect you, no matter what the future holds?"

Her focus drew inward, soul-searching. She regarded each of them for long moments, then grabbed an insta-dry cloth, and dried her tears.

Closing her eyes, she took a deep breath, releasing it evenly. When she opened her eyes, she was calm, centered. She spoke strong and sure.

"Yes. I trust you, my Mates."

She turned to Ha-Abassa Sarina.

"I Claim Ferrand Bon'Durel Bon'Fiel for my own."

Ferrand closed his eyes briefly, lowering his head, then put his hand over his heart. Opening his eyes, he gazed at Aubrey like she was his life.

"I Claim Léandre Bon'Durel Bon'Fiel for my own."

Léandre put his hand over his heart, eyes full of devotion.

"I Claim Jovian Bon'Ocal Bon'Fiel for my own."

Jovian eyes widened with joy as he put his hand over his heart.

Ha-Abassa Sarina intoned.

"You have laid Claim to these Lio Nel, Aubrey Newton Bon'Fiel. Ferrand, Léandre, and Jovian, you may approach your Honored Nessa and Honored Nel as Claimed Mates."

Their Lio Nel Mates rushed them from all sides, hugging, rubbing, and kissing whatever they could reach. Daniel petted, rubbed, and stroked, loving touching and being touched.

Eventually, they settled with Aubrey sitting in Ferrand's lap. Daniel snuggled into Ferrand's side with his arm around him. Jovian leaned against Ferrand's other arm, while Léandre lay his head in Aubrey's lap. The twins brought trays of food and drink.

Ferrand, Léandre, and Jovian took great delight in feeding Aubrey and Daniel morsels of food by hand, making sure they ate well. When their bellies were full and the food laid aside, Léandre tapped Ferrand's arm. Ferrand nodded and spoke for them both.

"Aubrey, there are many Pon'Durel Prides in the Known Galaxies and even more Lon'Durel Prides on Lio Colonies. Did you know this?"

She looked at him in surprise.

"No, I didn't!"

"Now you know. On Lio HomeWorld Bon'Durel Pride Mates live in adopted Prides or in the Cities. Our Pride has not rebuilt Bon'Durel PrideHome because we are not ready to do so. It may or may not ever happen."

Daniel petted Léandre's shoulder, a gesture he acknowledged with a gentle stroke of his tuft along Daniel's arm. Ferrand stroked Aubrey's cheek as he continued, his voice soft and loving.

"Léandre and I are happy as Bon'Fiel. They have welcomed us fully. I could not be Commander otherwise."

Aubrey took his hand in hers. Ferrand gave her a sideways grin, his expression a mix of humor and seriousness.

"It is not your responsibility to populate the Bon'Durel Pride. We have not expected this from you."

She peered down at Léandre, who shook his head, his gaze intent and sincere. She took a deep breath.

"Okay."

Jovian touched her thigh to get her attention.

"Hear me. I do not need young."

She blinked in surprise.

"Like you, they are not something I need to be happy."

Jovian stroked her shoulder, down her arm, snagging her hand from Ferrand's.

"Understand, too, I would have loved our young if you had them. But I don't need them."

He kissed the back of her hand as she accepted his words, her eyes glossing with tears again. Daniel grabbed her other hand.

She needs to know we accept her decision.

Daniel was firm and clear.

"We have what we need right here, right now."

Aubrey took a deep breath and nodded, prompting two silvery tears to track down her cheeks. Léandre rose and tenderly licked the tears away, then lay back in her lap.

Ferrand whispered into Aubrey's ear.

"We will not abandon you. You are ours and we are yours."

She scrutinized them all, one-by-one. She finally spoke lovingly.

"Mine."

She relaxed into her Mates' embrace, staying that way for long, happy moments before she turned her attention to High Nessa Katohna.

"I want to go home now."

The Lio around the room growled agreement, standing up.

Ferrand grabbed the gossamer fabric Ha-Abassa Sarina had covered Daniel and Aubrey with, folding it neatly. He took it and their folded insta-dry cloths to a colorful satchel, placing them inside, swing the satchel up on his shoulder.

Prime Cassian handed Léandre something, who then went to Aubrey, placing her Challenge-won Serc necklace over her head with quiet pride. Jovian dropped to one knee, helping Aubrey, then Daniel, put on sandals. Everyone else moved to the edges of the cushion, gathering their belongings.

High Nessa Katohna approached Aubrey, placing her hands on her shoulders, speaking in low, firm tones.

"You are a beloved member of Bon'Fiel Pride because of *who* you are, Aubrey, not the young you can bear. When the darkness seeks to use this and take you, push away the lie and remember the love."

Aubrey swallowed and agreed. High Nessa touched their foreheads together, and they shared air.

Next, High Nessa Katohna picked up Daniel's Chalel, handing it to him. He knew what to do with the garment, covered in symbols from his previous life, now embedded with the essence of his new one during his Call and Claiming.

He went to Aubrey, still dressed in her ripped gown, swirling it over her, covering her modestly by securing it at her shoulder, so it opened at her side.

Daniel's past now protected his future.

Aubrey smiled at him, leaning up to give him a kiss of thanks. Taking his hand, she looked at her Mates and friends.

"Let's go home."

Chapter 39
Aubrey

Aubrey and Daniel walked hand-in-hand behind High Nessa Katohna and Prime Cassian, flanked by the twins as they went through hall after hall of the Palace to get to High Nessa Katohna's personal Land Transport.

Raiida and Rahimi had their holo-comms open, speaking to people helping to prepare for their departure as they traveled. Their eyes constantly swept the perimeter, bodies tense and alert.

Stealth walked at Aubrey's side, while Travar was at Daniel's. Their Coalition followed closely behind them, hands on weapons, expressions forbidding approach.

Those who saw them stopped and bowed low in respect, waiting for them to pass. No one interrupted their progress. By the time they made it to the underground Transport Hangar, the Land Transport was up and running, prepared for flight.

High Nessa's Katohna's Transport was sleek white with purple and gold markings. It was compact, with one quiet turbo engine in the back between two stabilizers, and small curved wings on the sides.

The entrance to the Transport was open for them. As they stepped into the luxurious interior, a couple of Lio Nessas respectfully greeted them.

Kassie Keegan

They dressed like Raiida and Rahimi in clothes made mostly of straps. The Lio Nessas introduced themselves to Aubrey and Daniel.

"I'm Latah. This is Lulah."

The Lio Nessa Latah pointed at, who looked exactly like her, waved at them. Raiida and Rahimi went right up to the Lio Nessas, rubbing faces affectionately before stalking off to check the Bridge.

Daniel's confusion made Lulah explain with a grin.

"We are all sisters."

Latah smiled as she encouraged them to follow her to the Bridge.

"What will blow your mind even more is we are part of three sets of twin sisters!"

Aubrey and Daniel stared at each other, then at the sisters, in surprise. He shook his head.

"That's amazing!"

"We think so. And we are all in Security."

The walls and floor of the Transport were beige, marked with the Bon'-Fiel Pride symbol. The Bridge had a Captain's Chair in the center, which High Nessa Katohna sat in, cooly in charge.

There were four Pilot Stations near the front, two occupied by Pilots similarly dressed in black, one a Lio Nel, the other an Honored Nel. Both had their backs turned as they worked at their Stations.

The Bridge featured beige and coral colors, with the Bon'Fiel Pride symbol decorating the walls. There were four long, curved seating sections along the back wall.

Aubrey and Daniel sat on one end of a cushion next to Stealth. Léandre sat on the other side of Daniel, with Ferrand and Jovian taking the cushion next to theirs.

Rahimi explained to Daniel how to use his Shield to anchor himself to the contact point behind him like a seatbelt. Aubrey and the others secured themselves by their Shields while Daniel followed Rahimi's directions.

Rahimi gave him a satisfied nod of approval before going over to sit with Raiida next to Prime Cassian and Travar across the way. Latah and Lulah joined them, securing in.

When High Nessa Katohna began calling out final prep commands for lift off, the Honored Nel Pilot pivoted into profile, making Daniel freeze. He couldn't seem to hold back his shout.

"Jensen Buey! What are you doing here?"

Jensen swiveled his chair with methodical deliberation to face Daniel, still secured in by his Shield. His expression was rueful, with a touch of humor.

"Hi, Dan. How'ya been?"

Daniel stared at Jensen like he was from Outer-Space, which, considering the situation, was outright ironic.

"You leave without a word and now it's, 'Hi Dan, how'ya been?'"

Jensen pursed his lips together as he nodded slowly, looking around the Bridge before bringing his gaze back to Daniel.

"Yup."

High Nessa Katohna turned to Jensen, then focused on Daniel.

"How do you know my Pilot?"

"We got boosted at SpacePort Haddou together."

Daniel scrutinized Jensen, making Aubrey take a closer look, too. Jensen's complexion was sallow, and he had dark circles under his eyes. He was leaner than he had been before Prime Bastian went to the Fade. Aubrey remembered Jensen had been Prime Bastian's last PrideChoice. It had to be painful.

Hurt bled from Daniel, too.

"We were friends."

Kassie Keegan

Jensen's direct gaze stayed steady as he responded with emphasis.

"We *are* friends."

Daniel looked confused, shaking his head as his eyebrows lifted quizzically.

"We need to talk."

High Nessa Katohna cut in.

"Yes, you obviously do, but later. Now, we need to get going."

She faced forward.

"Jensen."

"Yes, High Nessa Katohna."

She paused, studying him with compassion and affection.

"I'm glad Daniel is your friend. He's a good male. Talk with him."

"Yes, High Nessa."

Jensen's gaze swept over Daniel, Aubrey, and the Lio around them. He smiled reassuringly, and returned to his Pilot Station. High Nessa Katohna and her Pilots worked together seamlessly to gain Permissions and ease out of the Transport Hangar into open airspace.

Aubrey dragged in a relieved breath when they were finally clear of the Palace, winging their way through Capital Maituri.

They were crossing lush open land when Aubrey perceived a low-level reverberation in the energy frequencies of the engine, as if its flow hit a wall and pushed back onto itself.

She was familiar with this Land Transport, and it felt off. She whirled to Daniel, who had a strange expression on his face, internally focused. Aubrey gazed past Daniel to Léandre and became even more worried.

Léandre sat stiff and still, frozen like ice. His eyes locked on Ferrand, ears down flat, tail utterly motionless, his mouth moving with words no one could hear.

She tried to holo-comm Léandre, but it wouldn't even ping for entrance. Something was wrong with comms. Aubrey's gaze swung back to Daniel, fear clutching her.

"Can you engage comms?"

He squinted. No shimmer appeared.

"No."

"We are in trouble."

Daniel's gaze held a calm-through-panic look, whispering.

"We are. What do you sense?"

"The energy hum is off. Like it's being stopped abruptly and being forced back in a negative wave on itself."

He completely understood.

"Like the flow of an energy ocean wave hitting a wall."

"Yes!"

They stared at each other and spoke in unison.

"Engine."

They disengaged their Shields and stood up. Everyone except Léandre and the Pilots, looked at them with surprise.

Aubrey threw off Daniel's Chalel, tucked her Serc necklace inside her gown's neckline, then knotted her gown at the waist. Daniel whirled to Lulah.

"Show us the engine, now!"

Jensen glanced back at him, eyes wide.

"What's up?"

"Trouble. Engine. *Now!*"

Jensen didn't hesitate. He swiveled to High Nessa Katohna.

Kassie Keegan

"Permission to leave the Bridge. If Daniel says there's trouble, there's trouble."

High Nessa Katohna responded quickly.

"Granted. Get them what they need. Stealth and Jovian, stay with them."

High Nessa Katohna looked over at her Lio and took in the state of affairs with a glance.

"Raiida and Rahimi remain with me. Lulah and Latah go with them. Ferrand, work with Léandre, he's become catatonic. Travar, med kit. Cassian, take Jensen's Pilot Station."

The Lio Nel Pilot spoke up.

"Altitude frozen! Comms disengaged."

Prime Cassian leaped to the empty Pilot's chair as Jensen ran to Daniel and Aubrey.

"This way!"

Chapter 40
Daniel

The Engine Bay was stark white with blue markings. Access panels were strategically placed in the enormous cylinder that encased the turbine of the turbo engine.

Daniel didn't hide his profound sense of urgency.

"We have little time."

Aubrey put her hands on the cylinder and closed her eyes. He watched her, his palms itching to touch it, too. She opened her eyes, her voice sharp.

"Daniel, I think we can do this together! Focus!"

He stopped ignoring his instincts and joined her. As Daniel touched the engine's cylinder he felt the hum of Aubrey's talent speak to him, similar to when they communicated during their Call to Mate.

Her frequency flowed across and through the engine, seeking its block. And she found it, like she could see with x-ray vision into the workings of the moving engine. He gasped at the new level of perception. When he took his hands off the cylinder, he lost the vision. Aubrey cried out frantically.

"Do you see it?"

Kassie Keegan

He put his hands back and perceived again with their combined talents.

"Yes!"

"I have to stay here. It's the best place to follow the flow! Remove the disruptor, Daniel!"

Jovian was at Daniel's side with tools, ready to assist.

"Where is it? Take me there."

He followed Aubrey's flow with his hands, skimming the cylinder until he hit a low access panel deep under the rear of the engine in a tight, almost hidden space.

"It's here, Jovian."

He stayed put with his eyes closed, concentrating his senses on Aubrey's flow, hearing the whir of tools, then the access panel falling to the floor with a metallic clang. Jovian's voice sounded muffled.

"Where?"

He shouted.

"To the left! Search for a blankness. A lack of light."

Jovian called out.

"Tools!"

Jensen dropped and slithered under the engine, grabbing the tool tray. They moved quickly and efficiently, handing tools back-and-forth with barely a word. Suddenly, the engine's energy raced forward into a smooth, easy flow that made Daniel's muscles relax in relief.

Jovian emerged with a bulbous piece of equipment covered with wired electrodes. A classic disruptor, easily programmable, and difficult to trace. Daniel noticed he smoothly, stealthily slipped something inside his ever-present tech-bag.

Jovian and Jensen crawled out of the tight space as Aubrey rounded the corner. They gazed at each other, eyes holding the knowledge that someone had sabotaged them. Everyone on board had been slated to die.

Daniel had one more thing to check.

"Check comms."

Comms were open again. They had not been Pulsed.

Jovian opened his arms and both Aubrey and Daniel stepped into his embrace, with Stealth coming in behind Aubrey. They held each other as it sunk in that they had come close to dying, but survived.

Latah and Lulah hugged Jensen. They broke apart, needing to show everyone what they found.

Daniel patted Jensen on the shoulder. Jensen spun, grabbing Daniel up into a hug, which Daniel answered with a tight grip of his own.

"Daniel. I thought I protected you. I'm so, so sorry. I know now, it makes no difference. I'm sorry."

He examined Jensen's face, lined with sorrow and pain. His friend suffered, and he didn't understand why. They would talk.

"Soon."

Jensen agreed as they separated. They were a somber group walking to the Bridge.

Daniel glimpsed Ferrand and Léandre as they rounded the corner. Ferrand had wrapped himself around Léandre, who lay against him facing out, gripping Ferrand's arms like a lifeline. Léandre watched the entrance leading to the Engine Bay like he was dying by slow degrees. Ferrand gazed at the entrance with blazing hope.

When Léandre saw them, tears welled up and dripped unheeded down his cheeks. Aubrey hurried to him, crawling into his lap to be enfolded in his and Ferrand's arms. Ferrand whispered in Léandre's ear, his face strained.

"See. I told you they would come. I told you this was different. We're alive. Our Mates are alive."

Kassie Keegan

Daniel went to Léandre, who peered up at him, his golden eyes holding unspoken knowledge and scalding pain.

I need to ease my Mate.

"We found a disruptor. It's okay now."

He swept his thumbs across Léandre's cheeks, drying his tears. Léandre accepted his words, but didn't seem eased.

Daniel moved to Ferrand, wrapping his arms around Ferrand's shoulders as he held his Mates close, bringing Ferrand's head to his chest so he could hear Daniel's heartbeat and feel the proof of his Honored Mate's care. Ferrand closed his eyes, burrowing closer, needing the touches and comfort.

He stood there for long moments, stroking Ferrand's silky mane as he listened to Jovian and Jensen explain what they had done and what they had found.

The Transport now functioned properly, and they were on course to arrive soon at Bon'Fiel PrideHome. High Nessa Katohna broke the silence.

"Sabotage. *Again.*"

The words fell like lead weights, full of implications Daniel was much too tired to deal with. He suspected his Mates felt the same.

"It's undeniable. This, after all that happened with the Call to Mate, is no coincidence. It would have been a crippling blow to Bon'Fiel Pride. High Nessa, Prime, Commander. Plus, our newly Mated Shaktah, with an Honored Nel of talent in high regard with the Crown Family. Then there's our highest level Security Officers and best Tech and Intelligence personnel. It might have taken two generations to recover from this hit."

High Nessa Katohna focused on Aubrey and Daniel.

"Aubrey. Daniel. Thank you. Thank you for listening to your instincts and saving our lives."

She swiveled to Jovian and Jensen.

"Thank you for helping them."

Low growls and stomps of appreciation sounded around the Bridge. Aubrey took Daniel's hand. It had been another close call they survived by working together and communicating.

Prime Cassian asked a simple question.

"Who?"

Jovian was thinking.

"Bon'Rocinal seems most obvious with Aubrey's recent Challenge Win against Judge Hulin. She would have had the clearance to sabotage our Mating, too, with access to the Catacombs."

Ferrand cut in.

"And they are still angry about the hundred year span Liani Combat ban."

What?

Prime Cassian explained without being asked.

"It occurred because of bad-faith Mate Challenges on Lio Fleet Kahlina for my grandparents, along with Travar's and Stealth's grandparents. The Training ban ended twenty year spans ago, but the Bon'Rocinal, Bon'Tecol, and Bon'Retal Prides are still woefully unskilled in hand-to-hand combat, and full of resentment for it."

"True…"

Daniel sensed Jovian's hesitation.

"But?"

Jovian regarded him, his thoughts heavy.

"But it's too obvious with the 'Rocinals. Too clear. I don't trust it. But I don't put this above them either."

High Nessa Katohna was decisive.

"I agree. We move forward with caution. We will not travel together like this again. No need to give them such a perfect target."

Ferrand's tuft stroked Daniel's leg as he moved to sit down. Ferrand had been thinking, too, his voice clear and strong when he spoke.

"We will check the Palace feeds and see if they caught anyone around the Transport, but I doubt we will discover anything."

Ferrand paused for a moment, his next words seeming pulled out of him.

"There are many similarities to the Transport crash Léandre and I lived through. The vibration felt familiar. We can only speculate about what happened with Jovian's family, but if this was sabotage…"

Ferrand closed his eyes and swallowed. When he opened his eyes, his face was stoic, his emotions buried deep.

"We should assume other strategically damaging 'accidents' in the past were potentially sabotage, too. We need to keep this quiet as we investigate."

High Nessa Katohna scratched her chin thoughtfully.

"Yes, we keep this quiet. Whoever did this can think their equipment malfunctioned. Meanwhile, perhaps they will make a mistake."

Everyone agreed.

"Raiida and Rahimi, we need more Security Teams."

Raiida thought for a moment.

"Kian's Coalition with Shiro Takeo and Marrok are rotating in. They've got a newly-boosted Honored Nel. He's their Coalition Brethren, and he has potential. Former Galactic Military, too."

High Nessa Katohna grinned.

"Excellent! Have Aubrey and Daniel meet them. If there's camaraderie, put them with Prime Cassian sharing Commons. I want a Security Team close to them. Janna, our Lead Honored, will be quite pleased her grandson Shiro Takeo is back at Bon'Fiel PrideHome. Everyone likes it when she is happy."

The twin sisters all agreed enthusiastically.

This Janna must be scary when she's unhappy. Guess I'll be meeting her grandson, too.

"Who else?"

Lulah spoke up this time.

"Bhaven's Coalition is available soon. Taryn has finished recovering from the thing that happened. Azhar's still fucked-up about it. He's moody, but his instincts and skills are sharp as ever."

"Put them with the Seconds."

"But their Pod already has six families."

"Send Tusse on assignment in the Capital. We have work for her and her Harem to do now."

"Yes, High Nessa Katohna."

"Cassian, Ila-Abassa Sarina is meeting us at PrideHome later. Send her to me as soon as you can. I must apprise her of what occurred."

"Yes, High Nessa."

"Any thoughts Prime Cassian?"

"Yes. Considering these events, I don't think Prime Bastian's disappearance was his going to the Fade. There have been too many dangers heaped upon our Pride and Pride Mates for me to believe it."

Daniel could feel the thoughts churning in everyone's mind about it. He knew nothing about what happened, but he sensed the danger to Prime Cassian, and he didn't like it.

Prime Cassian stood, giving Jensen his Pilot seat back. He went to Travar and Stealth, hugging them close before sitting on the cushion between them.

Kassie Keegan

Latah handed Jovian a cloth to wrap the bulbous disruptor in. He grabbed Ferrand's colorful satchel and carefully placed the disruptor within, keeping the satchel close to his side as he sat next to Daniel. securing himself in with his Shield.

It was time to go home.

Chapter 41
Daniel

Daniel's first sight of Bon'Fiel PrideHome would stay with him forever.

It was an enormously tall cylinder with discs appearing offset at the base and stacked on each other at the top with lots of gleaming, sun-reflecting glass.

Bon'Fiel PrideHome perched on a mountain peak halfway up a mountainous plateau with views of Capital Maituri in the distance. Sunlight bathed the PrideHome, surrounded by high meadows filled with trees, vines, flowers, and growing things on either side. A shimmering waterfall splashed into an oasis below.

Their landing, which was close to the Grand Entry of Bon'Fiel Pride-Home, was uneventful.

Jensen and his Lio Nel Pilot companion, Piron, would take High Nessa Katohna's Transport to a remote Hangar for a complete overhaul. They would not allow another sabotage of her Transport.

The group was quiet as they readied to disembark. Daniel swirled his Chalel over Aubrey, securing it on her shoulder. Ferrand and Léandre stood in a hug with Jovian. Then they separated and centered themselves into a more relaxed demeanor.

Kassie Keegan

Daniel called out to Jensen, who was working steadily at his Station.

"We will talk soon."

Jensen gave him a thumbs up.

Raiida and Rahimi took point with their sisters, Latah and Lulah, following at the rear, their companions taking up positions like they had going through Capital Maituri's Palace hallways. High Nessa Katohna followed the twins, Travar and Stealth flanking him and Aubrey, followed closely behind by their Coalition.

However, this time, those Lio walking on the edges of the group held out their hands to be touched by their Bon'Fiel Pride Mates as they passed. Only Daniel, Aubrey, and Léandre, who walked between Jovian and Ferrand, were untouched as they passed through the Grand Entry of Bon'Fiel PrideHome.

The center of Bon'Fiel PrideHome's Grand Entry shone like a stem made from light. It arched over their heads and opened to huge windows, and a domed ceiling formed with what seemed like glass.

Immense trees and vines grew in swaths throughout the vast open space. It smelled fresh and alive, and it dug into Daniel's heart with a welcome all its own. Aubrey squeezed his hand.

"It's beautiful, isn't it?"

He breathed his answer in amazement as his gaze explored everywhere while they kept moving.

"Yes."

"I'm still not used to it."

Daniel glanced over at Aubrey, and she smiled at him.

Now that *is a pretty view.*

He smiled back.

"Where are we going?"

She laughed.

"I don't know."

He kissed her hand.

"We will find out together."

They went to a large comm-activated lift, walked in, and swooshed to the top floor. There, they walked through a beautiful open-air park filled with trees, plants, and flowers featuring two huge pools of water with tinkling fountains where Lio and Honored sunned and swam.

The group followed Prime Cassian and Travar to an entrance off the park. There were distinctively beautiful flowering vines growing around the entryway. Daniel wondered who lived there.

Prime Cassian pivoted to them, posture alert and happy.

"Welcome to your new home."

Oh! I get to live here?

They stepped into a large room of warm, neutral colors. There was a long, low-slung, curved couch with tables and chairs near it in the center. On the far edge was a circular food prep area and an extended bar with tables and chairs made of exotic, light-colored wood.

What really captured Daniel's attention was the tree growing up through a tall, round opening at the side of the room. He broke off from the group to inspect the tree while Ferrand and Jovian went their separate ways, too.

Aubrey and Léandre wandered with him. He stared over at her in amazement.

"This is so great! We get to live with living things!"

She grinned back at him.

"Yes! It's wonderful, isn't it?"

A high-pitched purr, then a squeak sounded. There, high in the tree, was a tiny creature staring at him, bent low on a branch above his head.

Kassie Keegan

Daniel recognized the two coal-black eyes, the narrow snout with a tiny, twitching pink bead for a nose. The little guy's reddish-brown, woolly coat gleamed warmly in the sun, his long striped tail wrapped firmly around a branch. The high ears with red wispy tufts at the ends wiggled at him.

"Is that you, little fella?"

The little creature kept peering at him, his adorable nose twitching. Its eyes blinked.

"Remember me? I'm Daniel, little guy."

The creature gave another high-pitched purr, sat up, and preened its small face with its tiny three-fingered hands. He chuckled at the familiarity of the gesture.

"He's definitely the one!"

He looked around.

"Where's his friends, the Priti Sawat Azure?"

Ferrand returned and came over, peering up at the creature, who looked down at them, completely unafraid.

"This little Dharmik comes and goes as he pleases. Priti Sawat Azure is close. All is well."

Ferrand slid in behind Daniel, pulling him into a hug, facing out with his beefy arm crossing Daniel's chest. He spoke in Daniel's ear, causing shivers at the caress of breath over his sensitive flesh.

"Do you like the place?"

He glanced back over his shoulder at Ferrand, then over to Léandre, and a freshly returned Jovian. They wrapped themselves around Aubrey while watching his reactions.

"I absolutely love it!"

Ferrand's wide grin made him smile, too, as he faced forward again. Prime Cassian revealed part of why Ferrand was so pleased.

"In our PrideHome, each Pod has a Common Room, or Commons, surrounded by six private living quarters with private personal spaces above. Ferrand designed the Common Room, your living quarters, and the Private Offices."

Daniel and Aubrey gasped, scanning the Common Room with astonished eyes. Aubrey's gaze settled on Ferrand affectionately.

"You are a male of many talents, aren't you?"

He couldn't see Ferrand's face, but Aubrey blushed, so Ferrand must have shown a sexually sizzling expression.

"Many, many talents, Aubrey. I will enjoy showing them to you and our Mates."

Ferrand's comment made him join her in blushing, his nerves tingling with a low buzz of anticipation.

He glanced over, noticing Prime Cassian holding Stealth's hand while a happy-looking Travar snuggled tight under Stealth's arm.

"We share the Commons with your family. See there?"

Prime Cassian pointed to the right.

"That's our living quarters."

Prime Cassian paused, bringing Stealth and Travar into his embrace before licking up Stealth's neck with a grooming stroke.

Stealth's eyes closed at the caress, ears flicking in pleasure. When hiss eyes opened, he peered over at them with a sweet, shy happiness that made his heart melt for them. Travar practically vibrated with joy.

"I'd like you to be among the first to know Stealth agreed to join our Coalition."

Aubrey whooped enthusiastically.

"Go Stealth!"

They all laughed in the delight of the moment. Prime Cassian pointed directly ahead of them.

Kassie Keegan

"That's your living quarters. We will introduce you to the others we share Commons with later."

My living quarters. With my Mates.

His senses tingled harder. Rotating, he brought Ferrand's head down for a kiss, enjoying the enticing press of their bodies together. Velvet fur, soft facial hair, and gentle fingers caressing his back all added to the swell of sensation. Ferrand's flavor burst on his tongue, igniting a deep, aching craving for his Mates. Their lips separated with a slow lick of Ferrand's tongue along his lower lip.

"Ferrand, take me there."

He growled his agreement.

"Ferrand. Take me, there."

This time, he growled long and low with desire.

He picked Daniel up, wrapping his legs around his waist, swelling shafts pressed together, taking him to their rooms. Léandre did the same to a flushed Aubrey.

Ferrand and Léandre took them to a room full of peaceful beauty in warm earth-tones and cream colors with lush, green vines growing along the far wall. They lovingly put them down so they could wander.

Bending to remove Daniel and Aubreys' sandals, Jovian placed them near the entry. Léandre, Ferrand, and Jovian removed their Bandels, putting them on pegs by the entry, also scuffing off their sandals. Jovian smoothly took Aubrey's Serc necklace, hanging it beside their Bandels. It looked like a place of honor, which made Daniel smile.

He loved how well he and Aubrey fit into their Lio Coalition's quarters, their belongings easily fitting with their Mate's things. He looked around with wonder.

An enormous bed with rounded edges and a comfortable-looking padded backrest dominated one side of the room, seeming like it floated above the floor. Pillows and cushions of all shapes and sizes, covered with soft fabrics in tranquil colors, were strewn across the bed. It didn't surprise him to see insta-dry cloths stacked on a corner of the backrest.

On the wall behind the bed, there were long lengths of thin, cream-colored rope knotted to a frame and left hanging down. Beside the bed, recessed openings and exposed pegs held belongings, some of them open and available.

Daniel recognized his duffle placed along the wall next to a huge covered basket he suspected held Aubrey's things. Jovian took Daniel's Chalel off Aubrey and hung it up as they continued to look around.

Léandre activated the Solaray. From the happy sighs and growls, everyone felt refreshed.

Suddenly, Stealth stalked into the room, holding a pillow. He threw his pillow on the couch, then threw himself on it, rolling over to give them his back. He was still in guard-mode, but obviously did not need to protect Aubrey from her Coalition. Aubrey's tone was mild and a bit amused.

"Hey, Stealth. Nap time?"

He sighed and growled sleepily.

"Shumal is tired. No pestering. It's been a long night and a stressful day."

Tell me about it! At least Aubrey and I got some rest earlier. Poor guy.

It took but moments before Stealth relaxed completely and clearly rested.

Aubrey and Daniel continued to explore. There was a built-in table running along the opposite wall with a holo-vid screen. Trinkets and tools lay strewn throughout the room, little things, reflecting the person-alities of the Lio who lived there.

Draped in overlapping swaths on the ceiling were lengths of colorful fabric fluttering gently from a breeze flowing in from their private open-air balcony. An activated privacy field with sound dampeners let in light and air, but no one could see or hear those inside their quarters. Aubrey spoke with wonder.

"Hey, I remember this fabric! Léandre, didn't we have a picnic on it? And this one, too!"

She stared at Léandre, who grinned.

"You kept all of them?"

He went to her, giving her a soft kiss. Ferrand reached inside the colorful satchel, pulling out the shimmery golden fabric Abassa Sarina covered him and Aubrey with after they first Mated.

He climbed on the bed, reaching high, adding the fabric to an attachment point, then draping it across the space to another attachment point. The golden fabric now graced the ceiling above their bed.

Perfect!

Ferrand leaped down and grabbed the satchel, setting it next to an elaborately decorated box. He took out the dress Aubrey wore for their MateDance from the satchel and put it inside the box reverentially. Then, he added a handful of insta-dry cloths and the fabric which had wrapped their Mate Tribute Rings.

He put Daniel's folded clothes from last night to the side, along with Daniel's soft traveling clothes.

When he pulled out an insta-dry cloth with a ribbon folded in it, Ferrand gazed at Daniel, giving it a deep sniff, watching him with heated awareness, placing it on top of Daniel's pile of belongings with a sexy smile.

Creator, my gorgeous Commander makes me hot.

Ferrand rummaged in the satchel a little before bringing out a handful of glowing blue petals that appeared to be from Priti Sawat Azure, where Daniel and Aubrey had first kissed.

Jovian snuggled Aubrey and Daniel close as they all watched Ferrand.

"He went and got those after you both said, 'rest well.'"

Ferrand glanced back at them warmly, seeming to wait for more things to put into the box.

"He and Léandre are sentimental."

Léandre pulled Jovian's beard affectionately and walked over to a piece of random-looking tech, bringing it over for Aubrey to see, his eyes alight with mischief. She obviously recognized it.

"Hey! This is the first little thing we fixed together, isn't it? I thought Nasma needed it!"

Jovian chuckled at being called out so well by Léandre, who placed the little piece back where it had been.

"Yeah, well, she received a new one, and I kept this one because *you* touched it and we spent time together. We are all sentimental, huh?"

Léandre pulled Daniel over to him while Jovian untied Aubrey's gown where she had knotted it. Ferrand spoke, his voice deep, getting their attention.

"We need to add a few things to our mementos."

Ferrand untied his golden sarong, unwrapping it from around his hips, folding it, and putting it in the box. He pivoted so Aubrey and Daniel could see him easily.

Ferrand's balls were furred and large, his unsheathed length was thickly erect. Daniel couldn't take his eyes off it.

When soft, a Lio Nels' upturned sheath entirely covered and protected their shaft. But when hard, their erection emerged, and the sheath pulled back, out of the way.

Ferrand's hard cock was thick and long, its crown longer and more cone-shaped than a human's erection. However, the color and texture were truly different.

Ferrand's shaft had smooth gleaming skin the same dark-gold color as his fur, but there were small, intriguing darker-gold nubs in patterns across the top and sides, leaving the underside smooth. Daniel

Kassie Keegan

wanted to touch it. Experience its similarities and differences to his own body.

Then Jovian began kissing Aubrey. There were so many tantalizing things to see, he wasn't sure where to go or what to do. When Jovian lingeringly ended the kiss, he untied his sarong, unwrapping it.

Jovian's unsheathed golden yellow cock was deliciously long and hard, with dark-gold nubs in a different pattern than Ferrand's.

Jovian gave his sarong to Ferrand and went in for more kisses with Aubrey while their hands roamed each other's bodies.

Léandre took Daniel's head in his hands, bringing their lips together in a passionate kiss, stroking the insides of his wrists over Daniel's neck, shoulders, and arms, marking him with his scent.

Reveling in the kiss, Daniel ran his tongue along Léandre's fangs. His hands stroked Léandre's firmly-muscled, softly-furred body while Léandre explored him with a tingle-inducing touch. When Léandre pulled back, he licked his own fang for Daniel with his long, flexible tongue. Daniel's stomach tightened with need.

Oh, what he can do with his tongue.

Léandre grabbed Daniel's hand, bringing it up under his sarong, dragging Daniel's hand from his full, furred balls up to grasp his erection, watching his face with pleasured satisfaction.

Daniel explored Léandre's hot, silky hardness, touching a textured Lio shaft for the first time. Léandre untied and unwrapped his sarong, handing it back to Ferrand, revealing the beautiful, thick cock his hand explored.

Léandre wrapped his hand around Daniel's, gripping his length. Léandre's golden eyes blazed as he softly squeezed Daniel's hand around himself. Daniel understood Léandre.

"This cock is yours."

He whispered.

"Mine."

Léandre buried his hands in Daniel's hair, bringing their mouths together for another deep kiss while Daniel continued to caress Léandre's hard, hot shaft.

They both panted when Léandre leisurely untied Daniel's sarong, unwrapping it, then handed it to Ferrand, who folded it neatly, putting it in the box.

Léandre peered down at Daniel's erection, making him look, too. He petted Daniel's hardness with soft, caressing strokes, making him throb with arousal. Daniel used his free hand to put Léandre's hand firmly around himself and moaned at the pleasure as they held each other's cocks this way.

They enjoyed more passionate kisses. Léandre finally dragged away from their kisses to lead Daniel to the bed, his high, hard erection swinging heavily as he walked.

Léandre crawled up on the bed with Daniel, settling with him against the cushioned backrest, so they both had a splendid view of the room while they caressed each other.

Laying back, Daniel felt like a King with his Harem, all his fantasies about to come true.

Chapter 42
Aubrey

Ferrand approached Aubrey from behind, stroking gentle hands down her arms. She pulled away from her delicious kisses with Jovian to give him her attention.

Ferrand's voice was husky and deep, his heavy arousal echoing her own as his fingers toyed with the silky fabric of her gown.

"May I have this for my Box of Treasures?"

She consented. Jovian and Ferrand whisked the gown off her with a flourish, leaving her completely bare to her Mates. Jovian's hands settled back on her hips, his admiring gaze devouring her.

Ferrand turned, folding the long gown neatly, placing it lovingly with his collection of mementos.

She peered around Jovian's shoulder at Daniel and Léandre who were lounging decadently together up on the bed. Their eyes avidly roamed over her body, partially blocked by Jovian. They obviously wanted to see more by the way they moved their necks for better angles.

Ferrand returned to her, pressing her back against him, letting her feel the steely strength of his muscles covered in soft fur while his hot, hard, naked erection nestled into her lower back. She shivered, her senses overwhelmed with the resonant humming impact of his body flush with hers.

He looked down at her bare form over her shoulder. Bending, he licked her neck and rumbled in her ear.

"You are beautiful, Aubrey."

He reached around her to caress her breasts with his huge hands, adjusting their positions slightly so Daniel and Léandre had a better view. Jovian brought her attention to him with a gentle kiss.

"Gorgeous."

He kissed his way down her neck to her breasts while his hands roamed everywhere, leaving tingling trails of aroused awareness everywhere he touched. Ferrand held her breasts plumped up for Jovian, her hard tips inviting him to taste.

Jovian gazed at them like they were the best present he ever received. He swiped the soft end of his tongue across Aubrey's tender peak, making her suck in her breath at the sensation. Heat pooled in her belly.

He blew his breath across where he licked her, causing her nipples to harden more. She moaned, her hips moving restlessly, seeking.

I'm going to combust!

Jovian sucked her turgid tip into his hot mouth, laving it with his tongue. She arched, leaning back harder into Ferrand.

He switched breasts, hands on her hips, bringing her attention to the pulsing motions she couldn't control. Ferrand gently pinched the moistened peak Jovian had teased, making her cry out at the twin points of stimulation.

Jovian pulled off her breast with a smack and grinned wickedly as he kissed his way down her body. He settled himself comfortably on his knees at her feet, his tail swishing excitedly side-to-side.

Aubrey glanced over and saw Léandre licking and pinching Daniel's nipples in tandem with Jovian and Ferrand, causing Daniel to writhe on the bed. His pearlescent aura glowed a little brighter as he tried to hold back his moans, but she wanted to hear them.

Am I holding back? Is he echoing my response?

Realization struck her.

I don't need to repress my response. Let's open up together, Daniel.

Intentionally opening up her mind and heart to her Mates intensified her perceptions of their vibrant hums. Aubrey could sense the Resonance of their fierce emotions and consuming arousal, and it compounded her excitement.

When Aubrey felt Jovian's hot breath near her most private place, she released the eager moan she'd resisted as she watched Daniel being licked and stroked by Léandre. It aroused her higher to see her Mates pleasured, too.

Ferrand changed his grip on her, crossing one beefy arm over her chest, grabbing a breast in his hand while his other hand steadied her hip. Jovian raised her leg, draping it over his shoulder, and dove into her like he was starving.

Aubrey yelped in surprise at Jovian's first soft stroke along her seam. He spread her for his tongue and delved in. This time, she groaned, closing her eyes while she bent forward in reaction to the new sensations Jovian gave her. Her hands buried deep in Jovian's beautiful blond waves, grateful for her Mates' support.

I wondered what this would feel like.

His mouth was never still, licking and sucking everywhere, growling his enjoyment of her flavor.

It's wonderful!

Reaching up high into her, his long tongue stroked a sensitive spot that made her pant.

He pulled his tongue out of her with a slow, tender stroke and gave a perfect, gentle swipe to her clit, making her gasp and jerk. He did it again, making her moan.

He continued his ravishing assault on her clit as she moaned rawly in the grip of her Mates, her head tossing at the overwhelming sensations.

He's going to make me come.

Aubrey's inclination was to fight the build, but Ferrand and Jovian tightened their holds on her. The reverberating hum of their blistering sexual focus stole her mind.

Ferrand spoke to her, his voice deep, sexy, and reassuring.

"Don't fight the pleasure, Aubrey. Give it all to us. Give yourself."

The words, combined with an additional pressure at her slick entrance, then a thick push into her was all she needed. Aubrey gave herself over to the sweeping ecstasy, moaning low, her body undulating with the waves of it as Jovian licked her through her peak.

He growled contentedly as the thick pressure went away and he leaned in, lapping up the cream of her pleasure with his wonderful, flexible tongue, diving deep.

Aubrey opened her eyes, peering down at Jovian as he sat back on his haunches, licking his lips. His piercing blue and gold eyes glowed with carnal enjoyment.

"I love your cunt, Aubrey, and your cream."

She gasped at his graphic words. He grinned wickedly, kissing the small velvety patch of hair she had at the apex of her mound. Jovian's drenched sabah, hard and exposed, glistened with her cream.

His sabah was inside me!

She gushed again, gasping as Ferrand spun her, lifting her so her legs wrapped around his waist. Her hot, wet, needy core landed on the hard column of his shaft.

Ferrand held her tight against him, his huge hands supporting her hips, thighs, and flanks, both of them groaning at the heated press. He spoke deep and commanding.

"Jovian, stand."

Jovian rose, dragging his firm, velvety torso up along her rear and back, settling his hard cock against her rear.

"Give us your sabah."

She heard Jovian hum his anticipation as he brought his sabah between them.

"Aubrey, taste."

Staring into Ferrand's eyes, she tasted her own cream, licking Jovian's sabah from base to crown. Jovian moaned, pulsing his erection rhythmically on her while rubbing his chin across the top of her shoulder.

Sensually beguiled, Ferrand used the soft tip of his tongue to also lick Jovian's sabah with pure enjoyment. Jovian's moans became long and drawn out as Ferrand sucked all of Jovian's sabah in his mouth, laving it clean of Aubrey's juices.

Pulling off the sabah, Ferrand gave it a tiny kiss before looking deep into Aubrey's eyes, speaking in low, aroused tones.

"I want your cunt, too, Aubrey. May I have it?"

A new gush readied her for Ferrand's hard length. She wrapped her arms tighter around his neck and leaned toward his ear.

"Yes, Ferrand, my sensuous Commander. You may have my... cunt."

As soon as she gave her consent, Ferrand made a deeply aroused growl. He lifted her hips to a new angle and began filling her without hesitation, her eyes widening as she stretched open for him, his stroke smooth and steady.

When Ferrand was about midway, Aubrey tightened on him, causing him to grunt, then groan. He stopped, letting her adjust. Aubrey panted, eyes widening further when Jovian dropped and spread her cheeks.

He began licking and kissing her back entrance enthusiastically, swiping his fingers around Ferrand's embedded cock, gathering up Aubrey's cream. His thick, moistened finger pulsed against her tiny hole, making her tighten further on Ferrand, who growled again as he nuzzled her neck.

Jovian nipped her butt cheek, the surprise loosening her enough for his finger to breech her entrance smoothly. He pushed and pulled shallowly inside her, using circular motions that made her gasp.

The amazing, distracting sensations caused her to unclench, so Ferrand slid home with a deep, satisfied growl. Jovian slipped his finger out of her and kissed her butt cheek where he'd nipped her.

Standing up, Jovian whispered in her ear, his voice deep and enticing.

"You keep taking Ferrand's virginity while Léandre and I suck off Daniel for the first time."

Aubrey groaned and gushed at his words. Ferrand gripped her rear tighter in his massive hands, pulling his hips back, slow and gentle. He pushed back in harder.

Ferrand is inside my body like he is inside my heart!

He pulled back slow again, then pushed in hard and fast.

On the bed, Daniel moaned with pleasure.

Ferrand pushed into her with firm, steady strokes, making her moan and clench on his length. He kept up his strokes, pivoting so she could see what was happening on the bed.

She loved the carnality of the scene.

Daniel stretched out on his back, eyes riveted to her and Ferrand, mouth open on his moans as his back arched and hands fisted in the linens beneath him. Jovian and Léandre held Daniel's cock straight up so they could lick its length unobstructed.

When Daniel realized he had Aubrey and Ferrand's attention, he moaned low and long, prompting Jovian to take the crown of his cock in his mouth. Daniel cried out in orgasm as Jovian's throat worked, drinking his cream, while Léandre bathed Daniel's balls with his tongue, enticing him to continue coming.

Ferrand and Aubrey both groaned at the sight. She turned to Ferrand, eyes wide with her overwhelming arousal.

"I'm going to come!"

He pounded up hard into her as she shouted her peak and he roared his, filling her over and over with his thick cock, pumping her full of his nectar, ecstasy dancing throughout her body.

Aubrey hummed with energy as heat bloomed from Ferrand's nectar, bringing a second wave of bliss that made her cry out. He whispered praise in her ear as she rode him through her second peak.

"So beautiful in your pleasure, so sweet. Take it all. Own it. Own me, my Mate. So fucking beautiful!"

"Abah-Sah, help me! Does that happen every time you come, Ferrand?"

"I look forward to finding out."

"Me, too!"

Chapter 43
Aubrey

Ferrand kissed Aubrey while walking her to the bed where their Mates waited for them. He pushed her down onto her back, giving her his weight by degrees.

She loved Ferrand's bulk on her as he nuzzled her neck, giving her tender kisses. He spoke softly, glancing over at Daniel, making sure he had Daniel's attention, too.

"Aubrey and Daniel, Ha-Abassa Sarina has arrived."

They looked at each other and made to sit up.

"No. No, don't move. She requires nothing of you. Nothing changes, nothing stops."

Aubrey heard his hint of amusement as he returned his gaze to her.

"She meditates beside the couch Stealth is currently pretending to sleep on."

Ferrand spoke more seriously, his voice deep, soft, and compelling.

"We continue our Mating and complete our MateBond while Witnessed by a Pride Official and your Shumal, to protect you as Protocol demands."

Kassie Keegan

He kissed her with loving gentleness, then gave his gaze to Daniel, who was soothingly caressed by Jovian and Léandre.

"Please accept this aspect of Lio culture and bestow the Honor of Witnessing upon Ha-Abassa Sarina and Savion Pon'Salel."

Daniel took a slow, thoughtful breath, turning to Jovian for a warm kiss, then to Léandre, who gave Daniel a salacious kiss. When Daniel looked back at Ferrand, he spoke breathlessly.

"I accept."

Léandre reclaimed Daniel's lips.

Ferrand peered down at Aubrey, still inside her body, and buried indelibly in her heart.

"I accept, Ferrand."

He rewarded her with a slow, lush, melting kiss. She panted when Ferrand lifted, regarding her with respect and affection.

"Are you ready for me to pull out?"

Oh, Abah-Sah, this male is so amazing! Giving so much, showing such care.

She petted his cheeks, caressing him lovingly, gazing into his gorgeous light-green eyes.

"I love you, Ferrand."

He smiled sweetly and kissed her tenderly.

"I know, my beauty. I love you, too. You knew this, yes?"

Aubrey knew Ferrand loved her for a long time, and she felt glad she could finally tell him she returned his love. She kissed him with her entire heart as he growled his joy. After, Ferrand smiled while carefully pulling out and away.

Léandre and Daniel pounced on her, petting, kissing, and licking everything they could reach.

She peered down as they each plumped up a breast and gazed at each other over her body. They stared into each other's eyes as they gave her tips lusciously lingering licks, making her gasp and moan.

They licked more, bending closer to suck her nipples. The combination of a thick, velvet tongue on one hard peak and a soft, flexible tongue tip on the other was mind-blowing.

Needy again, she groaned with desire.

Ferrand sat on his haunches between her legs, pulling his tail forward, getting their attention. Everyone paused, riveted, as he removed his Serc, pushed his tuft back and down and secured it with the Serc. Ferrand's sabah emerged gradually, a dark-gold, nub-studded column of flesh made for pleasure.

Daniel whispered.

"Beautiful."

Ferrand growled his extreme arousal as he presented his tail to Aubrey, who grasped it gently, bringing his sabah close to her mouth. Jovian positioned himself at Ferrand's side, watching her as he spoke, Ferrand groaning at his words.

"When they lick and suck your sabah, Ferrand, you will release hard. I've been looking forward to tasting your nectar."

Daniel and Léandre slid up higher at her sides, leaning in so they could share Ferrand's sabah with her, waiting for her to give the first lick. She knew their hot breath tantalized Ferrand's sensitive, vulnerable sabah as he growled in anticipation.

Jovian locked eyes with Aubrey in sensual agreement as he bent low over Ferrand's throbbing shaft.

I want you to remember this, Ferrand. How we love and desire you.

Jovian flicked his tongue at her in a lascivious gesture that made her gush warmth. Aubrey winked at Jovian, then lifted her gaze to scrutinize Ferrand. She opened her mouth and licked his waiting sabah

Kassie Keegan

slowly, lingeringly, reveling in the unique tastes and textures of her big, strong, generous Mate.

She sensed Jovian mimicking her stroke and pace on Ferrand's thick cock. Ferrand didn't come, showing tremendous restraint, but he growled in agonized pleasure.

Daniel and Léandre joined her in lushly licking Ferrand's sabah, their tongues enjoying each other's flavors as they tasted his flesh.

Jovian had Ferrand's pointed crown in his mouth, moving in a circular motion as he, too, pleasured Ferrand.

It was all Ferrand could take. He released with a roar, his body curved forward, his muscles straining, showing in bold relief under his fur. His eyes closed, ears flattening as he pulsed into Jovian's mouth with small, controlled movements of his hips that went on and on.

Jovian swallowed fast and deep.

When Ferrand finally stopped coming, his ears came up, and he relaxed forward on his hands and knees. Jovian pulled off Ferrand's cock, appearing drugged from his nectar, watching Aubrey with heavily lidded eyes.

He knows I'm not done with Ferrand.

She took Ferrand's still throbbingly erect sabah and brought it to her core. Ferrand watched her ferally, breathing deep and fast, anticipation clear as he licked his fangs.

She pushed Ferrand's sabah into herself as Jovian capped Ferrand's cock again with his mouth just as Ferrand bent and sucked Léandre's crown into his mouth, moaning with abandon as he did so.

Léandre tensed, his face frozen for a moment of beautiful surprised bliss, transforming into rapture as he released into Ferrand's mouth, his lips open on a silent roar. Léandre's hips pulsed with the power of his orgasm, while Ferrand gave a second load to Jovian.

They collapsed to their sides together in the aftermath.

Savage Planet Embrace

Aubrey swept her gaze over her Lio Mates as they lay in a panting pile, their breaths churning in raspy gasps.

This is my favorite thing, seeing my Mates give and receive pleasure.

She pulled Ferrand's sabah out, her core tingling.

Daniel took it from her grasp, then sucked and licked Aubrey's cream off Ferrand's sabah with delicate fervor, savoring each lingering, cream-coated lick.

Ferrand and Léandre reached for each other, sharing a Lio kiss, which was all lips and licks, their fangs prohibiting the deep kisses they could have with their Honored Mates.

Breaking away from the kiss, Ferrand crawled forward, dragging his velvety, muscled torso over Aubrey's breasts as he dove into her mouth for a deep kiss, sharing Léandre's flavor with her. Ferrand then angled his torso over Daniel to share a kiss with him.

Aubrey rolled to Léandre to enjoy kisses, too. After long, sensual, lingering moments, she peered intently into Léandre's golden eyes.

"I love you, Léandre."

His eyes glowed, his resonant emotional tenor hummed warm and silky smooth as he kissed her lips softly, then charmingly kissed directly over her heart.

He loves me, too.

Ferrand flopped over behind Daniel, leaving Aubrey lying back with her legs bent and spread.

Jovian slid smoothly between her legs, giving her a deep kiss. She reveled in the delicious flavors lingering in his mouth. He pulled away and husked a question.

"Is your pussy hungry?"

It's a pussy now?

Kassie Keegan

"Yes. My pussy is hungry."

And it was.

I am insatiable!

Daniel surprised her with the intensity of his response.

"Good, because I'm hungry for pussy!"

Léandre gave a carnal grin, showing his agreement.

They picked her up and leaned her against a wedge-shaped pillow. It elevated her head so she could see down her body easily. Her bent legs spread wide as Daniel eased in-between on his stomach. He stared at her sex like it was the best toy ever.

She chuckled. Daniel glanced up at her with the same eager expression, asking distractedly.

"What?"

She pushed a lock of hair back from his forehead affectionately.

"You're looking at me like I'm some sort of playground."

He grinned broadly.

"Oh, sweet flower, you are most definitely a playground!"

Léandre settled beside Daniel, regarding her hungrily. Ferrand lounged higher up, giving her body slow, gentle, loving strokes, keeping her relaxed and aroused.

Daniel glanced over his shoulder at Jovian, who sat contentedly watching his Mates settle.

"Show me how you made her scream."

"You want her screaming?"

"Oh, yes!"

Oh, yes, indeed!

Jovian crowded in and gave her a long, slow swipe with his tongue, causing her to gasp. Daniel bent close and did the same, making them both groan at the sensations, Aubrey from the contrast of soft flexible tip to thick velvet and Daniel from his first taste of her flavors and textures.

Léandre did the same. Aubrey's eyes about crossed with the sparkling sensations they gave her, and the sexiness of being the willing subject of their licking lessons.

Daniel was fascinated and greedy.

"More. Show me more."

And that's how she became a highly aroused puppet on their strings.

Jovian showed Daniel and Léandre licks and strokes, where to put pressure, and where not to. She learned as much about her body as they did.

Placing his hand up at the top of her mound, Jovian thumbed the hood of her clit back, exposing its tiny, turgid, sensitive bud. He spoke deep and low while instructing Daniel and Léandre.

Ferrand got up and went around behind Daniel, lifting him to his knees in front of him, Ferrand's expression feral and focused, his tail high with excitement.

Daniel concentrated so much on her, he simply moved for Ferrand without thinking. He clearly enjoyed Ferrand's stroking pets up-and-down his back, hips, and flanks.

She glimpsed Ferrand's face, savage with want, as he targeted an unsuspecting Daniel.

They forced moans out of her mouth as her Mates began learning the best ways to suck her little clit. Jovian's voice was clear and commanding, pulling them back before she reached her peak, making her moan with disappointment.

"Léandre, bring her off and sabah-fuck her deep. She's loosened up and ready from Ferrand's load."

Kassie Keegan

Daniel's cry stole their attention. He arched high and back on his hands and knees, Ferrand making him grunt in pleasure with deep tongue thrusts.

Léandre licked, kissed, and suckled Aubrey's clit in the most perfect way. She felt a solid penetration, then something petting a spot inside her directly connected to her clit. She screamed with her pleasure.

Léandre continued to kiss her sex tenderly and pet her as she panted through the last of her aftershocks.

Glancing over at Daniel, who was still being enjoyed by Ferrand, Daniel's mouth was open, tongue out as Jovian rubbed the tip of his shaft against it, petting Daniel's curls back from his face.

"That's it. Keep it out so I can use your pretty mouth while Ferrand tongues and fingers your hole. He opens you up for cock."

Oh, Abah-Sah!

Heat swept over Aubrey in a hungry rush, and she moaned with want.

Am I really not satisfied yet?

Léandre grabbed her up and put her on her hands and knees, facing Daniel, their faces close.

He descended on her ass like a starving male. He spread her wide, licking, kissing, and teasing her back passage, opening her gently, but relentlessly with his fingers and tongue, stretching her.

Jovian pulled back from Daniel and contemplated the sexy scenes before him while leisurely stroking himself, leaning forward to coat Ferrand's and Léandre's fingers with nectar from his dripping crown when they reached out for it.

Jovian spoke huskily.

"Lio nectar is a perfect lubricant. We can fuck and come for hours and the ride stays smooth."

Aubrey and Daniel stared at each other, eyes wide, hands gripping the bed linens tightly as they were both eaten out and stretched at the same time.

Léandre raised up and edged close behind Aubrey as Ferrand lifted behind Daniel. Stroking his shaft over her rear, she felt warmth splash on her back entrance moments before he began pressing into her.

She cried out, blinking with surprise at the new zings of sensation. She jerked forward, but Léandre held her firmly still with his hands on her hips.

Daniel moaned non-stop.

Jovian petted them comfortingly along their back and shoulders.

Aubrey loved Jovian's sensuous commands. Closing her eyes, she focused her attention on his sexy, deep voice as his salacious demands ratcheted up the heat.

"Relax. You're open and ready. Time to be fucked, my hearts. Push out on their cocks as they penetrate you. Push out like that. Yes… It eases their path inside your hot, tight channels. Breathe. Good Mates, taking your first ass-fuck so beautifully."

Léandre's pointed tip slid smoothly, slow and easy inside her with his steady push. She obeyed Jovian and pushed out against Léandre's invading length until he was fully inside, the pressure and slight burn so new and overwhelming, she couldn't hold back her cries.

"Oh, Abah-Sah! Léandre! So full. Feels good!"

Léandre caressed her sides, back, and flanks, bending forward to brush adoring kisses along her back and shoulders as he paused for her to get used to him buried deep inside her.

She opened her eyes, relaxing into the feeling.

Daniel's eyes were closed in pleasured concentration. Jovian had his hands in Daniel's hair, guiding Daniel's mouth over his length to suck him deep.

Kassie Keegan

Ferrand thrust smooth and strong inside Daniel, his heavy-lidded eyes watching them, rapture clear in every line of his face and body.

Jovian's blazing blue and gold gaze focused on her and Léandre.

"You are so gorgeous, Aubrey, taking Léandre's thick virgin cock up your tight virgin ass. It's a fucking fantasy brought to life! I'm going to come, Daniel! Drink it all!"

Jovian closed his eyes, tilted his head back, and roared his release as Daniel's throat worked strongly, swallowing Jovian's nectar down.

Chapter 44
Daniel

Jovian's pleasured roar echoed in Daniel's ears.

His delicious, savory flavor strong as Daniel shivered in the aftermath of receiving Jovian's load of nectar. His belly heated, his body loosening up even more, pulsing with need, a tingling relaxation sparkling through him.

Ferrand growled long and low behind him moments before bathing his passage with nectar, making Daniel moan with another rushing wave of heated tingles.

Ferrand's deliberate, steady strokes hit his pleasure-spot relentlessly, his grip on Daniel's hips firm and in control. He felt breathless at the fullness of being taken. Ferrand bottomed out deep inside and growled in his ear.

"Your body is paradise, Daniel. I will have you day and night."

His shaft flexed at Ferrand's words.

Ferrand pulled out leisurely, then pushed back in, hard and fast, making Daniel moan at the pressure and the pleasure. Ferrand withdrew slowly and thrust in hard again and again.

Shuddering as sensation built within him, the flow of energy from his Mates building his exquisite peak into an all-consuming high.

Kassie Keegan

"I'm going to die!"

Jovian petted Daniel's hair and reassured him.

"No, my heart, you will be reborn."

Ferrand grasped Daniel's shoulders, bringing him up into a sitting position with Ferrand's cock buried deep.

He realized Léandre had done the same with Aubrey, who seemed as slayed as he was. Jovian kissed Aubrey, then helped Léandre bring her bent legs forward.

He could see the glistening lower stalk of Léandre's thick cock, still buried within her, as he shuffled on his knees to where Ferrand had him locked in place. Aubrey saw Daniel and moaned with want.

"I need your cock, Daniel. Will you give it to me?"

"I'm yours Aubrey. Always!"

Ferrand didn't pull out of Daniel, instead Léandre brought Aubrey closer and helped her wrap her legs around both his and Ferrand's hips. They reached for each other as Jovian positioned Daniel's cock to penetrate Aubrey, who was still full of Léandre.

Achingly, incrementally, her tight velvet sheath took his shaft. Daniel groaned and shuddered from the twin pleasures of filling Aubrey while being filled himself.

Aubrey kissed him. The hum of powerful feelings drenching his senses, her ardent kiss ending with a passionate declaration.

"I love you, Daniel!"

Oh, Creator, yes!

Profound love for her swept out of him in a crashing wave, making Aubrey jerk and moan at its power as she received it.

"I love you, too!"

Ferrand thrust into Daniel, which thrust him up into Aubrey, making them all cry out together. When Ferrand pulled back, Léandre pushed into Aubrey, making her channel tighter on Daniel. All of them moaned unceasingly as they continued their sultry rhythm.

Jovian stood up on the bed and put the tip of his cock at Aubrey's lips.

"Suck me, my heart. Suck me and bring us all into rapture as you drink."

Se spoke strong and clear.

"Jovian, I love you."

"Oh, my heart, my treasure. I am yours."

She opened her mouth and laved Jovian's shaft, pausing as she tracked Daniel's avid gaze, bringing Jovian's cock between them so they could share. Jovian watched them, growling his enjoyment.

Gasping with bliss, Daniel Resonated with Aubrey's powerful build-up as much as his own through the vibrant flow of her energy. He tasted Léandre, Jovian, and Ferrand's savage energy, too.

They were cohesive and strong together, an effortless loop of Connection and affection in an overwhelming pulse of sensation. As he put his hand into Léandre's mane, Daniel could see a white glow on his own arm.

The glow!

He groaned his words.

"Aubrey, I can see the glow."

She smiled at him vaguely, dazed by another hard thrust. She whispered, her voice barely there.

"I see it on all of us now."

She was right. They all held the glow as their pleasure rose. Aubrey looked up at Jovian, her eyes pleading.

"I need it, Jovian. Please."

Kassie Keegan

Jovian stroked her hair back from her face, gazing at her in carnal abandon as he brought his crown to her lips.

"Drink deep, my heart."

She moaned as she sucked Jovian as deeply as she could, one hand grasping the base of his cock to keep it close while her other hand gripped Ferrand's mane.

Their connection snapped sharply together, frozen on the precipice of an ecstasy that would forever bind them. Then they went over in a tremendous rush of joy. Jovian roared, pouring his nectar into Aubrey.

She swallowed greedily, triggering a white-hot, burning wave of decadent bliss to roll through them all, bringing them into each other's minds and souls as they all roared their release.

His Mates perceived and understood Daniel's fear of abandonment, treasuring his need to love and be loved.

He knew Ferrand's worry about safeguarding his family and Pride, and reveled in his unending nurturing care for them.

He experienced the depths of Aubrey's terror toward childbirth, feeling her fierce Claim upon them, combined with her bone-deep trust and love for each one of them as individuals.

He tasted the rage Jovian controlled through rampant, potent sexuality, understanding Jovian was sensually unleashed on his Mates, loving all of them with every piece of his soul.

He shivered with profound anxiety at Léandre's powerful, deeply buried, hidden fear that Ferrand and his loves would be ripped away from him. Léandre tried to protect them and abjectly failed.

He shivered again with extraordinary delight as he heard the roar of Léandre's rapture ripping through his mind along with words.

"I love you, I love you, I love you."

They repeated over and over in Léandre's amazingly musical, masculine tenor voice in their minds.

Léandre's authentic voice.

Their tremors of ferocious fulfillment and consuming Connection went on and on.

Gradually, the blistering intensity faded, and the white glow Daniel saw on them dissipated into a concentration above each of their hearts, absorbed there until it was gone.

They collapsed sideways in a heap of bodies, pulling out of each other, gasping for breath.

Ha-Abassa Sarina appeared beside their bed, an unexpected soothing presence. Daniel felt so mellow, he couldn't rouse enough to feel surprise. Her tone and posture were full of contentment.

"A beautiful Mating! This Coalition is Claimed and Sealed. Congratulations!"

Stealth quietly approached, bringing cool hydro-packs to them, for which they murmured thanks. He took their empty packs when they finished, his expression sincere as he spoke reverently.

"Thank you. Your MateBond is one of the most beautiful things I will ever Witness."

Stealth bowed low and left on silent feet. Ha-Abassa Sarina triggering the Solaray, then she bowed respectfully, exiting as quietly as Stealth had, securing the room behind her.

Aubrey cuddled close to Léandre as Ferrand moved to snuggle in behind him, pulling Léandre into a tight hug.

Ferrand must feel the echoes of Léandre's fear. We all do.

Daniel grabbed a pillow, getting comfortable next to Aubrey, their backs touching. Jovian dropped a swath of silky, silvery blanket over Aubrey and Daniel, and crawled into Daniel's arms with a happy sigh. Contentment flowed among them.

Mated, Connected, and beloved, they would face tomorrow together.

Chapter 45
Jovian

Jovian came to awareness, settled and satisfied.

He cuddled Daniel, who now slept on top of him, having shifted positions in the night. Completely relaxed as his mind engaged, he sensed and scented his Mates were all close.

Birds sang merrily.

Daniel will like the birds. He will love all the wonders of nature around him.

A lifetime of new experiences lay ahead for Daniel. Being with him was like experiencing everything fresh, too. Jovian swiveled to lay Daniel comfortably on his side next to him.

Aubrey's gentle fingers stroked through the thick fur on his back. He arched into her touch, rolling over to gaze into her sparkling blue eyes.

She smiled, scratching under his chin, making him crinkle his face in pleasure. He moved his head this way and that so he could direct those blunt little nails to his best places.

Aubrey kissed him, diving deep, her hands driving themselves into his mane as her body undulated against his with need, her arousal scent enchanting him. His cock extruded from his sheath, ready to please his Mate.

Sweet female, I live to feed your needs.

He skimmed her creamy seam, opening her, gently testing.

Lusciously ready.

He laid her on her back, unconcerned with the other warm sleeping Mates around them, his voice husky.

"You want this cock, Aubrey? You ready to be filled?"

She moaned.

"Please."

"Take it like the good girl you are."

He notched himself at her entrance and slowly pushed into her tight warmth, entering her leisurely, making sure his nubs rubbed against her sensitive spots as much as possible.

She arched into the decadent stroke, panting as he bottomed out.

"Jovian, it's delicious, so deep."

He pulled out unhurriedly again, enjoying the drag of the smooth stroke.

"Yes, my heart. This cock is yours."

Her nails dug into his shoulders, barely a prick through his fur. Aubrey wanted more, wanted it faster. Jovian wanted her to say it.

"What do you want?"

Achingly slow push, achingly slow pull.

"Please."

Jovian's inner sexual beast-nature preened with her sweet begging.

"Please, what, beautiful?"

Aubrey moved her hips faster to receive him, but he controlled her, making her take him slow. He spoke in her ear, his voice deep and enticing.

Kassie Keegan

"Give me the words. Make them nasty."

"Jovian… fuck me with your big…"

"My big?"

Slow pull. Slow push.

"Jovian!"

"Tell me what you want, so I can give it to you."

"Pound me with your big, thick cock and make me come all over it like a…"

Her voice trailed off, losing her thought as he steadily pushed in.

"Like a good girl? Or are you a bad girl, Aubrey?"

She had no more words, shaking her head, eyes closed as she mewled with need, too deep in her pleasure.

My sweet Mate. I will give you what you need.

Fucking Aubrey fast and smooth, he popping his pelvis against her needy clit, making sure she got every ounce of pleasure he could give her.

He reveled in her gorgeous sounds, and the voluptuous squeeze and gush of her channel as she came on him, but he didn't let up the fast, steady pace. He pushed her through more peaks before he let himself go, giving her his nectar as he drowned in the ecstasy of loving her.

Jovian stroked and petted her through her rush, whispering assurances while she shivered in reaction. They would become addicted to each other.

"Do you like the nectar-rush?"

Her body relaxed as the shivers eased.

"That's what it's called?"

"Yes. We Lio get a similar spike from your cream. It's a brief high. Mate hormones are powerful."

Daniel petted down his back as Léandre eased closer to their other side. Their Mates had been watching them enjoy each other. When a brief blue flash swept across Jovian's awareness, he knew Ferrand had triggered their Solaray to prepare for more sex.

Daniel kissed Aubrey's shoulder, his voice rough with arousal, as Léandre turned her head for a kiss.

"Yes, Jovian, Mates are powerful. Let me taste the rush you gave Aubrey."

His spine tingled at Daniel's sensuality.

Oh yes, my Mate. You will have everything.

Jovian licked up Aubrey's neck, pulling out of her moist heat, making her moan into Léandre's kiss.

Léandre eased up and onto her, deepening their soul-kiss. Positioning his shaft, he pushed deep, making her arch out of the kiss and moan with fierce pleasure as Léandre began a deep, steady, heavy rhythm.

Jovian glanced over at Ferrand, who watched while stroking himself lazily, a contented smile on his face, genuinely happy watching his Mates together. He gave Ferrand a loving scratch under his chin, earning him a lick on his wrist.

Jovian laid beside Aubrey and Léandre, Daniel sitting back on his knees, looking at Jovian's glistening length like it was a feast.

Feast all you want on my cock, Mate.

Daniel began licking the cream off Jovian's erection, moaning his enjoyment of the combined flavors of cream and nectar. Jovian took a swipe of juice from the root of his cock, and tasted for himself. Flavor burst on his tongue, making him close his eyes and crave more.

A shaft grazed his lips, softly waiting for Jovian to take him in. He opened his eyes, locking them with Ferrand's.

My dreams are all coming true.

Kassie Keegan

He had Ferrand's tip in his mouth, laving it with his tongue, reveling in his taste while the velvety heat of Daniel's mouth pleasured him. Jovian shivered with reaction and dedicated himself to pleasing Ferrand, while holding his own nectar back from Daniel.

Ferrand fucked Jovian's throat with deep, sure motions Jovian loved, wrapping two big fingers around Jovian's upper fangs, holding his mouth and throat open while using his other huge hand to burrow into Jovian's mane, controlling the angle of Jovian's head.

He enjoyed every prolonged, measured thrust. The tight grip in his mane. The sight and sounds of Ferrand's growling pleasure. He drank Ferrand's offering with ferocious delight, reveling in the flavor and warm tingling rush of his Mate's nectar.

Ferrand pulled out of Jovian's mouth lingeringly as he gave Ferrand's length a last lick.

They peered down at Daniel, whose big brown eyes gazed up at them mesmerized, his tongue barely touching Jovian's cock, distracted from watching his Mates.

Jovian and Ferrand had a new focus.

In short order they turned Daniel to his stomach, ass in the air with Jovian's tongue buried deep. From the tenor changes in Daniel's moans, Ferrand enjoyed Daniel's amazing mouth.

Jovian paid special attention to Daniel's sweet spot, using a twist of his long, flexible tongue to lave it over and over with the rougher center of his tongue. When he finally mounted Daniel and pushed in, his passage would feel ultra-sensitized, primed for fucking.

He took his time, using his own nectar for lubricant, stretching Daniel with his mouth, tongue, and fingers, readying him to enjoy his cock.

Ferrand gave Daniel his nectar with a pleasured growl, making Daniel shudder and relax in the throes of his nectar-rush.

Long moments after, Ferrand moved behind Jovian, taking his Serc, preparing Jovian's sabah. Jovian lifted, concentrating his excitement

Savage Planet Embrace

through his balls and aimed a burst of his nectar at Daniel's entrance before pushing in, slow and steady.

Daniel stilled, ass arched high to receive him, grasping the coverlet while he gasped his delight in being filled.

Jovian peered up to see Léandre sat with Aubrey on her knees straddling him, both facing them, watching. Léandre buried deep in Aubrey's ass, his tail reaching over her hip to her mound, the underside of his tail rubbing insistently against her clit as Léandre's sabah pushed inside her. He softly petted one of her peaked nipples and one of his own.

Aubrey hung in a suspended state of extraordinary rapture, skin gleaming, muscles tense, eyes glazed in pleasure as she reached for another peak.

His Mates' powerful excitement sparked his own.

Maybe they can accept the depth and breadth of my sexuality.

Jovian dove deep into Daniel, who took him easily with a cry of welcome, moaning.

"Yesss."

Daniel's head dropped forward when he was fully seated. Two hard thrusts were all Jovian got before Léandre seized Jovian's mane, pulling his body forward and down over Daniel, holding him there.

He felt Ferrand pull his tail up and bury his tongue deep. Moaning, Jovian pressed the fronts of his fangs into Daniel's shoulder, making Daniel cry out and clench on Jovian.

We have discovered a hot spot for Daniel!

Ferrand sat up, pumped nectar on Jovian's hole and filled him with his thick, hot, textured cock, stopping just after his crown breached, grabbing Jovian's arms behind his back in a restraining hold.

Jovian's mind swamped with searing submissive heat. Ferrand and Léandre controlled him, controlled the fuck, igniting all his darkest sexual triggers. Ferrand's deep, commanding voice made Jovian shiver.

"You take what we give, Mate. Do you hear me?"

Jovian nodded, feeling the pull on his scalp from Léandre's grip in his mane, gasping as his secret fantasies came to life.

"Say it. Your Mates need the words."

Ferrand leaned over him, pushing his cock in deeper while making sure their weight didn't crush Daniel.

"Give *me* the words, Jovian."

He gave Ferrand what he'd only ever given to one other being.

"Yes, Sir."

Léandre released Jovian's mane with a caress while Ferrand pulled Jovian up by his arms.

"You belong to *us*, Jovian. You are ours. Say it."

"I belong to you, my Mates."

"Don't forget it."

Ferrand gathered Jovian's tail, gripping it near his Serc, bringing their two sabahs together in a pleasurable rub, then growled his command.

"Time to fuck!"

Ferrand's powerful thrusts into Jovian drove his shaft deep into Daniel. Thrust after thrust, pushing them higher. Jovian dropped all his barriers and became elation personified, licking and kissing Daniel's back, neck, and shoulders with abandon.

Daniel reached his hands back, grabbing Jovian's hips and flanks to anchor himself as Léandre scooted closer, still pleasuring Aubrey with his cock, sabah, and tail.

Léandre and Aubrey helped raise Daniel's torso higher so he and

Aubrey could kiss. She stroked Daniel's length with one hand and lovingly caressed his face with her other.

Jovian pressed his fangs into Daniel's shoulder where it met his neck, ravished by the sexual decadence of being with his Mates, a wave of humming Connection overwhelming him as they climaxed together.

Jovian again experienced the truth of his Mates and heard Léandre's voice, raised in love and rapture. He would never forget the sound of it.

Coming down from the extraordinary peak, Jovian continued to softly suck Daniel's shoulder while he kissed Aubrey. Ferrand gently bit Jovian's shoulder in the same place Jovian sucked on Daniel, making him pull back and moan.

Ferrand spoke softly, but clearly.

"Did you think we didn't know? That we weren't with you as you explored and experienced?"

Ferrand's words froze Jovian.

No. No! Abah-Sah, no!

They instructed no one in the Dark Realm without an exchange.

Immobile, barely breathing, Jovian catapulted far-away as his mind raged with possibilities.

"Jovian, hear me now. Come back to us."

He tried. Ferrand bit him hard on the shoulder, finally gaining his attention. Jovian's wide-eyed, fearful gaze locked onto Léandre's open, direct one. They hid nothing from him. There was nothing different in Léandre's demeanor.

Confusion filled Jovian.

"I don't understand."

Ferrand gently shook Jovian with a loose grip in his mane.

"We are with you. You are ours. We have told you this."

"Yes, but not *there*."

"Everywhere, Jovian. Always."

"How? Why would they let you be there? What did you trade?"

Jovian closed his eyes at the last question, his mind wandering to what they might have given or done in the Dark Realm because of *him*.

Léandre pulled Jovian's chin fur in the loving way he had. Opening his eyes, Jovian saw Léandre's concern. Shaking his head, Léandre petted Jovian's mane back, his expression changing to loving care.

Aubrey stroked Jovian's arms while Daniel petted his flanks, their bodies all connected. Ferrand spoke, calm and reassuring.

"Nothing happened to us there. We protected our Mate while he got what he needed. The Dark Realm Prides understand devotion. Our care for you is boundless, Jovian. During that time, you needed them, not us. We understood."

Jovian tried to shake his head, astonished, a motion stopped by Ferrand's sudden, firmed grip in his mane.

"No longer."

Using his grip, Ferrand shook Jovian's head again, and bit Jovian's shoulder again, hard, his commanding words and actions making Jovian's cock jump within Daniel, who moaned at the pleasure of it.

"*We* see to your needs, all of them. Do you understand?"

Jovian's heart and spirit settled. His Mates knew what he needed, knew how to give and take from him, understanding his light, accepting his darkness.

Jovian spoke, every slow, deliberate syllable imbued with satisfaction.

"Yes, Sir."

"We love you, Jovian."

Léandre and Aubrey agreed, heat and affection in their eyes. Daniel moaned his approval.

I am truly loved.

Ferrand kissed where he had bitten Jovian and slowly pulled out. Jovian then pulled out of Daniel.

Aubrey whooped and laughed as Ferrand grabbed her up in his arms. He chuckled while sauntering toward the grooming room.

"Time to show Daniel the mysteries of a Mistaray!"

This made her shout with excitement again.

"This will be fun! Come on, Daniel!"

Daniel's eyes lit with amusement as Léandre helped him off the bed, strolling hand-in-hand toward the grooming room. Jovian paused, watching them, relishing the peace that settled upon him.

Léandre and Daniel turned, releasing their hands to reach out to him. He moved to them with a smile, taking their hands, walking together to the Mistaray.

Chapter 46
Commander Ferrand

Showing Daniel the Mistaray had been filled with laughter and love.

It took some time for Daniel to get used to the water spraying down on him. He enjoyed the rivulets on Aubrey's skin, and the patterns he could make in his Lio Nel's fur when it was wet.

Daniel and Aubrey decorated them all with fanciful shapes across their chests and backs, then rubbed them away, fashioning new ones. Daniel laughed, disappointed when their designs vanished as a burst of air dried and fluffed his Mates' fur. Afterward, Daniel triggered the Solaray, too, 'just to be comfortable.'

Ferrand gave Daniel an affectionate stroke down his arm while he remembered.

Five very clean, well-fed, and comfortably clothed Mates were now in Ferrand's personal private office.

Aubrey wore a pretty, mid-length, casual dress. He and his Brethren wore their regular Shendyts and gear. Daniel added a vest to his Shendyt and belt.

They sat across from Cassian, Travar, and Stealth, who also modestly wore a vest with his Shendyt. Everyone was patiently waiting for others to join them in Ferrand's plush seating area full of comfortable, low-slung couches.

Daniel snuggled in Léandre's attentive arms while Jovian had Aubrey ensconced in his lap. Ferrand sat close between both sets of his Mates, touching them contentedly with his hands and tail.

They'd used their personal entrance attached to their living quarters while the others would enter from a concealed external entrance downstairs.

Behind them stood a long group table. Off to the side was a smaller room with a holo-screen, desk, and chair where Ferrand often worked. As he looked at the cluttered desk, he thought of how his life had changed in only a few day spans.

Having Mates will do away with those late-night work sessions.

Looking over at his family chatting happily with their friends calmed him, firming his determination to make sure they were safe.

Ferrand shared the large, upper-level space with Jovian's secretive personal workshop. The office and workshop, separated by a wall, had distinctively different styles.

Ferrand's office sported charcoal-colored walls accented with warm woods ranging from blond to mahogany. The furniture featured black, gray, and natural leather colors. Windows were open all around the space, filling it with soothing, muted, natural light.

However, their business today was anything but comforting. Time to make plans because someone threatened his family, and Ferrand was going to fuck them up.

Ferrand's Lio Nessa Second-in-Command, Sec. Com. Savani said she had recent developments. High Nessa Katohna and Ha-Abassa Sarina decided to meet here, which was more discreet than their official Pride Offices.

Besides, most newly MateBonded Coalitions did not emerge from their living quarters for long spans after being Claimed. People would not expect Ferrand to be visible around the PrideHome yet, so they could keep this meeting a secret.

Katohna swept in with Raiida and Rahimi, grabbing drinks from the small refreshments area, coming over to join them. Katohna shared air with everyone, one-by-one. After, Raiida and Rahimi separated to lurk protectively near the external entry.

Sec. Com. Savani entered next with Scribe Divyah, who organized Katohna and Cassian's affairs. Cassian made introductions to Daniel, as everyone else knew them well. Ferrand shared air with Sec. Com. Savani.

"Well done, Boss!"

He grinned at her approval of his Mates.

Yes, I have chosen well.

Ha-Abassa Sarina joined them, sharing air with Aubrey and Daniel, greeting everyone. They settled in as Jovian engaged his extra privacy measures, Sec. Com. Savani's tone was warm as she began the meeting.

"Congratulations on your MateBond! Blessings upon you!"

There were roars all around and stomping of feet. He and his Mates laughed and smiled at their show of support.

Then Sec. Com. Savani became serious.

"We found no visuals revealing the saboteur of High Nessa Katohna's Transport. I'd like to bring Vivian into our investigation. She is a talented spotter and trusted Inter-Galactic Surveillance expert. Plus, she's very sneaky."

Their Lio companions growled with approval at Vivian's sneakiness, which confused Daniel. Ferrand grabbed Daniel's hand, giving it a kiss. He had so much to learn about Lio.

Katohna agreed to bring Vivian in, pleasing Aubrey.

Good, now Aubrey can confide in her friend. She will need to.

Knowing this prompted Ferrand to speak up.

"I would like to include all of those sharing the Common Room with my family brought into our confidence."

Aubrey and Daniel appeared quizzical.

Ferrand was about to reveal a big surprise.

They'd given Aubrey's best friends, Vivian, Talia, and Destiny, their own personal living quarters sharing the Commons with their family, along with Prime Cassian's Coalition.

Those Aubrey most cared about would live close to her.

"This means we disclose our investigation to Talia and Destiny, as well as Vivian."

Puzzled, Aubrey tilted her head, eyebrows furrowed, then her face cleared as she understood, a huge smile blooming. Jumping out of Jovian's lap, she leaped onto Ferrand with a cry of joy, seating herself on his thighs facing him, pressing her precious, warm, curvy body against him. His arms surrounded her, petting her back.

"You mean it! Me and my girls get to stay together?"

"Yes. We arranged it while we were still in Capital Maituri. We wanted to surprise you."

"I'm surprised and so, so happy!"

Aubrey gave Ferrand a lingering kiss.

"Thank you."

She angled sideways to kiss Léandre in thanks.

Giving Ferrand's face a sweet caress as she rose, she petted Daniel's arm as she walked past him back to Jovian, kissing and thanking Jovian, too. After, she settled back into his lap, again facing their friends. Aubrey smiled at Cassian, Travar, and Stealth, who smiled back at her.

"Thanks, guys."

Travar piped up, laughing as he teased her, patting his lap invitingly.

"Don't we get kisses, too?"

It surprised everyone when easygoing Daniel growled, his face hard, his eyes narrowed protectively in warning.

It was amusing to watch him realize what he'd done, smoothing his expression. Daniel cleared his throat, trying to act casual. Everyone chuckled. Cassian spoke dryly.

"That's a 'No.'"

He gave Travar a loving scratch behind an ear while commenting with affectionate amusement.

"Your new hobby is teasing growls out of Daniel, isn't it, Travar?"

Travar answered, full of anticipation.

"Oh, yes!"

Daniel muttered under his breath.

"Shit!"

Travar started belly-laughing.

"Now I have to keep score!"

Travar opened a holo-comm screen from a band on his forearm, making notes. Daniel watched Travar, shaking his head with a sigh.

Katohna brought them back to business, speaking decisively.

"Then it's settled. We will bring them in, but I want more here as a secret hub."

Scribe Divyah took furious notes on her tablet as High Nessa Katohna continued.

"We need to think strategically. I want Talia to prepare a fully stocked private Medical Clinic above her quarters."

Scribe Divyah was curious.

"Her Medical Team?"

"They can help her set it up. I'll talk with Perrin, Bahir, and Raaj. They know how to keep their mouths shut. I'll explain to them with Talia."

The Scribe continued her notes as Katohna spoke thoughtfully.

"Give Vivian a full kit for her personal Surveillance Intelligence Office, with codes. I want her searching quietly."

Katohna glanced over at Cassian.

"And while we are at it, bring Destiny's Studio into the personal space above her quarters, too. I don't want her having to wander far to do her work."

Stealth took a deep breath, exhaling while reaching for Cassian's hand, who took it immediately into his own. They'd been worried about Destiny. This would keep her close and secure.

Katohna is such a kind, wise Pride Leader.

Sec. Com. Savani glanced at her notes.

"We have Personal Security Experts, Kian, Marrok, and Shiro Takeo arriving back at Bon'Fiel PrideHome soon. They will take the final living quarters in Prime Cassian's Pod, with Commander Ferrand's family's approval."

She brought up the next item in her no-nonsense tone.

"Raiida and Rahimi continue living near High Nessa Katohna in her Pod. Tusse and her Harem Mates are off to Capital Maituri to gather intel. This opens living quarters for Security Coalition Bhaven, Azhar, and Taryn. They will live in my Pod with Scribe Divyah and her Harem Mates, along with Tapolah, Nasma, Litt, and their Harems. Is this acceptable?"

Everyone agreed.

Sec. Com. Savani put her notes down, peering over at Cassian, then Ferrand, and finally Katohna.

Kassie Keegan

"We have found unusual listening devices in some public spaces."

Jovian sat up straighter, his expression intent, making Sec. Com. Savani focus on him.

"Calm, Jovian. We've neutralized them, but left them in place, hoping the perpetrator will come to see why they are not functioning. I sent a full report to you and Commander Ferrand, with no alert. With you both so recently MateBonded, we didn't want to disturb."

Jovian glanced over at Daniel in Léandre's arms and relaxed back, pulling Aubrey tighter into his embrace as he accepted Sec. Com. Savani's words.

She turned back to High Nessa Katohna.

"A betrayer has infiltrated Bon'Fiel Pride."

Katohna showed no surprise. Instead, she seemed thoughtful.

Betrayal sometimes happened. Bon'Fiel PrideHome was huge, housing over five hundred thousand inhabitants who lived, worked for Trade Credits, and played on Bon'Fiel lands.

Bon'Fiel PrideHome was a thriving, independent entity.

Besides Pods of living quarters, each of Bon'Fiel PrideHome's ten levels had two large Dining Lounges with Food Prep Areas and Storage, and two huge Lounge spaces with enormous holo-vid screens.

Then there were the Tunnels, Gardens, Beehive Apiaries, Offices, Medical Clinics, Fabrication Rooms, Weapons Storage, Training Rooms, and the Skol-Ar school and nursery. The Undercroft was a vaulted storage area under the PrideHome for Land Transports and many adult-only areas.

Bon'Fiel Pride also oversaw Liani Combat, where they instructed Combat Training and Tactics, making them a formidable Pride, which also made many jealous.

Most of those who lived at Bon'Fiel were loyal and hard-working, but Lio also had beast-natures who needed structure and self-control. He, as

Savage Planet Embrace

Commander, and their Prime Ambassador, Cassian, along with their Teams, kept peace among Bon'Fiel PrideHome's inhabitants.

Ferrand had a great Security Team. They'd taken care of Bon'Fiel PrideHome while he answered the Call to Mate, becoming Claimed and MateBonded, but they needed him now.

He peered over at Daniel, who had his head on Léandre's shoulder, looking over at him, offering his hand to hold. Ferrand took it.

Aubrey's gentle touch on his arm had him turning to her as she grabbed his other hand, kissing the back of it. His Honored Mates understood his role and showed him much-needed support.

Sec. Com. Savani's next words hit hard.

"There's been unusual seismic activity in the Bon'Durel Sinkhole area. When a Bon'Proel Mineral Mines Team went to investigate, they disappeared. Bon'Terral Pride is preparing an Investigations Team."

Sec. Com. Savani looked at Ferrand with compassion.

"Commander Altair Bon'Terral has requested Commander Ferrand and Master-Tech Jovian to accompany their Team to the Sinkhole. Commander Ferrand because he knows the area well as his former PrideLands, and Jovian for his Tech skills."

Ferrand sat stone-faced.

Of course, I will go, but it will not be easy.

He looked askance at Jovian, who agreed with a silent nod, while petting Aubrey soothingly down her back. He felt Léandre's extreme unease and glanced over at him, realizing he also deeply sensed all of his Mates' varied emotional responses.

We are truly MateBonded.

Léandre stared at him with dark shadows in his eyes. They would need more Bonding and some sensual distraction before he and Jovian left them. Ferrand's voice rasped with buried emotions.

"When do we leave?"

Kassie Keegan

"Tonight. We will keep you cloaked. Hopefully, no one will know you aren't holed up with your delightful Mates."

Delightful. Yes, they are. And they need more 'delight.'

Ferrand stood up, releasing his Mates' hands, signaling the end of the meeting.

"Send us the departure details. We need some time with Aubrey, Daniel, and Léandre."

Everyone stood.

Ha-Abassa Sarina came to him, sharing air with him, then Jovian, blessing them. She gave Aubrey and Daniel gentle embraces before taking Léandre to the side near Ferrand.

Ha-Abassa Sarina's voice was low, but clear when she spoke.

"Now is the time for decisions, Léandre. Your path is their path. Their path is our path. We are together. We are with you. The time to trust is *now.*"

Léandre focused on her. His lips thinned, roiling emotions churning in his eyes, posture held in tight control.

Ha-Abassa Sarina gazed at him with love, then brought their foreheads together to share air. Léandre relaxed, but remained non-committal as they parted.

High Nessa Katohna nodded regally, and everyone quietly left. Ferrand took a deep, bracing breath.

Time to shake up this low mood!

"Aubrey, Daniel, we have something else to show you."

That perked them up. Daniel became intrigued while Aubrey looked grateful for the distraction, as Ferrand knew she would be. She spoke with interest gleaming in her pretty blue eyes.

"What is it, Ferrand?"

He made a sweeping gesture to Jovian's Workshop entrance.

"Lead on, Jovian!"

Jovian caught on quickly and led through the entry.

Jovian's Workshop was a sunny room of blond wood, floor to high-beamed ceilings open to a skylight letting in bright, abundant light. Tables full of equipment and organized tools lined the walls. In the center were multitudes of tables holding separate projects, all in different states of completion.

Ferrand's favorite place in the Workshop was a circular nook off to the side with a round window, a large, comfortable sofa, and a huge round cushion made for thinking or napping in the sun. He'd spent many hour spans watching Jovian work from the cozy alcove.

Jovian was uncharacteristically shy while showing Aubrey and Daniel his private space. He scrutinized Daniel's expressions as he peered around the Workshop with wonder. Aubrey leaned back against one of the worktables, arms crossed, a smile on her face as she, too, watched Daniel.

Jovian pointed to the far wall where two large new workspaces stood, speaking quietly.

"Those are for you, Aubrey and Daniel."

Aubrey lowered her arms and stared at Jovian as Daniel pivoted in surprise.

"For *us*?"

"Yes. You get to keep your Workshop in the Undercroft, Aubrey. Daniel gets one there, too, but I made this place for you here, so we could work near each other when we wanted."

His eyes twinkling, Jovian reached his hand out to Aubrey, who took it, together walking over to Daniel before he escorted them to their workspaces, showing them the set up. He had tools and equipment in each work area unique to Aubrey and Daniel's particular interests, a small but clear sign of how much Jovian paid attention to them, and how important they were to him.

Kassie Keegan

Understanding the magnitude of Jovian's gift as he opened his private space and his mind to them, as well as his heart and body. They hugged him, one hooked under each of his arms, giving him kisses.

"Thank you!"

"Thank you, Jovian."

Ferrand strolled to the sunny 'thinking nook' where Léandre laid in the sun on a cushion. He cuddled in tight to his beloved Brethren as they sunned, their tails twined together, the tips waving contentedly while they watched their happy Mates explore and talk about projects and plans. He looked forward to many such quiet, sweet moments.

Daniel wandered over to a table Jovian covered with protective fabric. It was common for Jovian to do this with his secret projects. He stooped, picking up a mysterious piece of tech off the floor. It had a bundle of tiny micro-wires attached to it.

As Daniel stood up, he examined the gadget closely, puzzled. His eyebrows lifted with revelation, then his face completely cleared of expression in a blankness Ferrand hadn't seen on his face since the Presentation at Capital Maituri's Palace.

Very curious.

Daniel glanced over at Jovian, who stared back expressionlessly. But communication definitely happened. He quietly returned the piece under the fabric with a small, secretive smile. Peering up, Daniel realized he and Léandre watched the interplay.

His beautiful brown eyes sparkling, Daniel gave them a slow-blooming, broad smile, coming over to inspect the circular, sun-filled room they lounged in. Ferrand spoke huskily.

"This is Jovian's 'thinking nook.'"

"Oh, yeah? What are you thinking about while snuggled up in the sun like that?"

Ferrand gazed at Daniel with banked desire, flirting back.

"I'm thinking about how luscious you taste and feel."

Daniel enjoyed the tease, answering coyly as he turned his back, peeking at them over his shoulder, affording them a lovely view.

"Oh! Are you feeling hungry, Ferrand?"

Léandre licked his chops lasciviously, making it clear he was 'hungry,' too. Ferrand felt starved for Daniel.

"Most definitely."

A low, pleasured feminine moan came from the other side of the room.

Ah. Sounds like Jovian already started.

Aubrey lay bent over an empty work table, her dress flipped up out of the way while Jovian ravished her with his mouth and tongue from behind. She cried out louder, her hips pulsing with an orgasm. Jovian licked her through the peak, rising as she relaxed. He moved his Shendyt to the side, aimed his thick cock, and pushed in with a groan as Aubrey moaned.

"Yes, yes, yes."

Daniel circled around to them, his cheeks flushed, his erection prominent under his Shendyt. Ferrand and Léandre raised their hands to Daniel, pulling him onto their cushion where they kissed and licked him. Daniel moaned, petting them back.

It would be a beautiful, sensuous interlude before he and Jovian had to leave.

Chapter 47
Léandre

Ferrand and Jovian filled them in on the reports, answering Aubrey and Daniel's many questions while preparing to depart. They were somber, but reassuring, sharing air and giving last hugs before donning their concealing cloaks, then quietly leaving.

Léandre knew the toll this trip would have on Ferrand, and tried not to worry. They would be here to help him after.

Aubrey's friends descended in a loud, happy distraction shortly after their loves departed. He took immense pleasure watching Aubrey squeal in greeting when Vivian, Talia, and Destiny arrived, settling in for a nice, long visit together. They scrupulously avoided speaking about why Ferrand and Jovian weren't there, Katohna and Cassian having obviously explained things.

Léandre showed Daniel how to work the food prep area, which was similar to what Daniel was used to, and they served a filling meal, while the ladies spoke about how they were setting up their living quarters and new spaces above.

They welcomed Daniel and Léandre into the conversation as they chose colors and expressed opinions. Aubrey frequently touched either him or Daniel, her unconscious, natural affection spearing straight into Léandre's heart.

Savage Planet Embrace

Soon it was time to rest, although he had no intention of sleeping yet. Escorting Aubrey and Daniel into their living quarters, he secured the entry. Removing his Bandels and belt, he placed them on their pegs while he and his Mates removed their sandals. Lowering the lights, he triggered the Solaray's brief blue beam, then went to his Mates.

Léandre intended to utterly satisfy them.

Aubrey and Daniel will know they are provided for, filled with love and nectar, whether they are with one Lio Mate or three.

They went into each other's embrace easily. Aubrey reached for Léandre's kiss as Daniel unfastened garments, their hands wandering freely. Clothing dropped to the floor with soft slithers.

Breaking their kiss, he grabbed Aubrey and Daniel's manes in gentle but firm grips, wanting their attention. They froze, hands in mid-stroke, eyes wide, their arousal scents spiking with his careful control, his nose twitched, his tail waving sinuously as he savored the heady mix. His mouth watered to taste them.

Léandre engaged his holo-comm and pinged.

They answered, along with Ferrand and Jovian, who were safely at their destination in the Mineral Mine Fields, resting for the night.

He engaged visuals for Ferrand and Jovian, wanting all his Mates to share this experience.

> LÉANDRE:
> I want your words. Tell me what you feel, what you think. Give it all to me.

Aubrey and Daniel's breathing increased as they absorbed his message, asking them to lay their thoughts bare through their words. To open themselves up.

> LÉANDRE:
> Can you do this for me?

He knew it wasn't fair to ask them to do something he himself could not do, but he wanted this, *needed* this.

Daniel hesitated, unsure of what he wanted, but also aroused and wanting to please.

"Yes. But how… I mean, what?"

Aubrey gave a wicked, sexy smile, her tone low, husky. Aroused.

"Yes, Léandre. The velvet of your fur feels so good against my skin. So soft! It makes me want to stroke and pet these beautiful muscles."

He released their manes as Aubrey did as she described, stroking her hands along the contours of his body, leaving a trail of fire.

His gaze ate up his Mates, loving how different they were from him, feeling a spiritual Connection to them as he stroked their beautiful bodies reverently, their skin gleaming golden in the low-light.

Their flesh marked easily, so tender, delicate, and vulnerable despite their Lio genetic boost. His bestial, protective, and possessive instincts ignited.

Daniel spoke huskily.

"I love how you look at us, Léandre. Like you want to shield us and devour us at the same time."

Léandre's gaze to flew to Daniel's face.

Very perceptive, Daniel.

Aubrey spoke.

"And your eyes glow all golden and predatory."

Daniel's deep brown eyes became wild.

"It makes me feel predatory, too!"

Léandre turned to Daniel, pulling him into an all-consuming kiss. Their hard, naked shafts and firm torsos rubbing together as they stepped closer to each other.

Aubrey pressed tightly to Daniel's back, her arms reaching in front of him, stroking their chests as she licked and nipped Daniel's skin.

"Daniel, you taste divine!"

Léandre broke the kiss and pulled her around, so they stood side-by-side in front of Daniel. He licked Daniel's nipple while watching Aubrey. Her eyes lit up. She leaned down to Daniel's chest, too, and gave his nipple a swipe with her tongue.

Daniel moaned, peering down at the two of them, the same expression of discovery in his gaze as was in Aubrey's.

"Oh, Creator! The different textures of your tongues make me weak-kneed. It feels so perfect!"

Time to get my Mates in bed!

Léandre took their hands, leading them to the bed, thinking he would be the guide.

Instead, Aubrey gave a whoop and jumped on him, joined by Daniel. They fell in a laughing heap on the bed together, stroking and petting. Pushing him down, both took one of his dark nipples in their mouths, swirling their velvet tongues around his tips.

He put one of his big hands behind each of their heads as they pleasured him, his heart bursting with love for his sexy, attentive Mates.

He reached over and grabbed Aubrey. Before her squeak finished, she was on her knees over his face, looking at Daniel, hands braced on Léandre's abs.

Swiping the soft tip of his tongue across her clit, he then ran a lingering stroke down along her sex to her creamy entrance. Aubrey's flavor burst on his tongue, and he settled in to feast.

"Oh, Abah-Sah! He's licking me!"

"How does it feel, Aubrey?"

"Like he loves my taste."

Moan.

"Like he can't get enough of me."

Kassie Keegan

Sudden cry.

"Like he knows exactly how to make me cream for him!"

He heard them kiss as he devoured her. Daniel spoke with anticipation.

"Oh, look what I have here!"

Taking full advantage of Léandre's exposure, Daniel stroked all over him with gentle fingers, digging into the thicker places of his fur with blunt fingernails, languidly petting the swells of his muscles.

Daniel sounded dreamy.

"I love your body, Léandre. I love touching you."

Daniel claimed him with his sweet touch while Léandre pleasured Aubrey, exulting in the music of her delighted cries as she reached her first shivering peak.

There will be many more, my beauties.

Daniel licked Léandre's cock with his soft, nimble tongue, causing his abdominal muscles to clench while Daniel stroked over his tightened abs.

Aubrey was breathless.

"Beautiful."

She leaned her weight forward, melting on top of Léandre. He opened his mouth wide on a soundless moan from the pleasure of her precious body on top of his. Léandre renewed his hungry pussy-eating as Daniel raised his shaft straight up.

Aubrey cried out with delight.

"Oh, yes, let's share!"

Léandre fisted the coverlet as they each took a side of his erection, mouthing and licking it, taking turns sucking his crown into their heated warmth. He could no longer focus when Daniel made a sensual demand.

"Give it to us, Léandre. We want to drink your nectar."

White-hot tingles flew down Léandre's spine with Daniel's words. He released his nectar to his Mates, his head swimming from the pressure with which he gave up his pleasure to them.

His Mates shared his nectar, licking it off his flesh and fur, moaning their enjoyment while tasting him, bodies jerking with the nectar-rush he gave them.

It was one of the most sensual moments of his life.

Concentrating on Aubrey's tender clit, he was determined for her to come on his face again. Soon, she did so with a cry, her body shaking with deep shudders pulsing along his torso where she lay. When she relaxed, he gently rolled her onto the bed.

Switching his position, he grabbed Daniel's hips, holding them steady and still, opening his mouth wide to engulf Daniel's length down his throat, swallowing hard repeatedly.

"Oh, Léandre! It's amazing! I'm going to... You're making me..."

Daniel stiffened and cried out his release, exploding down Léandre's throat in a torrent of cream. Léandre shivered at the deep, heated rush it gave him.

Hmm, tasty, creamy Mates.

He pulled off of Daniel's length with a slurp, watching them passionately kiss. Sliding behind Aubrey, Léandre raised her hips, so she braced on her knees, leaning her upper-body into Daniel's chest. He positioned his cock and slid in deep, Aubrey moaning her welcome.

Daniel kissed and licked the side of Aubrey's neck while she panted through Léandre's demanding stroke, making sure Aubrey kept talking.

"What is happening, Aubrey?"

"He's, he's in me."

Pull-back, thrust.

Kassie Keegan

"In you? Where?"

Kiss. Nip. Lick. A feminine gasp.

"Come on, you can tell me."

"He's in my… cunt!"

It was like the dam broke on Aubrey's words and she couldn't stop the flow, speaking without pause.

"It feels so naughty saying this. I can't believe how hot this makes me. If he stops, I'll die. I love cock. I need it. I didn't know it would be like this. I need my Mates in me, in all my places, in all my… holes, I need to feel your thickness, your hardness filling me up, making me scream."

She cried out at a deep, sudden thrust as Daniel grabbed her mane, tilting her head back, arching her neck, kissing and tasting, while his fingers pinched and rubbed her nipples.

"Drench me. I want it in me, on me, covering me, covering each other. I want it to never stop."

Slow, slow pull-back. Thrust.

"Oh, please, Léandre, fuck me! Fuck me *hard*!"

Yes, Mate. Feel this joy with me!

He fucked her hard and fast, bringing her to her first peak on his cock within a few strokes, then he slowed, adjusting their position by lifting her leg over Daniel's hips so she straddled him, Léandre riding her from behind. Aubrey's belly now pressed on Daniel's cock as Léandre fucked her hard and fast again, making them cry out at the exquisite friction.

There was no talking now, they were too breathless.

She peaked again, and Léandre joined her, his mouth open wide on a silent roar of desperate release, his body shuddering with its intensity.

Aubrey melted on top of Daniel, who stroked and petted her, giving her lovely, sweet words of praise. Léandre's heart bled with the beauty of them.

"You are so gorgeous, Aubrey. A dream come true. I love your flavor, how you feel, the way you think. Who you are…"

Léandre carefully pulled out, resetting her, lifting Daniel's shaft, so she slid onto him solidly to the root. They arched and moaned with the stroke, Daniel crying out.

"Oh, yes. Give me all of that tight, wet heat!"

They passionately kissed, Daniel thrusting up into her with smooth, steady strokes. Léandre helped Daniel ride her to peak, stroking and petting glistening skin, pinching stiff nipples, nipping flushed flesh.

As they relaxed after, he grabbed Daniel's thighs, hooking them over his forearms, lifting his hips at a perfect height, pressing the tip of his shaft against Daniel's entrance.

Aubrey braced herself with her hands on Daniel's chest as their hips tilted up and back, her knees no longer touching the cushion, so she hung her full weight on Daniel's cock, thoroughly impaled.

Daniel gasped, Aubrey moaned, and Léandre released a gush of nectar, easing his way into Daniel. Steadily, Léandre's pointed crown penetrated, sinking deeper and deeper until wholly embedded in his Mate.

Words poured from Daniel.

"Léandre! Oh, Creator, so thick. I'm so full."

He panted.

"I can't take it. It's too much. But I want it! I'm taking it… Ah… He's in."

Daniel groaned in agonized pleasure, Aubrey breathless.

"Watching you while you get fucked is amazing. It makes me feel feral."

She slid her hand to Daniel's throat and stroked him.

"I want to own you. Take your cock while they fuck you. I want to see the surrender in your eyes. I feel like a fucking animal!"

Suddenly becoming hesitant and shy, Aubrey sat up, pulling her hand away, sounding worried.

Kassie Keegan

"Is this okay? Is something wrong with me?"

Daniel took her hand, kissed it and put it back where it had been on his throat.

"I enjoy watching you get fucked, too, Aubrey. Don't pull back. It's okay to feel what you feel. I like how you are."

She spoke, sweet and solemn.

"I love you, Daniel."

Léandre spread his knees wide to lower his height and change his angle. Dropping Daniel's legs off his arms, Léandre wrapped Daniel's legs around his hips while supporting Aubrey so she could relax and enjoy the ride. He kissed her shoulder and petted her, wishing he could verbally reassure Aubrey she was perfect, her aggression and possessiveness natural for an Honored Nessa, and highly prized by her Mates.

He pulled back with slow deliberation, making Daniel moan like he was dying, then snapped his hips forward, thrusting deep, pushing Daniel's cock hard and fast into Aubrey, making her cry out. Daniel moaned.

"He's taking me!"

"He's taking us *both*! Take us, Léandre!"

"Give it to us! More! Give it *all* to us!"

He eased back slowly and snapped forward over and over, bringing himself, Aubrey, and Daniel through another mind-blowing peak, his loves shuddering and crying out in ecstasy as he silently roared his pleasure.

But he didn't stop with that climax, or the one after that. Or the next one, riding one peak after another until they were exhausted. Finally, Aubrey breathlessly cried out with a husky laugh.

"Enough!"

Léandre pulled out and away, letting Aubrey lay on Daniel as they caught their breath. Grabbing insta-dry cloths, Léandre helped Aubrey flop over beside Daniel. He cleaned himself, and then carefully, lovingly attended to his Mates before triggering the Solaray.

Lowering the lights, he slithered in-between his Mates, pulling a soft coverlet up to keep their pretty, furless skin warm as they snuggled into his sides in boneless contentment.

He heard Ferrand's quiet, deep voice in his open holo-comm.

"Thank you, Léandre. I love you, Mate. Sharing this was… I treasure it."

Jovian's voice was full of emotion.

"Love you, Léandre. Love all of you."

He only now noticed the two small audio-only monitor indicators of Aubrey's and Daniel's open shared holo-comms. Respect and joy filled Léandre's heart when he realized they had known and enjoyed sharing their play with their far-away Mates.

How I love my sneaky Honored loves!

Aubrey spoke with languid relaxation.

"It was wonderful. Get back here quick so you can have some in person."

Daniel spoke without opening his eyes, amused and content.

"Love you, guys. Can't wait to taste you again!"

Both Ferrand and Jovian growled in aroused agreement, then clicked off to find relief of their own.

Holding his satisfied Mates, Léandre relaxed, letting his heavy, buried thoughts finally come to the foreground of his mind.

He remembered Daniel's beautiful words while they made love.

Léandre wanted to say pretty words to his Mates, too.

He remembered their sexy commands as they reached for their peaks.

Léandre wanted to make those titillating sexual demands, too.

Kassie Keegan

He remembered Aubrey and Daniel laughing raucously with their friends.

Léandre wanted to laugh out loud, too.

He remembered Aubrey's and Daniel's beautiful cries of pleasure and how glorious Ferrand and Jovian roared as they came.

Léandre wanted to roar out his rapture, shouting his enjoyment to Abah-Sah like his Brethren.

He wanted those quiet moments with his Mates, where they whispered loving words meant only for each other.

Léandre could have those things, needed them from the depths of his soul.

But a promise bound him.

He had followed the rules to keep his loved-ones safe, maintained silence in all the ways required. Despite it, his family almost died. They surely *would* have died if not for Aubrey's and Daniel's special talents.

His secrecy no longer protected Ferrand or his beloveds, unleashing Léandre from his bond of silence.

He couldn't help his powerful, physical flinch as he remembered the slow cutting slice that took his voice. A drowsy Aubrey, eyes still closed, made a concerned noise, skimming her hand up over his chest, resting it comfortingly above Léandre's heart. Daniel slid his hand up Léandre's torso, placing his hand over Aubrey's.

My precious ones, cuddled so close, own my heart!

Even knowing the danger for his Mates, he could and would face anything.

No more silence. It's time to speak.

With the decision came contentment so profound, Léandre purred, relaxing his beloveds further, bringing smiles to their almost-sleeping faces.

Savage Planet Embrace

Incredibly, Aubrey and Daniel matched his purr with purrs of their own. Their soft rumbles a humming rhythm against him as they drifted off to sleep. Only truly happy, extraordinarily content Honored Mates purred.

A tear dripped down the side of Léandre's cheek, overwhelmed with gratefulness.

Thank you, Abah-Sah. I'm ready now.

Chapter 48
Aubrey

It had been a wild few week spans for Aubrey and her Mates!

Ferrand and Jovian returned with more questions than answers. Ferrand's knowledge of the area had been useful to the Investigators of the Bon'Terral Pride. However, Jovian's sensors picked up nothing unusual.

They'd loved Ferrand through the emotional backlash of returning to his sunken PrideHome and then loved each other through their joy and uncertainties when Léandre revealed he wanted his voice restored.

One of Jovian's secret projects had been perfecting the micro-tech to restore Léandre's authentic voice. They now knew what his voice sounded like. They'd heard it in their souls when they MateBonded.

Daniel had recognized one component in Jovian's Workshop on their first day there. Since Léandre's decision, Jovian and Daniel worked incessantly to get the perfect tones. Aubrey helped when she could.

Léandre gave final approval of their efforts last night.

He'd been amazingly calm about it all, considering how hard he fought it previously. To her, it showed how at peace Léandre was with it. He told them he would explain about his change-of-heart with his authentic voice when it was done.

Savage Planet Embrace

Their trust in Talia was absolute. She and her Medical Team were highly skilled and had the best equipment.

Still, Aubrey worried. Even as she knew her fear was irrational, it couldn't be explained away with logic, so her Mates didn't attempt to stop her concern. Talia and her Team kept them informed and close to Léandre, so Aubrey managed a measure of calm.

In their private meeting with Prime Cassian and High Nessa Katohna, everyone decided to keep the procedure a secret. For now, with Bon'Fiel threatened, it was an advantage, even if they weren't sure how they could use it. Léandre had been all for keeping it quiet, even more relaxed about having his voice restored after the meeting.

She had to go about her days as if nothing was happening with her beloved Mate. Daniel and Léandre made it as easy as they could by almost constantly staying close to her.

Aubrey and Daniel enjoyed working together.

Daniel met her Mech Tech Team and completed a few projects with them. He might stick there, but he had many areas to explore before deciding, and lots of time to figure it out.

She smiled, remembering when she'd taken Daniel to meet her Team. They saw her from far-off, walking toward them in the Undercroft beneath Bon'Fiel PrideHome, where the Team Workshops were.

Many Honored Nessas and Lio Nessas rushed Aubrey for hugs and pets, while the males followed at a measured pace.

One Nessa started it.

"You give me a…"

And the entire group yelled at the top of their lungs.

"Lady Boner!"

Everyone, including Aubrey, laughed heartily and hugged each other.

She'd introduced a grinning Daniel to her Team. Léandre standing proudly and protectively to the side, smiling as they warmly welcomed Daniel.

'Lady Boner' became a standard greeting for Aubrey in the PrideHome. Proud of the title, she laughed every time she heard it. Her latest pair of work overalls sported the title on them.

I love my Bon'Fiel Pride Family so much!

Daniel met with his friend Jensen, too. Aubrey sensed Jensen had a lot of damage, recognizing another bruised soul, like her own.

Daniel confided his hurt when Jensen left SpacePort Haddou without a word, as well as his hope their friendship could be renewed. It thrilled Aubrey when it went well.

Daniel settled into their new life nicely.

Because Jensen was one of High Nessa Katohna's personal Pilots, and had been on the sabotaged flight with them, they informed Jensen of their quiet investigation. Daniel could confide in him like Aubrey could with her friends.

Jensen stayed on alert for missions related to High Nessa Katohna's reconnaissance. He was on one now, or he would have been waiting with her friends in their Common Room as Léandre was prepped for surgery in Talia's sleek, new, compact Medical Clinic.

The Clinic had everything Talia and her Medical Team, a Lio Nel Coalition named Perrin, Bahir, and Raaj, would need for diagnoses and treatment on a small-scale. Talia had a full Surgical Suite and a Research Area on one side, and a couple of tidy offices on the other.

The entire space was in shades of white, light gray, and pale aqua-blue. Clean, professional, and soothing at the same time.

Besides the Treatment Area and offices, Talia had a cozy private Recovery Room with an enormous bed large enough for a full family to rest on in the center. Lio recovered much quicker when they were surrounded, groomed, and petted by family.

Aubrey sat on a long, curved couch, cuddled close to Ferrand, Daniel and Jovian entwined beside them. They took comfort in each other's nearness while gazing at Léandre through the clear barrier separating them from the Surgical Suite.

She reached a hand back toward Daniel, to be engulfed in his masculine warmth. Jovian's tail comfortingly wrapped around her ankle. She hugged Ferrand closer.

Prime Cassian, Travar, Stealth, Vivian, and Destiny waited for news in the Common Room below. High Nessa Katohna was with them, her Harem Mates dropping in now-and-then to show support, too.

Ha-Abassa Sarina serenely sat on a large cushion nearby. She'd shared air with them all, spending long moments with Léandre before sitting and closing her eyes meditatively. She was a source of calm for them. Aubrey could feel the soft hum of her reassurance flow through Daniel to her, and through them to their Mates. Even to Talia and her Team.

Because they were concealing Léandre's surgery, they carefully chose the site of their incision. Unlike Challenge scars or Honor scars, his incision would be completely healed.

However, typically, golden fur over a healed cut grew in with a slightly lighter color, which was a tell-tale sign of the procedure. Therefore, Talia would go in under his chin, where it would be hidden within his longer white chin fur and through his mouth.

Léandre regarded his Mates while they prepped him, his expression and posture full of love and confidence. Aubrey blew him a kiss, and he caught it, placing it over his heart like he had done the night of their MateDance.

She mouthed to him.

"I love you."

He smiled, and she thought about how soon she'd be able to hear Léandre say it himself. Anticipation raced through her in a tingling rush.

Kassie Keegan

I need to hear him say it!

Perrin, a Master Surgeon with light-gold fur, a short-cropped, golden mane, and big, serious ocean-blue eyes, would perform the procedure assisted by Bahir and Talia.

Bahir seemed the complete opposite of Perrin, with a shoulder length, wildly untamed, wavy mane in all shades of golden-brown. He had golden eyes, often narrowed in thoughtful concentration.

Raaj had a smoothly side-swept, multi-hued dark-brown mane, dark golden-brown fur, and golden-brown eyes. He loved to banter and used it to his advantage, keeping things light-hearted during prep. He would monitor vitals and answer questions.

Raaj smiled at seeing Aubrey and Léandre's loving game, amused when he spoke to Léandre.

"I see you catching those kisses. Did she steal your heart?"

Léandre grinned proudly, making a sweeping gesture of himself from head-to-toe.

Raaj understood.

"Aubrey has taken all of you, not only your heart."

Léandre gestured to Daniel, who had his hand over his heart while grinning at Léandre and Raaj.

"Ah, handsome Daniel, too, I see."

Léandre agreed with a chuff.

"Being MateBonded is wonderful, isn't it?"

Aubrey heard the longing in Raaj's voice as he gazed at Talia, who was off to the side preparing surgical arms.

Interesting.

Léandre touched Raaj's arm for his attention, nodding slowly. Raaj's eyes sparkled with humor.

"Did you know my blood-brother is Kian Bon'Rial?"

Léandre shook his head.

"He's returning home with his Coalition Brethren Shiro Takeo and Marrok. I will get to meet their new Honored Nel, Blaze, for the first time. They might live in your Pod and I enjoy visiting with my brother. He has been gone for quite some time."

Léandre's eyes twinkled. Aubrey suspected where this was leading.

"Perhaps you might need extra check-ups from your full Medical Team. You know, just to be sure. Don't hesitate to call us in."

Léandre swung his gaze meaningfully to Talia and then back to Raaj with his eyebrows up questioningly, Talia still blissfully unaware she was the subject of conversation.

Bahir answered Léandre's silent question.

"Very much, yes."

Then he sent a look so hot toward Talia that Aubrey was sure Talia's knees would've buckled had she seen it.

Talia has a Coalition in pursuit and doesn't even realize it!

Aubrey gazed up at Ferrand, who definitely took notice. The Coalition would be well-investigated soon. Ferrand knew Aubrey loved Talia, making her close family, which all Lio took seriously.

Léandre glanced back at Perrin, a question in his eyes.

Perrin peered up at Léandre, pausing his work for a moment to nod emphatically, his eyes full of heated determination. Then he cooly resumed his last minute diagnostic checks.

Léandre grinned up at Raaj and gave a 'we-shall-see' shrug.

Aubrey glanced over at Jovian and Daniel, who also caught every bit of the byplay. Jovian was amused, seeming to anticipate the shenanigans sure to happen. Daniel wiggled his eyebrows at her, making her chuckle.

Kassie Keegan

They looked back at Léandre, who wiggled *his* eyebrows, which looked absolutely ridiculous on a Lio's face, cracking them up.

It was with the sound of their laughter ringing in the room, and with a smile on his face, that her beloved Léandre lay down for surgery.

Chapter 49
Léandre

Léandre woke fully alert but relaxed, keeping his eyes closed. Aubrey snuggled close, sleeping on one side. Daniel slept near his other side. He scented Jovian and Ferrand there, along with Talia and her Medical Team.

He'd needed to be comatose and still for many hours until the neuro micro-wire connections fused into his body, activating his new voice.

Hushed movement alerted Léandre. From the scent, it was Talia moving close to the bed he and his family rested on. Subtle sounds and scents informed him Talia's Coalition quietly monitored nearby. She approached near his head, giving his forehead a gentle stroke. Léandre opened his eyes, but it wasn't Talia he saw.

It was Ferrand.

Ferrand leaned across a sleeping Aubrey to gaze into his eyes, seeking reassurance the device had not neurologically compromised Léandre. A very real possibility they downplayed around Aubrey.

He was sure Ferrand hadn't stopped watching over him for even a moment. Slow-blinking affection to Ferrand, he lifted his hand to his best friend and Mate, who took it, kissing the back, as was their habit now.

Talia murmured.

"You can speak, Léandre."

His voice, although breathy, was a resonant, deep, musical tenor.

"I love you, Ferrand."

Ferrand's face crumpled with emotion at hearing Léandre's voice. Tears filled his eyes and fell unheeded as he closed his eyes, clutching Léandre's hand tightly to his mouth for another kiss, this one fierce with joy.

Their precious Mates woke to the sound of Léandre's voice, Aubrey in awe.

"What a beautiful voice you have!"

She gave him a watery smile. Léandre gazed at Aubrey, his heart in his eyes.

"I love you, Aubrey."

She gasped, hugging him close as Léandre turned to Daniel, who watched them while hugely smiling, looking incandescently happy.

"I love you, Daniel."

Daniel lovingly caressed Léandre's face as he focused on Jovian, his voice becoming stronger the more he spoke.

"I love you, Jovian."

Jovian was solemn as he took Léandre's words into his heart, closing his eyes, savoring the sound. He opened his eyes while taking a deep breath, speaking for them all, his words heavy with gratitude.

"We love you, Léandre. It is a delight to hear your voice."

They cuddled in close. Léandre peered up at Talia, beyond grateful for her and her Coalition.

"Thank you, Talia. Thank you all. More than words can ever say."

She smiled softly, giving him another gentle stroke across his forehead.

"You are most welcome, Léandre. Rest now, all of you. You, too, Ferrand. Your family is safe and sound. Tomorrow is soon enough for tests."

Ferrand and Jovian made sure their blanket covered Aubrey and Daniel completely, then Léandre and his Mates rested peacefully.

They woke up happy.

Talia and her Team poked, prodded, scanned, and tested Léandre every way possible before announcing him healthy.

While a blushing Talia stood at his side, Perrin explained matter-of-factly that Léandre's only restriction was not to swallow 'large items, like thick cocks' until they cleared him. Léandre grinned and agreed.

He would always remember the faces of his friends when he spoke to them for the first time.

"Hello."

The myriad expressions ranged from surprised to overjoyed. They rushed forward to him and congratulated him with hugs and pets.

Finally, after all these years, as he and his beloved Katohna shared air, Léandre could tell her in his own voice.

"Thank you."

It was a profound moment for them both.

Although Léandre remembered how to speak and had no difficulty forming words, he wasn't used to it. It didn't take long for him to tire.

His attentive Pod Mates, Cassian and Vivian worked with Daniel and Jovian to quickly and efficiently prepare a meal for everyone. Including Perrin, Bahir, Raaj, and Ha-Abassa Sarina, who had smoothly arrived in the common room shortly after Léandre and his Mates had.

After cleaning up the meal together, their visitors took their leave with smiles on their faces. Their friends gave Léandre hugs, then quietly went to their own living quarters, leaving them alone in the Common Room.

Without speaking, Aubrey and Daniel reached their hands out to their Lio Mates and lead them into their quarters. They took off their sandals, Bandels, and belts at the entry. Jovian activated his extra security measures without being asked.

It was time.

Time to tell Ferrand the truth. A truth Léandre had protected Ferrand from for most of their lives.

He sat with Aubrey and Jovian cuddled up with him on the lounger they'd pushed close to the bed. Ferrand and Daniel curled up on the bed, facing them.

Léandre looked over at Jovian.

"Can you do me a favor? Explain to Daniel the difference between an Honored Coalition Mate family like ours and a Lio Harem Mate family, even if he's heard it before."

Jovian studied him quizzically for a moment.

"Sure."

He cleared his throat and began.

"Honored families are typically three Lio Nels who form a Coalition with an Honored Nel."

He glanced over at Aubrey with a sexy grin.

"Who are Claimed by their fiercely possessive Honored Nessa."

He reached over for Aubrey's hand, who took it, and faced Daniel.

"These families have Lio Nessa female young, who most often stay in the same Prides they are born into."

Léandre glanced at Aubrey, seeing she was fine with the comment, secure in their care.

"Lio Harem families, who have male young, are different. Did you know Lio Nel male young leave on Prowls when they reach maturity?"

Daniel shook his head.

"We Prowl, traveling from place-to-place, staying in Lio Nel Sanctuaries in the Cities or overseen by each PrideHome. Lio Nels often live and study at Liani throughout Lio HomeWorld with like-minded Lio Nessas and Honored. Or we go Off-World, to Lio Fleets or Lio Colonies, until we find our Coalition, our Harem, or the Pride we belong with."

Jovian gazed at Ferrand with warm affection.

"Ferrand, Léandre, and I were fortunate to find each other and discover our paths while we were still quite young, staying in Bon'Fiel Pride."

He swung his gaze back to Daniel, watching for confusion.

"Typically, in a Lio Harem family, there are three or more Lio Nessas who share five or more Lio Nels. Lio Nessas often begin Breeding Heat at the same time, which is why a minimum of five males is necessary to service Harem Mates."

Jovian paused, and Daniel gestured for him to continue.

"Lio Nessas are relaxed sharing Lio Nels with each other, something possessive Honored Nessas rarely do."

Jovian peered over at Aubrey.

"Would *you* share your Mates with another Nessa or Nel?"

She bared her teeth playfully at Jovian and mouthed her answer.

"Never."

Her Lio Mates grinned, whereas Daniel looked determined and protective.

"I don't want to share my Mates with other Nessas or Nels, either."

Kassie Keegan

Ferrand hugged him close, whispering in his ear.

"It was never an option, Daniel."

Ferrand gave Daniel a kiss on the forehead. Jovian smiled affectionately as he continued.

"Lio Harem Mates fully Bond to each other, like us Coalition Mates do. If they invite someone to join a Harem family, all must agree. They are often open to adding more. Most Honored Coalition families are not."

Jovian's eyebrows lifted as he looked at Daniel.

"Questions?"

"No, I understand."

Jovian turned back to Léandre, having done what he asked of him. Léandre took a deep breath, centering himself, and concentrated on Daniel so he didn't have to see Ferrand.

Keep it light. Keep it instructional for Daniel. Until it isn't for Daniel anymore.

Léandre wasn't used to his own voice speaking out-loud yet, and he certainly hadn't heard the names he would say in a very long time. He wondered how Ferrand would fare hearing his family spoken of.

"Ferrand's Lio Nessa birth-mother was Mayou, a fierce fighter. No one fucked with her."

In his peripheral vision, Léandre saw Ferrand nod in agreement.

"He had one Harem-brother, Fahalan, whose Harem Mate mother was a gentle soul named Coline."

Léandre glanced at Ferrand, who seemed to wonder where this was going, before giving his attention back to Daniel.

"The third Lio Nessa in their Harem was Wen. Quiet, watchful, and unassuming, Wen didn't have any young."

Léandre gazed over at Aubrey now.

"From the moment we met, Ferrand and I have been inseparable. We stayed together whether we visited Ferrand's family, my family, or snuggled down in a pit with other young at the Skol-Ar."

He peered down and smiled at those sweet memories.

"When Ferrand's family went to Telledea, it was a given I would join them there."

Darkness crept closer to Léandre.

His Mates must have seen it on him because both Aubrey and Jovian cuddled in. Their warm bodies pressed comfortingly against him.

"They got a comm about the Sinkhole disaster. We were on our way, speeding at our Land Transport's highest capacity, when we felt a shudder."

He looked at Ferrand, whose eyes were open wide, reliving the past with Léandre.

"There was confusion. They went to check the engine and then there was an explosion."

He and Ferrand both shivered in reaction.

Daniel plastered himself to Ferrand, giving him comforting strokes and making soothing sounds. Léandre was being lovingly cuddled, too, but he would not stop the words.

The tale must be told.

"I regained consciousness after being thrown from the smoking wreckage of the Transport."

He dragged in a ragged breath and let the ugly truth out.

"Just as Wen used her Rav Knife to gut Fahalan."

The words fell heavy from his lips, dropping like stones, crushing everyone's breath with their impact.

Ferrand blinked, uncomprehending, shaking his head, stunned.

"Léandre, what?"

He stared at Ferrand, tears welling in eyes that didn't leave Ferrand's face. He repeated his statement with plodding clarity.

"I came to awareness, as Wen, used her Rav Knife… to gut Fahalan."

Ferrand lowered his head and closed his eyes as the scene sank in. Their shocked Mates made no sound.

Ferrand opened his eyes, wet with tears, filled with pain, his gaze guarded as he crawled off the bed to sit on his knees at Léandre's feet. He softly caressed Léandre's silvery neck scar, his voice deep.

"Tell it all, Léandre. I believe you. Tell me."

He took Léandre's hands. Daniel moved beside Ferrand on the floor and cuddled close to his side, looking up at Léandre.

"The Transport burst into three sections when it exploded. It instantly destroyed the engine and Cockpit, along with your family. The only intact portion was where Wen sat, with us and Fahalan."

Ferrand nodded encouragement.

"We were thrown from the Transport as it went down. Do you know why the impact knocked you unconscious for so long, despite our Shields protecting us?"

Ferrand shook his head.

"No."

"Wen used disruptor dots on our Shields. Made us vulnerable to the explosion and impact. But you, me, and Fahalan survived anyway. Until Wen."

Léandre closed his eyes, seeing the slice kill Fahalan again.

"Wen killed him before I could move, Ferrand. I swear, I couldn't…"

Ferrand's fierce embrace interrupted Léandre, muffling his words. They dropped their heads back, roaring in a storm of anguish, their Mates joining them crying out. Surrounding them. Experiencing the depths of grief with them.

Long after, they were all on their knees together on the floor as Léandre and Ferrand stared into each other's tear-filled eyes.

"She was approaching you, Ferrand. I couldn't let…"

Léandre swallowed raggedly.

"Wen watched, amused, as I dragged myself to your unconscious body and laid across it. She looked at me with an expression I had never seen before, Ferrand. It was mean, cruel. Evil. It was like a stranger looking at me from a mask shaped like Wen's face. It was… She said…"

He couldn't continue.

Ferrand put their foreheads together, sharing air. After a time of scenting Ferrand's closeness and feeling his Mates nearby, he could focus again.

Gazing into Ferrand's eyes, Léandre gave his last truths.

"Wen asked me if I loved you. I said I did. She asked if I would die for you. I said I would."

Ferrand put his hand over Léandre's heart.

"Wen laughed and everything she said seared into my mind. She said, 'Yes, we do crazy things for love, don't we? If those idiots had been more open, more interested in advancement, we wouldn't be here, would we?'"

Léandre tilted his head, his ears lying back.

"Then she strangely asked me if I would live for you. Which, of course, I said 'yes' to."

Ferrand's eyes widened.

"She said it would amuse her much more to use my love to silence me for the rest of my days than to take my life in one enjoyable moment."

Daniel growled with ferocious anger, unable to hold it in.

Kassie Keegan

"I want to kill her so *much*!"

All his Mates, including Aubrey, growled their agreement.

Léandre hadn't finished.

"Wen said, 'Where's the fun in that? You keep quiet, Léandre, then you and Ferrand may live.'"

Aubrey spoke under her breath.

"That *bitch*!"

Bitch, indeed, Aubrey. You are correct.

"Wen said I must never speak of what I knew. If I did, she would torture you, Ferrand, and kill everything and everyone you and I loved. I believed her. I still do. Wen is alive. Somewhere. Watching. Waiting."

The possibilities froze Léandre. Ferrand prompted him to continue, determined to have the full story.

"What did she do, Léandre?"

"Wen told me to lower my Shield completely and raise my chin. She cut my throat slowly, enjoying her gruesome triumph over me, a youth who loved a male she should have loved like a son."

Léandre flinched at the memory. He would probably always have the reaction. His Mates hugged him tighter, surrounding him with care that he soaked in like a flower soaking in the sun.

"She didn't expect us to live, Ferrand, no matter what she said. Your Shield hadn't covered your head because of her disruptor dots. You were seriously concussed. Then she dosed us, spraying a hallucinogen up our noses. It's why you were so groggy and confused when they asked questions."

Ferrand encouraged him.

"But there's more."

Léandre sighed.

"Yes. She activated a final explosive on the surviving fuselage before walking away, like she didn't have a care in the world. I watched her leave, feeling the hot wash of my blood pumping out of my neck, my strength flowing out of me with it. I laid there helpless, waiting for the explosion to tear us apart."

He regarded Ferrand with astonishment and respect.

"When you woke up, Ferrand, I think you were sleepwalking. But you grabbed me and Fahalan and took us behind a boulder before the bomb triggered. You kept me from bleeding out. I am alive because of you!"

He grabbed Ferrand's shoulders.

"You saved me twice. Once by taking me with you to Telledea. I'd be gone with our Pride. Then you dragged me to safety."

Ferrand put their foreheads together again, speaking in a deep, rough voice.

"You saved me, too, Léandre. We saved each other."

Léandre eased. Ferrand finally knew the truth. Their Mates knew.

Ferrand and Léandre regarded each other before turning to peer at Aubrey and Daniel, Ferrand's voice rough.

"Then they saved *all* of us."

Ferrand knew.

"It was the sabotage, wasn't it?"

"Yes. I believe it was Wen. She's tired of playing, especially after seeing our MateDance with such desirable, sought-after Mates."

Léandre kissed Aubrey and Daniel's heads.

"Wen went after our family, went after Bon'Fiel. It would have been a perfect blow. She hasn't kept her part of the bargain, so I will not keep mine."

Daniel spoke solemnly.

Kassie Keegan

"Nor should you. We are with you, Léandre. We are together, and we are going to stay together."

They clutched each other, their minds sifting through what they'd learned. Aubrey peered up at them.

"Is it time to inform High Nessa Katohna and Prime Cassian of all this?"

Léandre shook his head.

"No. Not tonight."

He scanned the room, studying his Mates.

"We are safe here and have each other. I want us to *have* each other, to celebrate truly living life. The life we choose to live."

Crushing need for his Mates ripped through him. A need to hear their cries of pleasure, to feel the pulse of love flowing so beautifully among them.

"Whatever happens, we can face it together tomorrow. But not tonight. Tonight is for *us*."

He dug his hands deep into Ferrand's mane.

"Can we do this, Ferrand? Can we celebrate instead of morn?"

Ferrand pulled him close, keeping his eyes on Aubrey, Daniel, and Jovian over Léandre's shoulder. They spoke one-by-one.

"Yes."

"Yes."

"Yes."

Ferrand nipped Léandre's neck, making him melt deeper into his arms.

"Yes, my beloved. We can celebrate life and love."

Chapter 50
Léandre

Ferrand raked his claws down Léandre's back, causing him to arch, gasp, and moan. Jovian moaned, too.

"Oh, Abah-Sah, those are beautiful sounds!"

Daniel spoke eagerly.

"I want to hear more!"

Ferrand scraped Léandre with his claws again, making Léandre groan with sexual hunger. When he arched, Aubrey took Léandre's mouth in a blazingly passionate kiss, her soft tongue devouring his flavor as greedily as he took hers. She lingered, licking his fangs before pulling back, her tone husky with desire.

"We celebrate your life, Léandre. We also celebrate the life we get to have with you!"

Léandre growled deep and long in primal response, causing arousal scents to bloom strongly around him. He loved that his new voice was such a powerful force on his Mates.

Daniel went to him, wanting kisses. Their lips met in a gradual deepening, tongues teasing and stroking, unhurried. Their tongues met over and over, rubbing and tasting. They pulled out of the kiss by degrees, lips lingering. Daniel whispered, husky and deep.

Kassie Keegan

"I love your voice, Léandre. Give us the words, please. Tell us everything."

He gazed at Daniel, aroused and amused.

"Everything?"

Daniel treated him to another deep, slow kiss as his Mates adjusted their positions, Jovian moving behind Léandre, Ferrand behind Daniel, and Aubrey to the side, working to remove their Shendyts and her garments. As Léandre's kiss with Daniel ended, Aubrey whispered in his ear.

"We want *everything*."

I can give you everything!

Raising his tail, Léandre removed his Serc, pulling back the tuft. He repositioned his Serc, ready to reveal his sabah to his Mates. He'd used his sabah to pleasure Aubrey frequently, but had unobtrusively brought it into their bed-play. They'd said nothing, simply accepting what he wanted to give.

Another reason, among many, why I love my Mates so deeply.

His sabah emerged in a smooth pulse, a golden, nub-studded column of flesh, ready to pleasure his Mates.

His Mates had other ideas.

In short order, Léandre found himself bent forward with Jovian's tongue swiftly, but gently inside him. Daniel lay flat on his belly under Léandre, his cock engulfed in the magical heat of Daniel's mouth, while Aubrey and Ferrand shared Léandre's sabah.

Léandre panted and groaned as the exquisite sensations overwhelmed him all at once. Ferrand gripped his long braided mane, leaning close to his ear as he spoke, making sure he understood.

"Scream when you release, Léandre. Your Mates demand it!"

Aubrey sucked his sabah deep into her warmth as Ferrand spoke, their Mates' mouths working him. Léandre screamed, his body shuddering with the power of each pulse of his release. Daniel shook with the nectar-rush, sucking greedily for more.

When Léandre tried to relax back from his peak, it was obvious his Mates were not done. Ferrand and Jovian switched positions, as did Aubrey and Daniel. They pleasured him through another tremendous screaming orgasm. Wrecked, he panted, braced on his arms and knees, tail raised high with excitement. Ferrand spoke behind Léandre.

"Words, now, Léandre. Your Mates need the words."

Léandre began speaking.

"You are amazing, my Mates. There is nothing like feeling your tongues on me, in me."

Ferrand lifted Léandre's tail before he and Jovian pulsed nectar directly on his entrance. Daniel prompted.

"What's happening, Léandre?"

"Oh, Abah-Sah. They released their nectar on me. Gave me their tribute, their compliment through pleasure."

Léandre groaned. Aubrey had her hand on Daniel's shaft, his fingers buried deep in her while they feasted their eyes on their Mates. It looked like they were close. Aubrey was breathless.

"And now, what are they doing?"

A thick masculine finger pushed in. Then there were two, both his Mates using the lubricant of their nectar to stretch and prepare him.

"They put their fingers in me!"

Léandre saw through a haze of his own pleasure as Daniel and Aubrey rubbed each other and groaned, climaxing from seeing and hearing Léandre get finger-fucked, enjoying their Mates stretching and preparing him to take his first cock.

Aubrey took Daniel's cream, rubbing it on her belly in a primal response, Claiming Daniel's scent for her own. She seemed feral, gazing at her Mates with fierce ownership in her eyes. She urged Daniel down onto his back, lying in profile close to Léandre. She straddled him, taking Daniel's still-hard length inside her with a long, smooth push, making them both groan.

A burst of blistering heat shimmied up his spine, moaning in unison with them. His Lio Mates mimicked the deep thrust of Daniel's shaft into Aubrey with their long fingers inside him. Their sexual Connection sizzled bright and alive among them, their sensitivity to each other's emotions, extreme.

Aubrey and Daniel turned their gazes to Léandre. He could see them relish his moan with theirs. Aubrey grabbed Léandre tail with its exposed sabah, baring her teeth as she spoke, her expression savage in her pleasure.

"What are they doing now, Léandre?"

He became the embodiment of rapture stretched in ecstasy across the canvas of the scene.

"They are deep and still inside me. It feels like they are waiting."

Ferrand and Jovian took his shoulders in their hands to brace him.

"Waiting? For this?"

She lifted high up and dropped, hard and fast. Ferrand and Jovian did the same in him, making Léandre howl at their unified, hard, fast thrust within him.

Aubrey and Daniel fucked ferociously, growling and shouting with each deep, vicious thrust. Léandre joined them, receiving his own mind-blowing, vigorous finger-fuck.

Aubrey seemed close when she abruptly stopped, pulling all the way off Daniel's glistening length. Everything stopped except their deep panting breaths. Reaching a hand down to softly, possessively grip Daniel's throat, she got Daniel's complete attention.

"I'm going to come, but don't you come! Do you hear me?"

Daniel nodded in her hold, moaning his consent, looking enslaved by his demanding Mate.

Léandre's heart warmed and his shaft throbbed at how wonderfully uninhibited Aubrey had become in her sexuality with them. She now followed her aggressive, demanding Honored Nessa urges, unleashing them, to her Mates' utter delight, the trust she gave them to be free this way tremendous and treasured.

Aubrey lined up again, ready for another hard ride.

"I will come all over this cock and take my pleasure. But you will save your cream. Do you understand, Daniel!"

Daniel spoke in a breathless whisper.

"Use me!"

She growled her aroused approval, slowly lowering onto him while focusing her attention behind Léandre.

"Those cocks are *mine*. *My* nectar. Keep it for me until I *take* it from you."

Both Ferrand and Jovian growled their consent.

Aubrey grabbed Léandre's tail, bringing his sabah to her mouth, enticing him with her hot breath on his sensitive flesh. Her voice was soft, and even more commanding for its mildness.

"You will come for us, Léandre. Cover me and Daniel in your scent, in your Claim. Then Daniel will fill you with his cock and his cream, Claiming you for all of us."

Daniel arched and moaned beneath her, shaking his head and clenching his fists as he fought the urge to come just from her words. He managed it with brutal effort, panting, his eyes glazed.

Aubrey lowered Léandre's sabah, leaning forward, making Daniel growl at the friction. She gave him a sweet kiss.

"You are being so good! I reward good behavior."

Kassie Keegan

Léandre would remember that for further exploration later. He knew Jovian and Ferrand would as well.

I want to be good, too. I want to be rewarded.

He moaned as Aubrey sat back on Daniel and turned her attention to him. She brought his sabah back up to her mouth, gazing into his eyes.

"Roar."

She sucked his sabah deep. Léandre roared, pouring his pleasure out onto his Mates, Claiming them with his essence as his Honored Nessa demanded.

Aubrey pulsed and ground on Daniel in the throes of beautiful climax while Daniel screamed with his efforts not to come, his head rolling back-and-forth in pleasured agony.

Aubrey gave Léandre's sabah one last kiss, rubbing his nectar into the skin of her torso, then leaned forward to a practically crying Daniel. She kissed him softly as she pulled off him, making him whimper.

Ferrand and Jovian gradually emptied Léandre of fingers, their hands moving from his shoulders with loving, comforting strokes down his body.

Léandre peered down at Daniel, who looked up at him in helpless need.

My poor love.

Léandre gave Daniel his hand, and they both stood up. He went over to the bed, lying back on the edge, his tail draped down and out of the way, lifting his legs.

Daniel stepped between Léandre's legs, which he wrapped around Daniel, bringing him closer, arching his hips in invitation, gazing into Daniel's eyes.

"I'm yours. Take me. Claim me."

Desire ignited Daniel, but he was loving and careful, as was his nature. He took a large swipe of Léandre's thick nectar from where it landed on his chest and throughly lubricated his shaft, still liberally coated with

Aubrey's cream. His use of their combined essences as lubricant made Léandre shiver.

Daniel, poised and ready at his entrance, gazed once more at his face for reassurance. Léandre gave him a half-crazed grin and sexually begged for the first time in his life.

"Please."

Daniel pushed into Léandre slowly and steadily, not stopping until Léandre took all of him.

He heard Ferrand roar as Aubrey took his nectar during Daniel's Claiming stroke.

The stretched fullness was erotically new and delicious. Léandre gave himself over to the sensations, cherishing the gift of sharing this with his beloved Mates. Daniel pulled back slowly and thrust back in, fast and smooth, having learned the rhythm from his Lio Mates.

Jovian roared as Aubrey took his nectar at Daniel's first pleasure stroke.

When Daniel's beautiful, smooth length stroked perfectly again, tingling arousal struck Léandre like a hammer, sparking exquisite pleasure. He palmed his throbbing shaft, pumping his hand at the pace of Daniel's thrusts inside him.

It took only a few more strokes before Daniel and Léandre roared their own peaks, shaking in the tumultuous grip of delicious release, panting through the aftershocks.

Aubrey, Jovian, and Ferrand joined them, petting, kissing, and tasting Léandre and Daniel. Sharing Léandre's nectar, enjoying their own nectar-rush.

Aubrey kissed her Mates one-by-one, whispering words of praise and love.

"Oh, you are spectacular! I love your strength and the way you take care of us, my delicious Commander."

Kiss.

"You are amazing! Such an excellent Mate. An absolutely beautiful lover, and a wonderful man."

Kiss.

"I love your roar! You are magnificent, my beloved sexy beast."

Kiss.

"You make all my sweetest and most naughty fantasies come true, my beautiful, clever Mate."

Kiss.

"Thank you, loves."

Léandre spoke for them all.

"Aubrey, our love for you is soul-deep."

Their spirits, hearts, and bodies thrummed with humming satisfaction. Léandre felt full to bursting with love.

In short order, they cleaned up, triggered the Solaray, and piled into bed with Léandre in the center. Aubrey and Daniel cuddled him on each side, with Ferrand and Jovian nestled in behind them.

Supremely happy, it didn't surprise Léandre when his contented purr rumbled. Aubrey and Daniel snuggled deeper into Léandre as their soft purrs started, melting Léandre's heart with their unconscious, uncontrollable measure of happiness.

Jovian and Ferrand curled closer, purring, too. Léandre reached out to them, clasping hands as he and his Brethren shared their contentment, their family safe and secure in their arms.

The future may be uncertain, but their devotion to each other was rock-solid and never-ending. They would face the tremendous upcoming challenges together.

Strong in each other's embrace.

A Glossary of Terms

<u>A Glossary of Terms</u>
Alphabetical

Abah-Sah: *The Lio Source of Life.*

The Abassani: *The Priesthood who honor the Lio Source of Life called Abah-Sah.*

Bandel: *Wrist cuffs worn by Lio Nels in Coalition seeking Honored Mates. They cover the inside of a Lio Nel's wrist, one of their strongest scent-markers.*

Bereft: *Inconsolably lonely to the point of going to The Fade from grief.*

Buvol: *Dangerous, horned buffalo-like beast that runs in herds on Lio HomeWorld.*

Call to Mate (Honored Nel): *A Prize or Prime Lio Nel prepares an Honored Nel with a final hormone boost, sexually priming him, enabling him spiritually 'Call to Mate' his Honored Nessa, enticing her to Claim him and their Lio for her own.*

Chalel: *The half-cape unmated Honored Nels wear, designed by them with meaningful colors and motifs. Laid down for their Honored Nessa when she Claims them and treasured afterward when she wears it as a symbol of their MateBond.*

A Glossary of Terms

Declare: *Lio Nels offer themselves to an Honored Nessa for her Claim with a formal declaration. If the Honored Nessa does not complete the MateBond, the Lio Nels will become Bereft, never answering the Call to Mate again.*

Fade: *The Fade is what Lio call losing one's living spark and dying.*

Honored: *Humans genetically altered with Lio DNA to become a new race the Lio call Honored. Men become Honored Nels, women become Honored Nessas. Only Coalitions with MateBonded Honored Mates produce female Lio Nessa young.*

Liani: *A school that teaches a particular skill, overseen by a Pride. An example is Bon'Fiel Pride's Liani Combat, which specializes in instructing Shielded and Unshielded hand-to-hand combat.*

L.I.O.: *Lio Inquiry Office.*

Lio Coalition: *A group of three or more Lio Nels seeking Honored Mates. They typically wear Bandels to cover their strongest scent-markers so as not to irritate Honored Nessas who prefer such scent-claims only on themselves and their Mates. They produce female Lio Nessa young.*

Lio Harem: *Typically three or more Lio Nessas with five or more Lio Nels, producing Lio Nel young. Lio Nessas in a Harem usually go into BreedingHeat simultaneously. Sometimes includes Honored Mates.*

Lio Nel: *A male Lio. They have manes of all textures and styles. In a Lio Harem with Lio Nessas, they father Lio Nels. In a Coalition with Honored Nessas and Honored Nels, they father Lio Nessas. Until MateBonded, Lio Nels often Prowl the Worlds and Galaxies, learning and working as they go.*

Lio Nessa: *A female Lio. They do not have manes but often wear chains and jewels, or even paint their fur to adorn themselves. They typically stay within the Pride they were born but are known to Prowl before settling down with Mates.*

A Glossary of Terms

Locked into a Call to Mate (Honored Nessa): *A gift from Abah-Sah that quickly identifies an Honored Nessa's Honored and Lio Mates and her Shumal.*

An Honored Nessa sees a glowing aura around her fated Honored Nel Mate. This happens only when she has met both her Honored Nel and her Lio Nel Coalition. Upon seeing her Honored Nel, she becomes 'Locked into her Call to Mate.' The being who first finds her and brings her 'release' to release her from her Call, is her Shumal, who will protect her through her MateBonding.

MateDance: *When Lio Nels and their Honored Nel dance, displaying and offering themselves for an Honored Nessa to entice her Claim.*

Mate Tributes: *Tokens marking Lio Nels as Claimed Mates. It declares an Honored Nessa's intent to take them into her heart and body as Mates.*

Mimetic Mineral Shield: *All Lio and Honored are embedded with a small mimetic mineral disc in the delto-pectoral grove of their left upper chest between their collarbone and shoulder joint. Linked to their autonomic nervous system, the shield can be controlled with mental commands, creating a protective shield around their entire body or portions of it with a thought. It also uses their senses to detect danger and protect them before being consciously aware.*

Mistaray: *An elegantly curved freshwater shower which looks like a single giant free-standing white tusk suspended over a dip in the floor.*

PrideChoice Ceremony: *Upon first arriving on Lio HomeWorld or on a Lio Colony, Honored Nels and Honored Nessas choose their Pride by selecting the Prime Lio Nel Ambassador who suits them best. This prevents Prime Ambassadors from fighting and dying for Honored Mates their Prides need.*

Prime: *A 'Prize' Lio Nel who has fought and won a Challenge to become a 'Prime.' Usually destined for Pride Leadership.*

Prime Lio Nel Ambassador: *A Prime Lio Nel who has fought and won his position to lead and protect the Honored of a Pride. He represents his Pride at PrideChoice Ceremonies. A Prime Ambassador seeks Honored Mates, but it is rare for him to be Claimed by an Honored Nessa because of his obligations to the Pride.*

A Glossary of Terms

Prime Ambassador Name Change: *If a Prime Ambassador is MateBonded, the entire Pride celebrates this generationally by changing their name from Bon' (on Lio HomeWorld), Pon' (in space on a Lio Fleet) or Lon' (on a Lio Colony World) to Argen', Pargen', or Largen'. For example, should Prime Cassian Bon'Fiel be Claimed by Destiny (eyebrow wiggle), Bon'Fiel Pride becomes Argen'Fiel Pride until he is no longer Ambassador or he goes to the Fade.*

Prize: *An ultra-masculine, dominant Lio Nel. His pelt usually sports extra fur across his shoulders, chest, and abdomen and has a thick, luxurious mane. They provide hormones necessary to give Honored Nels their final boost to sexual maturity and Call a Mate. A 'Prize' Lio Nel has not fought and won a Challenge to become a 'Prime.'*

Projectile Weapons: *Projectile weapons are uncommon on Lio HomeWorld, although widely used Off-World. They are useless against Lio Mimetic Mineral Shields and gain no honor to the combatant. However bladed weapons are encouraged additions to fangs and claws and are widely used in Challenges.*

Prowl: *Until MateBonded, Lio Nels Prowl the Worlds and Galaxies, learning and working as they go. Lio Nessas usually settle within the Pride they are born into but they also Prowl before settling down with Mates.*

Rav Knife: *Upon maturity, the Pride gifts each Lio a Rav Knife, which is the only known weapon capable of penetrating Lio Shields. Rav Knives cannot be bought, they can only be given or bartered for through a sacrifice of time and labor.*

Sabah: *An additional cock Lio have hidden inside their tails. Their tail tuft fur must be held back by a Serc to allow an emerged Sabah to be fully visible. Many Honored do not know about it until they are Called to Mate.*

Serc: *The ring behind their tail tufts every Lio wears.*

Shaktah: *An Honored whose natural scent holds a fear-scent attractor so strong as to be almost irresistible to some primal Lio Nels. The scent can aid Lio Nessas in their BreedingHeat, inciting males to Rut.*

A Glossary of Terms

Shendyt: *Traditional skirt-like Lio wrap-around garment, usually belted, covering the groin and upper legs, worn by male and female Lio and Honored.*

Shumal: *Protectors and caregivers of an Honored Nessa, without the natural defenses of fangs or claws, making sure she stays safe and in control of a Mating, no matter how close to their beast-natures her Mates might become.*

Shumal's 'Release': *The Lio believe Abah-sah ensures an Honored Nessa's safekeeping by gifting her with a Shumal, who is usually the first person to find the Honored Nessa when she becomes unable to move, literally 'Locked into her Call to Mate.' The being who is their Shumal must give their Honored Nessa a 'release' in order for her to be released and able to move again.*

Skol-Ar: *Nursery, school, and/or housing for Lio young and youth. Usually at the heart of a PrideHome or Vessel.*

Solaray: *A laser that instantly removes sweat and grime, empties bowel and bladder, leaving beings refreshed. Scents remain undisturbed.*

Zumiel: *Lio Nels who are 'Found and Bound' by a Prize Lio Nel as a life-long companion. A Zumiel anchors a Prize Lio Nel's beast-nature keeping them from going feral.*

Character Summaries

Dearest Reader,

The Savage Planet Series has a MateBonded Coalition complete in every book, but there is an over-arching story arc for the Series. Therefore, characters from previous and future books play important roles in each story.

Because of this, I thought you would appreciate a summary of who the Coalitions from previous books are, along with some future ones.

Then I threw in some side-character summaries, because why not?

If it helps you, I'm happy.

When there's five Mates in each story, characters add up *fast*.

~Kassie

Character Summaries

Savage Planet Embrace

Savage Planet Series, Book 1

Aubrey Newton Bon'Fiel: *Boosted Honored Nessa from Pirate-ridden outpost SpacePort Omori. She is a Shaktah, someone whose natural fear-scent is highly attractive to primal Lio. Aubrey is an Energy Rider who senses hums of energy. She can repair anything mechanical.*

Daniel Shaw Bon'Fiel: *Boosted Honored Nel from SpacePort Arata. A SpacePort 'Rat,' he is an Energy Rider who can pluck energy to produce Energy Resonance he can follow. Daniel is a Mechanic and Inventor.*

Commander Ferrand Bon'Fiel: *Lio Nel from Lio HomeWorld in charge of Bon'Fiel PrideHome Security. Adopted from the Bon'Durel Pride that was destroyed by a Sinkhole. His family died in a Speeder accident on the way to help their devastated Pride, only he and Léandre survived.*

Léandre Bon'Fiel: *Lio Nel from Lio HomeWorld who is a MateDance Instructor. He is mute from the tragic accident that killed Ferrand's Family. Adopted with life-long friend and Mate Ferrand from the destroyed Bon'Durel Pride.*

Jovian Bon'Fiel: *Lio Nel from Lio HomeWorld who is a Tech genius adopted from the Disgraced and Disbanded Bon'Ocal Pride. Works Tech for Security and is an Inventor.*

Savage Planet Secret

Savage Planet Series, Book 2

Vivian Warner Bon'Fiel: *Natural-born Honored Nessa from Lio Alestia. A vivacious, curvaceous, smart-mouthed Surveillance expert, she works long-range mission ops for the Galactic Military in her private Surveillance Intelligence Office above her quarters. Gifted with sensing a person's intention before action.*

Character Summaries

Blaze Monroe Bon'Fiel: *Boosted Honored Nel from Earth. Former Colonel in the Galactic Military. On Prime Cassian's Security Team. BloodBonded with Prime Cassian. Gifted with sensing how people fit within a group, making him an unintentional matchmaker.*

Kian Bon'Rial: *Lio Nel from Lio HomeWorld. Former Team Leader in the Galactic Military, now on Prime Cassian's Security Team. Wears a Gauntlet on his left forearm, a weapon that also can engage Mimetic Resonance. The Resonance is keyed to Marrok's Mimetic Mineral Shield and helps Kian guide Marrok when he has gone Berserker.*

Marrok Bon'Vahral: *Lio Nel from Lio HomeWorld. Former Warrior in the Galactic Military. A Berserker, like many of his Pride, now on Prime Cassian's Security Team. A Master of the Shard Whip. BloodBonded with Prime Cassian to settle his Berserker beast-nature.*

Shiro Takeo Bon'Fiel: *Lio Nel from Lio HomeWorld. Former stealth Warrior in the Galactic Military. On Prime Cassian's Security Team. A Master of the Ribbons. He is Talia's Shumal.*

Savage Planet Discovery

Savage Planet Series, Book 3

Talia Mullins Bon'Fiel: *Natural-born Honored Nessa from SpacePort Vardar where her family runs a respected teaching Medical Clinic. Now lives on Lio HomeWorld with the Bon'Fiel Pride. Lead Medic to her private Medical Clinic at Bon'Fiel PrideHome.*

Valère Boudreau Lon'Salel: *Natural-born Honored Nel from Lio Intare where his family runs a prestigious teaching Medical Clinic. Completed Medic training at the Mullins Medical Clinic on SpacePort Vardar with twin brother, Valór. Served on Galactic Aid Vessel* Galactic Haven *with Valór.*

Character Summaries

Perrin Bon'Fabril: *Lio Nel from Lio HomeWorld. A highly controlled Master Surgeon in Talia's Medical Team Coalition.*

Bahir Argen'Tramel: *Lio Nel from Lio HomeWorld. A gruff Diagnostics Specialist in Talia's Medical Team Coalition.*

Raaj Bon'Rial: *Lio Nel from Lio HomeWorld. A good-natured Botany Expert in Talia's Medical Team Coalition. Raaj is Kian Bon'Rial's brother.*

Savage Planet Destiny

Savage Planet Series, Book 4, Finale

Destiny Dean Bon'Fiel: *Natural-born Honored Nessa from Lio HomeWorld. An artist with the gift of sensing truth. She is Vivian's Shumal.*

Prime Cassian Bon'Fiel: *Lio Nel from the Pargen'Fiel PrideHome on Lio Fleet Kahlina. He won Challenge on Lio HomeWorld to become Prime Ambassador of Bon'Fiel Pride.*

Travar Pon'Pomol: *Lio Nel from Pon'Pomol PrideHome on Lio Fleet Kahlina. Zumiel life-mate of Prime Cassian Bon'Fiel.*

Stealth (Savion) Pon'Salel: *Lio Nel from Pon'Salel PrideHome on Lio Fleet Kahlina. Stealth Warrior on Lio HomeWorld. He is Aubrey's Shumal.*

Other Important Characters

(Alphabetical)

Abassa Itakah: *Lio Nessa Abassa Priestess on Talia's Team. She brought Aubrey Newton Bon'Fiel from SpacePort Omori to Lio HomeWorld.*

Character Summaries

Bibi Sawat Azure: *The budding Sawat Talia's Team seeks.*

Captain Logan Landry Lon'Salel: *Natural-born Honored Nel, Captain of MediCruiser Vessel,* The CareTaker. *Uncle of Valère and Valór Boudreau Lon'Salel and many more.*

Ha-Abassa Sarina: *Lio Nessa Abassa Priestess, one of the Heads of the Abassani who honor the Source of Life called Abah-Sah.*

High Nessa Katohna: *Lio Nessa Leader of Bon'Fiel Pride. She formerly served in the Galactic Enforcers Fleet on the* Pitiless Enforcer *before winning her Challenge to become Bon'Fiel High Nessa.*

Priti Sawat Azure: *A Symbiotic Being. Sawat is a sentient tree-like being with huge azure-blue blooms who can walk on ambulatory roots. They only communicate with Priti. Priti is the ageless energy being who lives in the heart of Sawat Azure.*

About Kassie Keegan

USA Today Bestselling Author Kassie Keegan is the wildly untamed writer of the Savage Series featuring futuristic, bestial heroes and the beings who love them.

www.KassieKeegan.com

Sign up for Kassie Keegan's Savage News at:

www.subscribepage.com/kassiekeegan

You can connect with Kassie on Facebook at:

Kassie Keegan's Cosmic Lounge

Kassie loves to hear from fans!

author@kassiekeegan.com

Made in the USA
Columbia, SC
05 April 2025